PRAISE FOR *Sirena Selena*

"Santos-Febres examines questions of sexuality and power . . . blending lyrical hyperbole with social observation . . . in her lush and tragicomic first novel."

—*New York Times Book Review*

"This impishly sensual novel is an often hilarious anatomy of gender confusion and reminiscent of the classic silent film *The Blue Angel*. . . . The boy-girl Selena is as sweetly bedazzled as any hero-heroine out of a Shakespearean comedy."

—*Kirkus Reviews*

"What Puig did to transform the way we think of American film, Santos-Febres has managed for Latin music. *Sirena* is fantastic! Like Cesária Évora she'll come to haunt you, like Marc Anthony she'll steal your heart. The Grammys will have to invent a new category—Best Album of the Year in Fiction."

—Laura Esquivel, author of
Like Water for Chocolate and *The Law of Love*

PRAISE FOR *Any Wednesday I'm Yours*

"A fascinating look at life, crime, and journalism in San Juan, Puerto Rico."

—*Chicago Tribune*

"Santos-Febres shows a real skill for navigating the contours of urban loneliness."

—*Village Voice*

"An ambitious descent into the labyrinths of identity and desire. . . . Provides the reader with an adrenaline jolt of literary voyeurism."

—*Time Out New York*

"Santos-Febres seems to write with hot oils, and the page glistens."

—*Harvard Review*

© Nina Subin

About the Author

MAYRA SANTOS-FEBRES has won many prizes for her stories and was recently awarded a Guggenheim Fellowship and long-listed for the prestigious IMPAC Dublin Literary Award. She lives in Puerto Rico.

OUR LADY
OF THE NIGHT

ALSO BY MAYRA SANTOS-FEBRES

Sirena Selena
Any Wednesday I'm Yours

OUR LADY
OF THE NIGHT

A NOVEL

Mayra Santos-Febres

TRANSLATED FROM THE SPANISH BY
ERNESTO MESTRE–REED

HARPER PERENNIAL

NEW YORK • LONDON • TORONTO • SYDNEY • NEW DELHI • AUCKLAND

HARPER ● PERENNIAL

Originally published in Spanish as *Nuestra señora de la noche* in Spain in 2006 by Espasa Calpe, S.A.

HarperCollins books may be purchased for educational, business, or sales promotional use. For information please write: Special Markets Department, HarperCollins Publishers, 10 East 53rd Street, New York, NY 10022.

FIRST U.S. EDITION

Library of Congress Cataloging-in-Publication Data is available upon request.

ISBN 978-0-06-173130-3

09 10 11 12 13 OV/RRD 10 9 8 7 6 5 4 3 2 1

To what do we owe our great hunger for history, our obses-
sion with countless cultures, our incontrollable longing for
knowledge, but to our loss of myths, of mythical places, of
the mythical womb.
                    —Friedrich Nietzsche, *The Birth of Tragedy*

Nigra sum sed formosa . . .
                                        —Song of Songs

OUR LADY
OF THE NIGHT

Revelation

ATTORNEY CANGGIANO'S CADILLAC came to a stop in the driveway of the casino. A bellhop opened the door and reached out a hand to help the elegant lady who would surely emerge from that luxurious vehicle. He was surprised to see a gloved hand whose wrist was encircled by a solid-gold seven-day bracelet with a medallion of the Virgin of Charity dangling from it. Nor could he have expected that the glove would reveal, up toward the elbow, a firm black arm that shone against the overcast night, the lights of the ball, and the raw silk dress. A diamond choker adorned the lady's neck, which was also black. A cascade of curls fell level with that neck. The bellhop's eyes alighted on her chin and then on her face, as Isabel Luberza Oppenheimer emerged from the Cadillac. La Negra Luberza. The Madam from the Portuguese River. The bellhop had no other choice but to gulp.

At the same instant, District Representative Pedro Nevárez was entering the Red Cross ball, followed by Magistrate

Hernández and Senator Villanueva and his wife, along with Bishop MacManus.

They all looked on in fear as Canggiano offered his arm and led her past the wide door of the casino. At the entrance, La Negra handed a confused young man the invitation bearing the insignia of the cross printed on gold paper. He checked the invitation list and found her name on it. She then crossed steadily through the entrance of the casino, a steady hand on Canggiano's arm. He alone noticed the slight tremble in her fingers, her surging pulse.

"There is no hurry, Doña Isabel. The worst is over."

"Don't be so sure, Canggiano."

To their right, Representative Nevárez and his wife looked at them out of the corners of their eyes. It had been a week since he had spoken to La Negra. "I'll be by Saturday, Isabelita, so we can chat about the campaign donation." She already had had his meal ready. The girl Lisandra. She had brought her from Colombia for him. "Don't cry, darling, don't be frightened. Stop crying! If all goes well, this will be the last time that you have to sleep with the representative." A few steps ahead, the secretary of public works spoke with the engineer Valenzuela. "Doña Isabel, what elegance! I would like to come see you about a matter that might be of interest to you." Let them come see her the following week at her mansion in the Bélgica district. "I am always very interested in listening to proposals." At the end of the entrance hall the Ferráns brothers—Juan Isidro, Valentín, and Esteban—chatted. They flattered her with their smiles. Their wives remained silent and inaccessible, clutching their husbands' forearms tightly. The brothers commended her for her great heart, for giving so much of herself to those in need.

"How am I not going to give, when my own flesh has known what need is?"

Canggiano introduced her to the Colomés, the Tomés, the Valles; the cream of the crop of the town was there. At each spot, she paused with the attorney, who carried on with his introductions as if she had never seen any of these people, as if the day before, or last week, many of those men had not been at her bar. But she was making her debut in the casino, on the other side of the river, dressed in silk and diamonds. She had come in through the main entrance. No one had dared get in her way. She could not stop trembling.

Then she saw him, the worst one of all. Tuxedoed, with a broad chin, green eyes on white freckled skin framed by the blackest hair, greased back. His elbow rested on the bar, a drink in hand, probably a whiskey. He smoked. His wife was with him, snowy, prattling ceaselessly on some topic that led her to rest her hand on the shoulder of her beloved—"Don't you think, my dear?"—seeking his approval. It was the attorney Fornarís with his legitimate wife in his arms. The flattering gazes now seemed devious, revealing their mocking grimaces. "Even dressed in silk . . ." The attorney's eyes pierced her, at once, without warning, as if a strange power were making them gravitate toward her on the opposite side of the hall. He continued to stare at her and the sound of the conversations evaporated in the air. Isabel had to pause, feign. She pressed hard on Canggiano's forearm and he came to a sudden stop. She slowed her breath, *one . . . two . . . three . . . four . . . five*, but could not fall back into its rhythm. Fernando Fornarís made a gesture as if to walk toward her but held back also. With her eyes, Cristina followed the direction of the gesture. They both saw her, the lingering apparition. "Mother, attend to me in my anguish, protect me." With her gloved fingers, Isabel rubbed the medallion of the Virgin, La Cachita, which was always dangling from her wrist. She felt her face dissolve, wanting to float in the air.

Mayra Santos-Febres

The attorney Canggiano knew how to read her. "I beg your pardon, gentlemen, but I have yet to dance one number with the lady." He bowed to the guests and gently led Isabel toward the dance floor. Even with her back to them, the glares of Fernando Fornarís and his wife still burned into her, though less intensely. And with her back to them, she began to overcome that vision.

"Now we're going through the worst, Canggiano."

"If you are not feeling well, tell me, and we'll leave right away."

"I don't have that luxury, no matter how I feel. You hold me tight until they leave."

The Three Marys

THREE OF YOU went to the tomb at dawn. Mary the Holy Mother, Mary Magdalene, and Mary of Clopas, as if you were one. You went to grieve, sleepless, walking alone, as women have always done on the face of the earth. You came to face the sepulcher of the Son, scabbard of the flesh, the scabbard that the Lord renounces.

Three, and I kneel down before you and call you Virgin Protector. I kneel, because only you know of the sleepless flesh, the renounced scabbard. Because only you know what I have had to leave in my path to save me from the trash that they say I am. I go alone down my path like you. I come from the ball, from the grave, and from the void. Three Marys will be there when I come out of this grotto, keeping each other company, protecting me from this ill that besieges me. Protect me from the Enemy, all you women, Mother, Magdalene, Wife, together on the path among the beasts, shielded by their holy vesture.

If you help me, I will establish a shrine in honor of your name. If you help me, I will devote myself to the work that praises your glory, even though those who receive my gifts won't allow me in. Whip of the Enemy, tentacle of the Beast. I will do it though they scratch and bite me. For you, Holy Mother; for you, Fallen Virgin; for you, Wife. I'll do it though the last woman covered in drool spits on my grave. Help me find what I have lost. Don't let it be my punishment never to discover it. Only God knew the path that life had in store for me. Only you knew that I would fall prostrate at your feet. You know what is hidden in my heart, Mother. Grant me what I ask for and protect me in my tasks. One and three, the Marys that inhabit you, though you seem alone, seated on your throne among the stars.

Holy Mother.

Amen, Jesus.

One

The old lady awakes. Tower of patience, pray for us; mirror of humility, pray for us; cup of wisdom, pray for us, for me, a fly, or worse, a fly atop a bucket of shit, or the shit itself, me. The voices in her head are unalloyed. All night long the same thing, the old woman. By her side, the Child sleeps restlessly. He needs to sleep. Don't wake him, María Candelaria. Doña Montse, Doña Montse, Doña Montse, light the candles. Yesyesyes, no need to say my real name. Such an angel, the Child, as angelic as the angels when they rest from the vengeance of the Lord. Outside, the dew dries up in the underbrush. The beginning of another day. People from all parts will come to the sanctuary, the Shrine of the Holy Virgin of Montserrat in Hormigueros. The Black Virgin with the white child on her lap. The old lady knows it, feels it; today hundreds of them will come to make promises and raise their prayers to the Mother of All, the Intercessor of the afflicted. And may I be struck dead, the old lady says, may the sinister paw of the Beast

fondle the fervor in my crotch. She looks for the washbowl,
fills it with water using a rusty can, and washes her face. She
washes her arms, her droopy breasts, the skin of her belly, black
as the darkness after a lightning flash. She washes her crotch,
already gray. "You even look alike," Don Armando used to
say. "You have the same face and the same skin." From inside,
that human-like statue of a Black Virgin that he had left in the
house watched them. My sisters don't want it. Frightened, she
replied: Oh no, Don Armando, it's like she sees us. But— Don't
be silly, María Candela, he said. Hastily, he would climb on
top of her, and look, each day they let her get away down the
hill to the sanctuary less and less. He kissed her with hunger,
in a hurry. Those two keep me as a prisoner in their house;
they don't even let me breathe. Don Armando, the old man
who had brought her to this hill. He gave her a small house,
you will be my nurse, he visited her. But those sisters of yours,
those Harpies . . . If he could see me now that I have lost all my
looks, now that I am old. If he could see me now, with my head
in between my legs like someone who has eaten poisoned fish,
lighting candles. I fight them, today another one appears and I
will fight them, I straighten up, my skin lustrous because I use
oil of coconut and Palmer's Cream that I buy in town. Today I
will fight them.

"Mother, what are we going to eat today?"

The old woman washes her feet; she dries them carefully so
that the dampness doesn't stain her clothes. Grandma Rafaela,
Grandma Rafaela, you're going to come to no good, but she
never told me that it would be like this, with a different name,
taking care of a Virgin darker than soot in this shitty town. The
air seeps in through the planks of the room. Everything rever-
berates in the old woman, her steps, her guts, her wasted skin.
I, who came to take care of Armando. He was recovering from

a heart attack. With the medicine that he found in between my legs; how else was he going to recover? The Child tosses in the bed. He speaks, murmurs something. Hormigueros, for the ants that crawled on my back, Hormigueros, for the ants that crawled in between my legs, the Child is talented. The old woman watches him guardedly. She makes sure he is still asleep. Groping her way, she goes out of the one room of that house made of weathered wood. She walks toward the patio to light the fire. Could the Child be suffering the same nightmare? But she will chase it away. This kid is my son because he has the very same skin color as his Grandmother Rafaela. She will chase away his nightmares with hot orange-flavored cane juice that she will have ready for him when he awakes. I would have named him Rafael, but he is called Roberto. I call him the Child and he calls me Godmother and not Doña Montse, Doña Montse, as if that were my name, and me, yesyesyes, I am coming, what can I do for you, madam, what can I do for you, sir, to that melancholic attorney who bought the finca from the Harpies. I hope he returns soon. Our monthly supplies are all gone.

A little more tinder and the fire will be ready. The old woman grabs a piece of grease-stained cardboard. She fans the fire. It ignites. The house of nailed planks squeaks in the breeze like a rusty machine. The old woman walks toward the grotto of the Virgin. Holy Virgin of Montserrat, Mother of Mercy, Honor of the Caribbean, Protector, your People laaa-aaud you, whore of a Virgin who left me without a name. Near the grotto grow curative plants—basil, thyme, witch's oregano, aloe for the cough. She rips a few leaves from the orange tree. Lord, Lord, safeguard us, Lord, Lord, protect us, Lord of the green eyes, whose all-powerful presence is lost in the plains. She walks again toward the fire and throws the leaves in a pot

of boiling water. She frowns. Soon her head will begin to ache.
The Harpies, Eulalia and Pura . . . the Harpies . . . We'll take
care of the little boy, we'll raise him, Mr. Attorney, don't worry,
while it is I who gets up at dawn, lights the stove, and strains
his orange cane juice, the one flavored with *guanabano* for in-
digestion, *hierbabruja* when his ears almost rotted. Every day
the same thing, first the "helpless" brother and now the Child,
if only he wasn't such a beauty . . . The voices don't stop; the
pain in her temples makes them want to burst. The old woman
walks toward the makeshift clothesline in one of the corners of
the little house. She unclasps a dry rag and soaks it in the green
water of the cane juice. She goes back toward the sanctuary,
toward the plants that grow alongside the grotto, picks two
mulberry leaves, wets the underside with saliva, and glues them
to her forehead. She ties them on with the lukewarm rag soaked
in orange water, making two tight knots against her head. The
warmth of the rag, the odor of the leaves, ease the throbbing
a bit. They talk to the attorney, their rosaries in hand, and
they keep everything that he leaves for the Child. Virgin of the
Sanctuary, strike them dead and disembowel them! The voices
die down; they are her own.

"Godmother, I dreamed a scorpion stung me."

The Child appears in the doorway. The old woman approaches him, lifts him in the air, and presses him to her fallen
tits. "It's all right, my Soul, don't worry. I am here. Come and
drink your juice." Old María de la Candelaria looks at the Child,
at the Child's gaze, his big green eyes, from which the same
question as always will eventually seep out. Leave the question
alone, María.

"In the dream, what happened to the scorpion?"

"I stepped on him, Godmother, over and over, until it was a
little flat lump on the floor."

"Very well done, my love. Death to whatever stings the Child."

"I'm hungry, Godmother."

"I'll see if we have cornstarch, so I can make you a *cremita*. Do you want *funche*, Child?"

"Give me some . . ."

The Child looks off into the distance and the old woman knows what he is going to ask. When is Papa coming? She won't know what to say. Why doesn't he live with us? Why does he come in such a big, big car and leave in the same car? Why are my eyes green like his, but my hair curly like yours? Red flame within, you'll burn me to the ground, Mother. What have we here, a piece of coal? The old woman goes inside the house. She shakes a can; there is a little bit of cornstarch left for the Child.

"I'm walking up to the big house today to ask the Harpies for your allowance."

"He always leaves."

"We're out of rice and *bacalao*. The hen is about to lay; we can't throw her in the pot yet."

"Godmother, are you my mama?"

Virgin Protector who appeared to the rancher, Mother who saved him from the wild bull, that was over a century ago. Whom are you going to appear to next? She has gone mute mute mute inside the old woman.

"The mother is the one who rears, Child."

"But who is my mother?"

"Do you love me, Child? Because I adore you."

The old woman embraces the boy, rocks him, fingers the tight curls on his little cinnamon-colored head. Black Virgin with a white boy on her lap. The Child fixes his eyes on her. If she could, she would kiss his eyelashes, the hair on his eyebrows, the pores of his eyelids.

"Do you love me, Child?"

"Yes, Godmother . . ."

"Then I am your mother. Come, let's go to the grotto and pray. And you'll see how your father will arrive soon."

The old woman walks to the grotto with the Child. She takes his soft little hand, cottony, smooth, light skinned but not white, a stain in the palm from the sin of the Lord. The Child's little hand disappears within the old woman's wrinkled fingers. She opens the door.

"Go and search for the Three Stars, Child."

"Are these the ones, Godmother?"

"No, the long ones. Come on, light one."

The Child strikes the head of a match against the box. It lights. In the back of the grotto, on a stone altar covered with wildflowers, is the Virgin, seated on her golden throne. The color of her garments snowy, spotless. Over them, a great blue mantle that covers her to the edges of her face. Only the dark hands are visible, the face almost featureless, dark as well. The lonely eyes sparkle in the smoothness of the black porcelain. Behind her, over her garlanded head, her crown of twelve stars sparkles. On her lap, as she holds onto him with one hand, the Divine Boy rests. Of light complexion, almost white, his hair is the color of honey, his eyes light green. "That is you and me, Godmother." The Boy opens his arms to receive the pilgrims, the abandoned. The Child walks toward the figure and hugs the Divine Boy.

The old woman lights the candles, changes the water in the flower pots, opens the only window in the grotto. A breeze smelling of pasture and cattle passes through. You saved the rancher from the charging bull, you saved the whole world, and what about me? They both kneel.

"Godmother, do you think my mama is as pretty as the Virgin?"

"Yes, Child, now let's pray."

Fountain of Grace, bless me; Staff of Patience, guide me; Cane of Jacob, lead me; Rose of the Winds, provide for me. Soothe the voices in my head. Soothe my ire. And protect the Child who is the only thing that I have. Black Virgin with white child on her lap, give me back the ability to say something else, stop giving orders, whatever you want, right away, stop worrying, yesyesyes . . . There is something else that I have to say: give me what is mine, what is the Child's. I cannot die without saying it. Here I light one of the two-cent candles, I light it for you, Virgin, Montserrat, Montserrat, jewel under the commotion of my legs. Let the Father come, let him present himself to the forgotten Son. Let him bring us manna and leave us riches, raising me to my rightful position. María Candelaria Fresnet on my throne of stars, let him free me from the Child and from the Child's questions. And I pledge to you, Mother, that I will not sell you out anymore, I'll retire you from the business and the grotto, I will give myself to you, yesyesyes, completely. No more candles and pilgrims, no more sanctuaries to exhibit you to the desperate. I promise, Holy Mother, and if not, you will see, you will see what will happen. We have to eat, the Child has to eat, and I will not have him go hungry. So see what you can do, Mary, Mother, jailer. Amen, Jesus.

"Let's go, Child, and I'll make you a *fuchecito*. And let's see what I can come up with for lunch."

THE FIRST VISIT

And this stillness of life did not in the least resemble a peace. It was the stillness of an implacable force brooding over an inscrutable intention. It looked at you with a vengeful aspect.

— Joseph Conrad, *Heart of Darkness*

One

THE FIRST TIME that Luis Arsenio Fornarís went to Elizabeth's Dancing Place he already looked like a man. He had the thick shadow of a beard pressing in on his face, the blackest hair, from his father's side, falling in short waves over his brow, and the small green eyes of a cornered cat. He was wide shouldered, not too tall, with very light skin full of freckles. It was the same skin that the Fornaríses had brought from Corsica and the same freckles that marked the forearms of the men of their species. On his face there was not one blemish. A thick beard protected his face from the relentless Caribbean sun.

It was 1936, and everyone went to Elizabeth's Dancing Place. Prohibition was over. It was still illegal to sell moonshine or serve alcohol to minors, but generally the place paid no attention to age, color, or place of origin. A hostess opened the door for clients as if they had come to the promised land. The only requirement was that they came to consume.

The hostess's welcome made him nervous upon entering.

But Luis Arsenio Fornarís knew he was carrying a winning hand. He was sure one of the girls from Elizabeth's would approach him before they did any of his friends, who were still virgins. They had been telling him so in the car.

"Why don't we leave Luis Arsenio behind? With that old man's beard he is going to take the most beautiful girls from us."

"They say that Isabel just arrived from France with a fresh cargo."

"Can you imagine, the first time with a Frenchwoman?"

"The European ones are expensive. Only the politicians can afford them."

"And the soldiers."

"No, what they want is local meat, preferably dark. As if rolling around with the black women in their country wasn't enough."

"They can't, it's against the law."

"What law?"

"Segregation, you asshole."

The conversation continued through their guffaws. They had to become men and, at the same time, soothe the nerves firing off beneath their skins. It was the best way to ward off fear. That night, if everything went according to plan, Luis Arsenio, Esteban, Pedrito, and Alejandro Villanúa would become men once and for all, according to the custom of the men of their stock. In other words, every one of their studied poses would no longer be considered empty. From that night on, the smoking of Tiparillos in the school courtyard, the sip of stolen rum from the family's liquor cabinet, the unexpected erections in the middle of mathematics class, would take on weight and meaning. They would be responding to concrete stimuli, as concrete as the memory of real flesh, open and spread on the sheets of one of the beds at Elizabeth's Dancing Place.

Luis Arsenio listened while his friends talked about politics inside the car owned by the Ferránses, and which Esteban had managed to get. It had cost each of them half of their monthly allowance to buy the silence of the family chauffeur. But it was worth it. They were about to escape to a whorehouse. The chauffeur passed in front of the Fox Delicias Theater (where they had agreed to meet), then headed down Calle Comercio toward the Portuguese River. They left behind the plaza, mostly full of soldiers with their civilian passes asking workers, "Excuse me, friend, do you know where I can buy me a good time around here?" All of the workers knew the answer, without a doubt: "At Elizabeth's Dancing Place."

The conversation changed subjects. Alejandro Villanúa played the devil's advocate, defending the Americans with the audacity of a new convert. Enough of small-town morals. Everyone had the right to be in the plaza. It wasn't true that the soldiers were contaminating it, strolling through it with ladies of the night. Moreover, strolling through the plaza is an indisputable individual right, no matter how uncomfortable it might make the daughter of some family. The modern pragmatism that had transformed America into a model of prosperity and democracy was based on the protection of these rights.

"'*And we the people, indivisible,*' Alejo, but that doesn't excuse that the other day a soldier grabbed Margarita Vilá by the arm and wanted to take her by force. That's not right, my brother."

"They treat us all like peons."

"If Don Franco knew what Margarita did behind his back, soldier or no soldier . . ."

"He'll never know. The only one who deals with Margarita is the maid."

"That's where she learned her bad habits; those *negras* are firebrands . . ."

"You sound like you want to sleep with one."

"Not me, Don Franco. They say that Isabel brought him one from Martinique. He has gone mad for her and loosened his wallet. And Doña Luisa . . ."

"You don't think she knows? Why rock the boat?"

They were in the middle of a country road, entering the neighborhood of Cuatro Calles. Little by little they lost sight of the shacks where the laundresses and laborers born in the backrooms of some stately mansion huddled. The branches of the royal poincianas braided into false roofs that sometimes tore open to the sky to reveal a cloud lit by the rays of the moon. For a moment he pictured the house of his friend Esteban, which was identical to his. Everything in its place, observing custom, the taste and the rigor of good breeding, the porcelain on the mahogany bookcases, the white lace tablecloths. The chandeliers were suspended from the ceiling by a thick cord that held up a weight greater than iron in suspended spirals of crystal bubbles. The windows of the china cabinet reflected a faint tremor, almost imperceptible, blurring the lustrous images seen by the observer who had suddenly discovered them. The lustrous checkerboard of the native tile marble floors formed an imitation Mozarabic arabesque beneath feet that refused to remain there. The tension and a yearning to flee: Why was it always like that?

Luis Arsenio remembered the exact day that he noticed. He was no older than nine. His father arrived at the house a little earlier than usual and found him awake, playing in the living room between the legs of the grand piano that his grandparents had insisted on buying for his lessons. Rather than playing it, Arsenio liked to twist himself into it, exploring the springs that came out of its belly. A dilapidated Noah's ark, a gigantic machine with bandaged keys, a shipwreck . . . That's what he was up to, imagining what the intestines of the piano might be, when his father arrived. It was rare that he heard him arrive. Luis Arsenio remained silent, still, as if waiting for an accident, for something on the point of falling to finally shatter on the floor. He felt guilty but did not know why, as if it were a transgression to be there in that mysterious moment when his father arrived home. Fernando Fornarís took off his hat, hung it on the usual hook, took a deep breath. He rubbed his eyes briefly, then opened them, blinking, regarding the space that was his home as if he were sleepwalking. His eyes were not his; the things in that house not his. And there, in the middle of his delirium, the attorney Fornarís discovered his son under the piano. Their looks crossed; the son, Luis Arsenio, and the father, Fernando Fornarís, fenced in by the space of the living room. His father gave him a slight smile and called him over with a gesture of the hand. Luis Arsenio walked slowly, and when he reached his father, he felt an enormous wish to hug his legs. But his father was a step ahead of him and lifted him in the air. He kissed him on the chin, a soft and meditated kiss, as when Arsenio was younger and his father returned from the long trips to the capital. Hugging each other, they both contemplated the room, wrapped in a complicity that made them nestle into each other, as if waiting for some vehicle to come save them from the hushed anguish of that house.

Esteban smoked a Tiparillo. Luis Arsenio asked him for one. He looked through his pockets for something to light the cigar that his friend handed him.

"Make sure you don't see any cassocks!"

They laughed in unison. That phrase was the one they used when they went out to smoke in the courtyards of the school. And it was perfect now that they were in the middle of their escapade. Luis Arsenio was able to block the breeze coming in from the window and light his cigar. He watched as the wind took the smoke-filled breath from his lungs out the window, who knew where. Fumes in flight.

"Let's go over our strategy, since we're getting close. We each pay individually so we don't get confused with the bill later on. We ask for drinks and a separate table."

"What do you mean, drinks? We're underage. I don't want trouble with the law."

"But, Pedrito, then why are we going to a whorehouse?"

"You go to Elizabeth's to do one of two things, to drink or to, you know . . ."

"What we have to do is get with it. We grab whoever we like right away."

"What if we all like the same one?"

"Not likely, since Villanúa likes only Martinique women."

"Stop fucking around, guys, all this gaggling is going to give us away."

"I hope I run into my father at Elizabeth's. Can you imagine how proud he would be?"

"Or relieved that he didn't have to take you himself."

"Yeah, but if mine finds me there . . ."

"Arsenio, you have nothing to worry about. Your father is the only man in Ponce who never goes to Elizabeth's. Everybody in town knows that."

The chauffeur took a local road that was as dark as a wolf's mouth. Near the end, they could hear music thumping in the distance and see faint lights emerging from the shrubbery. The road was tarred and paved, which was unusual in the country;

but even so, pothole after pothole made the springs in the car reel. It tossed like a yawl advancing against the current. "This Isabel is right around here," said the driver, who hadn't uttered a word since they left town but now let out curses right and left. They went up a hill and came down a slope to a big ranch that looked more like a tobacco plantation than a place for trafficking flesh. The chauffeur turned off the motor and got out to open the door for his passengers. Esteban tipped him again, "So you can fill the tank and no one in the house finds out," and reminded him what time they were to return. The chauffeur fixed his eyes on each of the boys, choosing not to display the lowered gaze or the obsequious smile of a hired servant. It was clear that this place had emboldened him. It was also clear, Arsenio thought, that Elizabeth's followed different rules than the rest of the town, that there the distance between servants and masters was altered, that the body and its humors dared to be more familiar with each other. It was advisable to have that thick beard of the men of his stock, to raise the chin, to hold the chauffeur's stare defiantly, if one wanted to survive the untamed territory of Elizabeth's.

In the distance, as a chorus to the car's engine, they could hear the murmur of the river.

The whole town knew it. His father, the attorney Fernando Fornarís, would not set foot in Elizabeth's, even if his life were at stake. Though it would have been so easy for him. Elizabeth's was right on the banks of the Portuguese River, in a plot adjacent to the family's ranch. All he would have to do was say that there were land disputes he needed to settle, that he had to stay in the country, and cross over. His mother, Doña Cristina, would never have known, suffocated as always with caring for Luis Arsenio, the only child. And when not, suffocated by other spirits. It would not even have been necessary to lie to escape to the Dancing. And Arsenio would have understood. His mother's kisses frightened him.

It would have been so easy for his father to go to Elizabeth's. Perhaps because of this, Luis Arsenio found himself getting out of the car with Esteban, Pedrito Serrano, and the boorish Alejo Villanúa, standing right in the middle of a rocky path, with their backs to the crude driver, who moved away without saying goodbye. Perhaps because of this he committed to the adventure without even thinking what he was going to do once he crossed the threshold of the whorehouse. But they had to cross it before anything else, span the twenty steps from the road to the door. And so he did it. And so did they all, propelled by the same current, tossing their cigars on the ground, smoothing down their vests and their hair, balancing their weight on each of the stairsteps that led up to the door of the entrance. There a hostess, a diminutive figure, was leaning against the banister. She had long black hair that brushed up against the rise of her buttocks and an oriental dress, worn so tight that it seemed painted onto her very skin. Only her stiletto heels made clear that she was in battle gear, that she wasn't a vision. Luis Arsenio swallowed his fear and thought that the time had come to establish the presence of a Fornarís within the walls of Elizabeth's. In this, he was mistaken.

Inside, he saw what he saw and had to admit he was astonished. The swept floors, the well-stocked bar, the spacious, dimly lit dance floor, made him understand why Elizabeth's was so well frequented. It was another dimension. The tables were covered in linen with small candles propped up in the shadows. A stage, big enough to accommodate a *charangas* band, was illuminated with floor lights. The proscenium was adorned with bamboo chips and a strange mural of glittery yellow butterflies on a green background representing foliage. False columns, painted in gold, decorated the ranch house. The ceiling was clean and high, filled with clouds of smoke from dozens of cigarettes. And there was alcohol, rivers of alcohol. Beer, *aguardiente*, moonshine rum, whiskey, wines that mocked the laws that had converted them into illegal elixirs. What had caused this miracle of the transmutation of those waters?

The crowd laughed loudly, drank freely, in that place with the air of a fluffy divan, of a throne without eyes but replete with hands and skin, and with a ruckus that camouflaged words spoken without reservation. On top of this, the girls were there, Isabel's pupils, goddaughters, protected ones, wandering through the room like gifts of flesh. It didn't look anything like the men's-only bars in town—dirt floors, a few stools, and a greasy bar where they put out Dutch cheese and mortadella in the middle of the afternoon. It was not a place for men in short sleeves, with straw hats pushed back and vests draped over their forearms if they were well-off, or handkerchiefs tied around their heads and feet hardened by the earth if they were poor. There was none of that look of an animal corralled by fatigue and tension that reigns over men who cannot alleviate their sleeplessness. It was another dimension, different and joyous, like the festivals where pairs of lovers walk hand in hand toward the game tents and the men chat leaning against the showcases. But no. It was a different kind of joy at Elizabeth's, an overflowing joy that was yet aware of its almost impossible state. The joy was a gift, along with laughter, with women as diverse as one could imagine, ready to talk and to freely give of themselves for the entire night, to listen attentively and gaze deeply into one's eyes, to look away only to begin a game of give and take that would end up gracefully on the bed. These women were responsible for breaking down the tightness in men. There was no tension, no sleeplessness, no silence. Isabel's girls strolled through the ballroom covered in rustles of taffeta, with ample cleavages and carmine lips, brandishing shrieks and laughter and swaying in their high heels, perfumed with a thousand fragrances and with smoke and with the smell of desire given off by those who arrived at Elizabeth's in search of a place where they could loosen the bindings of their decency.

IN THE MIDDLE OF THAT ballroom, an impressive woman smoked, seated on her straw throne. Her eyes open, two deep-set almonds that watched over the place, alert but spilling over each fellow, over each dancing couple, over the hand that opened and closed the cash resister at the bar, over the dark-skinned men, tall as towers, who sipped their drinks with apparent indifference, positioned near the entrances and exits of the room. She passed her eyes over everything as if she were evaluating a variety-show performance and at the same time weighing strategies for defending a mining territory. Her eyes covered everything. Her skin was blue, panther blue, blue like the shadow of a hungering eye. The yellow dress in raw silk made her stand out, as did the solid-gold bracelets dangling on her arm, which held a cigarette holder. Her short, stiff hair framed a face with fleshy lips, a doll's tiny button nose, with a strong chin, more or less squared. Her skin was so glossy that it was difficult to believe it was skin. There was something disturbing about her body, with a minuscule waist, wide hips, and firm, springy breasts under the dramatically low neckline that announced the deep blue of the skin. Her pointed chin moved up and down as she sucked in the smoke from the cigarette holder. No shock, since that lady seated on that throne knew how much of a woman she was. She also knew that her skin was a temptation and that a mere gaze at it would impress anyone.

"My father says that the first thing that we have to do is go say hello to Isabel."

So Esteban incited the action. His friends adjusted their neckties and crossed the ballroom toward that version of a throne. Luis Arsenio wanted his steps to seem insolent, accustomed to the transactions of that bar, but his heart betrayed something contrary. It started beating to the rhythm of a stampede and tangled his walking. He had to close his eyes. It was only for a moment, but it was as if the air were being let out of the room. It seemed as if he could hear Esteban, Alejo, and Pedro from very far away saying hello to the madam. When he opened his eyes, Isabel Luberza was looking directly at him with a defiant smile on her lips. His friends were introducing her.

"Fornarís? Very pleased to meet you. I know your family well, even though they don't frequent my house."

Isabel's eyes were filled with a dazzling ferocity. Luis Arsenio did not know what to make of that welcoming look. In the etiquette manual that he was rehearsing in his head there were no specifications on how to chat with a woman so illegal, so powerful, so blue. Isabel Luberza Oppenheimer, alias Isabel La Negra, alias the Madam, continued to stare at him, reading him through and through. The young man's heart again emptied. Esteban, Pedrito, and Alejo started to become uneasy, infected as well by the distressing thrust of the lady's eyes. But just at the moment when it seemed they could not withstand it any longer, Isabel's eyes shed their intensity. They turned bright and sunny, as if it were another person who was watching them from that dark and solid body, not beautiful at all, no hint that it was the body of a woman desired by thousands, adored by thousands, capable of founding an empire on the shores of a river. Isabel became the benevolent *patrona* again, seated on her straw throne, transformed into a spectacle herself and transforming everything that she could hoard with her gaze into a spectacle. The simple and odd madam of a brothel.

"Boys, order whatever you want. The first round is on the house."

Luis Arsenio was relieved and went with his friends to grab a spot at one of the tables in the back, on the far side of the dance floor. A girl took their order. She was tiny, very young, and a foreigner, which they could tell from the accent with which she said her name. "Altagracia, but you can call me whatever you want, handsome," she responded to Alejandro, who was warming up his lover's engines while she wrote down the drink order. The boys ordered a pack of Lucky Strikes and rum on ice. The band played a popular *pachanga*. Luis Arsenio looked around the place. The bar was packed with soldiers. They had already hoarded many of the girls. Some businessman or other in a linen suit and with a wedding ring drank at one of the tables in the back, like them. In between the shadows of the dancers' bodies, they could spot the presence of someone famous now and then.

"Isn't that Bobby Capó?"

"That's not him, Pedrito!"

"They say that he and Tito Rodríguez come here a lot to live the bohemian life."

"That's all they come here for?"

"What I want to know is why we came, to watch people strolling around as if it were a Sunday after Mass or to get us some nice ass?"

Alejo Villanúa was getting up from the table, taking a last drag from his cigarette. He was pretending not to be, but Luis Arsenio would bet anything that Alejandro was cringing as much as the rest of them, like him, who had barely recovered from having met Isabel La Negra. But for once, Alejandro was right. At the pace they were going, there wouldn't be any girls left when they finally agreed upon why they had come. Raising his eyebrows, Esteban let Arsenio know that he, too, was jumping in. Pedrito, lingering, was the last one to abandon the table. Head down, he made his way toward the dance floor like a dog following the scent of scraps. The *charanga* musicians began to play a bolero by Benny Moré.

Esteban was the first one to take out a pupil to the dance floor. She was a fragile and yellowish girl, a little hick recently arrived in the city, you could tell. Her demeanor was of someone who finds herself suddenly in a strange place. Seated at the table, Luis Arsenio watched them dance. He still didn't feel like getting up. He took a deep breath. At that moment, the laughter of a woman flooded the room like a trumpet solo. Startled, Luis Arsenio looked all around, trying to find its source. Then he saw her. She was a young *mulata*, a replica of the madam, but with a more yellow cast to her skin and looser, the nose pointier, the chin rounder. She was approaching him. She couldn't be older than him, but she walked with the sureness of centuries. She was dressed in green. "Like your eyes," a voice whispered in his ear and that was all he heard. The music and the laughter evaporated in the ballroom like an echo at the bottom of a flaming cup. The girl crouched beside him and murmured a few words, something like, "I've been watching you since you walked in." She took him by the hand. He let himself be taken. He followed her through a corridor full of doors. They went into a small room, separate from the others, but with a ceiling fan and open lattice windows from which a night breeze, common to the shores of rivers, entered. The girl turned around and looked at him over her shoulder, offering him the opening of her outfit so he would undress her. Luis Arsenio put his hands on each button, on each fastener and zipper, amazed that he did not make a mistake on any of the steps. His hands acted on their own, and on its own his blood found the place to ignite his cravings. His limbs gently pushed the girl toward the four-poster bed in the center of the dingy room. Her face crossed great distances and buried itself in a curly lock that smelled of smoke and need. But the need that was imposed was not hers but his; he opened his mouth and planted a kiss right on her face, right on her eyes that he closed with his lips, right on her flesh that he devoured bite by bite, her lower neck, her bitten nipples, her licked and trembling belly, until he could find the riverbed of the flesh within, which Arsenio lapped calmly, not knowing what he was doing, not knowing, in fact, that what he was doing was possible, right, advisable, not even asking him-self. He began to hear groans and responded to that signal as if he had been waiting for it forever. He knew that he had to take up her whole body, open a path through the legs of the *mulata*, bury himself in her warmth until it completely enveloped him; folds and heat would close in around his need. He pushed up and down, finding unsuspected rhythms. He found a place for his tongue, as it twisted itself into the skin of the girl with the yellow skin, the color of pumpkins, with a sweet and sour flavor that reminded him of his mother's desperate kisses. His tongue was mad and his eyes another cloudy madness. He could only open them little by little, perceiving disconnected images. Here a nipple right by his nose, there a knee moving toward his hips, somewhere else nails scratching his forearms, and his freckles jumping from his skin to her darker one. A shock of frizzy hair blurred his vision, a mouth, fleshy and full of folds like the one below, whispered words, then it broadened into a smile, letting him know clearly that this battle was lost, that his will was only this rhythm of pleasures, and that with her he would pay the price for giving in to his need. Luis Arsenio felt the presence of his defeat and grew afraid, a terrible fear that curdled with a greater fury inside his body. He closed his eyes and saw himself from within as the same person, but different, between the legs of another woman but the same one, drowning in tears that weren't his but that invaded him with a sense of nostalgia that he could not explain. Below him, entangled in the sheets, the girl continued to whisper words. He had to give in, he had to fight and give in, he had to understand that defeat was the only possible way out. His manly desires would end up as sweat and milk between the legs of a *negra*. His pelvis emptied in spasms against the body of the girl, who looked at him with more satisfaction than he thought proper for a lover on a fixed salary. A delicious defeat shut his eyes anew.

The girl nestled in his arms. The room smelled like the slime of the riverbed where amoebas and water worms begin a vital cycle. Luis Arsenio Fornarís knew that he had crossed a threshold. Was that perhaps what it was to become a man, that sense of feeling like another, literally another, in the skin and in the moment of another? He put the thought out of his mind and breathed in a moment of tranquillity. But he soon felt the memory of his father's looks seeping into the sensations of his body. Everything happened in an instant. It was the memory of that one look when he was under the piano during that anguished afternoon, that he did not fail to recognize ever again, not even when he bumped into his father in a hallway, or when in the middle of some Sunday dinner, his father returned from his silences and collided with Arsenio's eyes. Luis Arsenio Fornarís, naked, was returning to his body next to the adolescent *mulata* with whom he had made love for the first time. His father looked at him. What was his father doing in that room? How long had he been there?

"Too much excitement," he thought and decided to get up

from the bed. "My father has never set foot in this whorehouse," he almost said out loud, as he slid into one pant leg and then the other, buttoned his shirt and tied his shoes. He was going. He wanted to wash his entire body with lye. He wanted to rid himself of the woman's aroma. And with the aroma would go the memory of the touch, the weight of her legs on his back, the warmth of her crotch swallowing him whole, and the eyes of his father looking at him sadly. Returning to her role as rented woman, the girl watched him get ready. Arsenio found his wallet, took out the money, and placed it decorously under a pillow. The girl took the bills, turned her back to him, and counted them as she twisted herself in the folds of the sheets. Afterward, she crouched by the four-poster bed and pulled out a washbowl full of water. She washed her face, her arms, her thighs, her crotch, and watched him with a vacuous expression. Arsenio could not stand it any longer. He quickly left the room. Behind him he heard a door closing and silent mockery biting at his heels.

"Let's go," he said on returning to the table.

"We're not moving from here until we find out what happened back there."

"I'll tell you on the way."

"Well, since the gentleman Fornarís is intent on protecting questionable honors, I better tell you of my adventures . . ."

"*Ay,* Alejo, but you didn't even last fifteen minutes back there."

"Fuck off, Esteban."

"Isn't it true, Pedrito? We hadn't even finished the drinks that you ordered us and you were back. And the girl looked rather bored . . ."

"Not tickled at all."

In the distance, a rumble of engines muzzled the echo of

farewells. Afterward it was all silence. Hurried steps resounded on the sidewalks of the deserted street and went up the steps of the mansion accompanied by a rattling of keys coming out of a pocket. Luis Arsenio Fornarís arrived at his home. He hastily crossed the quiet living room scarcely feeling its reverberations and quickened his pace. It was imperative that he reach his bedroom, take off his shirt, get under the shower, and let the water soothe the sensations of his skin and his chest. When he passed the study, he found it lit and his father within, engrossed in the reading of some documents. Head bowed, the blackest hair streaked with a gray that gave him an air of both solemnity and fatigue, the whitest skin, freckled all over, a thick beard protruding from his chin, he had been kept up late that night by office matters. His tortoiseshell glasses framed eyes as green as those of Luis Arsenio Fornarís, perhaps a bit less so, the dim hue of already dying weeds. There were those eyes, trapping him again.

His father looked at him. He opened his mouth as if to say something, but the son cut him off with an "I'm home. I'm going to bed," and walked off steadily toward his room. To hear his father's voice at that moment would have been unbearable, because suddenly and without reason, he felt as if all the hatred in the world fell upon his shoulders. That man in that chair was a wretch. Why would he want to talk to him now, what would he say to him, now that he had just made himself a man in between those thighs at Elizabeth's? Why break the silence now, if he could not have warned him beforehand what is lost and what is gained in between those thighs, in between those bodies apparently diverse but that replicate the same woman? It is Isabel's laugh that entangles itself in between men's legs and follows them home like a vengeance. It entangles itself in between the legs, doesn't it, Father? And even if you never again step into the shadows of its dismal rooms, it never lets you stray too far from the Portuguese River. You will always be by its shores.

Luis Arsenio showered. He slipped under the sheets of his bed, but the brush of the fibers made him feel as if he were somewhere else. And again he was where he wasn't supposed to be. He had to return to his home, his bed, and his own body, to sleep, forgetting that night, regaining the prudence of his ways, and becoming Luis Arsenio Fornarís again, son of his father and father he himself would become, link in the Fornarís chain, the eternal chain of men of his stock. He jumped out of his bed and headed toward the kitchen, specifically toward the cabinet where his mother kept the bottle of "cordials" with which she baptized every coffee, every fruit juice, every one of her sad breaths. He put the bottle to his lips and a burning gulp soothed the anguish in his chest.

Now he could sleep, forgetting everything. Fleeing.

Two

"ISABEL . . . GET back here, girl. The river will take you."

"But it's hot, Godmother."

They had spent the whole day washing. The waters of the Portuguese shone brightly in a sun that pecked at the skin. Godmother had chosen a bend where the river turned before emptying in the Salistral neighborhood and the beach at La Guancha. They arrived very early in the morning, "before all of the other washerwomen, *mija*, because if not, the waters get all soapy and the clothes come out grimy." They took out the most delicate items and soaked them in a deep pool. Her Godmother prepared her a dish with parboiled bananas and butter, and a cup of sugar cane juice. Then they set to work. Maruca scrubbed each piece of clothing against the rocks and then went over them with a blue bar of soap, rubbing off the rings around the shirt collars and the mud crusted on the hems of pants. Isabel was in charge of hanging the clothes, the women's undergarments, the underskirts, and of making sure that they were completely clean. But the river was so cool and the sun burned so hot. The waters sparkled as if they, too, were made from fragments of the sun. The girl became distracted. Then Godmother Maruca was calling for her. "Don't make us fall behind, *muchachita*." She tugged her by the arms, put another article of clothing in her arms, soaked with little shards of the sun. She had to resort to a couple of smacks on the bottom when Isabel began to cry because she wanted to go back in the river no matter what.

They finished washing the four baskets of clothes from the ladies in town, the sheets and pillowcases from the Tous residence, the grand Señoras Catargenas' outfits, of the widow and her sister, "who always bring me these petticoats that feel like tents, they're so heavy." Isabel laughed, imagining the widow Cartagena camping under her petticoat. She tossed stones into the Portuguese; she was pretending to be on a camping trip and the stones were bullets. Godmother Maruca folded the clothes that she had laid out to whiten on the rocky shore. "Now we'll see if we can get some starch so I can iron all these clothes. Help me here, *mija* . . ." The girl began to gather the ladies' undergarments and nightgowns. "You take the smaller bundle. Let's go, before it gets too late." The stretch back was long. They would walk by the shores of the Portuguese until they reached the Constancia neighborhood. From there, they would take a shortcut through the Fornarís farm, descending along its outer edges and crossing a bridge to arrive at San Antón.

The royal poincianas, *capás prietos*, and almond trees provided a shade that made the way back easier. The girl Isabel played a winking game, following the rays of the sun, until she could see through the branches that sometimes covered the sky. When she caught a ray of light, her sight broke up into bubbles of color and the outline of the leaves dissolved into a mist. Godmother Maruca went up in front, her dark neck taut as she balanced the immense bundle of clothes on her head. Erect as a wading bird, she sank her long legs into the ground as the light fabric of her blouse fluttered like feathers in the breeze. They, too, dissolved into bubbles of color.

They turned into a stretch of undergrowth that took them away from the river. From beneath them, the murmur of the waters guided them. They could see the bodies of other crouched washerwomen from the high grasses, sleeves rolled up to the shoulders, madras handkerchiefs on their heads to ward off the hot sun. They were all big and dark. All of them were awkwardly crouched, busy at making the clothes fly in the air, the water fly in the air, where rays of light burst into unexpected rainbows.

"Maruca, woman, drop that bundle. You're too old to be a washerwoman."

"And to steal your husband, too, but I did that last week."

Roaring with a sluggish laughter, Lucía, the washerwoman from San Antón, caught up to them. From other bushes emerged Casilda from Merceditas, Carolina from Vista Alegre, and Toñín from Contancia, all with their bundles of clothes freshly laundered, fragrant of river water and sunlight.

"I'm telling this one not to accept any more *reales* from the *patrones*."

"*Reales* are money as well."

"Spanish money. The dollar is the money now."

"And if I get all fussy and they end up not paying me?"

"But, woman, don't you see that you end up losing with the exchange? Casilda, do you know what she charges for the wash? Six *reales* per bale."

"Toñín, you're letting them swindle you. Six *reales* isn't even seventy-five cents with the exchange. I wouldn't even work for the mother who brought me into this world for that."

Isabel grew confused among the chorus of washerwomen. She tugged at her Godmother's skirt. "I'm hungry, Go . . ." Her stomach was rumbling.

"Don't worry, Isabelita, we're almost home. Teté must have already made dinner, and if not, I'll fix something in no time."

The other washerwomen continued chattering. When they reached the bridge, they each went their separate ways.

"So long, Maruca. And you, Isabelita, don't ever become a washerwoman. This is no life for anyone."

"No, my dear, this *negrita* isn't going to be withered by the sun. I already have her spoken for in a house."

"Where? In town?"

"Yes, sir."

Isabel tugged at her Godmother's skirt again. "What does that mean, 'spoken for'?" Maruca's face grew utterly dark. She snapped the hand away from her skirt with an abrupt gesture that frightened the girl. "Don't meddle in the conversation of grown-ups. Bye, dear." Lucía laughed in her face. "*Ay*, Maruca, you're going to have to train your *negrita*, because they'll give her back after a week." With two long strides, Godmother moved ahead of her. Isabel recognized the gesture. Godmother did not want her to hear what they were saying.

They continued with Lucía on the last stretch toward the barrio. From behind, her Godmother and the other washer-woman looked like the same person. Dark flesh, two enor-mous bales of clothes on their heads, cotton blouses, and print or gingham skirts. They walked with measured steps, swaying their hips, moving at a steady pace yet barely lifting their feet

from the ground, finding the perfect rhythm
load. All the washerwomen that Isabel had ever
the same manner. The same as the walk of tha
Godmother had told her was her mother.

It was at that bend in the river where Isabel saw her for the
first time. She was big, with tightly packed flesh and yellow eyes.
Isabel saw her carrying a hemp basket brimming with clothes,
without letting one single piece drop to the ground. Her wide
lips let out a small bright smile, and her straight teeth went well
with the sparkle in her eyes. She wore her hair braided closely to
the skull with a madras handkerchief over it. The wide rump of a
mature woman did not at all match the manly hands with which
she fisted the bar of soap as if it were a pistol. She crouched, set
the basket on a river boulder, and began to beat an article of
clothing against the stones of the current. Water splashed on
her face. The suds of the soap ran up her naked arms, creating a
transparent froth on her wet skin, dazzling in its darkness. Her
arms were upside-down lightning bolts.

The day that Isabel saw her mother, Godmother Maruca
called her over, taking her firmly by the shoulders. She squeezed
harder than usual, as if the girl had done something wrong.
Then she turned her around until Isabel was facing the opposite
shore of the river, and said, pointing with her finger, "That is
your mother." And she told the girl that the crouching washerwoman who made the clothes fly through the air was called
María Oppenheimer and that she was born in the San Antón
barrio to a black Englishwoman who came to the islands to
cut sugarcane, after her man. The woman became a migrant
worker and followed the path of the harvests. She could not
raise a child. María Oppenheimer had been given away forty
days after her birth.

They accompanied Lucía to the outbuilding of her house.

...ke some *panas*, Maruca, before they rot. The tree bore so much fruit this year. They're so good . . ." Her Godmother took the bundle from Isabel's arms. "Here, girl." She handed her two of those round green fruits. They continued home. On two sides of a dirt road, San Antón rose before them. The majority of the town was composed of *bohíos* made of wood planks and thatched roofs, raised on stilts to keep out the critters. Some had cardboard walls and zinc roofs. Each house had an outbuilding, with its fire pit and makeshift ovens where pots brimmed with the day's dinner. It was the time when everyone returned. Bricklayers, launderers, workers from the Mercedita sugar mill, stretched their whole bodies and left their tools at the steps of their houses. Inside, some woman prepared something to put in their mouths. The neighbors greeted Godmother Maruca. The girl Isabel also responded to the greetings, carrying her two *panas*, relieved of the burden of laundry from the river. At the end of the road, children chased after a metal hoop. A lame old woman shouted at them. One more house and they would be home.

In the outbuilding, Teté Casiana was carrying one of her stepchildren whom she cared for. Isabel loved to watch her smoke her tobacco pipe as she watched over the children's games. Every afternoon she sat by the door of the *bohío* waiting for them, Godmother Maruca and her, to return from their washing. She sat on a stool that she herself had carved from the trunk of a balata that had fallen during a storm.

"In San Ciriaco, *mija*. This was the tree that did me in. The Americans had just arrived. And my sow escaped. My sow, *nena*, the only thing I could get out of the Spaniards who left in a cloud of dust when the other white people arrived. They didn't pay anyone, not even with food coupons. But the strong winds worsened. I went in to secure the cistern, for the love of God, and I left the gate of the corral open. That sow was shrewd as the devil. She escaped, you know."

HER OTHER LITTLE BROTHERS, THERE were four, returned to the patio with the metal hoop. One was chasing a hen. Godmother Maruca said hello to her sister and went into the house.

"God almighty, it's hot. Is dinner ready, Casiana?"

"I soaked a *bacalao*. And those *panas*?"

"Lucía gave them to me. Is Mariano home yet?"

"Not yet. Come here, *nena*, sit here. I am going to tell you the story of when you were born and came to live with us."

The girl Isabel let herself be led by the hand, let herself be embraced. Strange, because Teté Casiana was not prone to offer such endearments. In the arms of the old woman, she smelled the smoke that frolicked in the graying coils of her hair. Casiana gave her a timid kiss and sat her at the foot of the stool. Isabel readied to listen to the story as she picked at her toenails.

"You were born on the exact day of the storm. So, *negrita*, that means you have to be respected. When you were born, the Portuguese overflowed. It flooded houses and harvests. Even the Americans had to seek refuge in the brick carriage houses in town. There was hunger for months. That's why I wanted to keep that sow, because I knew that it would be needed after the storm. After the first winds abated, I went out to look for her. The rain pricked at my face like the thorns of wild roses. But I didn't care. I looked and looked for her until I found her. She was by a pickax, shielding herself from the wind gusts. I was going to get her when the sky tore open in two and the bolt that split open the balata struck nearby. I took the blow right on the hips. It went *crack* very clearly, as if it came from within . . . and, oh, what pain. I had grabbed the sow tightly by the rope around her neck, and look here, it was she who saved me. She dragged me toward a cave. It was there that Arminio found me, already thinking himself a widower."

Isabel knew the story by heart, in all its variations. In some, to rescue her, Arminio made a stretcher with branches from the same balata that brought her down. In others, she doesn't know how she awoke the next morning with that balata on top of her. In all of them, Teté later carved things from the balata until her fingers bled. Stools, little animals, cooking spoons. Carving and carving until she could shake the only habit that she had known all her life, which was to work, going crazy when thinking about their condition, the face on her husband counting out pennies so they could eat.

"Forty whole days and nights passed and on the following morning, very early, I awoke to carve from my balata. I was almost finished with the stool. And then, Isabel, my fingers took on a life of their own and began to carve a figure of the Virgin. I started to pray. 'Holy Mother of God, watch over me in my hour of need.' When I was finished carving, on that very road that you see there, your mother appeared with a little bundle of flesh in her arms. It was you, *mija*, and she was bringing you here, on the very day of the end of the quarantine, because she had to go back to work and there was no other family to take care of you. She put a silver dollar in my hand and promised that she would pay me every month for taking care of you. For a whole year she did not miss a payment. Afterward, it became more difficult for her, because she kept changing houses and *patrones*. But the important thing is that she came here and that after her there came other women who wanted me to care for their children. Once again, I put food on the table, until God decided to take Arminio and I brought all my children here. It was then that Maruca saw you and went crazy for you. In an instant, she asked to become the Godmother in your baptism."

"Casiana, stop distracting the girl. Isabel . . ."

"Yes, Godmother."

"Go to Don Demetrio's house and take him this little bit of food."

Isabel got up from the ground beside Casiana's crippled hips. She walked toward the fire pit where her Godmother was serving two dishes with a mixture of fresh vegetables and a little bit of rice. Her Godmother still had a somber look on her face. So, careful not to drop the goods, Isabel ran to Don Demetrio's. The cigar roller's house was the only one in the neighborhood that the girl was allowed to enter without Teté or her Godmother. It did not look like any of the rest of the *bohíos* in San Antón. Anyone would say it was the poorest, if it weren't for the books, stack after stack of books leaning against the plank walls of his little house. Don Demetrio didn't even have a stove, but he had plenty of books. "They are nourishment for the soul," he said. "Well, let's see if you put something down the hatch, so that well-nourished soul doesn't go fleeing from you," Godmother would gripe in reply. In the afternoons, when he returned from the tobacco factory, he transformed his house into an improvised school for the children of the area. Her Godmother—"Let's see if you can show her to read the letters, Demetrio; I think the *nena* is very intelligent"—took her there whenever she could. And even if Isabel missed a few weeks, Don Demetrio never complained—perhaps because her Godmother paid him with food. The first dish served in their house was always for him.

Isabel had to maneuver to get the hot meal to the cigar roller. She had to slip in between bodies, say excuse me and even push one or two workers who were in her way to the steps of the entrance. A group of people crowded around the outbuilding of the little house.

"Holy Mother."

"But why did she kill her?"

"Let me see, give me the paper."

Demetrio Sterling read the news.

On the thirty-first of January, Luisa Nevárez Ortiz, a servant in the Quebrada Honda de las Toas sector, had been sentenced to hang for the murder of her seven-month-old daughter. Never before in the island's history had a woman been sentenced to die. The daily *La Correspondencia* said that when they asked the accused how she got along with her daughter, she replied that she did as well as any mother, she had wanted to move with her daughter out of the house of her uncle, a man named Eduardo Ortiz, where they lived off his hospitality since she had lost her job because they didn't want to give her the back pay that was owed to her. Sometimes she became desperate because the girl would not stop crying. The accused one's breasts were dry.

"I can see why she murdered her."

"That's no excuse to take the life of a child, even if one has given birth to her. You have to bear things and leave it up to God. You have to become resigned to things."

"Ay, Doña, resignation doesn't solve anything when a child is starving to death."

There was a picture with the story. Luisa Nevárez Ortiz, a lost look in her eyes. Her face even more somber than her God-mother's, looking beyond the paper. Isabel imagined it was the same way that the accused would look at the jury, the defense attorney, the judge. As if they were ghosts, or as if she herself were a spirit responding to a far-off call, with her skin turned to sheer rind. She managed to touch the photograph, pass her fingers over the ink that coagulated on the face of the accused.

Then the paper passed from hand to hand, smudging with ink the rough fingers of washerwomen, bricklayers, cane cutters, and cooks from the neighborhood of San Antón.

She would have stayed there by the outbuilding listening to the people talk. She would have stayed to listen to the explanations of Don Demetrio, who always took his time to find a fifth leg on anything. "Here, the true crime is ignorance and exploitation," the cigar roller began to respond. But Isabel's guts were rumbling. She hoped that Mariano hadn't arrived before her. Why couldn't her uncle Mariano get lost forever in the cane fields?

Inside the *bohío,* her Godmother shredded a piece of *bacalao* in a dish.

"Here, *mija*, keep on boning this, but don't throw out the water; it's to finish boiling the vegetables."

"What about the *panas*?"

"They're almost ready."

"But he always eats them all."

"I'm going to take out a little bit for you right now, so you can eat it before he gets here."

He was the man who arrived covered in quicklime, in dust, in scratches, with the smell of rotten fruit in his mouth. Mariano Moreno. Perhaps he had been a good man once. Perhaps there had been a day when his cinnamon complexion and his black eyes had made his sisters laugh. But that must have been before Isabel was born. Now, Mariano Moreno gave rise to a long weariness and a furious yearning not to be wherever he was. It was noticeable from the moment he approached the *bohío.*

There were some seasons when he was hardly at home. He came to eat after work and would take a bath that used up all the water in the cistern, then put on a clean shirt that Godmother received as payment, and go out to be swallowed by the night. He would disappear for weeks, for months, and his absence marked the good times. But sooner or later, he returned. He came back with his eyes red as a demon's. This is why I break my back, so this house fills up with blood that is not mine? He threatened to throw out all the children that the Godmother had taken in from the street, Isabel first, "that fucking *negrita*, such a vain little soot smudge." Godmother Maruca shouted at him that the girl helped with the laundry, with the chores. Furthermore, soon Isabel could begin working as a servant in some house and that salary would help as well. But Uncle Mariano roared over her Godmother's voice. He grabbed things and threw them on the floor until he passed out in his tattered sackcloth bed. He would awake in tatters the next morning, to put his shoulder to the wheel, to look for manual labor in the town, digging pathways, paving roads with stones, until he made enough pennies to disappear for another period of time and try out a different life than the one that he was fated to live.

In the days after he returned, the sisters cared for him as if he were an ill-behaved child, saving the best vegetables for him, the most succulent plate of food, the freshest cane juice. To ingratiate themselves, they made Isabel take his bowl of dinner to the table very carefully, so that not one drop of soup would be lost in between the boards of the *bohío*. Mariano stared at Isabel. Those looks made her uneasy, and it was not just her. Godmother Maruca always appeared when she noticed her brother looking at Isabel in that manner, waiting for the girl to put the bowl on the table without saying a word. Isabel did not forget the insults and the unpleasant experiences, or that slimy thing in his stares. "Don't you look at me that way," she wanted to say him. "Don't look at me; it's not my fault." Afterward, she would go as far away from Mariano Moreno as possible, in case one day he found out what she wanted to say to him and made her pay for it.

That afternoon, Mariano Moreno arrived as always, dirty and scratched. But there was something strange about his mood. So strange that he gave the most tender piece of *pana* to the girl. He also brought cane juice from town. Isabel ate and then went to relieve Casiana from watching the children. Inside the *bohío*, the conversation was for adults.

"Did you speak to Doña Georgina?"

"She said to bring her the girl, not a problem."

"There will be a problem when she sees her. Isabel is far too young."

"When did Mama send you off as a servant? I wasn't even born yet."

"That doesn't—"

"You tell her not to be fooled by appearances. That Isabel knows how to sew and even cook. That she does laundry too."

"Still, Maruca, why don't we wait a little bit? Let her grow up some."

The children were chasing the hens in the dirt patio. Five—with her, six. Isabel counted heads, as Casiana had taught her, to make sure that none of them would escape through the thicket, where a spider could bite them. There was one missing, Julito, the restless one. Isabel saw that the boy was walking toward the steps of the *bohío*. He was almost at the first step. She imagined Mariano's shouts if he saw him. She ran and grabbed him and picked him up while making signs to him to be quiet. But she couldn't help hearing part of the adults' conversation.

"No, Casiana, we have to get that child out of here, before something terrible happens."

"Why are you both looking at me? I haven't touched a hair on that *negrita*. Even though she's a brat. Do you see how she looks at me?"

"Like you look at her."

"All right, enough . . ."

"The truth is, Casiana, that Isabel is going to be better off in town. She will be fed and housed. Mariano, did you tell Doña Georgina to enroll her in school?"

"Yes, Maruca . . ."

"If they enroll her in school, then I'll go along with it."

"Every time I return the laundry, I'll stop in and see her."

"And bring her here, so that I can see her."

"Good, I'll take her tomorrow."

"No, Mariano, I'll take her. I'll bring her to Doña Gina, see if they still want her."

"Even better."

"But they have to enroll her in school. If not, I'll take her back."

THE SUN WAS IN THE middle of the sky. Above the clouds, dark birds glided, as if held up by invisible strings that twisted in the wind. Isabel looked at them, squinting so she could see them get lost in bubbles of color, in the haze of the sun, but it was not working. Godmother Maruca walked a few paces ahead. In her arms, Isabel carried a small bundle of her clothes. She had not thought they were so few. She walked wrapped up in silence. And that silence was different than usual, when the hush would have been a response to an "Isabel, enough with all that racket," or when it was a game, like the one she tried to play with her eyes. But it wasn't working. Above her, the birds remained attached to the sky with their wings, and Isabel would have liked to ask her Godmother, "What kind of birds do not allow themselves to be erased?" But her chest did not let her. It felt so sealed off that she could barely breathe.

"Come on, girl, pick up the pace, we'll never get there."

Isabel would have liked to respond, "Yes, Godmother," and at the same time name the birds that glided in the air. Perhaps they were mangrove birds. Maybe if she figured out how to open her mouth and breathe again, swallow air to break that silence, she could tell her Godmother, "Up there," and her Godmother would see the birds and read their designs in the sky. She would say in a low voice, "No, not today." And they would turn around. They would return to San Antón to chase after the hens, to listen to Casiana's stories, to watch Julito so he would not run into the steps of the *bohío*. They would find a way to avoid the vengeance of Mariano Moreno. Perhaps the birds would inform her Godmother that the solution was a simple one: close the door tightly once the uncle had left the house and never let him in again, or poison his food and the next day make him a balata coffin to bury him in the cemetery. Say a rosary over him and that's it. Then, Isabel promised, she would take care of all the chores, mop the floors, scrub them with a brush. She would make the juiciest omelets over the wood stove so Teté Casiana did not have to sweat, she would learn to balance baskets full of clothes on her head, like her mother, and she would care for her Godmother so she could rest. She would become the hardest-working washerwoman in town. She would make a lot of money, go to Demetrio Sterling so that he could finish teaching her how to read and write, and then she would never have to go to a stranger's house, with people she didn't know, who would never understand the silence that was now gnawing at her throat and would not let her speak.

But her Godmother was not looking up at the sky. She walked steadily. She had taken off her only pair of shoes so they would not become soiled with the dirt from the path. Her eyes were fixed on the road, beyond the wind and the pastures. It was a look that did not notice anything, not even Isabel, who walked behind her Godmother, hoping to catch up with her but always falling back, behind that look that did not notice anything because you had to walk forward, always forward, trying to catch up to something that left you behind, outside of time, suspended in the air like a mangrove bird, soaring far away, behind everyone else.

A PAIR OF BLACK HANDS reaches up for the bronze knocker of a mahogany door with carved overlay and stained glass. As the door opens, an old servant in a shapeless dress moves her hands from the doorknob toward the pockets of a floral print apron. She wears a white handkerchief on her head. It is Lorenza, Isabel would later find out. Outside, at the entrance, she had stood there solemnly by her Godmother, waiting for the door to open while Godmother played with her hands, rubbing them together, nervous. She said hello to Lorenza. That is the name of the old woman who opens the door; don't forget it. Godmother looks at her and makes a gesture with her mouth, something like a smile. But she frowns on the verge of some uncertainty. Lorenza clicks her tongue, looks at the floor. Then she looks at Godmother again.

"So you made up your mind?"

"Well, *mija* . . ."

"Don't worry, she'll be fine. I'll get Doña Gina . . ."

Two silhouettes appear on the floor. One walks slowly a few steps behind the other, which happens to belong to a white woman, tiny, with chestnut hair and brown eyes, her hair up in a high bun. Her outfit, with a round neckline and lace, makes her look older than she is. It covers almost her entire body, sleeves to the elbow, hemline down to the ankles. Isabel thought that any moment the lady would drop to the floor from the heat. Too much clothing . . . Perhaps because of this she could not stop fidgeting, smoothing the skirt, the pockets, her hair, with the hand which displayed her wedding band, and nervously fingering her earrings. She arrived with loud footsteps that echoed against the ceiling of the mansion. Lorenza led her to the door and remained back in the shadows broken up by the sunlight through the patterns of the stained glass.

"Maruca, I think I have some sheets that need to be washed. Come in through the servant's entrance."

"No, Doña Georgina. I've come to bring Isabel. She is very obedient and hard working. You would do us a great favor."

"Isn't she too young?"

"Not really, Doña Gina. At her age, I was in charge of an entire house. But it's up to you. If you like, I'll take her and bring her back . . ."

"The truth is that Lorenza is getting old on us and could use a little help. But I can't pay her much. A dollar a month."

"And will you enroll her in school? You said that if I brought her, you would enroll her."

"Of course. That way she can keep my daughter company and help her with her homework. The things that they teach in school today . . . Who understands them? Don't worry, Maruca, I will do you that charity. Lorenza go get Virginia."

Lorenza gazes at them from the shadows. Then Isabel watches her disappear into the drawing room of the house to do as she is bidden. Her Godmother continues talking with the lady in a tone that Isabel has never heard before. It seems that she has become shorter, as if suddenly she had shrunk before that tiny woman, almost a midget, who right away saw herself as taller than her Godmother, with more flesh on her bones. It is difficult for Isabel to believe that such a woman speaks forcibly, that her words are heard as more potent compared to the murmur that trickles from the mouth of her Godmother, Maruca Moreno, the only one who knows how to stand up to the bestial roars of her brother. It is very strange. Her God-mother has shrunk irremediably before Isabel's eyes.

Lorenza returns holding a girl by the hand. Two long chest-nut pigtails, a sailor's suit with white socks, leather ankle boots with black string. They are worn by a stocky girl, of a some-what spongy plumpness that contrasts with Isabel's thinness. And there is Isabel, in the doorway, her arms like sticks for chasing cats, her little legs underneath cowed under the skirt of a shabby dress, fraying at the sleeves, with oil stains on the chest, and in her hands, a bundle with the few things she had in the world. She never knew she owned so little. The girl in the pigtails, by contrast, owns the very sun. She shines encased in her little sailor's suit, her hair tied with lustrous ribbons, her plump, rosy skin free of blemishes, hand in hand with the old woman who drags her feet and avoids looking at Isabel's God-mother. Mama Maruca continues to shrink before the lady as she squeezes her hand. Isabel sees everything as if she weren't there but in a long bright hallway, from which she can look at everything with a cold curiosity. At the end of the hall-way, she sees herself—skinny, dirty, with nothing she could call her own. The only thing that is hers is her Godmother, who has now shrunk as if she were about to disappear and become nothing but a tenuous sensation in her hand. The Isabel from the hallway reaches out her fingers and tries to touch the dirty, skinny girl who is her, but halfway there she stops. "No, I better not." Her eyes pull back from the empty air that separates the two.

"So, child, what is your name?"

The Isabel in the doorway looks at her Godmother, who makes a gesture with her chin, so she answers the lady's question.

"Isabel."

"Well, Isabel. This is Virginia, the girl of the house. Do you want to play with her?"

Isabel looks at her Godmother again, who gives her a shove so that she goes in.

"Go ahead, *mija*, you stay here and I'll come back for you later. Do everything that the lady asks. And behave yourself. You are going to enroll her in school, right?"

"You can count on it . . ."

Lorenza takes Isabel by one hand and Virginia by the other and ushers them inside the house. Meanwhile, the Isabel from the hallway sees how the other Isabel drifts away into the house; she turns, expects to see her Godmother with her eyes teary at least, expects her to look up at the sky so that the mangrove birds would tell her no, that she has no right to leave her with these people who make her feel as if she has so little. But Godmother does not cry, or look at the sky, or do anything. She merely turns and leaves, down the steps, in her clean shoes that she will take off when she gets to the outskirts of town so as not to wear away the soles or soil them in the dirt. Lorenza smiles compassionately. From the hallway, Isabel watches the silhouette of her Godmother move away past the beveled brilliance of the stained glass.

Doña Georgina's heels click urgently, and before the shadow disappears she commands: "Lorenza, start running a bath. This girl needs to be washed before she dirties the whole house."

Engines

THE PURRING OF an engine approaches from the road on the hill. The old woman sees the blue Packard arrive against the green of the shrubbery, winding down the curves. The Child is making sand castles in the dirt, his mouth dirty with mud. The old woman runs to find a wet rag, runs to find the Child his nice clothes, the ones he always wears to meet the Señor.

"You see, Child, I told you. If we kept on praying, your father would come."

The Packard parked near the big house. Doña Eulalia and Doña Pura approached the balcony and once there smoothed the pleats in their skirts, fixed the hair in their buns. The old woman saw them from where she was bustling to get ready below on the hill. The chauffeur got out to open the door for the attorney. Mr. Attorney, Mr. Attorney, to what do we deserve this pleasure; she heard them. What brings you here? Are you visiting Robertito? We'll let old Montse know right away. They are the old ones, falling apart in wrinkles, with their papery skin, like the wings of an albino cockroach . . . Pretending they know nothing while we wither from hunger down here. But today is the last day, I'm telling the attorney, telling him everything. You will give me strength, Mother.

"Come, Child, let's change your clothes and comb your hair so your father sees how pretty you are."

The old woman puts the linen pants on the Child, passes a tortoiseshell comb with chipped teeth through his hair.

"No, Madrina, it hurts."

"Stay still, *muchachito* . . ."

The Child's tight curls get all tangled up in the comb. The old woman puts brilliantine on it, passes her fingers over the hair to straighten it. How long has it been since she last combed it? Yesyesyes, centuries, but I always bathe him, de-lice him, and feed him, I am the loyal slave, the humble respectful one, may the will of the attorney be done through me. And why is the Child in the sanctuary *bohío*? The old woman hears them. Doña Montse can't handle too much commotion anymore. That *negra* is stronger than a balata. I wish you could have seen how she cared for our late brother. She is a pure soul.

God the Father, God the Son, God the Holy Spirit, have mercy on me. Intercede, Mother, with the force of your crystal staff. Strength. The voices in the head of the old woman come together with her own voice.

Do you want a little haw soda, a *mamey* shake? The attorney does not want anything; he doesn't want to set foot in the big house. With a flick of his hand he dismisses the Harpies. He descends the hill toward the old woman's *bohío*. She sees him, hears his footsteps. How does she hear so well? She holds the Child's cinnamon hand in her own veined hand. The Father will come and save the Son. He will legitimize my position. She, too, smooths the pleats of her thin blouse, which flutters in the wind, unwashed. Black Virgin with the white Son on her lap. Standing in front of the *bohío*, they wait for the Señor's visit.

The Child frees himself from her hand. He runs to meet the Father.

"Child, ask for your father's blessing."

The Father lifts him up in the air and looks at him. Green eyes against green eyes; they are the same. A few more freckles on the Father, a toastier shade on the Son, but the broad chin, the oval face, the blackest hair, the arched eyebrows, and those green eyes like glass. It is confirmed by just looking at them. The attorney cannot deny his germinated seed.

"So good you have come. The Child was beginning to miss you."

"This boy is so big and so strong."

"Look how fast I can run, Papa."

The boy runs downhill toward the grotto of the Virgin. He touches the stone wall and returns. The attorney looks at him and smiles, that fatigued smile that is never erased from his countenance. Green eyes of the Son, sparkling, green eyes of the Father. The Child returns gleaming and throws himself around the papa's waist. He laughs. Pitcher of water, promise of joy. The Father shakes off the far-off look in his eyes and laughs as well, placing his white hand on the head of the Chosen One.

Yesyesyes, whatever you say, whatever you want, I am here, ready, upright, newly a slave, Virgin, open the grotto, yesyesyes, sir. The Forgotten One . . . The voices in the old woman's head confuse her. Did the attorney say something? He wants some water. Does he want me to brew him some coffee?

"No, Doña Montse, I have come to spend the day with Robertito. I want to take him into town and buy him whatever he needs. He is about ready for school. I am going to see if I can talk to the principal to enroll him."

TELL HIM NOW, OLD WHORE, tell him that the Harpies won't let you enroll him, that they have you serving them day and night, day and night, Doña Montse, Doña Montse, light another candle for the Virgin, the other one went out; change the water in the flowers, it stinks. Up there in the big house, the chapels with the blond Virgins, immaculate, sheltered from the eyes of the pilgrims. And you, yesyesyes, dumb old woman, the flame you are named after corrodes your insides, yesyesyes, so you can go then and do the same thing to Montserrat. Come light the candles for me, come, bring my lace coif. They are going to kill me, all these Virgins, sir. I am old, Mr. Attorney, I am old and I don't even have a place to drop dead. Not even this shack is mine, tell him, stupid old woman, damned to hell be all these Virgins.

"Why don't you come with us, so you can tell me what the Child needs."

The old woman takes two hesitant steps on the dirt in front of the *bohío*. Did she hear right? The attorney wants her to go with him, to leave the place where he has her buried, leave the sanctuary, the neighborhood of the sanctuary, next to Salsipuedes, up the road from Miosotis, that it be she and not the Other Ones who sits in the chauffeured blue Packard and accompanies him to town. You see, I told you, if you recite the rosaries that you owe me . . . Mother who wraps me in her mantle, the prison of your skin lifts me to the clear blue sky of the Packard. The old woman climbs up the steps of her little house as fast as she can. From below, the laughter of the Child hastens her. The laughter of the Child and his papa, Son of the skies, visitor Father. She puts on her best print dress, with tiny flowers, pearl colored, a black handkerchief on her head, and plenty of talcum powder on the flaccid skin around her neck to prevent sweat. She can't find her shoes, the black ankle boots that she wears with her stockings to church on Palm Sunday. She looks for them under the bed. There they are. She puts on her stockings and goes outside with the boots in one hand, wearing sandals. She will put them on in the car, so that the impious dirt will not soil them.

They climb the small hill. Doña Eulalia and Doña Pura watch her get in the car. "We'll keep your lunch warm, Mr. Attorney, for when you return . . ." They're going to have to stuff their lunch up their asses, damn them. The old woman looks at them, smiles within. The chauffeur turns on the engine. The attorney lets the Child sit near the window so he can look at the scenery. He steps aside to let her in, for you, you wily old woman, Mother. The old woman sits cautiously on the leather seats; don't stain them with anything: with her own skin? Take us into town, Juancho. They leave behind the big house, Don Armando's two sisters, tools of the Beast. They are nailed on the balustrade balcony like pillars of salt. The Child sticks his hand out the window, "Be careful, Robertito," and plays with the wind currents. Rafael, I would have liked him to be named Rafael, Angel of Vengeance. The chauffeur takes the road toward Camino Grande. They turn on San Antonio to get to the office of the superintendent of the school.

"The principal owes me some favors. Let's see if we can enroll the Child, even though the term has begun."

The town through the window. Calle Ruiz Belvís, the plaza, the library, the works of Our Lady of Montserrat.

"Doña Montse, why don't you bring the Virgin from the sanctuary here?"

"And what do I keep, Mr. Attorney? How do I make a living?"

"Isn't there enough with the allowance that I leave with the ladies?"

"Those two old women don't give us anything."

The Child saves her, the Son redeems her, the Child says what can't come out of your mouth, you old whore. Yesyesyes, the Child is your rage and your vengeance. The old woman says nothing while the attorney looks at his son's green eyes, looks at the old woman's black eyes. A sweet, bovine smile on the old woman's face. Accept everything, old woman, accept everything, like the Virgin, let her will dissolve in you.

"What did you say, Robertito?"

"That those women don't give us anything, and Godmother and I sleep in between sacks. I am afraid, Papa, that I am going to get stung by a scorpion. The other day I dreamed that—"

"Juancho, you better turn here and take me to the Casa Alcadía."

They stayed outside with the chauffeur. The attorney gave them some money. The Child felt like having sesame cakes, "and some sugarcane toffee, Godmother, and sugar cookies." "You can't swallow everything, Child. What an appetite!" Not even the holy hunger that your word makes Law. The old woman walked proudly, taking the Child by the hand. Let's get you an ice cone; what flavor do you want, my cuckoo? What about you, Godmother, what are you getting? The old woman asked for coconut, in honor of the coast she was from. That shitty hillside. She watched the vendor shave the ice with his metal comb till it became a see-through dusting. In a paper cone, he colored it with sugar syrup and fruit juices. Now the water will melt in your mouth, naughty one. The old woman laughed on her own, while she let the Child of her heart taste

her cone, Rafael, Rafael, my angel, then she took the cone to
her mouth, slurped up the watery juices from the cup. Don't
stain your shirt, Child; come, let's go around the block.

The Child threw stones at the pigeons, climbed up the
rubber trees in the plaza, jumped down from the walkway
benches. *Muchachito*, for God's sake, stay still . . . He wet his
hands in the fountain. The attorney was still in the Casa Alcadía. The Enemy is Doña Eulalia and Doña Pura asserting
themselves with the Word of the Absent One. The Enemy is
the place at the bottom of the hill, at the end of the farm in
this shitty town where I said yesyesyes, Black Virgin with the
white boy on your lap. Black Virgin, white boy . . . How long
would the attorney be? Suddenly, she saw him walking out
toward the car where Juancho, the chauffeur, awaited him. If I
were younger, I would grab that Juancho and take him out to
the fields and show him some things. The old woman called
the Child and they walked toward the blue sky, the Packard.
Strength, Candela. Put out the voices. Don't let the gentleman
hear them from inside your head; don't let him see you moving
your lips, alone, lost in murmurs.

"Montse, why didn't you tell me before?"

"What, Mr. Attorney?"

"That your real name is María de la Candelaria Fresnet."

"No, Papa, her name is Godmother."

"It's because of the pilgrims."

"I'm not following you."

"The pilgrims to the grotto. They started calling me after
the Virgin, and I let them, not to contradict them . . ."

"But if I had known your real name we would have been
spared several hours at the Registry."

"Now it is me who isn't following."

The attorney responded by handing her some documents.

You don't know how to read, you old idiot, you don't know how, O Mother, watch over her ignorance, her absolute disturbance. The old woman looked at him, her eyes empty, and empty the name in your name, Amen. The Child took her hand and she squeezed his fingers, dirty and sticky with fruit juice.

"What are those papers, Papa?"

"Doña María Candelaria, here is the title to your property. The grounds on the hill are yours and so is the monthly allowance for the Child. Now, let's go to the school, and on the way see if we can talk to some builder that you know. What that little house needs is someone to fix it up."

The Father took the Son's hand and they walked in step toward the Packard. He made a gesture of disgust and surprise, taking out a handkerchief and wiping the Child's hands with a frown. He cleaned his own hands as well. A look of affection reappeared on his face, but the distance in the eyes remained.

"You will never be stung by a scorpion," she heard him whisper. "I promise."

La Cachita

THREE JUANS SAILED on the sea. A tempest of wind and rain approached. It overturned their yawl and they were drowning. Since they were devotees of the Virgin, and they wore her on a locket, when they saw themselves lost, they clamored for her. The Virgin appeared and saved all three of them, Juan the Hateful, Juan the Indian, and Juan the Slave. After she had saved them, she told them: "You know, my dear children, that I am the Queen Mother of God the All Powerful; those who believe in my great power and are forever devoted to me will always carry my likeness stamped on a medal so that it keeps them company and free from evil. They will be free from sudden death; no rabid dog will bite them, nor any other animal. They will be free from accidents, and even though a woman be alone, she will not be afraid, because she will never see visions of the dead." I will respond: "All shadows will dissipate in my path, Amen, Jesus, the Virgin of Charity is with me." Afterward, she addressed Juan the Slave: "Juan, here I leave you, with the Holy

Gospels and the Cross on which my Son died, this prayer for a woman in labor, or she who feels afflicted by the throbbing in her heart, for a bad labor of any type brings bad consequences. Let her put this prayer over her belly, making the sign of the Cross, in memory of the seven sorrows that struck me. From on High will come God's blessing. Let her pray a Hail Mary to the Holiest Virgin of Charity. Her pains will vanish immediately, those of her heart, those of her belly, both. May the blessing of God the Almighty descend upon you. Amen, Jesus."

And she disappeared.

Three

HE AWOKE KNOWING what he had dreamed. The smell told
him, the smell of old sweat, as if he had spent all night tossing
inside a giant pumpkin whose pulp caressed every inch of his
skin. This is how he woke up, smeared with something thick
and vegetal, somewhat with the acidity of nausea, somewhat
with the sweetness of a thing that dissolves slowly in the mouth.
In between his legs, he felt something like the white of an egg
beaten on a burning surface. The dream repeated itself; it had
been chasing him for a few nights. It definitely occurred for the
first time after Arsenio had gone to Elizabeth's. In the dream
he was on the farm near the Portuguese River. Someone was
calling him from a distance. All he could discern was the echo
of that voice screaming his name from beneath air turned into
water. The echo was the voice of a woman, calling him like
a lost child. He was supposed to return, not walk any farther
into the high pastures. But he was not going to obey. He never
obeyed in the dream.

Behind some recently cut banana trees, the sky filled with butterflies. The smell of pumpkin sweat had just condensed in the air. Out of nowhere, the smell of the butterflies became thick weeds. And then the dark hand of a woman pushed him through it. His chest filled with horror because of the strength of that hand, which led him into a limbo where his entire body floated on the leaves. Those leaves had the power to scratch his skin, but he didn't feel anything behind him. All the heat was up-front, where that hand rested, grabbing him in between the legs. Something clinked. The dream filled with metals, perhaps of distant bells, accompanying the echo of that woman's voice that warned him not to go there, but it was too late. That thing the hand grabbed hardened and filled with sap, a juice that ached in between his legs, a fluttering in his belly that made him want relief, any relief. Over his bloated belly rose a dark face, the face of a black woman who looked at him from below, where the hand jabbed at the clothes until it found that piece of flesh that cut short his breath and burned him. She looked up from below, full of power. He, lying there, could do nothing but fear and yearn.

The woman opened her mouth slowly and brought it close to his flesh, which jumped as if alive in the plants that were her hands. Then the smell of exposed pulp clouded his vision. He awoke, startled, with the feeling of a million wings of insects ricocheting off his face.

He struggled to sleep all afternoon. But he did not want to get up. He could indulge himself. He had been on vacation for a week. Christmas was coming. It was his mother's feast. Doña Cristina Rangel took advantage of the Christmas holiday to remind everyone that she was the señora of the house, a true lady, the giver of domestic commands, who ordered the ham, the cuts of pork loin, the punches, the marzipan, and the hazelnuts to offer the guests who passed by the house with their good wishes. New outfits had to be tailored for midnight Mass; she had to buy a new mantilla, since her old ones had been seen too often by her friends at church. She needed an embroidered tablecloth for the center table and had to put together the nativity scene, which was essential to give the house that pious touch. Doña Cristina Rangel de Fornarís would assume her role of the guardian of tradition. Daughter of Mary, Amen, Jesus; Follower of the Mother, Amen, Jesus; Horn of Plenty, Amen, Jesus. She would not be corrupted by the new Christmas fashions that the Americans had brought over—those horrendous pine bushes that they decorate with paper garlands and lights that go on and off, and . . . they turn their houses into brothels—but maintain modesty and good manners, so that family and friends could see that in that house life was lived spectacularly, full of harmony and family unity, like in a dream.

Luis Arsenio knew the script by heart. His whole life he had seen it repeat itself again and again. His father disappeared early in the morning, announcing that he would not return for lunch, that he had a sea of last-minute clients who wanted to put their legal documents in order before the end of the year. After saying a rosary, his mother would come down to the kitchen to have her coffee and breakfast alone, that coffee that always smelled like something else, those strange cordials that she offered visitors—the grapefruit one or the star anise one or homemade cherry cordials. The cupboard was always full of colored bottles that emitted an aroma of the slow fermentations with which his mother baptized her coffee every morning to begin her day. During the holidays, things became worse. One, two cups. Then the torture began. Doña Cristina pursued her son throughout the house. She wouldn't leave him alone even in his bedroom, or on the patio, not even in the bathroom. She insisted on rinsing the suds of foam from his jawbone. She paid no attention to the shadow of a beard that he already shaved and treated him like a child, asking him insistently what he wanted as gifts for Three Kings' Day. "Mother, it is almost two weeks until the sixth of January; leave me alone . . ." But no, she would not rest. You had to be on guard. You had to go to the store beforehand, find out if they had what was needed, and if not, send out for it somewhere else. "And you know, my angel, that on this island everything takes forever, so that it may not be here by the sixth . . . Remember how much you wanted that little electric train, the one with the red cars? If you knew how much I suffered so that they arrived on time and not shatter your illusions . . ." Luis Arsenio ground his teeth, trying to get his mother's hands off him, taking away the comb with which she tried to part his hair correctly, trying to prevent her from throwing a tantrum with Casiana because there was not enough linen in his pants.

"I don't want anything, Mother. Leave me alone, leave me here dreaming of a *negra* sucking me off . . ."

He swore to himself he would say it. If she forced him to get out of bed, Luis Arsenio swore that for the first time he would be vulgar with his mother and say it. But that is exactly the gift that he wanted: to slip away from that emptiest of beds, run toward San Antón, and dive into Minerva's dark body. That was her name, Minerva. He had known it for a few weeks, since the day he had seen her in the light of day walking in the plaza toward the same shop where his mother bought lingerie. She was with another girl from Elizabeth's, he was sure, because they clasped each other's hands, their arms interlaced as if working up the courage. The men in the plaza looked at them suspiciously, afraid that one of them would dare to say hello. The women looked back at them in disgust. He saw them cross the plaza with an excessively determined step, their chins defiant. His girl was dressed simply, in a floral cotton dress and shoes with black stockings. She had braided the dark honey of her hair under the nape of her neck. And her skin, which was exactly the same hue as her hair, made her look like a toasted sesame seed glazed with sugar.

They had almost crossed the plaza onto Calle Perla, to the block with the lingerie shop. The girls opened a path amidst the crowd of shoeshine boys, lottery ticket, ice cone, and vegetable vendors, and were getting ready to cross the street. Luis Arsenio saw how the vendors said hello to them, free of tension or fear. An everyday hello. He saw, in fact, Esteban's chauffeur, the same one who had taken them to Elizabeth's almost a month before. It was the chauffeur who in a lively voice shouted, "Minerva," and made a gesture that made the girl spin abruptly on her heels. Her cotton dress also spun in the wind and revealed a little more of the sweet sesame seed of her calves. At once, Arsenio's vision grew blurry and his blood simmered as if he had swallowed fire. He turned. And he too went after the girl. He couldn't help it. He paused only when he saw himself reflected in the windows of the lingerie shop, just as he was about to touch her on the elbow before she went in. It was the terror, the echo of laughter biting at his heels, the suspicion of the stares of the passersby who recognized him . . .

"There goes the attorney Fornarís's son . . ."
  "What is he doing with that *mulata*?"

"That girl works at Isabel La Negra's bar."

"Today's youth has no respect . . ."

The terror made him cover up his intentions, keep on going, find refuge in looking at perfumes in the shop window of the store next door, thinking he needed half-cent stamps. He passed by the lingerie shop again but did not see Minerva, with her defiant chin, walking with a resolute step through the aisles of the store. He didn't see her looking out of the corner of her eyes at the attendants, who smiled, sneering and attentive to any movement the girls might make that would give them the opportunity to put them in their place with some hurtful remark. He didn't see her confronting the decency of other women, the sound proof of the superiority of other women of the species. They were all superior to her, because Minerva was a whore and she was black, and those were the worst two things you could be on the face of the earth. He didn't see her. But afterward, the dreams by the river became more frequent.

He finally decided to get out of bed. He would shower. Go by Esteban's house. He had to convince his friend to go with him again to Elizabeth's. Just the two of them, without Pedrito and his stray-dog face, and without Alejo Villanúa and his mischief-making. He was counting on Esteban's loyalty to bring him out of this trance. He had to go see Minerva, be with her one more time, at least. He would find a way to tear her from his dreams and his hunger afterward. He would find a girlfriend, perhaps, a proper girl he could kiss chastely and introduce to his family. But he didn't have the nerves for that now. Now he had nerves only for Minerva, to lick the sesame seed in between her legs, ask her to suck him, penetrate her, put the backside of her calves around his neck. But first he had to slip under his mother's surveillance and convince Esteban to come with him.

Thank God, his mother was busy putting up the nativity scene. Doña Cristina pestered Delmira and Carmela. She had them high up in the ladders of the back courtyard bringing down boxes full of old newspapers that protected the porcelain figures. From the shreds of paper, full of lizard droppings, there emerged the Virgin with Son, Saint Joseph, the mule, the cow, the sheep, and the shepherds. You had to be extremely careful and take obsessive care lest one of the figures break. Luis Arsenio stuck his head out the door at the moment that his mother berated the servants, that "then you have to order them directly from Spain, and you don't know how much trouble that is, of course you don't, you don't even know for certain where Spain is."

"You see, Carmela, the paint on the rooster's beak chipped off."

"Don't worry, Señora, I'll fix it with a drop of nail polish. No one will notice."

"Nail polish? This is a very expensive figurine. Mother of God, grant me patience with these creatures who do not know the value of things . . ."

Delmira and Carmela sighed. Luis Arsenio watched them, kneeling among ceramic figurines and old newspapers, squinting their eyes, looking everywhere for the patience, the strength with which "to please the señora." But it is impossible to please the señora. That is part of the game. Pleasing her is impossible because her standards are unattainable, the señora's tastes most excellent, the señora's sensibility fragile as glass. The señora's sacrifices those of a mother most loving, the señora's sorrows those of a martyr of the home. The señora will always be unsatisfied and the world eternally in her debt. Only her balm will console her. The balm of her liquors, that daily squirt of the secret concoction with which she perfumes her coffee. Luis Arsenio knows this and is embarrassed by it. He is embarrassed to see the servants kneeling and looking through shreds of shitty paper. He is embarrassed to see his mother with her drink in one hand and a handkerchief in the other covering her nose from the dust of the boxes. He is embarrassed by himself, trying to escape on tiptoes down the stairs, fleeing to Esteban's house to convince him to go with him that night to Elizabeth's Dancing Place. But he suffered more from hunger than from embarrassment. He managed to slip out the servant's entrance.

Taking Calle Almenas, Luis Arsenio turned on to Sevilla. Two more blocks and he would be at Esteban's. Canted Majorcan entrance, bronze knocker, a house so like his. But he was out of luck. The Ferráns family's residence was full from top to bottom, left to right. From the large wrought-iron gates, he could see the bustle of people. Luis Arsenio had to wait for more than fifteen minutes in the entrance vestibule while Esteban pulled himself away from his family. This couldn't be a simple Christmas visit.

"My uncle Jaume has arrived from Barcelona."

"Who?"

"Haven't I told you about the uncle in Catalonia?"

"I thought you were Corsican."

"And Catalan, on my mother's side. Uncle Jaume has come seeking asylum, Arsenio. They say that things are hotter than the devil's tail over there and that it doesn't make sense to send me to set up a career in Spain because it is in the hands of the anarchists."

"Fuck, no."

"Come, so you can meet him."

Esteban dragged him by the hand just as he was about to say

something about their proposed escapade. If he wanted to win his friend over, it looked like he was going to have to meet Uncle Jaume. But there was enough time to kill until nightfall. Esteban's house seemed like a safe enough refuge from his mother's holiday obsessions. He wouldn't lose anything by listening to conversations about the outside world, cooling the fever in his flesh that came from his dream of the river and the memory of Minerva. Luis Arsenio let himself be taken through the corridors of Esteban Ferráns's house (so much like his).

All the men of the family were gathered in the library. The elder Esteban had brought together all his brothers, who had come from the farm in Tibes and the business in the capital as soon as they had heard the news that Uncle Jaume was coming. They had had plenty of time to prepare for his arrival. The uncle had left by train for Cadiz the moment that he posted the letter announcing his exile. In the letter, he said that he would soon leave for Havana to visit family for a few days, and from there decide where he would settle. If he did not stay in Havana, he would pass through Puerto Rico. It would take him fourteen days to cross the Atlantic. The letter arrived when the uncle was approaching the coast of the island next door.

> *General Trujillo is offering incentives to any Spaniard who wants to move into Dominican territory. I haven't decided, but I am definitely leaving Barcelona. The son-of-a-bitch Andrés Nin has all the workers riled up here. He has been taking advice from that Trotsky. He has created some "soviets" and swears that he will take over the republic, and that he will spread communism to where the sun sets, depending on what happens in Germany, of course. Last year, the "brown shirts" lost the election. But not this year, no way . . . These imbe-*

ciles sow terror in the streets. The only good thing about them is that they have taken the banks from the Jews. They will definitely win the elections this year, and then the communists are done. But I can't wait so long. They have already declared martial law in Barcelona and worse, because there is gunfire everywhere. Twenty dead so far this year. That's the way it is, cousins, this country has gone to shit.

Luis Arsenio remained leaning on the doorframe beside Esteban. The men spoke in loud voices. Arsenio saw by the look on Esteban's face that he did not want to miss out on what the grown-ups were talking about. This was clearly a conversation between men, a class in process that instructed his friend on the procedures and customs of the men of his stock. Noises from the kitchen could be heard. Meanwhile, Uncle Jaume had worked himself up into a state. Huge. Severe. He was overdressed, as if his suit, though custom made, belonged to someone else. The jacket and vest were made of a lightweight brown cloth, but they nevertheless suffocated him. And from that casing Uncle Jaume unsheathed the arms of a bull, with the gigantic wrists of a mountain peasant, the neck of a bear, with hair sprouting out every which way. The men had just brought him his coffee. The uncle grumbled, as the rest of the family laughed and sipped from their porcelain cups, "How can you drink this?" "You'll get used to it, Jaume, and you will find that there is no better cure for the heat than a demitasse." His watery, beady eyes gleamed against his fat cheeks, which were somewhat reddened with the afternoon's wheezing. But those beady eyes also took measure of the men of the Ferráns family, as if searching for something in particular, something beyond the proposed after-dinner conversations. The three brothers smoked cigars that the uncle had brought from Havana. A whole box of Montecristos, the ones for export.

Jaume was saying that he had given up on the idea of staying in Havana. With a hand whose fingers were much too wide, he pulled on his recently filled belly.

"The banks, gentlemen, have hit bottom and there are no signs of recovery. They tell me that it has been like this since twenty-nine. Man, it has been three years and nothing."

"The plunge hit the Cubans hard."

"I'll say, because I've been told by Emilio, a cousin on my father's side, but, well, he's like a brother, ten years ago it was marvelous. Calle Comercio was as bustling as any business street in New York or Germany. German banks, Flemish banks, Spanish banks, from Vizcaya . . . But now who knows what is going on there, who's in control? And how are things here?"

"Very bad. The socialists won the last election."

"You're kidding!"

"Don't exaggerate, Valentín, it was actually a coalition with our party."

"And are there brown shirts here, by any chance?"

"Here they are black. But don't worry, Jaume, the nationalists don't have many followers."

"I don't know, Esteban, between the small business owners and the workers from the mountains . . ."

"Yes, Valentín, but most of the people are terrified of them after what happened this year. Riggs's execution was a mistake. Why would they want to go up against a colonel from the Yankee police? They are directly at war with the Americans. And they are going to have to deal with them."

"The thing is that there are strikes everywhere, in the tobacco industry, in the ports . . . Even the women have gone on strike."

"They have decided to emulate the American unions. They demand the same rights. No, Jaume, it's the same as in Spain."

"The world has been turned upside side down. Birds firing at shotguns."

"Those bums are all the same, ingrates . . ."

So spoke Uncle Jaume, Don Jaume Pujols, born and raised in Catalonia, who before this trip had never set foot on the soil of the Americas. Luis Arsenio couldn't help looking at him when he spoke, when he pronounced that word "ingrates." He couldn't help asking himself if the peons and workers, the furious and gloomy strikers, had anything to be grateful for to these ancient masters. Perhaps they did, the men of his stock. At school, they stressed this unquestionable heritage. And perhaps it was true, that the Masses and wakes, the language and customs, spun together a way to experience life that was "derived uniquely from the island, influenced by the climate, the geography, but that was deep-rootedly and decidedly . . . Spanish." So said the priests at school. And so had he observed his mother stand up for every time that she saved the Virgin from the nest of lizard shit. So he had seen at dinners, and weddings, in the house decorations, and ladies' dresses.

But Luis Arsenio had gone to Elizabeth's. And there was no doubt that something else bustled there. At Elizabeth's the bodies moved to some other sound, and customs were dictated by other laws. Some other music knitted the hours and the rituals of existence on the earth; some other skin colors and textures imposed themselves on the eyes. That thing, what was it called? That thing that drew his will toward Isabel La Negra's house, toward the shimmying, the laughter, the smell of Minerva, what was it called? What was the name of that thing that made him fear his prowling about in the darkness, while in the clear light of the plazas the looks of his peers applauded the chaste spectacle of the rituals of his clan?

"The Americans are in a similar mess. With both houses

of Congress now solidly on his side, Roosevelt can pass any socialist law he comes up with, so many he had to invent a Second New Deal."

"Things are not looking good."

"But perhaps not so bad. I hear rumors that change is in the air. But pay attention; the winds of change will blow from another direction."

"Why so much mystery, Juan Isidro? Tell us, man, this is family."

Juan Isidro laughed. He put the cigar to his lips and took a deep drag while his uncle and brothers hung by the hair of his silence. He was the oldest of the Ferráns. He had been forced to emigrate to the capital and work like a peasant grocer when the coffee, sugarcane, and small fruit harvest hit bottom after the double blow of Hurricane San Ciriaco and the arrival of the Americans. It was mere luck that the patriarch (whose name he had inherited) had some small land holdings in the capital. They weren't good for anything but quarries. But it went well for Juan Isidro. He sold stone and landfill for the first projects of the new masters. He saved some capital. He married a daughter of the Fernández family, of doubtful racial origin, but very wealthy, from a family of Creoles who owned stores and had recently taken over the coal business. He consolidated his store with theirs, convincing his father-in-law that he would buy all the supplies at "preferential" prices from his brothers in the south. Then, he slowly acquired parcels of land bordering the stone quarries that he had inherited from his father. Everyone told him that he was crazy, that nothing grew there, and that people who wanted country houses wanted them in other parts; but Juan Isidro considered another possibility. His business was not building or growing but selling—oils, buttons, a sack of stones, or his own mother, if need be. The Americans had arrived promising the dawn of progress, wasn't that right? Well, you needed a lot of stones to erect a future like the Americans were promising.

"Construction."

"What?"

"Everywhere in San Juan you hear rumors that Roosevelt is going to revive the economy, and that he is going to do it one way: spending on public works. He is going to use the federal funds to pay contractors, build bridges, dams, roads . . ."

"And how many others will they invest in?"

"I don't know, but there will be a lot of building."

"So what we have to do is make sure that we supply the stones for all this construction. Build a strong alliance with the party . . ."

"The parties. We have to buy the Unionists and the Republicans."

"Our seams will show."

"But aren't there three of us?"

Luis Arsenio sighed deeply. He had never been much interested in politics and he was already bored. Besides, he wanted to tell Esteban about his plan. But he couldn't leave his friend just standing by the door. He almost darted in to offer himself as a player in the farce orchestrated by the uncle. Juan Isidro would announce his conversion to the Republican Party. He would make campaign donations, sign up for the political rallies, take press photographs with Don Celso Barbosa. They would buy it more from him, because he lived in the capital and was married to a *mulata*, and that has to look good to "that black doctor who gave rise to the party." Esteban and Valentín would continue to support the Unionists just as they had done with the Liberals before, as all landowners did.

"Still, I don't like it. Nationalism everywhere, even America, you with gunshots, strikes, and dungeons, when what I have come looking for is exactly the opposite . . . At least Trujillo was welcoming Spaniards to save his country from barbarism . . . What I would like to do is open a savings account over there, because I am tired of selling olive oil."

"Well, we're going to need capital to run the quarries."

"You'll find me on the island next door. I will advise you to start looking for those who will offer you the best contracts and show you about 'legal shortcuts.'"

"We already have that . . . the attorney Fornarís."

"Malleable as mud and mute as a grave . . ."

Luis Arsenio jumped in his spot, as if a spring had come loose in his body. He could not contain himself. The looks directed toward the doorway could not be contained either. With their eyes, the Ferránses told each other all that needed to be said. There was an intruder among them.

Esteban the son interpreted the awkward energy in the eyes of the grown-ups very well. He immediately gave an explanation for the young Fornarís's visit. He was a very close friend, and when he stopped by the house, Esteban told him about Uncle Jaume's visit. Arsenio stayed to offer his respects. But the uncles were so engaged in their conversation that they didn't dare interrupt it. As Esteban explained, Luis Arsenio shrunk by the entrance to the Ferráns's parlor. If he let go of the door, he would fall, he was sure. But he heard Esteban the father chastise his son, asking him why he had not offered his friend a drink, or an hors d'oeuvre; what was the boy going to think, that visitors don't eat in that house . . . He tried to speak, to turn down the invitation, but he could not articulate a thing. Mute as a stone. His friend took him by the arm, led him gently to the center of the parlor. Somebody there extended a hand; he extended his. It was the fat fingers of Don Jaume Pujols. They felt viscid, mollusk-like. He

gave a short bow as a greeting. He didn't say anything, couldn't
say anything, but let himself be guided.

That's what Esteban did. He took him toward the kitchen
as if he were a rag doll. Luis Arsenio suddenly found himself
seated, sipping a glass of cold lemonade before the eyes of his
friend, who calmly let him drink. "It is nothing, my brother.
They haven't said anything except that your father knows how
to do his job." But Arsenio knew otherwise; something was
going on with Fernando Fornarís that was not right; it wasn't
just he who noticed. Other men knew he was different. Because such other men existed, forged in iron, beyond suspicion, like Uncle Jaume, cunning men like Juan Isidro Ferráns,
swaggerers like Don Esteban and Don Valentín. The world belonged to men like the ones in his friend's house, ready to take
advantage of come-what-may and scream insults at the tops of
their lungs as if they knew they were the owners of the world.
Not like his father, who did not talk, his father, who did not
have matter from which to subsist, who was only good to be
the mute shadow who searched for the most legal manner to do
the will of these other men, those who sell the innards of the
earth, and of the men who inhabit it without giving it a second
thought.

"And why did you come?"

He almost forgot why he came. But Luis Arsenio remembers. A skin like toasted seeds, a light cotton skirt floating in
the air, a chin defying the stares of others. Minerva. His father's
opaque silhouette dissolved in front of him.

"Let's go to Elizabeth's again."

"I'd love to, but it can't be today. You see how busy I am.
Why don't you ask Pedrito or Alejandro? They have a chauffeur as well, in case you don't dare take yours."

"No, my friend, it has to be with you."

"You're on fire . . . Be careful, my father says that when one acquires a taste for ass . . ."

"When are we going then?"

"After the Day of the Epiphany."

Luis Arsenio made the calculations. Ten days. His skin will grow sore. He can't wait that long. Too many days and nights, too much disturbance through which the dream of the bells can slip in, the dream of the dark, the powerful hand that drags him to the pasture, touches him in between the legs, on the root of his terror. Still, what choice does he have but to wait?

Four

THE TOUS GIRL was still an amorphous jumble of flesh. Isabel, on the other hand, was growing a slender body, with hardy flesh, and her breasts were at the point of shooting out from her ribs. Her hips were beginning to widen, announcing the woman who would live in her flesh, in that shade of burnished blue. Her skin shone with the beads of humidity. The young woman grabbed a shabby towel, dried her body thoroughly. She couldn't help looking at her flesh and smiling, making mental calculations of how it was superior to the girl Virginia's. Stronger, "hardier."

She had just taken a bath. She had broken such a sweat mopping the floor of the entrance hall that Lorenza herself proposed it. "Freshen up, girl, the afternoon is going to be warm." Lorenza would be waiting for her so they could start sewing side by side. She had likely settled herself in the service balconies, seated with her sewing basket by the straw rocking chair. Isabel stopped looking at her body as she dried it. "Not a drop

of fat . . ." She put on a dress handed down from the Tous girl.
The fabric rolled on her hip and around her back. But a few
stitches on the bottom and two or three patches here and there
and it would fit her like a ring on a finger. "Better than it fit the
girl." There was a reason she strove to learn the lessons from
Lorenza. "I'll take the dress in later." Isabel left her little room
toward the back patio of the Tous house.

"Here, *mija*, because this is ruining my eyes."

Lorenza was trying to pass a thread through the eye of a
needle. "Oh, ma'am, it's not like it's a camel." Isabel sucked on
the string in a showy manner, and threaded the needle on the
first try. "Perfect eyesight, child, perfect." She sat down next to
Lorenza, who had already divided the sewing work into three
piles: Mr. Tous's socks, the girl Virginia's uniforms, and the
hems of the lady Georgina's skirts.

"More hems, Lorenza? What's wrong with that woman?"

"I think she is shrinking."

"Sshhhh, what if she hears us?"

"She's going to grow tiny as an ant and one of these days we
are not even going to notice when we step on her."

They bad-mouthed their *patrones* all afternoon, in whispers.
"What they should get for that young lady is a barrel, which
is the only thing that's going to fit her soon, for the love of
the Virgin." Isabel listened to Lorenza's witticisms while she
concentrated on the task of mending Mr. Tous's socks. The old
servant watched her closely out of the corners of her eyes, in-
sisting that "it didn't matter if the stitch is not straight; no one
is going to notice." But Isabel wanted to do it right. With her
fingers, she measured each stitch on the opposite side so that it
would fall exactly where the point of the needle had entered
in the previous stitch. "It's not like your life depends on those

socks." It didn't depend on them, but she wanted to do it right. So that when Mr. Tous stepped into his socks, he would know, or at least imagine, that the stitches were sewn with care.

"Let's see, put this old shirt over the archway, so that the busybody thinks we are working on her rags and leaves us alone."

They put away the patches and began to embroider. "This is a Richelieu stitch. It begins like the French stitch but then gets thicker." Isabel fixed her eyes on Lorenza's hands. Perfect eyesight. She knew they were big and almond-shaped, her eyes. Sometimes the girl's little friends were captivated watching her curvature, like a date, a seed of the desert. And it wasn't just Virginia's friends who watched her. She had caught Don Aurelio, the señor of the house, resting his pupils on hers, on her ass pressed in by the outfits passed down from his daughter that she would alter. All the way down went Don Aurelio's eyes, as she passed by five steps behind Lorenza with the tray of meats and vegetables.

They had taught her to count them, five steps behind, with the soup bowl or other victuals in her hands. Counting out in her head, one, two, three, four, take a breath and begin to step, five, following Lorenza in the duties of serving dinner to the family. She followed behind and behind each of her steps followed the eyes of Mr. Tous. But this was only recently, ever since she started growing into that hardy woman's flesh. Doña Georgina's eyes also followed her; she griped aloud, "We have to order a service uniform for this child. Virginia's old dresses don't fit her anymore." But Isabel found rhythm. She ignored the *patrona*, and at the same time responded out of the corners of her eyes to Don Aurelio's stares. She looked at him looking at her and a smile spread on her face. Warm dessert, *arroz con leche* just out of the oven in the señor's looks.

"You are looking for a beating on your behind . . ."

"But I'm doing everything you said, Lorenza . . ."

"*Mija,* you know what I am talking about."

Lorenza had been silent for a while. She had let Isabel get lost in the stitching. With a gesture of her chin she pointed to the stack of Don Aurelio's socks, all mended by the young woman's hands, each pair smoothed and folded carefully.

"All you have to do now is perfume them and take them to his room. I've got my eye on you . . ."

"Lorenza, you're wicked . . ."

"I'm old, is what I am. You think that you are the first *negrita* who's had her flame appraised by the don?"

"You worry too much. As if something could happen."

"You better shut those legs tight. And be careful, the busy bee sees everything . . . Well, let's see if it's true that you were paying attention. Show me the Richelieu."

Night surprised them on the balcony of the back patio. Lorenza got up from her chair. "It's getting late. I'll be going to sleep like the hens. I'll see you tomorrow." Isabel walked peacefully to her room. She lit a candle and the whole room brightened, wall to wall, especially where she had glued up a likeness of the Virgin of Mercedes that her Godmother had given her a few months before. "Here, so that she protects you." She changed. A loose cotton robe covered her hard, mature flesh. "Refuge of sinners, Mother of mercy, Holiest Virgin Mary, here I am, contrite and humbled, begging for your patronage." Isabel kneeled to pray. She secretly asked to be freed from the shadow, for the Virgin to get the dark vengeances that she plotted against the girl Virginia or Mrs. Tous out of her head. "Lift my thoughts, let me not wish ill on anyone, for my señoras to be trampled by mules, or perish from the plague or a slow death. And protect Lorenza and my Godmother." She only needed to survive the night, "Amen, Jesus," and for another day to pass. Then she would see her.

The following afternoon, after school, she was scheduled to visit her Godmother. For three whole days and their nights she would sleep in a straw sack at the *bohío* in San Antón. After her visits each month, she was sure to end up with pains in her hips and mosquito bites all over. Teté Casiana teased her. "This *negrita* has grown too classy. She can't live with us poor folk anymore." Isabel pretended she was bothered by it. "Go ahead and keep on bothering me, and see if I don't ever come back." But the truth was that she counted the days leading to the last week of the month, when she could finally rest from the Tous family. Before she went to bed, she put together a bundle of things that she would take home. She would give one of the altered dresses to one of Teté's girls, a quarter pound of Dutch cheese that Lorenza had "put aside" for her from the *patrones'* pantry, a handkerchief for her Godmother. Isabel brought the candle closer until it shone in her eyes; she sat on the bed. Dark almonds, perfect eyesight. She threaded the needle. She would finish embroidering Godmother Maruca's initials on the handkerchief, even if she stayed up all night. It would be a surprise.

A loud bell announced the recess hour. Isabel headed for the shade of the poinciana, her favorite spot in the school. She would entertain herself there, almost always alone, playing marbles with the river stones or reviewing some lesson. The Tomé sisters, Paulina and Matilde, approached her. They were *mulatas*, daughters of the medical doctor who worked in the Ladies Hospital. Sometimes she played with them, and with a white girl, Eugenia, that the Carmelites had taken in as an intern but who had disappeared like a ghost that year.

"She had tuberculosis."

"You think she died?"

"Oh, I don't know, Isabel. The nuns say that she was taken to her parents' house, that she was very ill."

"I imagine that they will cure her there."

"My dad says that that illness is not curable, and that it is contagious. If he finds out about Eugenia, he will probably take us out of the school."

"No wonder the nuns haven't said anything."

"But you'll see when I am a doctor. What about you, Isabel?"

"What about me?"

"What would you like to study?"

"Well, I'd like to open my own seamstress shop."

"Not me, as soon as I can, I'm leaving this town, to the capital or to the United States. My father studied there. And don't worry, you're going to make my trousseau."

"Isabel."

It never failed. There was the fat one, interrupting her. What could she want now? Leaning under one of the arched hallways of the school, the girl Virginia made a great fuss of calling her over. Isabel had to leave the conversation half-finished. How much she yearned to leave the town, go far away, leave to study, leave San Antón. She lowered her head, preparing herself to listen to whatever fresh whim. "Where did you leave my umbrella? You know the sun is not good for me. Look for it, Isabel, and while you're at it, ask the nuns if there's any lemonade left. I'm thirsty." Isabel headed for the rooms of the school building. She was about to pass by the girl when Virginia grabbed her by the arm, grabbed her so tightly it hurt.

"And don't let me catch you talking to them again. Mama

has said not to mingle with such trash as the Tomés. And if I can't, you can't either. Now go, get me the umbrella."

Isabel was on her way back, with the parasol under her arm, when the nuns opened the main exit doors. That was the sign she was waiting for. The day and the torture were over. Isabel saw the gray head of her Godmother on the opposite sidewalk. She ran toward her *patrona*. "Here. My Godmother is here for me. I'm leaving." And she left the girl Tous with her mouth open, about to say something. She crossed Calle Estrella at the front of the school. It was clear that Godmother Maruca was getting older. Her flesh was not as solid as before. It jiggled somewhat on her bones. "God bless you, my dear, and may the Virgin protect you." She had noticed it more during the past months, when she embraced her by the neck to ask her for her blessing, as she did now.

They walked toward the plaza. "See if I find a cut of meat. I got paid for laundry today. Let's celebrate, Isabelita." Now she had to count her steps not to get too far ahead of her God-mother. Maruca walked slowly and seemed tired. They crossed Calle Atocha, then León. At the end of Intendente, the plaza was buzzing with business. Rows of vendors extended the lengths of the quadrangle sidewalks. Isabel recognized two or three neighbors from San Antón crouching next to their baskets of harvest goods. They were full of yams, sweet potatoes, and plantains from the private gardens, laid out over pieces of cloth. The women were squatting in that position suitable for work, like the washerwomen, feet apart, skirt in between the legs, knees to the elbows. They shooed away the flies that settled on the merchandise with a straw fan or dried branches. "Two cents for yams, two cents a pound, two," they announced prices. "Sweeeeet cane juice, take some." From a distance, the young woman heard the sweets vendor. "Wait, Godmother, I'll be right back." She left Maruca behind haggling for the price of a side of kid.

"Can you give me the coconut sweets, five pieces of sugarcane toffee, and a packet of ginger cookies."

When she had finished paying, the Godmother had caught up to her, weighing her with a sarcastic smile.

"Good God, are you a lady of means already? Where did that money come from?"

"What money?"

"The money you used to buy those sweets."

"They're for the children. I make a little bit helping Lorenza with her embroidery . . ."

"And since when do you embroider?"

"Lorenza is teaching me. See, Godmother, we don't need to have me work for the Tous family anymore. I can sew from home . . ."

"Isabel, you are forgetting the most important . . ."

"No, I spoke to Lorenza already; she can refer some clients."

"And school? Who will pay for school?"

A silence grew between them. They crossed Calle Salud, toward the shores of the Portuguese. They walked slowly, listening to the river. Finally, they reached San Antón.

Teté Casiana smoked her tobacco pipe on the balata stool. As soon as she saw them approaching, she made as if to get up but sat back down. Teté Casiana was old as well. "Bless you, Teté." Isabel sat on the steps of the *bohío*. She opened her bundles. The godchildren whirled around her as soon as she took out the packet of sweets.

"I brought you Dutch cheese; and for you, Godmother, a handkerchief. I forgot to give it to you."

"Look, Casiana, the girl knows how to embroider."

"G. M. Those are the initials of your name."

"How pretty. When are you going to bring me one?"

"Next time, I promise."

Julito had grown up. He could finish a whole *tirijala* sweet on his own and had even shown the disposition to get his hands dirty eating the taffy with coconut and *melao* sugar. Night fell slowly over San Antón. Isabel watched through the smoke from Casiana's pipe, eating a *tirijala* herself. Her Godmother stoked the fire under the goat casserole. There was something, or someone, missing who would transform the evening's atmosphere into the tense but familiar. Better to do without what was missing.

"Where's Mariano?"

"He hasn't come by in months. He's mixed up with a young girl who came down from the hill in Tibes."

"Poor girl."

"Mother of God, Isabel, you never got along very well with Mariano."

"It's a matter of knowing where he comes from. He has suffered much in this life."

"Well, then let him be happy with this woman and leave us alone."

They looked at her, surprised at how mature she sounded. "This one has grown up," they told each other with their eyes. Isabel took another bite of her sweet. The *melao* stuck tastily to the roof of her mouth. She got up from Casiana's side to stretch and to help with watching the kids. "Julito, come here, let me clean your hands." Uncle Mariano was not going to show up. Those three days in San Antón would be glorious; she felt the sweet taste of her return trip in her mouth. She hoped it would last forever.

"Here, girl, take some goat stew to Don Demetrio."

The Godmother put three platters in her hands. Isabel smiled.
The pretext was perfect. Dusty road, sugar towns side by side
with *pana* or mango trees where the afternoon grew muddled.
Isabel almost ran to the house of the tobacco roller. Demetrio,
Demetrio Sterling. The whites in the town couldn't so much
as look at him. Strikes, centers for workers. Everyone talked
about his union adventures, his ties to Alonso Gaul, the editor
of the newspaper *El Águila,* another presumptuous black man
who insulted the owners of the farms and factories whenever
he felt like it, denouncing them for anything in the court of
public opinion. Lorenza had warned Isabel. "Don't even mention him to Mr. Tous. He almost had to close the factory this
year because of that man." She found him leaning on the door
of his little house, reading next to an oil lamp. Isabel thought
that the teacher was thinner than before. That fibrous body of
his bent like a reed by the doorframe and revealed bones that
she had not noticed before. Maybe it was his reading posture.
With three long strides Isabel reached the front of the *bohío.*
But Demetrio didn't even notice her. "Hello," she had to say to
bring him down from where those pages had hoisted him.

"*Muchachita,* what a joy to see you. You have grown into a
woman."

"Godmother sent this."

"But why? You don't take classes with me anymore."

"Old debts. The ones you can never settle."

"How deep. Did you learn that from the white folks?"

"No, Demetrio, I came up with that on my own."

"And have you learned how to read?"

"Some time ago."

"Well, here."

He put a pamphlet in her hands, "Free and Sovereign Love."
It was by a woman named Luisa Capetillo. "A workers' play,"

Demetrio said. "Because marriage is a contract of buying and selling where often the woman ends up losing. I bet that they haven't taught you that in your school."

She responded, "I don't think about love, Don Demetrio. I want to be a woman of means, start my own business."

"Well, for that you have to find a partner who understands you and respects you."

"Oh no, no partners, no kids, nothing. I don't want to end up having to give up newborns because I can't support them."

"But that's a very lonely life, Isabelita."

"Like yours, teacher?" A moment of astonishment dilated his pupils, forcing him to smile contentedly. Maruca hadn't been mistaken. This girl had a good head on her shoulders.

They talked a while longer. Isabel let herself speak because Demetrio listened to her, without correcting her or scolding her, without trying to make her do "what was best for her." With him, she was an equal, a whole woman who could decide her destiny. Night closed in over San Antón. "I have been working in tobacco factories since I was your age. I have been everything, picker, roller, leaf dryer, reader. That's why I notice the abuses." Isabel listened to Demetrio's measured voice. How old could he be? Not one wrinkle showed on his skin, nor one gray hair in his tight curls. That thick caramel skin did not give away an age. He had seemed the same her whole life. A little thinner now. And yet he seemed so old. How old was Don Demetrio? She didn't dare ask.

"Isabel, they're calling for you. Godmother is serving the stew."

They had to send Julito to look for her. She would have stayed the whole night talking to the tobacco worker. Isabel returned to the *bohío* with Demetrio's pamphlet under her arm. She was going to read the whole thing, staying up all night if necessary. Perhaps between those pages she would find the argument that she lacked to convince Godmother to let her return to the neighborhood, to be free and to soar.

In the blink of an eye it was Monday. On the way to town, Isabel stopped at Don Demetrio's to return his pamphlet. "What did you think?" She had to promise him that they would talk about the reading assignment later, because she was late. She liked that Luisa Capetillo. "Unionist, and she was a tobacco worker as well." A woman of means, Isabel thought as she left San Antón behind. "We'll talk to each other as equals because my rights are the same, and not those of a serf as you would have me believe," the protagonist of the play had said, who to top it off had the same name as hers. Isabel. Woman of means, independent, free. There were others who had achieved it. The steps to be taken were one after the other, without counting. The river moistened the air and cooled off her long walk. She crossed the bridge of the two lions and took Calle Montaner. In four blocks she would be in her little room in the back patio. In her house? No, her house was the one she had left behind. "But I will return soon, soon and on my own two feet," she almost murmured, pushing open the back entrance. She didn't know just how soon that premonition would come true.

She found the Tous house upside-down. "Get ready, the busy bee is angry," Lorenza brought her up to date. The lady had been acting possessed, "since you know this week is the seal's party. She had to return her dress because it was so tight that she couldn't get into it." It was true, she had forgotten, that week they were celebrating Virginia's entrance into society. The preparations had been going on for months; they had sent away to make the dress, gone searching for cheeses and preserved meats, ordered a cake. It seemed that during those days, sneaking around in the middle of the night, Virginia had eaten the courses for the party. "Now the seal can't get into her dress and the mother is furious. Stay away from her. She stings." As soon as Doña Gina heard Isabel arrive, she whisked her away to go shopping in town.

Two, three, five steps. They took Calle Reina to the Vilarís seamstress shop to watch over the alterations to the girl's muslin dress. Four, five steps, they crossed from Calle Cristina to check on the order of fine pastries. Two, three, they returned through Comercio to order the crown of orange blossoms for the debutante's hair. Five, six steps. From there they crossed to Las Delicias; they had to arrange the Mass before the ball for the girls in the casino. Isabel followed Doña Gina everywhere. "Come on, young lady, no time for laziness. I give them three days of rest and they want to take forever." The girl bit her tongue and heard the voice of her Godmother in her head. "Isabel, the school." She took a deep breath and said to herself, "Soon, hold out."

They returned to the house carrying a thousand packages, plus a box of high heels for the girl to try on. They were going to go straight up the stairs to the second floor bedrooms when they were detained by the rattle of dishes from the kitchen. "Virginia," the mother called, "where are you, young lady?" Pieces of bread with honey were scattered on the tiles of the entrance hall. A jar of olives sat half-opened on a living room table. "I am going to tear you apart, I swear, if that dress doesn't fit you again . . ." Doña Gina rushed down the hallway looking for her daughter. She pulled her out from the shadows of the kitchen, yanking her by the arm and pushing her up the stairs. Isabel smiled within, as she heard the mother unloading her anger, rearing on her hind legs.

The next day she and Virginia stayed home from school, "because there is so much to do, you won't have time. Besides, I can't let this one out of my sight." Doña Gina gave orders like the captain of a man-of-war. "Iron these petticoats, starch these shirts, put this lace edging on the collar of my organza dress." And to Isabel, "Girl, you go look for the dress at Don Antón's, see if now . . ." She had to walk fast, one two three four five, quickly. Isabel returned with the muslin order in her hands. She immediately went up to the rooms where they had Virginia imprisoned so that she would not gain any more weight. She knocked on the door—"Come in"—and unloaded that vaporous foam on the bed. Without meaning to, she caressed the cloth underneath and imagined herself covered by those added pieces, which would fit her like a ring. Virginia grabbed the dress from her and looked at Isabel with such disgust that it would have been better if she had punched her.

"Let go; you're going to soil it with those sooty hands."

Grab the girl Virginia's flabby neck, pull apart her tiramisu curls, bury a pinky in the eye sockets. She saw herself squeezing her throat until none of those words would ever come out of her mouth again. "Me and you, equals now, you imbecile. Come on, you and me, now." With one hand she held the other so that they would not fly to where the girl Tous had begun to undress. Her hands trembled. Her mind trembled. Isabel opened her mouth. One by one, she thought of the insults that she should say, the ones that she and Lorenza went over every afternoon in the service quarters. "I'm better than you, you flabby seal. Even your father knows it. I'm stronger, tougher; you are worthless, ungrateful, useless." She had them all in her head, clear as can be; the slaps were vibrating in her wrists. But an invisible force made her fall silent. "Dare, Isabel, like in the play." She could only quiver against it, bite her tongue, wanting to rip out her own eyes not to see, not to watch herself. Her Godmother's voice hummed against her skin, "How will we pay for school?" That voice echoed undaunted under the look of disgust, complicit in the insult.

Lorenza found her weeping by the baskets of dirty laundry on the back patio. Isabel tried to cover her face and hide her tears. But the old woman noticed and read the fury in her eyes. "What did the seal do to you?" she asked, with a serenity so like tenderness that Isabel could not hold back the rush of emotions. Without even thinking about it, the young woman buried her face in Lorenza's breasts, her soft breasts that took her in as if she were a newborn. Lorenza led her slowly to the backyard. They sat where no one could see them, next to the sewing chair, Lorenza with her arms thrown over the girl's shoulder, soothing her hiccups, Isabel not able to stop crying. The old woman began to sway, one way and then the other, she rocked with Isabel in her arms. She didn't say a word. The wind was the one that spoke through the leaves in the trees. The laundry hung to dry also spoke in the breeze. Lorenza swayed. "Don't blame anybody but them." Isabel raised an eyebrow.

"Don't blame yourself or anybody else. That's the way they are. That's what they do to make themselves feel better. They do it to everyone."

"But if Godmother hadn't left me here . . ."

"She would have left you with Doña Pura, who would treat you just the same or worse. Or with Doña Estela, who has three daughters like Virginia. Not one, but three. Can you imagine what that would be like? You, having to attend to three seals . . ."

Isabel let out a guffaw. She immediately covered her mouth, looking everywhere. But Lorenza remained calm.

"That's the way the ladies are. They have nothing else to make them feel good."

Isabel thought about the dresses and the embroidery, about Virginia's outfits and the house, with its china cabinets, its mahogany furniture. She thought about how those women could walk through the plaza with their heads held high, throwing around the names of their parents and godmothers without having to hate them. No one ever abandoned them to fate. Isabel gave Lorenza a look of disbelief.

"To me it seems as if they have everything . . ."

"My dear, if you knew what my eyes have seen. The kicks and slaps that some of them have to put up with. Remember that I have been a servant in all those houses . . ."

"It doesn't matter, Lorenza. There are blows that are more painful. Nobody insults them to their face."

"No, they insult each other behind their backs. Wait till you are older, young lady . . . but don't be in a hurry, because I am not going to help you. And don't think that I have been a servant all my life. If it wasn't for this rheumatism. I was one of the most famous seamstresses in town. Ask around, go ahead, ask in the shops who Lorenza Angulo was. I am going to teach you how to sew like the angels in heaven, so that when you get out of here, you will be a master. So you don't have to take anything from anyone."

"God and the Virgin willing," Isabel murmured, drying her tears with the back of her skirt.

"Even if they aren't willing . . ."

That's how Lorenza responded, with the same calm with which she had rocked her. Blasphemy, self-assurance, habits as strong as tenderness. Lorenza did not commend herself to the Virgin. "You'll see how I teach you the tricks of the profession, and that to sew well you don't have to bother with the angels." Isabel gave Lorenza an impious look, Lorenza who would teach her how to fight. She stopped crying.

* * *

THEY HAD FOUND HER LYING in her sackcloth bed. Teté Casiana had gone into the bedroom to wake her up, surprised that she had not yet risen. Godmother did not react. Her hands were cold as an ice block, her jaw open, as if on leaving, her soul had wanted to open a hole from inside. Her cheeks were deflated and looked sooty and gone gray. That's what Isabel thought when she saw her later. Her Godmother's skin had gone gray.

They sent Demetrio Sterling to go look for her. Teté Casiana stayed in the house, keeping vigil over the body with the neighbors and preparing the burial. She was anxious for Isabel to arrive, so she would help to dress her Godmother, set up the home altar where they would recite the first novenas for the eternal rest of Maruca Moreno's soul. They had to iron all the white clothes for church, the big poplin skirt with starch water, the crisp crinoline slip, the peplum with brown loops, and Teté Casiana could not do it all by herself. She would take forever with her shattered hip. They had to put up Godmother's hair with a tortoiseshell barrette, the kind sold by the traveling Lebanese. Isabel had the barrette with her. Put the scapulars of the Virgin of Mercedes around her neck and bring the large likeness from her servant's room. And loop a rosary around her cindery fingers to ward off evil and draw in light. María Maruca herself had gone over the instructions for the day of her death a thousand times. "It's your duty because you are my only goddaughter. Let there be fresh flowers on the altar, white lilies and carnations because white is the color of the Virgin of Mercedes. Set up a clear glass container with perfumed water and nine candles. And in another separate cup, a Jericho rose. Don't forget to use the lace tablecloth that's in the trunk and make an arch of fleshy leaves and Indian coffee branches."

When Lorenza told her that a tall black man was waiting for her in the garage, she had a premonition. An insect with transparent wings inside her made her go mute. She went directly to the garage where Demetrio Sterling fidgeted with his felt hat, knitting his brow. Seeing him confirmed her suspicions. Godmother would never have sent him to the house of the *patrones*. If she was fine, she would never have sent for her in town.

Demetrio stopped fidgeting with his hat and looked at her. He looked directly at her, with his pointed face, his stiff neck buttoned up in a striped cotton shirt, with his shabby but ironed pants, his tobacco worker's boots. Isabel knew. She went to look for Doña Georgina, who agreed to advance her the pay for the week so she could go back to San Antón. She had just seen her, had just hugged her such a little time ago, two weeks at the most. Now she was going back with Don Demetrio. Something was amiss, seriously amiss, with that destiny to which she now offered herself without looking back.

The *bohío* in San Antón seemed poorer than ever to her. But there was no other place to keep vigil over the body. The church was in town and it was to keep vigil for the rich. Those floorboards would have to do. Isabel arrived in the ox cart, and with the help of the neighbors, Teté had already bathed the deceased. They still had to comb her shaggy hair, put the barrette and the big skirt on her, prepare the altar. They also had to place her in the box that the neighborhood carpenters had not yet varnished. Even when she saw her thrown in her sackcloth bed, Isabel could not cry. All she did was watch in silence, ask what still needed doing, and begin to work diligently. She heard the children and Teté Casiana crying from a distance, but she swept the floor of the *bohío* with great zeal, watered down the entrance, lit the fire, cut the Indian coffee branches, and looked around the house that had once felt like her home. "I'll return on my own two feet." But now her feet couldn't find a place to rest. The *bohío* felt like a disgusting hovel to her. She kept on asking herself how she had lived there, how you could live in this manner, an entire life, like her Godmother's, in between those four walls of cardboard and wood, that frond roof where rats scurried, those sackcloth beds where lice and scorpions burrowed. Perhaps Godmother had her reasons. But now without her, that place could offer no shelter.

"We'll have to keep vigil for Godmother outside, Teté. Everyone won't fit in here."

And so they did. Once the carpenters had finished with the wood box, Demetrio helped them put the body inside and looked for two benches to hold up the coffin. They put the mosquito bedding from the bed on top of the body to keep the flies out of Maruca's mouth. They set up the altar against a wall in the house. It was a rustic table covered with the lace tablecloth. At the top of the vault made with fleshy leaves, exactly as Maruca had indicated, they put the likeness of the Virgin of Mercedes. Isabel was in charge of that. But there were other Virgins on the table, a statuette of Casiana of Providence and another one that the neighborhood prayer leader had added, "so they keep each other company."

"It's the Mercedes one, but it doesn't matter. In the end, they are all the same, like God, who is one and three. But the Virgins are even more."

Carved in wood and painted in brilliant colors, a blue, gold, and white robe, she wore a crown of rays topped with lace. The neighborhood prayer leader brought the figure wrapped in votive cloth. Black Virgin with white boy. Holy Virgin of Montserrat.

By the time they started the rosary, Godmother had begun to reek. They had to stop her mouth with cotton soaked in eucalyptus and grains of Paradise alcohol, as well as her ears and her nostrils. They lit two big candles nearby, mounted on *tabonuco* handspikes, to keep masking the smell. Teté Casiana brewed coffee and brought out a large decanter of distilled alcohol. Isabel mixed the rest of the Dutch cheese that she had brought from town with some "hors d'oeuvres" that Lorenza had given her before she left for San Antón. That night, gathered around the grounds of the *bohío*, under the stars, they recited the last rosary for Maruca Moreno. Then everyone left her alone. Isabel spent the night with her Godmother, keeping vigil over her final sleep.

I BELIEVE IN ONE GOD, the Father Almighty, Maker of Heaven and Earth, and of all things visible and invisible. They heard the murmurs of the congregation in the distance. Isabel and Lorenza returned to the house with measured steps. They had listened to almost the entire Mass from the back pews. The debutantes sparkled beside the altar. They all wore immaculate dresses and were surrounded by tall candles and flowers. They were contrite virgins under their mantillas. "Except the Tous girl, who looks like a badly wrapped legume in that dress, for the love of God." Isabel and Lorenza watched from the rear pews where the help sat. Near the end of the ceremony, Doña Gina had dismissed them. The casino would provide its own troop of white-gloved waiters. "Trained expressly for events like this," the señora said, "so I won't be needing you." Good. Isabel wasn't in the mood for parties. They would have the Tous mansion all to themselves.

It had been four days since the Godmother died. Lorenza lit the oil lamps in the living room. "Today we'll dine like queens. Look at all the meat left over from the luncheon." They pulled out the entire service and set the dining room table. Isabel didn't care if they got caught. She didn't care about anything lately. Her steps weighed heavily on the floor tiles, on the carpets, on the sun-scalded floors. "Slow down, dear, today we are alone. Let's not make it a chore." Lorenza disappeared through the hallways of the house just as Isabel served the dinner plates. When she returned, Lorenza had a bottle of wine in her hands, looking at her through mischievous eyes. "This is for later. We're going to have a few glasses in honor of your Godmother." They put music on the Victrola and ate until they were glutted. Isabel thought of how much she would have enjoyed the presence of her Godmother that night, there with her.

They went to the parlor. Lorenza joined arms with her, imitating the stiffness of the *patrones*, who wouldn't move their hips if their lives depended on it, as if they had poles up their asses, "Hello, and how are you, Mr. Attorney . . . Oh, yes, ah, distinguished señora . . ." She imitated them and Isabel broke down with laughter. She needed to laugh. She watched as Lorenza threw herself on the straw seat of the mahogany armchair, took off her shoes, and put her feet up on the coffee table, in just the way they had told Isabel never to dare do. "Your glass, dear." From her aged hand poured streams of wine from the bottle that she had "rescued" from the shopping for the party. "Oh, what a fine bouquet," Lorenza mimicked the *patrón*, raising her pinkie and puckering her mouth as she blinked. They laughed some more, a soothing laughter. Isabel drank until she felt her head floating.

At midnight, caught up in their own party, they noticed headlights approaching the garage. They ran to turn off the Victrola, take away the fine china on which they had dined, hide the table linen, and empty their glasses. Isabel went shooting down the hallway to get in her bed. Lorenza stayed busy in the kitchen, pretending she was cleaning up, not to give rise to suspicions.

It was Mr. Tous. He was alone. He arrived a little tipsy from his daughter's debut. Doña Gina had asked the chauffeur to take him home. She had to stay, to make sure that the room in the casino would be left in good shape. Virginia had gone out with her friends and the chaperone, as was the custom of girls on the night of their debut. But Don Aurelio needed to get home. It was evident that he had consumed too much alcohol. And Doña Georgina didn't want any problems with him, "Go to bed, Aurelio. You get so obnoxious when you drink," or with the authorities in the casino.

He came into the dining room, saw Lorenza timidly wiping down the table, and ordered her to leave everything for the following day. He went into this room and shut himself in there, asking not to be bothered. Lorenza shut off the last light. Don Aurelio then walked toward the room in the back and knocked on Isabel's door. For a moment, Isabel thought that it was Lorenza, but that sort of knocking wasn't the way they did it; the old woman would have at least stuck her head in. She got up. She was wearing a striped cotton nightshirt that had once belonged to the girl of the house. She walked toward the door slowly. She held her breasts with one hand and with the other one she turned the bolt. She was met face to face with Aureliano Tous.

The *patrón* wore long sleeves. His deep black hair shone more than ever, matted with grease. But even so, a grayish curl

fell over his brow. Startled, Isabel took two steps back and left
the entrance open. Don Aurelio approached her. Her, Isabel
Luberza. Her heart wanted to leap out of her chest; it beat in
between her temples, cut off her air, did not let her think. But
at the same time, Isabel did not care that the *patrón* was there.
She did not care about anything. She closed her eyes. She felt
Don Aurelio grab her by the hips and bring her toward him. It
was a slow but firm embrace. Now she would know, now she
would truly feel how full of sorrow she was, how her heart was
bursting. Don Aurelio brought Isabel even closer to him, sur-
rounding her firmly with his arms. He began to breathe on her
neck, smell the tops of her shoulders. And she, immobile there,
could only feel that "nothing matters." Perhaps she should call
Lorenza, run out of there. But where? What other arms would
take her in? It was better if she stayed there, very quiet, breathing on Don Aurelio, who kept on hugging her gently, smelling
her all over. A warm embrace that perhaps would bring relief.

Don Aurelio began to walk her toward the bed. "Everything is all right." He gently guided her with his body. "Don't
be afraid, girl." He did everything so slowly that Isabel felt as
if she were suspended in air. Aureliano Tous picked her up and
put her on the mattress, took off her nightshirt, threw it on the
floor. Isabel kept her eyes closed, but she felt the exact weight of
Don Aureliano's eyes deliberately looking at her, as if wanting
to memorize the contrast of her skin with the bedsheets. With
the ends of his fingers, he touched the skin of Isabel's wash-
board belly, the roundness of her small breasts, the erect nipples, the neck above, the chin, and the lips thick as a sigh. Now
her whole body beat beneath her closed eyelids. She opened her
eyes only when she sensed that Don Aurelio was getting up. He
pulled off his suspenders, unbuttoned his shirt, and proceeded
to slowly undo his belt. So slowly that the room filled with

the smell of leather and vetiver. So slowly that it distorted the echo of steps approaching in the hallway. To Isabel they seemed slow and distant steps, as if from another time. Godmother, nothing matters anymore, steps that approach through the back corridors, heels that reverberate on the parquet floor, stopping in front of her door. A light seeped in through the crack, outlining a silhouette by the door frame. Doña Georgina's voice made itself heard on the walls of the little room, from end to end, and in Isabel's heart that skipped a beat. "But it doesn't matter, Godmother," although she could hear only the echo of that other voice.

"Aurelio, I think that you have the wrong room."

The rest was shouts behind closed doors, then murmurs.

The following day, Doña Georgina waited for her in the vestibule of the house with a face of stone. Beside her, Lorenza held on to a cloth bundle with all her belongings. This time the bundle seemed bigger than the first time she had done it. How many years had passed? Seven? Eight?

"I must inform you, Isabel, that we no longer require your services."

Doña Georgina turned away and disappeared down the hallway. Lorenza handed her the bundle of clothes. She let her fingers rest on the girl's hands. She smiled sadly as she deposited a worn thing into her palm. It was cold and metal. Isabel felt it slowly. Later, she looked at it. It was a medal of the Virgin of Cobre. Safeguard for travelers. Shelter for those beaten by the storm and high seas. Lorenza, the blasphemer, was giving her a medal of the Virgin? Isabel wanted to ask. She wanted to get closer and rest her head on Lorenza's chest; she wanted to embrace her but could not. They both could not. They took each other's hands under the bundle of clothes and let them rest on each other for a while, as when Maruca had abandoned her there and Lorenza had grabbed her hand to bring her inside. Now she held on to her hand at the threshold of the door.

"You were saved by a hair. If the doña hadn't arrived in time, the *patrón* would have eaten you like a little bird. At the plaza you can always find out who needs servants. Let me know where you end up. Take good care of yourself, Isabel."

Lorenza's face changed suddenly. She took two steps back inside the Tous house and without looking at her closed the door.

Joyful Mysteries

"THIS IS THE joy you send to me, Lady? Is this the only joy for me? It seems so, as it was for my mother, and my mother's mother. But I search for something else among the libations, something sweet at least, unlike the fruits offered to me by the Beloved."

I APPROACHED HIM. I WAS pure and pale like you, Mother, wrapped in tulle, like the images of you that the nuns gave me in the school where they locked me up to adore you. They didn't want me mingling with trash; they didn't want to blacken and sully my skin. Immaculate One, I saved myself for the Beloved, I crossed the islet of the Church of Providencia, Holy Mother, Mirror of Patience, Protector of the World. I was going loyally toward your lap and you gave me up to the Beloved. I put my faith in you and you gave me up, Señora. I repeated your words to him, "Here is the slave of the Lord." First joyous mystery.

The nuns taught me that. My mother's mother taught me that. You taught me that with your example, "Your will be done through me." That night I undressed before the will of the Beloved and the Beloved penetrated me while I closed my eyes, my flesh burned, I bled, babbling and in pain, waiting for the kisses that would reward my obedience. But the Beloved stuck his crippled, hard, coarse will in me. And he didn't even kiss me. I didn't know what to do. He looked at my pale flesh and didn't kiss me. He looked at my blond curls, like the ones in your lap, and at that very moment I saw how his eyes strayed out the windows of the room. We were in the Meliá Hotel. The next day we would board a ship for our honeymoon. The Beloved's eyes fled out the window, and even at sea I never recaptured his gaze.

"What happened to your eyes?" I asked as he tried unsuccessfully to fix them on me. "Grant me your true love, Señor." My second joyful mystery. I asked him, shuddering. I implored him, convinced by your example. "Lamb of bitterness, pray for us. Scales of justice, pray for us." I did not know what else to be besides a maiden become a wife. When we returned to the mansion that my father gave us, I looked for the best cooks in town. I instructed them: "Carmela, that's not how you prepare the rice for the paella." "Delmira, the marzipan has to be kneaded with the fingertips." I became as vigilant as an eagle. Those two darkies had to listen to me so that their hands, which were extensions of mine, could produce the delicacies for the Beloved.

And the libations, let there be libations. I sent them to the dusty streets that could not soil me, to the stinking markets that I should not set foot in to look for the libations that I would render for the Beloved. I sent for the mangoes and cherries, the passion fruits and the guavas, the sea grapes, the grapefruits with the best pulp for a slow fermentation. I sent the darkies, from their sweat, from their fire. Let them go directly to search for me and in the pantry I would bottle the liquids of various colors. Grapefruit wines, orange cordials, cinnamon and lemon *aguardientes*. All illegal, it was said, alcohol was illegal in your Kingdom, but the wines that I made were not. The libations for the Beloved were untouched by the laws of man, by the laws practiced by the Beloved that made men subjugate themselves under the burden of Order. "Señor, help me obey the just laws . . ." But that's my fourth joyful mystery.

"I shouldn't," he would say to me when he saw the fermentations taking shape in me. My belly also taking shape and in the wind the shape of an elusive rumor that ruined all the plans for recovering the Beloved. My belly expanded and in the streets a reptilian hiss, "This is the Señor's second son." What do you mean, "the second son," Mother? How did you allow this? Why did you let me become the Displaced One? I, the child of your sorrow, the image of your likeness, pale and Immaculate like you, queen among women like you, meek sheep who would be rewarded by the one and only gaze of the Beloved. I could not become the one condemned to forgetfulness, to the absence of the Beloved due to another who could not even touch the hem of my lamentation. No one suffers more than me; no one relishes more the painful mystery of his rejection and turns it into joy. I am the queen among queens, as I should be, it was the reason that I was born and conceived. It was the reason that my mother suffered, and my mother's mother, and her mother before that. It was the reason that bitterness settled like a ballast stone in my belly. I am the Queen among all women and the Beloved has to put his seed in my belly, over my head a crown of a dozen stars, under my feet a resplendent moon, on my robe rays that dress me with light. To reach me with his gaze and tell me in a sweet and most loving voice, "Woman, share the crown of eternal life with me."

Mother, how did you allow it? Why don't you make the heavens rip open and shatter her in pieces with a lightning bolt, she who dares drag my place in your Kingdom through the mud? Mary, be my Mother. Avenging, let the heavens rip open. Inquisitional, to crush my enemy. Just, lend me your scepter to pierce her belly. Her and that fruit of her savage paunch, blow up both of them and bathe myself in the river of their blood. May their blood dye the length of the Portuguese River, Mother, their impure and disgusting blood. Don't look at me like that, demanding mercy. Don't point me toward the path of forgiveness. For once in this life, let us not forgive, let us not suffer in silence, let us not patiently await the Beloved's return. But let us commit ourselves to fulfill your Word, to ratify our place in your Kingdom. Please, Mother, please, Mother, please.

I am the image of your likeness. That is why I was born and conceived, to be like you, and like my mother, and like my mother's mother. If not, how would I be able to distinguish myself from other women? What other value do I have, if not suffering? If I had renounced sorrow, if I had not been this guiltless steer walking toward the slaughterhouse, how would I be better than the other one who saves herself for No One, who doesn't wait for the twelve stars, or the robe of light, or the moon under their feet? But then, if she didn't do this, how did she seduce the Beloved, how is it that though Absent she keeps him within her yearnings? Mother, why her and not me?

But I get ahead of myself. I always get ahead of myself. Third mystery and libation. "Lord, grant me poverty of spirit." Is this the only joy for me? The Beloved made me poor. The Beloved took my being in his hands and made it smaller. I couldn't do anything; no, because of your mandate, no, because of your faith, no, because of your example. O, Beloved. My spirit is the offering and the bond. Not desire, guilt, not desire, guilt, not desire. I, Cristina, crystalline and crucified, cup full of libations that have not been savored, the more you defeated me, the better, the more I could show the Beloved the scabs of my suffering. The longer my spirit fermented, the sooner he would have to come to save me. He, Mother, my only sustenance, because you forgot about me.

But what about her, Sacred Virgin? Couldn't the author of my infamy have been someone else? Couldn't she have been someone close to her who from the day she was given to you kneels at your feet in adoration, who donned the mantilla of the Mother and wore orange blossoms in her crown? I, the Immaculate; while she bears on her skin the stain of the cauldron that burns the sins of man. She, daughter of Seth, condemned to roam without a home over the face of the earth. I, daughter of Mary. Not her, impossible. Black Virgin with white boy on her lap. Black Virgin with white boy on her lap. But they are not you. They are not the images that come from you on High, that the Church ratifies and puts on its altars. They are a disruption of you. I would be humiliated to compare myself to that Other One. Couldn't someone else be the author of my disgrace?

After the fifth month of gestation the name of the Vile One who stole the gaze of my Beloved reached my ears. After you demanded that I become Immaculate. After you demanded that I become Untouchable. She, the Fondled One, the Lowest. Why should I lose myself in the soot of a mortal sin? Let me not lose myself, Mother, nor lose the son in my innards. The true Son of the Beloved. Let me not lose myself, who followed your example.

Here I am, fermenting in this glass that has become my flesh.

This is the joy that you have in store for me? Is this the only joy for me, now that the Son has grown up and goes looking for his own way. Stop time, Mother of Mercy. Break up the course of Destiny with your kindness. Don't let him separate himself from me. To live side by side with the Beloved is all that this impoverished heart can stand. Don't take away my only sustenance, the only thing that anchors me to this earth. Let the mystery of my lap continue to burn in me with the sorrow of joy. You, who abandoned me to my fate, listen to me, you who made me into you to spit on me, protect me. Grant me this last wish. You owe it to me.

Five

THE BAR WAS full of young men, not one soldier from Loosey Point, not one merchant, not one traveler, only young men. Some must have been five years older than Luis Arsenio. The only one there who was properly a man was an impressive *negro* man almost two meters tall. He was by all measures a man and so erect that the years did not seem to weigh on him. It was difficult to guess how many he bore on his body, but at least forty. Forty something.

The Victrola was on. It was too early for the hired musical ensembles to be playing, for the hostess to be working the door, and that's why she was seen taking her time smoking, leaning over a chair, amusing herself by watching the spirals of smoke in the candlelight. It was a slow Wednesday night at the bar, the middle of a holiday week in which the soldiers went home to their families. Those who remained in Loosey Point or in Camp Santiago could not leave their posts. The civilians had made New Year's resolutions that they would soon forget, but which for the moment made them feel guilty about their desires. It was Christmas. There were family feasts and the whores were loose. Only the young men came to the bar. Some of them were migrant workers. Others Luis Arsenio had seen selling fruit in the plaza or working somewhere in town. Their skins were like a rainbow of toasted wood, with the red hues of ripe fruit beneath a precarious brown, which sometimes became yellow or an intense blue. Some skins were very fair, as fair as his, but they betrayed some other sort of origin against the bone. It was as if, from underneath, they emitted a shadow, like the skin of a drum stretched over the frame. Their hair was as varied as the skins. Very dark straight locks, others coiled and coarse as brushes, loose curls of a surprising copper hue, others tight like sanding scrubs. The lips and the eyes took on unexpected shapes, thin on faces dark as tar, thick on skins that were almost white, freckled with red kinky hair and the greenish eyes of a crouching cat, like the eyes of the Fornarís men. The young men drank beer and chatted loudly. About the fact that it was thirty-five cents an hour that they charged for their labor. That it was about to be lowered because of the banks. That there was talk of a general strike if they couldn't resolve the salary reduction. That they were opening more alcohol distilleries and that this would bring down the price of moonshine. "Listen, would you like to buy a little carafe while you wait for the girls? I can sell it to you cheaper than you can get it here." The fibrous *negro* man pulled away the one soliciting Luis Arsenio and told him not to bother the clientele, without even looking at him. He left Luis Arsenio with the thank you on the tip of his tongue.

The girls had not come down from their rooms in the back. You could hear no music, smell no alcohol. But it was the holidays. What were those young men doing there? Were they fleeing like him, seeking some refuge? Could they be tormented by the claims of the flesh like him? Once again Luis Arsenio was a mute witness to the rage of others. But then Minerva came down, still not suited up, no lipstick, no silk dress. She looked better than he remembered. Luis Arsenio stood up like a harpoon, went toward her, sleepwalking. He clasped onto her waist right there, in front of everybody, not caring. He didn't care about anything. Only Minerva. To consider the hue of her toasted skin, suck on her lips, bite her sweaty neck. That's why he was there. He had fled his house, anxious. It was impossible to wait until after the holidays.

He had taken advantage of the situation. It was the day before the Epiphany and the father had not made it home. On Christmas Eve, Fernando Fornarís made it a point to get home early from the office. He had dinner, the table set up with the best linen and silver, and the family present. The uncles, aunts, and grandparents had shown up, with all the grandkids, nieces, and nephews, who ended up breaking the mother's nativity scene. Fernando Fornarís put up a good front, spending time with his brothers and even playing hide-and-seek with his nieces and nephews out on the patio. At a given moment, he put his arm on his wife's shoulder and even made soft caresses on her back. Luis Arsenio watched the scene, astonished. That day they seemed like a happy family.

But on New Year's Eve the father's absence was devastating. He arrived half an hour before the end-of-the-year dinner that was always celebrated at the grandfather's house. Doña Cristina waited for him already dressed, holding her shawl, about to burst into either a rage or tears, Luis Arsenio was not sure. All night he feared that his mother would lose her composure and make a scene in front of everybody, right there, at the entrance to the mansion. But Doña Cristina Rangel was able to contain herself. She behaved like a lady on the way there, during the whole dinner, and on the way back. She held back until they returned to the house. Then, behind closed doors, she let out from her chest the thread of a broken but fatal voice. Her hands shook, her eyes were glassy, and her clenched jaw gave her a serene and apocalyptic air. She announced that she was never again going to go through anything like this, and "this time there will be no reconciliations, and that it will well serve you, Fernando, to shape up, because if I decide to go to my father's house, I won't return, I swear. The first time I did it because of the boy, but Luis Arsenio is grown up now; so watch it, bastard. Sleep with your eyes open. And think about what you're going to do."

"What are you doing here?"

"I came to see you."

"Just to see me?"

She didn't slip into the role of femme fatale easily, not like the night when dressed in green she had dragged him into the room in the back. She didn't slip well into the role of rented woman. Minerva. Perhaps because she wasn't dressed for the part, her face without makeup, her tight curls gathered up in a little bun, like a country girl. She passed her hand over her hair, smoothing it, over her worn skirt, trying to make it hang more seductively. She even raised her chin in defiance, as he had seen her do that afternoon in Las Delicias. But no, this was another Minerva. One more. The one in green, the one like toasted sesame seeds with her leg of blossoms, and now this Minerva facing Luis Arsenio at the bar, stripped and deprived of something. The multiplicity of the young woman should have frightened him. But the effect of Minerva's nudity without choreography made Luis Arsenio even more aroused. He couldn't let go of her waist. "Can we go up, alone?"

"I haven't started to work yet."

"I'll keep you company while you get ready."

His pockets were full of money that he had taken from his mother's purse. He didn't know how to tell Minerva. "Here are all the bills, they are yours, but take me into your bosom, Minerva." But it seemed as if the girl guessed it from the expression on his face. She took him by the hand and led him to one end of the bar, where the corridors led to the assignation rooms. Toward the back were the stairs that Luis Arsenio had climbed with Minerva a month before. But she took him another way. They came out at the patio and, through some side balconies, went up to the next level. They crossed through a kitchen where some coffee grounds were steaming in water. They left behind a small parlor and a hallway where the voices of other girls getting ready seeped in. Minerva finally pushed open a small door. "This is my room, *niño*, the real one." It would have been just as well if she had thrown open the door to heaven.

The day before, Luis Arsenio had woken up to the aroma of New Year's Day lentils. He smelled olive oil, hot beans, and pieces of ham. Arsenio arose at once, with an uncomfortable void at the base of his chest. He went to wash. The water streamed down his face, but his mother's words resonated in his head, other snippets of her harangue. "Think about what you are going to do, bastard, because this time I'll leave and not return." Cristina Rangel stood her ground, erect, solid. She confronted her husband like never before. Today perhaps Luis Arsenio would see the outcome of that fight that he had been deaf to all his life. His father, as always, had tried to escape, but his mother had cut him off. Perhaps this was the decisive moment. He went downstairs to the kitchen. His mother was in the center of the room, seasoning the lentils, her face a little puffy but smiling. "Did you sleep well, my dear?" At the service table, his father drank coffee while he read the paper.

Family arrived, this time fewer of them. The attorney Fornarís greeted the guests—"Excuse me a moment"—and went to change. Cristina busied herself with the guests and Luis Arsenio—"Mother, beware"—wanted to warn her about something. But he couldn't, there were too many witnesses. But he smelled him in the air, escaping through the aroma of the lentils. The attorney Fornarís was fleeing from the house through the back patio. Luis Arsenio watched him go away in his blue Packard, with the chauffeur at the wheel, the windows rolled up and his briefcase resting in the backseat. He heard his mother call for her husband at the top of her lungs throughout the house, because she wanted to introduce him to such and such Ibañez, a friend of an aunt who had a legal question, "Because my husband is a top-notch attorney, my dear; he knows everything. You'll see how he'll solve your problem in a second. Fernando!" He had to pull away from the window, return to the deaf and mute lie, rescue his mother from embarrassment. "Don't you remember that Papa had an urgent appointment with a client in his office?" Cristina, playing it up, rolled her eyes and said, "Mother of God, of course. This head of mine, each day it remembers less." Luis Arsenio arched his eyebrows sarcastically. Everything returned to normal, his mother included. It was shameful.

He waited until the guests left. He saw his mother say farewell to the family with her hand and a smile held up by two safety pins on the back of her neck. When the audience had left, Luis Arsenio saw Doña Cristina sigh. His mother sighed, his mother's whole world sighed with her, and it seemed as if she

were left suspended in air, as if she would never again set her
feet on the earth, or her touch over things, or set her steps to
the minutes and seconds that govern the world of the living.
Doña Cristina Rangel de Fornarís sighed and locked herself up
in her bedroom. She remained there the whole day. She didn't
try to go looking for him, Luis Arsenio, her first and only son,
as she always did. She didn't try to fix his hair or ask him if
he was hungry, or sleepy, or felt like having an ice cream. She
didn't look for a pretext to call for the servants and begin the
tireless task of harassing them till they could take no more.
Doña Cristina Rangel did not do a thing. She simply took a
deep sigh and fell away from herself. Luis Arsenio watched as
she dragged her defeat to her room, to hide between the sheets
of her bed.

He wandered around the deserted town. When night fell, he
returned home and locked himself in his room to wait for his
father's arrival. He did not hear the Packard during the night. He
sensed, however, that the door to his mother's bedroom opened.
He went to see if she needed him. But no. Cristina did not even
look at him. She walked past him, down the stairs, her eyes half
closed, toward the kitchen. He saw her open a cupboard door
and bend down to find something. Somehow, there in his mother's hand, was a bottle of moonshine rum cured with dried fruits
and cinnamon sticks. That drink came from only one place—
San Antón. The blacks in San Antón owned distilleries that they
hid in the pastures next to the cane fields. Everybody knew that.
Even the authorities. But nobody gave them any trouble. The
sale of illegal rum made up for salaries that otherwise would
not have been enough to blow smoke on their hunger. It was in
the best interest of the *patrones* that the workers had something
with which to make a few pesos. Moonshine everywhere, and
his mother, Doña Cristina Rangel, was partaking as well. She

had probably sent Carmela or Delmira to buy it. She didn't even try to hide it. Her son watched her drink one, two, three glasses of liquor, seated at the kitchen table. He saw her drink without pause until she had downed half a bottle. He could smell the rancid aroma of his mother's perfume mingling with the fermentation of that rum. He saw her head droop until it fell on the table. He saw his mother drunk as can be, forgetting herself, thrown like a rag; and he felt ashamed.

Luis Arsenio walked toward the kitchen table, picked up his mother, and took her to her bed. He had to keep watch over her that night, listening to her murmur unconnected phrases, something about María, something about a staff and a mirror; looking out to see if the shadow of the car's headlights illuminated the stained glass of the windows. Nothing. Fernando Fornarís did not come back that night. The second of January passed. His mother remained drowned in an alcoholic stupor. He took the bottle from her, emptied it. He didn't know how, but another bottle appeared, hidden in a new place, in the linen armoire, in the chest where she kept her wedding dress, under the pillows. His father did not return. He tried to force his mother to eat lentils. Doña Cristina choked on them. He called Delmira and asked her to prepare a chicken consommé for the *patrona*, "because she is not well." He thought he saw an incredulous and mocking gesture cross Delmira's dark face, as unexpressive as a cold stone. He felt rage. How dare Delmira laugh at his mother? How dare she, after supplying the alcohol herself? Under what pretense, on what moral ground? Who was that presumptuous *negra* who dared mock Cristina Rangel de Fornarís? Ingrate . . .

IT WAS THE AFTERNOON OF the third of January when he saw his father's sky-blue Packard, covered in dust, enter the garage slowly. He saw the chauffeur shut the front gate, his father get out of the car, take his hat, his briefcase, and look inside the house like one who has been defeated. He then swore that his father would find him in the house only over his dead body. He had fulfilled his duty. He had taken care of the mother three days and nights. He had cleaned the vomit from the corners of her mouth, fed her, sat with her, hid as many of her drinking bottles as he could. But whatever else broke out would not be his fault or his responsibility. In a few minutes, those two beings who were his parents would face their prison and their sentence once again. He did not want to be there to have to clean up after the carnage. Because now he was sure, nothing was going to change. His mother, perhaps, would throw a tantrum one day. His father would try to leave but would end up returning, cowed by the terror of taking a false step outside of the prescribed and accepted fold granted by the name he had and the position with which he was fated. He himself, of course, was leaving. First, to Elizabeth's Dancing Place and then as far away as he could get from that house of lies.

The light came in through the window lattices. He didn't know where it came from. Maybe from the moon. Maybe from some lantern that flickered at the entrance of Elizabeth's. It was interesting. There was no light or even electrical wires in the whole neighborhood of San Antón. But near the river, in that remote and backwoods whorehouse, there was a generator with a light post, the type installed by the government. He hadn't noticed before.

Minerva looked at him straight on while Luis Arsenio thought about the origin of that light that fell on their chests and reduced their flesh to shiny droplets of sweat, a shadowed nipple, a mound like a ripe fruit, a face covered in a haze.

Minerva looked at him curiously from the half-light of the room.

"Are you going to stay a while?"

"All night if I can . . ."

He thought that suddenly there was haste in Minerva's voice. Perhaps another client was waiting for her, one of the young ones that they had left shouting at the bar. Those young men, how far away they seemed now that he was with Minerva. But she was in a rush. Luis Arsenio felt it. He looked at her suspiciously, rising up on his elbows to better read her face.

"If you want, I'll pay you more."

"It's not that . . . it's that I never finished the garlands . . ."

Then, from under the bed, Minerva pulled out a jute bag filled with scarlet crepe paper. They were for the Feast of the Kings. She was still naked, but now she seemed more so. A strip of paper rolled up in the hinges of her flesh, as she explained to Luis Arsenio, "I hope that Isabel doesn't find out, but anyway it's her fault; first she sends us into town to look for toys, then we had to go shopping, order pastries." A thigh shudders against the red; her thick mouth does not stop vibrating, "Syrup for the ice cones, blocks of ice . . . then we brought the toys here . . . Oh, they are so pretty." Minerva's mouth opens, she smiles, "Balls, fire trucks, these blond dolls that were a dream. I kept one, because I never had such a thing . . ." Luis Arsenio looks at her; he cannot stop looking at her. It is the first time in days that he sees something that makes him smile. "But now, how do I finish the garlands?" He promises to keep the secret. He even offers to help her. And so they sat there, coiling crepe paper, both of them naked on the bed. Minerva took out a pair of scissors to cut strips. Luis Arsenio twisted crepe paper until his intentions became twisted and he could not help jumping on top of Minerva again, on top of the garlands that wrapped around their bodies.

"Boy, we are never going to finish this way."

"Don't worry, I'll give you all of the money I have to buy more paper."

"It's better if you don't give me any money. Remember, the Three Kings have come."

"You don't have to give me a gift."

"And who said that the gift was yours . . . ?"

Minerva arched her back and gave Arsenio a taste of the gift. Luis Arsenio dissolved into a thousand tremors that plowed through his skin. Minerva offered him her rump, her wide and wet hips. When he was on top of her, Arsenio felt like multiplying that gift for her, making it lasting. He adjusted himself on her back, keeping rhythm with his Minerva, who was now many Minervas, all with their back to him, the horrible Minerva of the bar who offered him her zipper, the one in the cotton dress fluttering in the breeze of the plaza, and this Minerva of the garlands, who dissolved underneath him, her back to him, open for him in a bed decorated for the Three Kings. Luis Arsenio let out a long guffaw and remained there, clutching those hips, breathing heavily, lost in the curves of that dark-skinned back, in the little pearls of sweat that emitted from the pores, in the moans of that woman whose face he could not see, but as if he could see her, see her closed eyes and half-opened mouth seeking air, and the hands burying themselves anywhere, lost in her rhythm, in her wetness, lost in the rubbing and battering that he was not going to let up on, not until he heard her scream, not until he felt her backing up in search of him, wringing herself from the inside and then opening up with palpitations to snatch from him, from Luis Arsenio, all of the juices that were left inside him.

They finally came down from the dingy room. Luis Arsenio felt light, weightless, as if he had just been born. He wanted to continue to be that person that descended from Minerva's pleasures. On the way, Minerva told him that it had been on a Three Kings Day that Isabel brought her from the barrio to work for her. "I was fourteen years old, with an uncle who was breaking me to bits. But Isabel took me to a doctor who made me better and brought me here. I worked at the bar first and doing errands. But you make more on the dance floor." Luis Arsenio frowned. He didn't want to hear these stories. Too much reality. But he was not going to interrupt if the stories allowed him to hear Minerva's voice, accompanying him to the bar to grab a drink. Now he would have some sugarcane rum and put some coins in the Victrola to celebrate the holidays his own way. There were few of the young workers left who had been shouting at each other when Arsenio arrived. But the tall *negro* was still there, imposing, like an ebony spike. The young men who were left had quieted down and listened attentively. About then, Isabel La Negra stood up.

"The next time you get in trouble, I am not going to send money for the bond. You are already in hot water. There is not a tobacco owner who will give you a table. And still, you volunteer to organize workers . . ."

"But what would you have me do, Isabelita? Those assholes want to starve us to death. What? Are they going to lower our salaries? The next thing you know they'll be charging us to work for them."

"Don Demetrio is right. You should read the Manifesto that we were studying the other day."

"What studying, studying . . . as if you were señoritos."

"Well, believe it or not, Doña Isabel, we do teach ourselves. That's what the labor center is for. You should come by. We educate many ladies of your profession there."

"Careful, Jonás, don't cross the line."

"Don't worry, Don Demetrio, nobody crosses the line with me because I stop them, at once. Anyway, boys, in this establishment there is a strict rule, no talking about politics. And I called you over to help with the Feast of the Kings, not for you to convert me to that socialism of yours, because I already have my religion."

"And an expensive one at that. How much are you going to give to the cassocks this year?"

Someone else who referred to the priests by their skirts. Arsenio felt like smiling, offering his immediate sympathy to that fierce man. Just as he was going to be from now on, now that he held on to his Minerva, sated. But an annoying buzzing sullied the air in the bar. Minerva stopped caressing him. She lowered her eyes. The pair of workers who were left joined that uncomfortable silence that infected Luis Arsenio. All he wanted to do was look at Minerva. But he had to consider the madam, that other dark woman who cut a path through the men, like a fish swimming in the turbid waters of that silence.

"Look, Demetrio . . . My last days will be spent in that refuge; they will say Masses in my name in that parish."

"You are going to donate a lot for those puny priests to say rosaries for you."

"And may I ask why you say that?"

"Isabelita, there are things that money doesn't change."

Luis Arsenio leaned on his chair, preparing himself. He wasn't exactly sure for what, but something was simmering in the air. Minerva kept her eyes fixed on the floor. "This is the anguish," he thought. But the opposite occurred. Don Demetrio Sterling extended his hand. He caressed Isabel's cheeks with his rough fingers, as if he were brushing away a straw. But the straw would not come off, the color would not come off. Demetrio smiled as he looked at her, amused and saddened at once. Suddenly, Isabel La Negra shrank, became nothing but a tiny woman, with the face of a girl who has just been scolded. She sighed a little.

"Don't be getting in any more trouble, Don Demetrio. Remember, you are the only one that I can call family around here."

"Don't worry, Isabelita, nothing is going to happen to me. But I see you walking into a fire."

"Teté and Godmother used to say that I was daughter of the storms. I won't burn . . . Go on, Demetrio, help me set up for these Kings. Time flies."

Minerva's tense fingers pressed against his thigh. A whisper said, "The garlands." It was time to go. But Luis Arsenio did not want to leave. He had been a witness to something, a nameless alliance, a little light he wished to remain under. There were other ways in which blood knotted, other links that could create profound alliances. "What if I stay a little bit and help you with the garlands?" "No, you better not," Minerva said and turned away. Luis Arsenio grabbed her by the waist and with a breath took her in completely. That night he would have given anything just to be another worker, any neighbor's son, a stray with no name. Not to be burdened with the name that anchored him to his stock and his caste. He would have given anything to remain within the walls of Elizabeth's Dancing Place until the world that beckoned him from outside turned to wind and dust.

Montaraz

THE CHILD GROWS, the Child grows, the Child grows. The old woman sees him approach on the hill path. I'm here, God-mother. He throws himself on the steps of the little house like a bundle of clothes. Oh, Mother, how big he gets. Each day he looks more like him. You're hungry, Rafael. Roberto, God-mother. How many times do I have to tell you? Or call me whatever you want. Why do I get angry at you, foolish old woman? Maybe you should light another candle for me. The old woman walks toward the fire, lifts a lid from a smoking pot. I'll serve you now, Child. How was school? I didn't go. What do you mean you didn't go? I'm not going anymore. After every-thing your father did to enroll you . . . Oh, Child, if he finds out . . . And how is he going to find out, if he hasn't been here for months? The old woman kneads her hands. You burned your-self, dumb old woman. It hasn't been months. Or has it? The voices don't let her keep track of time, of the passing of days. It can't have been months, there is still food in the pantry.

"I brought that food."

"How, Child?"

"Doing errands in town, Godmother. Doing favors for the girls of Tres Marías. We don't need him to return. I am a man already. Whatever you need, ask me."

A full grown man, a full grown man, the Child grows. The phrase flutters like a horsefly in her head: a horsefly that perishes in midflight because the Child said he worked at Tres Marías. Whory Mother of God, concealed without sin. That was the place Don Armando took her out of. It was from there that she ended up on this hill. This will not end well, will not end well. The old woman feels new again, recently arrived from the coast, from the sands of Hatillo del Mar. Once again she feels the earth under her bare feet. She had been a migrant worker, a coast runner, finding her way in the mountains. She milked cows, raised pigs, and went to the country to pick coffee. Hormigueros was smaller than a mosquito bite, tiny, but behind Calle Ruiz Belvís was Tres Marías. She started by taking out the washbowls of the hookers who worked there selling themselves to the cattle ranchers. Later, she even sold herself until she went to pick coffee at Don Armando's farm. She kept both jobs. It was convenient.

A full grown man, the Child grows. But he doesn't even have hair on his legs, must not even have hair where he should on his dick, wretched brat, let him bow before me, before you, Mother. Since when are you not in school? Since last month, the Child says. And the old woman: But, Rafael. Why don't you call me what the hookers call me? Bobby, they say, when they pass their hands through my hair, when, well, I better stop, Godmother, because you are an old woman. I don't want to offend you.

The old woman stops stirring the fire and approaches him.

From a distance, the many smells hit her. Smoke, alcohol, a mixture of perfume and cheap powders. The Child's eyes are red. He's drinking, he's drunk, stupid old woman, because you took him from your lap. Now the boy will be lost before he arrives at the temple of my protection. I can't allow it, I can't allow it, beloved Virgin. The old woman covers the eyes of the voices, covers her eyes. Damn, if he perishes, it is your fault. Walk as fast as you can to the grotto. My grotto, to my grotto, you had better resolve this. The Child laughs behind her back.

Staff of patience, hear our prayers.

Mother of perseverance, hear our prayers.

Mother of forgiveness, hear our prayers. I don't want a message or proof. Please intercede before Him.

The old woman does not need to light candles. Inside the stone grotto a fresh breeze blows and the shadows eat away at the corners where the votives of the pilgrims flicker. Little tinplate arms, legs, reliquaries of the Virgin with Son, dried bramble crowns. Like you, old whore, who thought you were going to escape your torment. The Father won't come, the Father will punish you with the whip of his scorn, after he put the parcel in your name, sent you allowances, after he liberated you from the slave quarters of the Harpies, and now you repay him with this. No, Mother, let the Father return, I am old, yesyesyes I am the Señor's slave. Don't you dare not tend to me in this hour, don't you dare, because you and I are made from the same material. Skin like prison, skin like shadow, skin like wood eaten by the fire. You are nothing without me here, so let's see if you shimmy that ass from that throne and present yourself to the Father. Tell Him the Child is in trouble. Tell Him he is frequenting Tres Marías. Tell Him to make a move. To forget about what is happening in his other Kingdom. To show Himself and tame the Enemy who wants to possess his

Son, the Beloved. Mary, Amen, Jesus. The Virgin of Montserrat looks at the old woman darkly from her reserved porcelain face. The old woman lets out a sigh of relief. Perhaps she won this dispute. She must obey and listen to her, or else leave her chores for some other *negra*, someone else to water her bushes and attend to her pilgrims. Her knees hurt. She doesn't know how long she has been there, kneeling, fighting with the Virgin through prayer. How many days, how many weeks? The Child must be numb from hunger.

She comes out of the grotto and closes the door carefully. With her hands on her back, it's going to crack, it's going to crack in two, old woman, you'll see, climbs the hill to the house. The truth is that the house has grown. It's painted white and the planking is new. The air and the rain and the quiet of the night do not seep in anymore. She fixed it up good with the allowances sent by the Señor. Each month it arrives and she hides it under a plank beside the bed. "Here, Child," she gives part of it to her angel Rafael Bobby Roberto. She gives him enough for his expenses, his sweets. But never for rum. Never for the Tres Marías—the one Mary in the grotto is good enough and she herself had been all three Marys before Don Armando took her out.

She finally makes it to the top. She almost smiles. She won the battle. Yes, she won the battle. The Virgin will intercede. She will bring the Father, tame the Son. Black Virgin with white boy on your lap, Black Virgin with white boy, the charging bull of her fury will save him. No more neglect, no more neglect, no more. Do you want your dinner, Child? The old woman speaks to the air. She looks for him everywhere in the little house, the living room, the two bedrooms just finished.

The Child is not there.

SECOND VISIT

Ask myself nothing.
I have seen that things
Searching for their path
　　Find their emptiness.

　　　　　—Federico García Lorca, *Poet in New York*

　　Noli me tangere

The Enemy

SHE THINKS SHE has a big enough mouth to say "this is mine." She thinks she can hold her own against me, and against the plans that were left in my hands by my own.

That's what the Enemy says. He awakes with the dictum on his lips. He goes to his office with the dictum on his lips. He lunches, dines, watches television, now in color, goes to bed with the dictum on his lips. Isabel has become an obsession. But I remember well, lest she forget, when I was a boy, she was the one who came to pick up the dirty laundry, my father's sweaty underwear, the soiled petticoats, just so she could have enough to eat. Don't let her forget. Every Friday afternoon. She couldn't look us in the eye. So what is this now about rights, about titles of properties, thinking she has a big enough mouth to speak and respond? The Enemy gets up from his desk. He sees to the secretary who comes into his office, signs a few documents that require his signature. Takes the mail addressed to him, a man of influence, a man of business, son of his father.

"Señora Castañer on the line."

Let the damn mother who gave birth to her answer it, the Enemy thinks, but responds.

"Tell her I'll call her at home later. I am very busy."

Damn that Norma. From the day he married her all she does is ask for his advice. Tinito wants to change careers for the third time. And Mariela will graduate soon and we haven't done anything about the prom . . . As if he cared. The Enemy scratches his head and asks himself why his wife does not understand that he should not have to worry about those things. That's what she is there for. And he thinks it's great that she leaves all the business decisions to him, that she had even granted him the power to manage the sections of the importing business and profits that were hers. I don't have a knack for those things, Norma had said after they married. He never loved her as much as he did that moment when she gave him full authority. Absolute trust in him. A complete handing over. What he never got from his uncles, his father, he came to get from that wife.

What he never imagined was that Norma Castañer, of the Castañers from Guayanilla, didn't have a knack for almost anything, that others had to make important decisions for her; that's how she had been raised, paying nuns, tutors, and chaperones, paying etiquette and manners coaches, to cleanse Norma of every decision, show her how to cede her rights, hang herself from the arm of a man; harmless, she was, with that air of a deer lost in the woods, like the ones in Maryland. So harmless, calling at every hour to ask for advice, to announce catastrophes, to weep. At least his mother put up a struggle; she fought inch by inch with the Father, even if she didn't talk to him about anything else, even if she let him come and go with other women and didn't take the fight to that level, because she was the señora of the house, and as the señora of the house she behaved.

He scrutinizes the letters addressed to his office. Copies of account statements. Minutes of managerial meetings. His office, with his desk, his phones, his secretary, his personal things, all constructed to his liking. Everything responded to his plan, the plan that he saw his uncles devise in their offices thirty-five years before and that he finally convinced them to entrust to his hands. It had been a struggle; for though he hadn't yet married, didn't whore around, with a degree in hand and working like a dog for them, they didn't want to let go of the steering wheel. He had to wait until they grew old.

His father finally retired, almost blind. Uncle Valentín had died the previous summer after a long illness. A letter arrives— the widow and her sons asking for their allowances to pay bills at the universities and house expenses. Let them hold back a little bit, that's what he would like to tell them, take it easy with the spending now that the uncle is not with them. Now he's in charge. Now it is he who has to deal with the taxes, the strikes, which were back after two decades of calm, and the Party that lost for the first time in history. With this kind of political instability you had to be careful about the construction contracts that fell into your hands. Call the secretary to order a check with a copy from accounting to send the allowance to the widow Valentín and her son who is studying abroad. The check should come from the construction company, so they can be deducted as expenses later. The widow is listed as a manager, so is the cousin. Let them get paid from that. But don't let the check go out today or tomorrow. Let them wait.

In his hands he holds an official envelope with standard postmarks and the corresponding signatures.

"Canal construction and other work pertaining to the de- viation of the Portuguese River's bed have been indefinitely postponed until the allegations of inappropriate indemnity of land have been cleared . . . ," the letter says, "to elucidate the errors in the deeds of the property that Fornarís alleges to have ceded, in August of 1932, to Isabel Luberza . . ."

He takes the envelope and crushes it. Unbelievable. Someone has reopened the investigations of the land deeds on the shores of the Portuguese. The last administration had approved the change of deeds for a considerable amount. The transaction had been done so that they could hook the fat fish of the canal construction. "You hand over the land to us; we'll pay you top price and favor the firm for the digging of the new riverbed. That's if we win the election," they had told him. "But fuck my unlucky stars, they lost." The forces became immense on the other side; somebody, damn them, evened the scales for them. Uncle Juan Isidro was too old. They listened to him out of respect, but he no longer had the power to straighten out the opposing party in favor of the family business. When did the power of influence slip through my hands? "And now look . . . they want me to return hundreds of thousands of dollars, as if they had their hands in my pockets," the Enemy murmurs. As if I had not already invested in union bonds so that they convince the workers to accept the new agreement, in machines and parts for the water pumps, on the same commission that became *donations* for senate electoral campaigns.

Who the hell dares to go over his head, who did that vile whore manage to buy off, for how much and with whose flesh? That's what he wanted to know.

The Enemy picks up the receiver, dials, and waits.

"My dear Bishop MacManus . . ."

"Always a pleasure to hear from you. Just right now I was thinking about the plans to expand the university. You know that without the lands that your family donated to the archdiocese . . ."

"That is exactly why I am calling. You know that those do-nations depended on the business with the canal construction on the river. Now they have opened an investigation; I am afraid that we are going to have to put off the plans for a while."

"What, Señor Ferráns? But we have already begun the cam-paign for funds to expand this educational center."

"It's just that there are certain factions in this city who are sticking their noses where they don't belong. A certain lady of business of dubious reputation. In fact, your archdiocese accepts her substantial donations."

"You know well that the church feeds from all of its parish-ioners."

"You misunderstand me, your Excellency. I know that we are all welcome in the house of the Lord. I am only calling to warn you of this delay. You pray for me so that I can straighten this out and keep my word. If not, I will pray so that you find another family to donate lands for this important work of yours."

He has to make another call, but the Enemy feels like spit-ting. His mouth fills with an acrid taste, like the sourness and bitterness of the smell of flies flitting over fresh garbage. But the men of his stock don't spit, so he gets up and goes to the small bar twinkling with high-end liquors in one side of his office. A man of business needs such a bar, well placed in a corner, for situations like this. He makes himself a whiskey with water. He has to get rid of the taste of tar from his mouth. With a long gulp from the glass, he refreshes himself. He learned it in Mary-land. The opponent has to be destabilized so that he doesn't see where the next attack is coming from. Bishop MacManus, Bishop MacManus, the pawn to destabilize La Negra. But there is one move left to play. They have opened an investigation. Well, he'll attack with another one. He dials.

"Alejo, how are you, my brother?"

"You must mean Senator Alejandro Villanúa."

"Oh, sorry, Mr. Senator."

"What can I do for you?"

"They opened a new investigation about the lands on the Portuguese."

"About Isabel La Negra's little lot? Weren't you buying it from her?"

"She's not cracking, the sly one."

"If you want, we'll do the same thing we always do. But remember that the Party controls only the senate. The secretary of public works is not ours, and they can catch you."

"Damn, Alejo, what do I do? Give some advice, for the love of your mother."

"Let's subpoena her again."

"But you've never been able to convict her. That woman has more senators in her pocket than whores at Elizabeth's."

"Probably. But we can't lose anything by trying."

"Well, go ahead, man. What else can we do?"

It is hundreds of thousands of dollars that he has committed to other things. The business will crumble if the construction of the new riverbed falls through. Because the worst part is not the lands, or the investigation, or the nuisance about the tomatoes. The worst part is that he already bought new machinery and bought unions and bought senators. And this investigation opens a Pandora's box. Other investigations about things nobody needs to know anything about can slip in through there. "Then what?" the Enemy asks himself. "Then what do I do so details about the quarry, the rebuilding of the central airport, and the stretch of Highway 876 don't rise to the surface? No, I can't let it happen." The Enemy throws back the rest of the drink. "This bitch will pay." He needs to concentrate on the solution, not the problem. La Negra must have bought someone. And he has to find out who. "I swear she will pay. Wait until I get out of this mess."

But who would have imagined it? No one, really. For that man never had any character. He let everything be taken from his hands. They had to sell the farms in San Antón in order to care for the madwoman. All that land where cement and stone grow, roads so that things come and go and circle. We made good deals with the outgoing government. The bad thing is that we signed contracts. I told Uncle Isidro, I told him plainly. Let's not do it until we have gone over the deed. But who knew about that parcel, right on the river. It's worthless, but it is there, right in the middle. Quite the song with which they bought that groveling *negra*'s mouth. So don't let her pretend she has a mouth to speak with now. She sold it a long time ago.

"You and I both know that decisions made on the spot are the best to make the profits grow," he had said in a message sent to her. The madam did not want to accept. "It is not for sale." With that mouth, as if it were hers. So the reply was sent back, and to confirm that he had received the message through her lawyer, Chiro Caggiano, she herself haughtily appeared in his offices. "It is not for sale." She pronounced each syllable firmly, then turned around and walked out of his office, leaving him with the words caught in his mouth. Damn her, and damn Uncle Juan Isidro. "Why do you worry so much about such an opponent?" He had been taught in Maryland that no competitor is too small. He had underestimated her and now was going to have to shake up his influences, buy more functionaries to stop the investigation.

The phone rings. The Enemy checks his fancy watch. It is

time to attend to other business. He is going to have to postpone his battle with Isabel. "Times have changed," he tells himself. Times change and he is going to have to change along with them. If La Negra doesn't sell, let her not sell. He will find other ways to make her concede.

Egyptian Mary

HOLY MOTHER, EGYPTIAN Mary, Holy Virgin who sold yourself to cross the sea. Sinful was the knowledge that you used to reach Jerusalem. You wanted to see what everybody saw, know who they were talking about when they fervently murmured, "Al Nasir." Al Nasir, you murmured, and you knew that that was the lost seed. The son you had and did not have, that your body expelled, the soul that blankets the body they gave you to eat and drink. Hail, Egyptian Mary, it is to you whom I direct my prayer. To you who are one of the three, one of the thousands who have lived the life that I live. Sinful is the knowledge that guides those women who walk alone in this vale of tears, slaves who find sustenance in the only places they can. And then they call out to them, "sinner," knowing the road they have taken.

You are my guide. You know me. You were loyal to your premonition, for which you abandoned paints and perfumes, left behind your rich merchants, your jewels. You wandered on the roads, subsisting on whatever you could earn with your body, offering it to travelers. You offered yourself to the ship captain and he crossed the temperate sea for you. He led you to other roads, like the ones I look for. Show me the way, Mother, show me the way to recover the wasted seed. Al Nasir, you murmured, Al Nasir, you who did not have the luxury of being the Immaculate One. Just to see them open the doors of Alexandria for you, see you cross its threshold without having to hide in the shadows. You, who know what it is like to have to live in the shadows, watch over me, Egyptian Mary, watch over me.

Fate and premonition. That is why you abandoned your house, canceled your meetings, went on your way. You fell to your knees before the Holy Sepulcher on seeing the Mother. Not the Son, the Mother, not the Son, the Mother, a woman like you, her breasts torn by a thousand sorrows, as if a sword was plunged into her heart. Nobody knew about your pains. Not even you, as you quietly continued to work on failed appetites, not knowing of the sea loosened in your crotch, flooded as if with anxious tears. You fell on the ground, devastated, swearing to be a slave among slaves, the lowest. Amen, Jesus, and you were. You never returned to Alexandria, your city.

You wandered in the desert for forty years. Only your hair shielded you, and the tears on your burning face, and the rags on your dry sex. Egyptian Mary, Gypsy Mary, Mary Magdalene. You were as beautiful as the Queen of Sheba, as the Sybil of Eleuthera, Sacred and Wise like them. As soon as the Mother appeared to you, your heart remembered the pain. You dried up, Mary. Your long, braided hair was your only mantle, the nakedness of your flesh the tunic that covered you. You ate three loaves of bread in the sixty days, your chosen martyrdom. You accepted penance and cleansed yourself, at peace among the beasts, naked as you came into the world. In this grotto, I light you candles so that you remember that you are capable of giving birth, capable of cleansing me once and for all, in case I am visited by the Seed. I want to follow your example, Mary. Don't forsake me now.

That is why I send you this prayer . . . Don't let the forty years that I have been wandering multiply themselves by forty more. Don't let there be another forty for the forty that I carry parched within me, naked, my skin boiling in the pool of my discontent. I have paid my debts. I have done my penance. For my error and my wisdom, for my error and my wisdom, for my arrogance in thinking that I could free myself from the shadows because it was only the Son who tied me down. That I could forge some other path than this grotto that is ours. I have seen you everywhere, and have followed you everywhere, Mary. You watch over the gloomy waters, the sighs of hunger where men are slaves and open themselves to darkness. But they do not want to plunge into the beautiful abyss. They don't want to let go of the name of names. There was light, but they do not want it; that is why they want to keep us alone and fallen. I fell into the trap, all of us alone and contaminated by the light. I want to be the dark soil where the Seed ripens again. Or at least where it sends out its transplanted roots. Listen to me, Mother. I am abandoning my home, my fortune, my jewels. I am casting out my arrogance and offering it to the unfaithful. Don't forsake me at this difficult hour.

Holy Innocents

I AM THE only one in this grotto; come see me, old woman, come, Candela, you ball of fire from hell, light some candles, kneel before my sacred mantle. But the old woman won't go. Virgin of Montserrat, stay in your shoddy kingdom, Virgin of Montserrat, burned-out one, shroud yourself with your mantle. Let God descend and suck on my dry tits, God Almighty, Father, Son, and Holy Spirit, but not like the Child because God is white and like the whites He takes what He wants and then says, "This is your place. Don't ask for anything else." Let her go fuck herself back there in the bushes; I am not going. She has to prepare delicious meals for the Child, to celebrate his saint's day and his birthday and his spirit made flesh. See if he calms down. See if he returns to the fold.

IT IS THE DAY OF the Holy Innocents. The old woman sweeps the floorboards of the house with a broom made from leaves.

Little balls of dust are stirred up with each pass of the fibers. The Child is not there. She sweeps the dust toward the entrance and pushes it outside. Let the breeze take this dust, the dust of the steps of the Son looking for his dwelling before the Lord. The dirt fell on the top steps of the house. The old woman sweeps them one by one, leaning against the railing. The Fall is coming, old woman, as she puts her hands on her hips to hold on to herself. To myself, Mother, I don't need you anymore, you can rot in your grotto, hollow as you are inside. Doña Montse, Doña Montse, Doña Montse. Someone is calling you. I said I am not going. But I have a promise to keep. Everyone has kept their promises. Except the one to me. O Virgin of Shit. Well, I'm not going down until you take care of what I have asked for and bring the Señor here.

The old woman gazes toward the bottom of the hill. A silhouette appears among the bushes, leaning on the gate. She walks with all the patience in the world. The pilgrim waits for her.

"Didn't you hear me?"

"Yes. But since I saw you talking to yourself, I thought it wasn't meant for me."

"Well, it was. The sanctuary won't open until after the Feast of the Epiphany."

"Can I leave you my offering for the Virgin? I've come from very far . . ."

"Give it to me, I'll take care of it. You can leave the flowers at the entrance to the grotto."

The pilgrim placed three cents in her hand. Three candle stubs and three pennies. The old woman almost burst out in guffaws. This is what a kept promise is worth, look, Virgin, what they come to pay you. She put the three pennies in a pocket of her ragged robe. I'll get some rum, you'll see, yesyesyes, three cents of booze down the gullet, that's why I am called what I am called. Doña Montse, Doña Montse, Doña Montse . . . That's not my name. María de la Candelaria Fresnet, Candela, fire, for the Christians at Tres Marías. Watch me go, I'll find the Child and drink with him.

She climbed the hill, but this time took another path to the stove in the back patio. She had put rice in the pot, and it was just about sticky enough. You are going to make rice pudding, huh, old woman? The Child's favorite delicacy. You are going to add dried fruits and shaved coconut, cow's milk and cinnamon powder. Cinnamon like the color of the boy's skin, which had acquired its true color. The old woman grabs a can of milk, pours it in the pot, grabs the grater, and works on a dry coconut. The pulp of the coconut is white, white the grated bits, like vaporous clouds and feathers. When they first brought him, the Child was almost this fair, rosy even. But you could see other hues coming from inside. Yesyesyes, in his tiny balls first, you could see the mixture there. The señoras noticed his sooty balls, dark as grapes. Armando would tell me the same thing, open your legs, you devil, allow me into my fruit dark as a muscatel grape, and it was the same with the Child's tiny balls. The old woman grates, grates . . . the hollow skin of her arms trembles with each pass. Armando was dead. The Child had an ear infection. We will take care of him, we will take care of him. The attorney dressed him in linen, in cambric; he tied bows on the Child's sleeves. And the Child sick. That's not how you raise the Child of the Virgin of the low valley. Although I am neither the grandmother nor the Godmother, that's not how you raise the Child of this Sheep of Bitterness, bitter as fury.

She stopped when she felt the teeth of the grater against her knuckles. She put all the coconut gratings in a dish and went to the cauldron. Because the Child is not the Son or the Father, and never the Holy Spirit. The Child is the Mother freed from the Virgin, the Mother freed from the grotto, the Mother freed from the Son. She took off the lid of the cauldron and threw in the coconut and the cinnamon; she mixed it all together with a wooden spoon and put out the fire. It finishes cooking best in the embers. The Child approached the hill. She watched him stumble against the wooden gate, strange, although not drunk as he usually was when he came home now, he was losing his footing and balance. She watched him teeter, open the door to the grotto with a shove, and close it.

Maybe he is praying. Maybe he will find his way again. She would not bother him. See if you grant me what I am asking for, Useless Virgin, and return him to the fold. Because these days the Child is more agitated than usual. These days the Child disappears for long stretches. And she is old, I am old already, and too dried up to be dealing with these frights. Sometimes she has to put her hair up, slip into her good dress, and go look for him at Tres Marías, drag him out of there. It's shameful that they have to see her like that, like a grimy and black dried fruit, but if I withered up lighting candles, you are going to wither as well; remember we are made of the same material, Montserrat, Montserrat, Doña Montse, because we are made of this wooden skin that catches fire instantly. My breasts withered from so much lighting and putting out candles, from so much reciting and unreciting rosaries, from so much tending to others. But you are as old and dry as me. Your favors are also worth three pennies.

It was the day of the Holy Innocents. This time the old woman kept track of time; the voices would not confuse her. She was aware of the passing of the days. I told you to do something, Montserrat, so that before the year ended the attorney returned here. Perform one miracle, if you have it in you. The Child does not come out of the grotto. She sees some candles being lit inside, smoke coming out of the only window. He must be hungry. I am all the nourishment that your Son needs. Whoever has me on his chest saves himself from all evil. Damned be the one on the throne. The old woman makes up her mind and goes down to the grotto. She knocks on the door, but there is no answer. Roberto? Are you hungry? Do you want to eat? I saw you go in; tell me, Child, do you want to eat? I made you a rice pudding you'll be licking off your fingers.

Doña Montse, Doña Montse, Doña Montse. No, it can't be. More pilgrims. The old woman hears them call for her. The sanctuary is closed until after the Day of the Epiphany. But the shadows remain in the bushes; the shadows wait for her at the gate.

"Do you know where your godson is?"

"The Child? Why? Who wants him?"

"We are from the police station . . ."

"Holy Virgin, what happened?"

They prodded her into town. At the police headquarters were the superintendent, two policemen, and a Eusebio Cintrón, a cattle rancher. Your godchild attacked the son of this señor, Doña Montse. That's not your name, Godmother. What do you mean attacked? Bet it was at the Tres Marías, huh, old woman? Bet it was at the origin of your stain. It looks like a fight about skirts. Lito Cintrón insulted him about what you can guess and Roberto jumped him. Nobody saw where the knife came from. The best thing would be for him to turn himself in, Mother of Purity, watch over him, Tower of Strength, hide him until the señor comes. Don Eusebio can take justice into his own hands. It's best if he turns himself in. Let them get the attorney, dumb old woman, you shut your mouth, and call Fornarís. The old woman grabbed the superintendent by the sleeve. Did you call the father? Yes, Dõna Montse, he says that as soon as he can, he'll come running.

One

"HEY, LOUIE, THE dining hall is closing soon. Are you coming down to eat?"

Luis Arsenio jumped. He snuggled into his coat and went down the stairs. His friend Jake was calling him. If Fischer Hassenfield had become more tolerable, it was because of Jake. He had been assigned to a modest room with a big window and a single bed, in what was known as the Quadrangle. The oldest buildings in the university were there—The Fischer Hassenfield House, the Ripe House, the Ware. His room was in the first house. The only inconvenience was that he had to cross the Quad to go eat at Ware, where the dining hall was. The law students were in his dorm. *Res Publicae, Res Populis*, the coat of arms said, irises gracefully displayed on a background of blue ribbons. Luis Arsenio passed under that coat of arms and decided to cross through the dry leaves of the Quad. At the end of a hallway, a crowd of people gathered in the dining rooms. He got in line for his spongy chicken, no salt, his mashed potatoes, his watery vegetables. His taste buds were growing accustomed to the flavor (or lack of it). On the opposite side of the line of diners was another line of dark, expressionless faces that served them their steaming dishes. Faces like Delmira's and Carmela's. Faces like Minerva's.

Minerva naked against the plank walls of the little room at Elizabeth's. Luis Arsenio entangled in her legs, trying not to lose control. Minerva scratching his back, biting his shoulders hard enough to leave the marks of her canines. Arsenio sucking on her neck until he left the print of his passing on her. Minerva pushing him off naughtily, murmuring in his ear, "Who said you could?" Luis Arsenio thinking about her, with his hand lost in his pants, smelling her on him until he arrived in Philadelphia.

"They accepted me to study abroad."

"Where?"

"At the University of Pennsylvania."

". . . I am going to miss you."

That wasn't exactly the farewell. But Luis Arsenio superimposes it on the "maybe I'll surprise you and show up next Saturday" that he deceitfully told her before he disappeared from the town forever. He would have liked to have dared more. He would have liked, for instance, to have sat naked on the bed, leisurely smoking a Tiparillo, while he informed Minerva that he was leaving, that the meeting with the boys who were waiting for him at the bar was his farewell party. That he had sneaked from the house for the last time and he did not know if he would ever return.

Carrying his tray, he looked along the tables for where Jake Barowski was seated, his books beside him, as always. Jake Barowski—they had become friends instantly. He was carrying his chest up the stairs to the second floor of Fischer Hassenfield when he stumbled up against a thin tower of gawky bones, which greeted him with a welcoming smile, "Hola, are you a Spaniard?" "Corsican." It seemed better than saying, "From the islands." At Fischer Hassenfield almost all the students were Anglos, but there were some from the odd countries: Danes, a certain Chilean Comte de Lautréamont. Very rich Mexicans who kept to their own closed cliques, two or three Russians, and Jake. Jacob Barowski, a Jew from Philadelphia. On that day, as he helped Luis Arsenio with his chest of clothes, he explained his background. His father was a member of the Congregation Mikhev Israel, the second-oldest in the country. Aside from the study of the Torah, Barowski dedicated his life to studying all kinds of books. He loved them so much that he became a librarian by profession and worked with the legendary Cirus Allen on founding the Free Library of Philadelphia. Abraham Barowski instilled in his sons (there were three) a love of the written word. Perhaps it was because of this that Jake had wanted to become a lawyer, and it may also explain what the Jew was doing in Philadelphia speaking to Luis Arsenio in Spanish.

"Family language. My father's other surname is Machado. Galician-Portuguese. He did not want us to lose our heritage."

He saw him in a corner of the dining room and walked toward him. A chorus of young women passed in front of him, also on the way to the tables. One of them held her gaze on him. Her face was the color of alabaster. It wasn't the dark-haired fairness common with women of his class or the anemic paleness of the country girls. Her skin was translucent; something like mother of pearl shone from under the indirectly glowing skin, letting through a shine that beat from under the blush of the cheeks, and against the temples framed by terrifically red hair and brown eyes. The young woman looked at him with a self-confidence that not even Minerva would have wielded. She shot a smile at him and continued with her friends to an adjacent table.

When he got to Jake, he found him laughing in a low voice. "Don't even bother," he said, and for a second Luis Arsenio did not know what he was talking about. Jake looked in the direction of the girl.

"She's out of your league."

"You know who she is?"

"Maggie Carlisle. Second year. But you shouldn't bother."

"Why not?"

"Can't you tell? You're not her type."

"She looked at me as if I were."

"If you really were, she wouldn't have looked at you like that."

Pure milk from full breasts. Her hair and her pubes in flames. But he shouldn't think that. She was a university girl, dedicated to her studies, her intellect, a decent girl. You could tell from looking at her. She brushed back a lock of her terrifically red hair. She cut her meat delicately, chewed it with her rosy lips, her perfect little porcelain mouth. She leaned her head on her hand, attentive to her friends' commentaries, surely intelligent commentaries; she chewed and swallowed slowly. The young woman looked at him again. Luis Arsenio surprised himself, thinking about the warmth of the contact with those cheeks that seemed to swallow him, the feverish graze of those lips, how they could quell the hunger crammed in his soul. No, impossible. You don't think those things about such refined girls.

He had arrived in Philadelphia at the end of September, set to stay at the house of friends of his grandparents, formerly owners of a tobacco factory on Fourteenth Street in New York City. The Viñas, both Corsicans from Cuba, moved to Philadelphia when they realized the change that was coming, which would sink many others. The tobacco importing industry was going to be struck by gale-force winds. The Southern states asserted themselves with tariffs that raised the price of imports, making Havana cigars a luxury item, removed from daily life by cigarettes mass-produced from leaves grown in Arkansas, Mississippi, and Louisiana. A top-quality Montecristo could cost as much as a dollar at that time, while the Pall Malls, Lucky Strikes, and Marlboros sold for pennies a pack, a consolation preferred by the thousands uprooted by the Depression. Action was needed, and quickly. The Viñas (now Mr. and Mrs. Viner) sold the land where their tobacco factory was located. They wanted to go far away from the city with the money they made. They moved to Philadelphia, thinking it would be a stopping-off point, and opened a smoke shop. But their plan was to acquire capital to build something else in Florida, in the middle of the mighty city that was being forged out of the little coastal town of Miami.

"This has no flavor."

"Wait until you come to our house to eat real food. You'll be licking your fingers."

"Jake, seriously, I don't want to be a nuisance."

"Oh, please, Louie. Besides, there are no ceremonies during Rosh Hashanah, no prayers, no acts of penance. You don't have to convert to the faith of the chosen people if you come to eat at our house on Thursday."

Luis Arsenio interrupted the spell cast by the girl's gazes in the middle of the Ware dining hall at the University of Pennsylvania. His friend Jake was inviting him to celebrate the Jewish New Year. That Thursday would be the first day of the month of Tishri. October. The nights were growing cooler and the leaves were changing color. Philadelphia was dyed in orange and ochre, a new light sifting through the leaves over its asphalt streets. This was a not a town lost in the tropics. This was a true city. Tall buildings made of glass and metal, cars everywhere, stores with the most unique items, the most unique people. Luis Arsenio got to know Philadelphia bit by bit. He improvised routes from City Hall or from South Street, where the jazz bohemians milled about. After classes or on weekends, he threw his scarf around his neck and set off to walk the city. He crossed west until arriving at Market Street, went up from there to Chinatown, and then crossed diagonally toward the east and the university. It was a beautiful fall and a beautiful city. He wanted to celebrate Philadelphia. If his mother could see him now, her precious prince baptized in christening gown and mantilla in the most Catholic of traditions. "Oil and vinegar don't mix," she would warn him. "Oil with which you were anointed and vinegar that the godless gave the Son of God to drink . . ." Some idiotic gibberish like that from his mother, if she only knew. But in that city he was free, swift, and volatile. Here he didn't have to cling to the customs of the island.

Maggie Carlisle got up from her table. Luis Arsenio couldn't help but notice her. And she him. She walked with her friends toward the exit. Just before losing herself in the hallway, she stopped again to look at him. She and all her friends looked at him and burst into laughter by the doorway.

"Allen's making it difficult for us, but I'm going to give it all I've got. Did you finish studying for the exam tomorrow?"

"That's what I was doing before I came down to eat."

"What if we meet in a corner of the library at Fischer and go over the governmental law material?"

"Go look for a spot, and I'll go get the books and meet you."

"Hurry it up, Louie."

"Luis Arsenio."

"Don't waste your time; no one here is going to get used to calling you that."

He didn't like the nickname, but it was worse with the other name, correcting the few who found the time to talk to him, trying to make them pronounce the *r* of Arsenio properly, or making sure they didn't finish the name with an annoying *u*. He couldn't fathom why the Yankees couldn't leave their mouths open at the end of his name. His last name was a lost cause. With luck, it was transformed into a stammering *Forneress* that made any of the girls who heard it burst into giggles because of the vocal proximity to the whole family of fornicating words. *Louie Forneress.* That was his new name, a name without lineage, swift and volatile.

The exam on governmental law had been a killer. But they survived it. Luis Arsenio went up to his room in Fischer to change his shirt, look for his jacket, and put on a tie. Jake waited for him in the vestibule. When he came down, Jake greeted him with a frank smile. "It's clear that they've taught you well. You will be a hit with my mother. But no one will save you from the food at Ware."

They went up Spruce Street to Thirty-sixth and turned left into the Jewish neighborhood. At the Mikhev Israel they made another left. A short lady with a gray bun opened the door to the three-story brick house where they arrived early in the afternoon, although it was already getting dark. She was the mother, Ruth. Right afterward, his steps echoing from the stairs on the second floor, Abraham Barowski came down. He led them into a room where a large group of guests was gathered. Luis Arsenio sat on a chair upholstered in dark velvet, near a stone fireplace. Heavy curtains covered the windows. Everything seemed to be made of a dense material, composed of thousands of layers. In the back, framed by two doors of carved wood, he could see the dining room. "I am in an old world," Luis thought, remembering the rooms of his dorm, Fischer Hassenfield. Walls covered in mahogany panels, dark hues, the smell of trapped air. This was a place protected from the air and the light.

The Barowski clan gathered in the living room—the oldest brother, Elisha, the sister, Doris, and the mother. Abraham Barowski introduced him to Mircea Dauberg and his wife, Nelly. It was a good thing that he wasn't the only guest, or the only foreigner. Mircea had just arrived from Austria and he brought news of some family members to the Barowskis. "Thank God they are all right. Ruth, my wife, was raised in Vienna, but her parents were Polish," the old man explained. "We are Corsican," Luis pointed out. He would not mention the islands. There was no need. That dinner gathering was an encounter of thousands of journeys and thousands of old worlds. Vienna, Lisbon, Amsterdam were geographic spots that came up in conversation, becoming points of reference. Because what brought those guests together was a ritual that had nothing to do with the proceedings on earth.

"Now that everyone is here, let us begin with the *brajá*."

The clan gathered around the patriarch, who began to recite a prayer in Hebrew. "*Baruch atah Adonai, Eloheinu melech ha'olam.*" The intonation made him lower his head. To Luis Arsenio it sounded like a lullaby, and enchantment, a blessing. He wished that the illumination of the candles lit by Ruth would dissipate all the fogs of the world, that it would spill over all the dear ones who walked on the earth—the absent ones, the present ones.

Jake whispered in his ear. "They are the lights of Yahzeit, for those who are no longer with us."

"There will be many to light this year."

Doña Ruth had just finished her prayer when Mircea Dauberg let the comment escape. The Barowskis grew tense in the middle of their undertakings. The room almost cracked under this new weight. Elisha, the oldest one, cast a furtive glance at his father.

"There is no cause for alarm. They are just work camps . . ."

"There does seem cause. They say that in Dachau they are building enclosures that can hold thousands. And that in Breitenau you can see the black smoke from the chimneys from miles away, fires going night and day. The air stinks of scorched flesh."

"That's impossible, Mircea. It has to be an exaggeration."

"I believe it, Elisha."

Old Barowski closed his eyes to let out a long sigh. Mircea continued to recount how they had taken the Bonns, the Gorodischers, the Maddens in the middle of the night. "We escaped through the French border. We were lucky. From there we passed to Canada." And now they had come to that warm living room in Philadelphia.

"The Erenbergs were leaving the day after. And the Kraussers were still in Canada."

"This is your home, Mircea. You can stay here as long as you need to."

"We can save them one by one, Father."

Jake spoke now. He looked at the old man with shining eyes and a tense expression that Luis Arsenio had never seen. He did not even recognize the tone of his voice. The patriarch grimaced, snorting through his nostrils.

"And what would you suggest? That we go shouting through the streets demanding that the government do something? Jacob, just look at what governments do. The Russians, the Germans, the Americans."

"Here they have to respect our rights. The constitution . . ."

"The papers that constitutions are written on withstand everything. But power is power. What we need is some land, a place to finally rest after so much persecution."

"A nation is nothing but a pretext for people to pummel themselves to death. You yourself taught me that."

"Well, I was wrong. Now I would gladly offer my life for a Jewish nation."

The lintels, the curtains, the heavy velvet of the furniture, became for Luis Arsenio a tomb over his chest. Outside, the streets of Philadelphia were sure to be fresh and busy. He wanted to lose himself in that commotion. He was about to make up whatever excuse he could to get out of that living room. But Doña Ruth saved him. "Come now, Abe, Jacob, we don't have to decide the fate of the world right now, not the world's, nor ours. The desert can wait for us, but dinner cannot."

They went into the dining room and the banquet began. Round challah bread, smoked salmon, carrot salad, apple and honey cakes. Luis Arsenio's palate woke up from the stupor into which it had sunk with the food at Ware House. Flavors dancing in his mouth anew. They were foreign to him, but there was something familiar about these people to whom food meant something. Luis Arsenio listened to conversations about the Rabbi Joshua, whom he did not know, about the synagogue on Union Street, where he had never been. He relished the flavors of his food. Mircea spoke of the progress of his son Daniel's studies. "Too bad Doris won't be able to join him at Hochschule für Musik. I am sure she would have been admitted." Jake did his best to keep Luis Arsenio informed on the minutiae of the conversation. "That rabbi is a scoundrel, a boyhood friend of my father. Daniel is a genius on the piano. If you could only hear him play, Louie, how his fingers fly over the keys.

Doris could only wish to play like that." Luis Arsenio laughed, amused to lose himself in the details of the conversation. He chewed, pleased. But the previous conversation kept beating at his temples. The death of the Jews, the exodus, the nations. Everything went on at the table as if none of this had ever been brought up. Better not to question it any more, better to let the omission weigh densely on the succulent Barowski table. Better just to chew, taste, swallow.

IT WAS AS IF HE had the power to invoke Maggie Carlisle. He thought of her name and she appeared. Maggie Carlisle. And there she materialized, red and alabaster through the halls of the university—through Mayer Hall and Stouffer Hall. She kept on casting those inviting glances toward him. But Luis Arsenio remained mute. It was a question of finding just the right moment, he told himself, planting himself in front of her and beginning a conversation. "My name is, your name is, it's cold, winter closes in so quickly, in my country time passes by differently; it's not that it is slower, but more circular." She would keep her eyes fixed on him, perhaps swiping a red curl from her face. "Circular?" "Yes, you don't notice how one month spills into another because there are no seasons." "No seasons? Where is this?" Maggie would ask him. Then he would explain that on his island . . . but wait. Speaking about his island first thing would not work at the University of Pennsylvania. It would be impossible then to get close to her. Impossible to take those four or five steps toward Maggie Carlisle, who did come from a solid place on this earth. He could tell.

"And if I ran into her on the street?" From there he could make the leap. Luis Arsenio was on his way to Sam's Soda, on Fortieth Street and Spruce. There, in the middle of that city, all contexts vanished. The black young man with the bread passed by, the man with the hat on his way to Woodland Avenue crossed. Someone asked for a sausage from the street vendor. A woman scolded a boy who was begging for ice cream. Cars took off, the street lights changed. A ham sandwich, a hamburger, some French fries, an apple pie. Luis Arsenio went into Sam's Soda Shop, thinking about what he would order. Everyone ate quickly and spoke shrewdly. Jake had shown him the spot.

"I've been coming here since I was little. They make the best chocolate malts in the world."

Sam's was a swarm of little conversations. Luis Arsenio had agreed to meet Jake at the end of the day and had found a table and was taking out his books on commercial law as the waitress approached. There was no time to lose. The whole school was on tenterhooks. Although midterm exams were coming up, no one responded to those rhythms, because everywhere the only talk was about war. Even there, in his sanctuary of Sam's Soda Shop.

"We won't be able to stay out of the conflict for long."

"I think that they've already sent some troops."

"And what about what's happening in Poland?"

"No one can confirm it; you know how the Jews are, you have to take everything they say with a grain of salt."

A group of young men gathered around the curved counter, talking in loud voices. The war, the Jews. Again the same topics. Who was the one who said such an idiotic thing about the Jews? He passed his eyes over the malt counter and saw all those similar clean faces. Reddish plump cheeks, well-groomed hair, solid shoulders, young men probably from Anglo-Saxon families in Maine, or Irish families in Delaware. He watched the door anxiously. It was better if Jake didn't come, if he didn't have to listen to this. To come across this would be to breathe in again the dense air of that night in the living room, beside the candles of Yazheit.

Luis Arsenio opened his books and plunged into them. He finished his drink. Jake never came. He began to gather his things to go somewhere else, to the Fischer Library, maybe, or the campus, under a tree, where the talk would be about less pressing things, sports, for example, or some dance given by some fraternity. He wanted a light murmur to serve as background for his reading. But some classmates who recognized him arrived. "Come sit with us, Louie," a freckled kid from history class insisted. He walked toward the group's table just as the entrance bell rang from behind him. The door opened. Maggie Carlisle walked in.

She was with some friends and she knew all of the young men who had invited him to join them. He was the only one who had not met her. So then—"Louie, this is Maggie"—the necessary introductions were made. Finally, the desired bridge spread between eyes and eyes, mouth and mouth; a bridge of words. "You eat in Ware, right?"

"Yes, the cafeteria in the women's dormitory is a real disaster, not that Ware is fine cuisine." Laughter. The friends went over to look at the selection of music in the Victrola. But Maggie stayed put. It was just for a moment, and Luis Arsenio took the opportunity to offer her a vanilla soda.

"Do you have a lot of exams?"

"Plenty. But I think I'll do all right in almost all of them."

"I don't see your friend, the one who's always with you."

"Who, Jake? He's very busy."

"Are you Jewish too?"

"Me? Not a bit."

A sting of resentment ran through Luis Arsenio's entire body. How was it that they confused him with a Jew? His mother had warned him: "Tell me what company you keep, and I'll tell you who you are." But he was Luis Arsenio Fornarís, son of the lawyer and grandson to the businessman, of the Corsican Fornaríses from a town very far away from Sam's Soda Shop. The context of his life was distant, incomprehensible, impossible to name. Especially now, when he had finally opened the lines of communication. Luis Arsenio needed to follow his plan. Not to mention the islands.

"You're keeping other company as well."

"What's wrong with a single woman going out with her friends?"

"Don't you have a boyfriend?"

"No."

And she lowered her gaze to her straw. Coy, perhaps, elusive, but casting out an invitation. Right there, in Sam's Soda Shop, Luis Arsenio Fornarís invited Maggie Carlisle to the movies.

Maggie's arm in his, a first approach. Her hands taken, another. His nose twisting itself on a red curl, in the fragrance that emanated from her neck as they said their goodbyes at the stairs of the dormitory. "See you later." Maggie smiled, while her eyes peered at him with a tiny flame that he had forgotten could exist in the look of certain women. They had walked through the Old City, by the Schuylkill River, sat on the grass. It had been their second date. Afterward, there were many more. He and Maggie in the darkest part of the movie theater, in the last row of the balcony so no one would see them. Seated up there, with Maggie's face in his hands, Maggie's lips on his and Maggie's whole body smelling just like her; and he, trying to coil himself in her smells without startling her, to cover himself with them and take them wherever he went.

"Careful, Louie, don't let her break your heart."

Jake Barowski appeared at the end of the month of Tishri,

it seemed, just to warn him and throw a bucket of cold water on the fire that was Maggie. The November chill already bore down on one's face. Each breath turned into evaporated ice. Thrashing through his drawers at Fischer Hassenfield, Luis Arsenio looked for his checkered scarf. He wanted to give it to Maggie so she could have something of his. Jake leaned on the doorframe. Luis Arsenio heard the commentary behind him and decided not to turn around and look.

"Don't worry about me. I know how to take care of myself."

"In every situation?"

"In more than you can imagine."

"The rules are different around here."

"When two people like each other, the rules are the same everywhere."

"You're sure that she likes you for the same reasons?"

"What do you mean, the same reasons?" Luis Arsenio was about to ask, but he found the scarf and put it around his neck. Maggie was waiting for him at a little restaurant on South Street. They would have a light dinner, go window shopping, and stroll through the city. That is why Maggie Carlisle liked him, to take him by the hand, to lose themselves in the crowd. There was no need for context.

He went down the stairs flustered. What did Jake care what he did with Maggie? He didn't need his advice or warnings. He had Maggie now. Although sometimes he felt something strange in her. Sometimes, hands were let go in the middle of the street— "Hi, Collin"—if someone she knew passed by. Sometimes the trips to the movie theater were too many, alone, to the most deserted showings. So much timidity was disconcerting, because in private Maggie was another person. Her kisses more freely given each time, her looks inviting him deeper within.

He turned on Thirty-third Street, near the park. He wrapped the colorful scarf around his neck, on top of the other one he was already wearing, and buttoned his coat all the way to the top. It was going to be a cold winter. He finally arrived at the restaurant on South Street where he had agreed to meet Maggie. Her neat red hair picked up the last light of the afternoon as she waited by the tables. Luis Arsenio remembered that he had two gifts to offer to her. He had just received good news. He walked to the table where Maggie shone in the cold Philadelphia afternoon. A waiter brought them the menus.

"My grandparents are coming to visit me in Philadelphia. Why don't you come with me so you can meet them?"

"Your grandparents?"

"I want them to see the red-haired goddess who goes out with me."

"And meanwhile, my father will put a price on my head. If I don't go home for the holidays, he will lynch me."

"You're exaggerating . . ."

"You don't know my father. His family is one of the ancient ones around here. Very conservative, although he allowed me to come to the university. If it had been up to my mother . . ."

"Mine is a problem too."

"Does she want you to get married as soon as you graduate?"

"Well, no . . ."

"Mine does. Luckily, my father determined that I should live a little first."

"What you need to do is introduce me to your parents and tell them that you already have a fiancé."

"If they even set eyes on you, it would be the end of me. They would lock me up in the attic."

"Are they so horrible?"

"The worst . . . ," she tells him coquettishly, hurling herself on his neck, grabbing him by the colorful scarf to kiss him. She doesn't let him complete his frown, begin to feel an annoying sensation that rises to his throat in the form of a question, "The worst?" reticent, "Why the worst?" but a bridge again spreads between arms and arms, lips and lips. A bridge of shared saliva with a little essence of fruits, of vibrant breath, of a tickling that awakens the skin and makes them fight the mild cold of the docile winter that blankets them. The contact interrupts the question, the question that vanishes in the air, like a compressed breath, like smoke.

"Here, this is for you."

"What a beautiful scarf. I'll put it on as soon as we finish eating. They say the meatloaf is good. I'm very hungry. What are you getting, Louie?"

Two

THE IRON WAS heated in a charcoal stove. And in a pot, the starch water cooled. First, the finger to the mouth, and then on the hot metal to test the temperature. With the other hand she would spray the piece. Perhaps she should add a little essence of Katanga to the mixture, the one she bought at the drugstore on Calle Virtud. But maybe not; it could cause stains. She fans the charcoal with a piece of cardboard. The iron needs to be very hot to smooth out the wrinkles on the cloth. So that it comes out perfect, spotless, fragrant. She had made the dress of gauze cotton herself, with a low open neckline and the waist also low, like the suits Don Antón had shown her that were tailored in Europe, after the latest fashion. Pleated skirt to the halfway point of the calf. Loose fit, it was perfect on her, highlighting her hips but making her appear slender, modern. She would cover the exposed part of her legs with lace stockings, bought with an entire month's savings. The only thing that didn't match was the shoes. They used to belong to the girl Virginia.

Isabel had dyed them white and changed the lacing for more refined buckles so they would look more like the ones in the magazine clippings that Don Antón had shown her. "This is how people are dressing now and not with those shawls and long dresses that the doñas in this town have me cut for them." Isabel had to take the clipping to the shoemaker so he would know what she was talking about. So much ignorance. The first chance she got, she would leave forever.

She had not returned since the burial of Godmother Maruca. Since *that* had happened. But that night there was a dance at the center that Don Demetrio and his "illustrive" tobacco buddies had put together. These people lived their lives celebrating events. She was not interested in visiting the library or participating in the study groups or the conferences. But a dance she would go to. She wanted to show off now that she could, that she was getting used to her new life amidst fashion clippings, appliqués of the moment, the artifice of luxury that any person had at their disposal, no matter where they were born. "What you need is inventiveness and good taste, my dear, like few have in these rough parts. Look how they dress, ready to go clear chopped trees. Oh, if I could go to the great city, the great city." Isabel transported herself with her new boss to the parks of the Retiro, the plazas packed with people, where each article of clothing could count on a window display to be seen and admired. "Good taste to use as an introductory card, nothing else is necessary, my girl, not lineage, or family, or eight bedrooms. Demeanor and elegance, like any civilized people. But around here, it is asking too much . . ."

Finger to the mouth and then finger to the metal. The sizzling let her know that the iron was ready to smooth out the pleats of the dress. With her eyes steady, she passed the hot iron over the cloth until the creases of the pleats stood out and the seams were smooth. Everything had to be exact, so the night would be as well, smooth and light against the wind. She looked for the shoes and the lace stockings. As much as she explained it to the shoemaker, the buckles were not exactly like the ones in the clipping. While her dress cooled, Isabel began to put on her stockings.

She had been lucky. After *that* had happened and Doña Georgina threw her out of the house without another word, Isabel had found herself on the street not knowing where to go. She could not go back to San Antón, now that her Godmother was not there. She wandered through the streets of the town the entire afternoon she was evicted, all her clothes in a bundle, until she arrived at the shop.

She had been attracted by a cut of yellow cloth. She had never seen anything like it. Those fibers shone of things that have not yet achieved their proper luster, but which nevertheless, raw still and wounded, show their essence. Isabel wanted to pass her fingers over the wounds of that piece of cloth, caress it, know what it was called, at least. She walked in just at the moment when the dressmaker was mentioning the opening of La Catalana—a tobacco factory that was expanding—"and that stole the best one of my girls . . ." Don Antón was complaining to a client, "because women leave seamstress work behind to go toil like men, of course, they have the right; I'm not such an old fogey, but to go work in those factories full of bat droppings to strip tobacco leaves, no. It was better that Cecilia left. I need girls with different sensibilities." The dressmaker sighed, nervously smoothing out a roll of cloth and dragging a piece of onionskin paper with the heel of his boot. Isabel listened to him, not daring to interrupt, and Don Antón said: "But, you see, what a spot they leave me in, because in one week the military ball will take place in the casino. The colonel has invited the cream of the town, and I, thinking I had an assistant, accepted an order that now threatens to do me in." Isabel had already given up. She would never know the name of the cloth. Then Don Antón turned around right in the middle of the shop and exclaimed, "And what do you want? Looking for a job? I better make the sign of the cross first. Tell me, girl, how good are you with a sewing machine?"

The surprise appearance of her lucky star gave her courage. As a reply, Isabel sat down at the seamstress's table with a scrap of that cloth that had attracted her. There was a little piece thrown down next to the sewing machine. "That's raw silk, girl. Start with something easier." But no. Isabel passed her fingers over the surface of the fibers briefly, long enough to read it, establish a complicity with its brilliance. She took a pair of scissors and cut it on the bias. She looked for the proper thread with the other hand. Without blinking, she passed the thread through the eye of the needle, lowered the fastener, making the pulley turn. She set up the cloth with such perfect direction that the seam came out in an exact straight line, without wrinkling the surface, and with each thread a continuum, just as she had learned under Lorenza's tutelage. Don Antón was impressed. They talked about salary, a dollar more a month than she earned in the Tous house, a room at the back of the shop for her use. "And I hope that you can take care of yourself, girl. But what I am talking about? You're a grown woman." Isabel counted her years on the face of the earth. Fifteen, was it? Or sixteen; she wasn't sure. She smiled. So that was how long it took to become a "grown woman." Knowing it was no small thing. Not to have to answer to anyone for her comings and goings, free of attending to the girl Virginia, and of being hounded by Doña Georgina's looks. Is that what it was to be a "grown woman"? It was no small thing.

Dressed and ready to go, Isabel made sure that everything was in its place. She closed up her little room, being sure to turn each lock twice to the right, as Don Antón had showed her. She began to walk toward the outskirts of town, taking the path on Calle Comercio to San Antón. She wasn't alone. Small groups of servants were dressed up in their finest outfits to go to the dance. Demetrio had convinced the most famous of the musicians to brighten up the festivities at the workers' center: Bumbúm Oppenheimer. His fame (and his infamy) was the bait. A drinker, quarrelsome and insolent, he wasn't one of those park musicians, those mulattoes with greased hair, members of the fire department, who insisted on breaking the chords of the polkas and contra dances that white people listened to at their balls. Bumbúm was a musician from the tough neighborhoods around the sugar mills. To listen to him blow by blow was a delight, with that rhythm that he pulled from the goatskin stretched over the wooden frame. Wherever Bumbúm went, three others followed—his three drums like barrels, but portable, the bass, the *dos golpes*, and the *requinto*—which in Bumbúm's hands spoke. He crept up on top of the bass to peal with sharp strikes, improvised contrapuntally against the bass that beat like a heart. Bumbúm's fingers shuffled on the drum like the feet of a dancer. Bumbúm's voice was the proclamation of what was happening in the neighborhood, news that was not published in *La Águila* or *La Democracia*, or any other newspaper. He was adored throughout the coast, in the public dances that were celebrated in the sugar mill towns of Vista Alegre, or Joya del Castillo, or in the very Bélgica barrio. All the young men wanted to play like Bumbúm, drink a whole sea of moonshine like Bumbúm, after they themselves had sung their hearts out, with their veiled attacks on the señoritos and their commentaries on the uproars of the neighborhood. They all wanted to be Bumbúm Oppenheimer. He too had emigrated from the English islands, like Isabel's mother, looking for work. Perhaps they were even related.

The majority of them were women. Here and there a man walked on the streets toward the dance, but in front of her, all around and behind Isabel, a mob of women. The most striking were the whores. They had an attitude about them. Isabel heard them laugh louder than the others, call each other with higher pitched shouts. "Camburi, girl, don't get too far ahead." Fierce, excited mules. They had to be like this. Wandering alone at night in those times was motive enough for the police to accuse anyone of "dishonest solicitude." And it was worse if they were of "unknown profession." They would take them to the Ladies Hospital and lock them up there for up to a year and a half, without trial, or pressing charges, or family visits. "Hygiene regulation," they said, "to heal our pustules, but it's all lies." That night, the women told the stories to each other and Isabel overheard. "Yes, honey, and they stick it to you by force, a thing like a steel scissors that splits you open down there to see if you are ill. It doesn't matter how much you scream. A cousin of mine, *muchacha*, who hasn't been touched by even the air, was grabbed one night she had to stay late because her *patrona* made her darn some sheets. My uncle and two neighbors had to go claim her at the police station and even then they didn't let her go. 'But you see, my daughter is a virgin,' Uncle Chabelo told them, and my cousin screaming while they stuck that thing in between her legs. When they found out that it was true, they let her go. But she didn't come out of it well, because everyone found out about it in the barrio, and out of shame, she fled to the mountains where nobody knew her. Now she is starving, picking coffee beans by the bale. And it was going so well for her in town . . ."

They talked loud, laughed hard, hurled shouts from one side of the road to the other. If some man happened to step into their bounds, the others surrounded him, screaming improprieties.

"The Americans are still bloodthirsty after the war."

"And what is that to me? I'm not an American; nor do I have weapons."

"Not counting the one between your legs . . ."

"Excuse me, O saintly one, but these are the instruments of my profession."

"That's just why they're making it difficult for us, because according to the guards, we wheedle away the boys that the Americans need to recruit."

"It's not like they loose their limbs after a little tussle on the bed."

"Well, they better stay away from me, because I bite, and now I cut."

"What did you say, woman?"

"Just yesterday I bought a knife at Don Neco's hardware store. And the first cop that puts his hands on me, I swear that he is going to remember me every time that he looks in the mirror."

Something silver caught the lights of the road. It was the girl, who, to show off, had unsheathed the knife. The others gathered around her to feel the weight of the metal.

She recognized a voice. A few steps ahead walked one of the seamstresses from the atelier Vilarís. Leonor. She had been working for Don Antón longer than anyone. "This takes a French stitch," and, "You do the buttons and I'll finish the buttonholes," were the only comments that they had exchanged.

Isabel approached her. She greeted Leonor with a somewhat timid hello and the girl let out a smile. It was another sparkle against the dangerous night. "This is Teresa," she introduced a friend. They talked about the possibility of Don Antón hiring Teresa as a seamstress, if only for a month. Teresa had just fled from her parents' house.

"What happened?"

"Well, honey, some man promised me the moon and the earth and then couldn't even put a roof over my head, so I left him. I'm tired of chasing after men. Now I just want to take care of my things until a made merchant shows up. For him, I'll give birth to a few kids and that's it."

"This one thinks it's easy."

"Giving birth is very easy . . ."

"No, honey, finding a made man."

They laughed, joining the ruckus of the road. The entrance to the barrio could be seen from afar, a frame of streets with straw *bohíos*, the little plaza near the ancient ranch house where they stored the work tools that all the neighbors (and their parents) used in the cane fields that surrounded San Antón. Some said that the house had been the slave barracks. But it wasn't anymore. They had made it into the center where the public dance led by Bumbúm Oppenheimer was celebrated.

"We look like the three Marys." Isabel, Teresa, and Leonor each paid a cent to get into the dance. The barracks was lit with oil lamps and torches. In the back you could hear the men tuning their drums. In the middle of the chorus, pouring drinks out of a carafe, was the famous Bumbúm. Broad like a tightened muscle, black, gray haired. He wasn't tall. His smile stayed with everyone in the patio, setting the rhythm for all the other malicious laughs of the men in the building, concentrating on their ritual of improvising full quartos and defying the imagination, letting the eternal essence of competition throb between them.

In the opposite corner of the yard Demetrio was busy with other men from his cigar factory. They had set up a table with a white tablecloth. On top they had placed pamphlets from the "Free Pages," "Daydreams," "The Worker's Union" and a copy of the "Program for the Free Federation of Workers," according to Don Eugenio Sánchez. Next to the table, a group of women from the federation sold *bacalao* fritters, *yutía* and plantain croquettes stuffed with crabmeat, and sugarcane juice for a half, one, and two cents. A swarm of people lined up for their refreshments. Isabel's insides began to churn right then. She walked over with the girls. The aroma from the corner had awakened her appetite. And not just hers.

"And who is that?"

"Demetrio."

"Well, he looks like a made man. If I get close to him, you think he'll notice me?"

"But, Teresa, weren't you going to concentrate on doing your own thing?"

"Yeah, but look how handsome he is."

"Well, go see, because he's very strange. His whole life is concerned with strikes and books that he buys himself, sometimes not eating because of it. I don't know, Teresa. I think he's a little crazy."

"He's not crazy, Leonor. It's just that the thing he likes is to read, to think. And he says that if he hadn't been born poor, he would have studied law like the Tomés."

"Who told you that, Isabel?"

"He told me. I know him."

"Oh, baby, introduce me . . ."

They had to deal with their hunger. It was best to introduce Teresa to Demetrio to consolidate the friendship that she was seeking. Isabel let the girls take her by the arms on the way to the tables. "I have friends," she said under her breath. She counted all the things that were a first that night. The dress, the dance, the company, the longing to enjoy herself. "A full-grown woman," she said to herself and smiled. The night was going perfectly.

The playing of a *bomba* made the walls of the barracks vibrate. The leather of the drums resounded in the box of her chest. Isabel ate her stuffed croquette and drank her cane juice intending not to move, not to sweat or soil her newly made dress, but her feet got away from her. "You imagine what you want the drum to play and you tell it with your body." Isabel wanted to tell the drum that she was happy. That she had survived *that* moment in the embraces of Don Aurelio, the wounded pride of Doña Georgina. That she was now in a better place, to let her Godmother know. Leonor noticed her itching to dance. Gently, she pushed Isabel toward the center of the ring formed by the dancers. Isabel took off her shoes, her stockings, "because you can't dance a *bomba* wearing shoes." She made the required turn, very erect, arrogant. She planted herself in front of the bell player and began to spell out the rhythm of her recently discovered strength.

A pair of eyes followed her every movement, looking at her assertively. They fell upon her like a warm wave, and at the same time like a breeze and like burning coal. They weren't the eyes of any of the musicians. Nor were they by the tables, in the faces of Demetrio's friends. While she searched for the eyes, a vivacious *negrita* stole the attention of the bell player. Disconcerted, Isabel had to exit the ring. Whose eyes were following her? She went to sit on the stairs of the ranch house, to clean her feet and put her stockings back on. Teresa stayed behind, chatting with Demetrio: "Because, listen, now that you've explained it to me, I, too, have had my rights violated." Leonor

stayed behind also, trying to figure out a way to steal the spotlight from the vivacious one, preparing to show herself off.
Isabel sat on the stairs, carefully slipping on her stockings. She
had paid more than a dollar for them, a whole month's salary.
She would hate to tear them.

"*May I?*"

Rising straight up to the heavens and dressed in a military
uniform, a man offered a handkerchief. His hair was greased
and parted at the middle; he wore an olive green shirt, buttoned to the top, with a heavily starched narrow collar. He
smelled like aftershave. Light-colored eyes, perhaps yellow,
shone against his skin. Isabel couldn't quite make them out in
the dark. The man made gestures for her to take the handkerchief and was jabbering something in another language. He
saw that he wasn't being understood. So without hesitation he
began to lower himself toward the feet of the *negra*. He began
to clean them with his handkerchief, and waited for her to put
on her stockings and her shoes. The loops, the strap of the heel,
each gesture was meticulously executed by fingers, long as a
bird's wings, that lifted the metal buckle and inserted the strap
through.

"My name is Private Isaac Lowell. I am from here, but my
mother was born in St. Croix."

"Where is that?" Isabel asked, waking as if from a lethargy
when she heard him speak Spanish. In response, the soldier
pointed toward the east, past the cane fields, to where the sea
opened up. He pointed toward someplace far away with his
fingers, but with his eyes he spoke of things nearby. They were
definitely yellow eyes. Isabel remained on the steps. She wanted
to better listen to what those eyes had to tell.

"First, they sent me to Alabama, to a training camp that was
pure hell." Screams at four in the morning, races in combat

gear, with helmet, boots, backpack, and rifle. "Never, not even when I was kid in St. Thomas, had I been so overwhelmed by the heat." And to top it off, the sergeant in his regiment let his fury loose on him. "When he found out I was from the islands, he wanted to show me how things were done on his turf. I peeled more potatoes than anyone, kept the most impeccable uniform, and still that drill sergeant wouldn't take his boot off me." He would make sure that the "little island nigger" would learn how to be civilized. "Now that I think about it, the worst part of that hell was the sergeant."

Isabel did not know where her friends had gone. She saw them vanish in the barracks amongst the bodies of the dancers and the guests. She thought she saw Teresa disappear outside in the bushes with Demetrio, and Demetrio smiling in the darkness. She was at the mercy of Private Lowell's story. At the mercy of his yellow eyes, which told her about his grandfather, an Episcopal minister who immigrated to New York, fleeing the enclosure of the islands. He never knew any other father, though they told him that his own was a Basque grocer who never offered him his surname. He grew up between the island of his grandfather and this one, where his mother still worked as a seamstress. It was his grandfather who provided him with an opportunity when he set sail for the big city, invited by a congregation with which he corresponded. He asked him to be his pastoral assistant, and his mother, full of pride, gave him her son, to try out his luck in the North.

"I wanted to go to flight school, but before I could be accepted they transferred me here. At first, I was happy, because I would be near my mother. Work has aged her . . . But my orders are for the camp in the South. Here, all I do is run errands for the officers."

When he came to the end of the story, it was after midnight.

Private Isaac Lowell accompanied her the entire way back to the door of her little room at the atelier. His words flowed without cease. Isabel was transported by the stories of the soldier, but at the same time she found herself very much there, sure-footed on the ground beneath her feet. Not detained, or out of place, or obligated to be there. While the soldier told his story, Isabel felt at peace where she was.

She turned the locks twice as needed and opened the door to go in. It was already three in the morning. But those yellow eyes still watched her.

"Can I see you the next time I have a pass?"

"And when will that be?"

"In two weeks."

"By that point, you will have forgotten how to get here."

"I won't forget. I promise."

"Promises are swept away by the wind."

"Mine are heavy as stones. You'll see."

That is what the soldier said. Isabel leaned on the doorframe. Isaac put his hands on her waist and she found the rhythm of that embrace. She did not feel anguish. She wanted the warmth of those fingers on her back; she was waiting for it, fostering it little by little. She knew exactly what the warmth would bring, bodies scarcely coming together, the raising of her chin so that her lips would be exposed, a closing of the eyes without shutting them, a squeeze of saliva calmly settling in the mouth. Her first kiss to which she had consented. Her first encounter as a woman with a man she liked. To the many gifts of the sleepless night, now this one was added. That soldier promised to look for her in two weeks and, meanwhile, to keep her occupied with the days of the calendar. If he kept his promise, perhaps Isabel would have a familiar face to wait for. A life beyond the shop, again. But it was better not to get ahead of herself. "For now, I have it," she told herself. As she saw the soldier vanish into the night, the door closed by itself through her fingers.

It was nice to wake up with the memory of the soldier in her mouth. Nice to sleep in without having to get out of bed. But Isabel had to go to work. Don Antón fretted relentlessly in the shop and called her urgently. He woke her up with three knocks on the door of the shop.

"Isabel, come on, girl. Bad day to get stuck in the sheets. All hell has broken loose."

He began to toss things around in the shelves, throwing the wax pencils on the floor, the pens to mark patterns. "Special order." She could guess what he was up to already. Don Antón always acted like this when they were faced with urgent orders. He raised a ruckus, throwing everything on the floor, calling for them at the doors of their rooms before they were due in. Isabel put on the first outfit she could find, put on her lace-up booties, and almost without fixing her bun left the little room to see what had Don Antón in such a state.

"What time did you tell Leonor to get here?"

"Same time as always."

"Well, look, that was wrong, because yesterday at Mass I bumped into Don Luis, who put in a very special order, very urgent."

How was she to know that at eleven o'clock Mass her work plans would be changed? Don Antón dashed like a bald hummingbird to look for a roll of blue cloth. "Three wool pants and a marine blue checkered vest. They are celebrating the arrival of their son, who has just become a lawyer. Holy Mother, where did I put my scissors?" Isabel put them in his hands right away, making it seem like she, too, was agitated. Don Antón furrowed his brow and his little mouth; he took deep breaths and ner-

vously adjusted his well-tailored vest and matching pants, somewhat too tight around that waist of a buzzing bird. "All hell's
broken loose, now we're in for it . . ." But Isabel knew that it
was all part of a false hysteria to make her hands and Leonor's fly
over the handle of the machine, so that the haste would vibrate
in their hands while Don Antón cut out patterns and compared
measurements and crooned out light songs and prayers to the
Virgin, filling the entire shop with a faltering buzz that mixed
with the murmur of the needles and the scissors.

Leonor finally arrived, exactly at eight, as usual. She came
in surprised that the shop was in full working mode. "Finally
you get here, girl. I was getting desperate." Don Antón ran
up to get her started finishing the cut of a sleeve according to
the measurements that he would call out. Leonor looked at
Isabel. "What is it with this bird?" She had to crouch to hide
her guffaw. Then, recovered from the laughter, she cut a piece
of black satin that she would sew on as lining for one of the
pieces.

"They say they saw you in the hands of someone in a uniform."

"There are a lot of nosy people in this town."

"So the prisoner gave in . . ."

"What are you talking about, Leonor?"

"Oh, Isabel, don't play the fool. Are you a soldier's woman?
Come on, tell me, I'm dying to know."

They couldn't keep on talking because Don Antón approached them, clapping and egging them on in a jargon that
he said was in French. He concluded with, "I promised Don
Luis that everything would be ready by tomorrow. Come on,
girls, because we also have to finish what we've fallen behind
on . . ." Leonor took this instant to get the details of the date.

Between one stitch and another, Isabel told her about the dance, about the kiss before he went off to his new camp.

"And nothing happened? Lord, how chaste . . ."

"Give me some credit. I'm not like others who jump in at the start."

"Holy Virgin, Isabel is getting hitched, in white and through the church."

At the exact moment of this chiding, Don Antón walked in to look for a spool of thread and heard Leonor. He gathered himself in front of the work station, clutching his chest, with the face of a very startled old maiden, and said through his lips, "Is it true, Isabel?" "No, Antón, this one is making things up . . ." But she had to listen to the dressmaker's scolding anyway. "You have to be careful with men; they like to take advantage. I know by experience, as a man, and a young woman like you, so serious, so alone in this world . . ." Isabel nodded, "Yes, Don Antón," swearing vengeance on the other one, who played dead beside her. They were just about done with one pair of the very special pants, from the urgent order, that Don Antón would begin that morning.

The wife of a soldier. She hadn't thought about it until her new pal said something. What would it be like to be the woman of a soldier? Would she go with Lowell throughout the world, wherever they sent him? Would she live in a base, in a house like the ones they gave the lieutenants at Loosey Point? Would she travel to distant countries, throughout Europe? She would leave that town forever. She would leave behind the dusty streets and the thin, baggy-eyed women walking barefoot in the streets. She would leave behind the death of her Godmother, the memory of the calumnies of the Touses. She would miss Don Antón, but she would write to him, detailing the fashions that she would see on the streets of New York, the colors of autumn, the latest in feathered hats and organza embroideries of flowers for the necklines of dresses. She would miss Leonor, although the only thing that she wanted to do now was step on her corns for having exposed her. But it didn't sound bad. The wife of a soldier. It was no small thing.

Going up Calle Salud to Guadalupe. Crossing the Portuguese. Isabel got up early. She lit the charcoal for the iron to sharpen the crease of the pants, the lapels, and the sleeves of the suit jacket that she had to finish. She starched and folded the clothes. She sprayed the whole bundle with lavender water that Don Antón kept in the shop. It was a long stretch to the Fornarís house in La Alhambra. She would deliver the order very well ironed to make a good impression. Hopefully, they would give her a tip. She had seen a piece of tulle that she could embroider and make into a shawl for the next date with the soldier.

It was still too early. Isabel decided to kill some time by choosing other clothes to wear, one of her best day dresses. Afterward, she would go to the house of Luis Fornarís. Isabel had heard the name in the shop. A prosperous merchant in the import and export business. It was said that some of the young men in charge of his stores were his illegitimate sons. He had multiple businesses, but he took care of all of them himself, because his only legitimate son, who was a prince, was reserved a better destiny. He had to sell some lands to send him to study in the capital, pay for his whims. But Don Luis didn't care. His spoiled child would never be able to disappoint him as long as he kept on studying, as long as he brought back a professional title. It seemed that the plan had been accomplished. The young man was coming back as a lawyer. Isabel pressed the bundle of clothes against her chest. Yes, it smelled rich. Now that she had to bring it to them, she asked herself whether she had starched the lapels of the suit sufficiently.

A young woman opened the back door without looking her in the eyes. Isabel entered through the kitchen and waited with the package in her hands. The young woman slipped away through the hallways of the mansion and an uneasiness settled into Isabel's body. The rooms of the pantry, the kitchen, the porcelain dishes in the pail of soapy water, the china cabinets with their silver. That feeling of entrapment. Isabel almost thought that she heard Lorenza calling her to come and help her pick up the remnants of the breakfast that were left cold on the mahogany table (she was sure that it would be mahogany) of the dining room. But there was no reason to be anxious. She could leave there and go back to the shop at any moment. She didn't have to lower her eyes like the servant girl and hide in the silence of her steps, go confront the owners and importune them with the message that someone was waiting for them in the kitchen. One of Don Antón's light songs came to her lips.

The tulle shawl that she would throw over her shoulders to wait for him, the tulle shawl that would match his yellow eyes. Isabel breathed in the fresh fragrances wafting from the bundle of clothes. She would embroider some red flowers in the center of the shawl, no, maybe some pale white lilies with green leaves that would coil around the border. Then she would attach fringes to the ends. She heard some steps approaching. A swift silhouette advanced down the hall. Isabel smoothed her skirt, adjusted the barrettes in her hair. She was rehearsing her line, "Don Luis, this is from Don Antón," when she was left with the words in her mouth, flabbergasted. Green eyes that looked at her directly, the shadow of a heavy beard on a young face, the whitest hands.

"These are the pants?"

"Yes, señor . . ."

"Let's see if you don't have to take them up. My father insists that I am taller than I really am."

Fernando Fornarís took the clothes from her hands. He gave her a definitive smile and went down the hall again. Isabel could not forget those eyes, that face that had just been scrubbed, although a dark shadow still lingered in the chin. It caught her unawares and she had not been able to protect herself. She wanted to run out of that house.

Don Luis's son returned wearing the pants. He was also wearing the vest. He looked good. The lapels crossed his chest completely, revealing a slim figure. The opaque buttons, which Isabel had convinced Don Antón to use to heighten the elegance of the outfit, glittered. "What do you think?" And he made a gesture with his arms to make sure that the vest wasn't too tight. He lifted a leg, then the other, somewhat wrinkling the crease in the pants. This time she kept her eyes lowered. Concentrating on the clothes and not the face of the model, on those green eyes.

"A real attorney." It was Don Luis who approached. Gray at the temples, thick eyebrows. The father was a double for the young man, only older. There was, however, something hardened in his look, which was missing from the eyes of the son. Isabel breathed a sigh of relief on hearing him arrive. She knew how to abide with this man, to deal with him.

"The vest fits me perfectly, but the pants . . . Don't you think they have to take up the hem a little bit?"

"They look fine to me, but ask your mother. She will know. And you, young lady, tell Don Antón to come by for payment this afternoon. I'll give him the full sum."

"Aren't you going to tip her for the order?"

"Here you go, for your efforts. This son of mine and his customs from the capital . . ."

Isabel took the coins from the hands of the father. She gave a slight bow of the head and went out through the service door. Once on the street, she could breathe again with all of her being. She put the coins in her pocket to keep them safe. It would be more than plenty to buy the materials for her shawl.

On the way back, she stopped at the Zaragoza goods warehouse. Because she was an employee of Don Antón, they gave her discounts on the cloth and on the lace edging. There was embroidery thread in the shop, but she decided to take some imported ones that glittered under the light. She bought a spool of very pale yellow thread and a green one for the leaves of the vine in the design. The memory of the eyes of the merchant's son seeped into her mind. Green eyes with fulgent rays the color of moss and honey.

That afternoon, Don Antón closed the shop early to allow him to pass by the Fornarís house and get paid in a timely fashion. "Because you know how the rich are, girl. They have a party for the son, and in the end spend their money on this and that and then I have to wait months before they pay me for the job." Isabel watched as Don Antón put on his vest, perfumed the collars and the sleeves with his lavender water, and crossed with a light step toward Calle Reina, flitting past the benches in the plaza. She closed both of the latches on the door and went to her little room, carrying a basket set up with needles and frames. There were still a few days before she would see Isaac. She would surprise him wrapped in her shawl. She would cover her shoulders with it. She would listen to him speak while she showed him the fine piece that had come from her hands. Then, slowly, she would get closer to him. She would put on and take off her shawl so that he would see how well she could shelter him. Because she could do it, so skilled that she could embroider an entire house around them. "Wife of a soldier. Not a bad idea." Isabel pulled over a sewing bench. She put the cloth in the round frame. The wood made it taut. "Perfect vision." Isabel focused her eyes on threading the needle. She chose a spool of green thread to begin her embroidery.

Avenging Angel

RAFAEL, I WANTED him to be named Rafael. Full name: Rafael Fernando Fornarís. Terrible Mother Mary, keep him in your grotto. Wrap him in your mantles and make him invisible. Shelter him in your shadow because I am your devoted slave. Yesyesyes, the sanctuary will not open for pilgrims who come seeking your favors. Your doors will not open because you will be busy protecting the Son on your lap. Black Virgin, Carbuncle of Hope. Now you throw yourself before me, old woman? You who had forgotten me, who would not come down from the hill to offer me lit candles or flowers for my altar. And now you come? I advise you to attend to me. You are made of wood and a candle can be knocked over very easily. Reliquaries catch fire very easily. My trembling hand will administer vengeance if they find him and submit him to ridicule. If I were you, I would do what this old woman asks. If I were you, I would already shut up. Women shouldn't speak in church. If I were you, I would remember that my place is to serve. Yesyesyesyes, watch over the Son. Now and forever, Amen, Jesus.

The old woman lets go of the beads of the rosary. She looks up the road again. The Father shouldn't be long. The Enemy. They were the Enemy. Doña Eulalia and Doña Pura never gave me the Father's number. They never told me where I could find him. You tell me what the Child needs. How are we going to allow you to dial the number when you don't even know what this paper says? What? You don't know how to read, dumb old woman, you don't know anything. Over there, in Hatillo del Mar, they raised you wild as the beasts. In the coconut groves, dark as a bug. Coal that burned within my flesh when the Harpies would deny me access to the Señor. Go take care of the Child, and me, yesyesyes. But inside Candela, a fire, María de la Candelaria. Smoke escapes from the only window in the grotto. The Child should be there, curled up in the mantle of the Holiest Virgin. A cloudy blue sky approaches through the bushes. Thank God, the attorney is here.

"Good God, finally."

The old woman lets herself breathe.

"Where is he?"

"I don't know for sure, somewhere in the woods."

"It's better that he turn himself in. Then we can negotiate."

Is it the business of the Father to sacrifice the Son? Is it the way the Son must take to realize that the Señor abandons him again? And what about her? What about me, Señor, who have served you all these years? I carry the Cross of your ignominy; in my skin I keep the stain of your flaws. I told you, old woman, I told you, I am the only one who can intercede. I told you, Montse, that's the way it is, María. Never trust the Señor.

The old woman looks at him and doesn't say a word. Her eyes roll back in her head. The attorney notices her eyes popping, her hands shaking, the mouth that moves mutely without murmuring a word. The face furrows in grimaces, a concentrated scowl, the threat of tears, with only the shine of fury in her dry eyes, lips bitten down to the red core.

"I'm going into town to talk with them. But before, I'm going by the hospital."

"On my knees, over my dead body, without the Son . . ."

"If the boy from the cattle ranch doesn't die, we can raise some sort of defense."

"Without the Child, Virgin, then who? Yesyesyesyes."

The attorney shakes her lightly by the shoulder. "Don't fall apart now, Doña Montse, we have to be strong, for Roberto's sake." Roberto Fornarís, his full name. Angel of Vengeance should have been Rafael's name. And look what the Father asks of you, as if your back hadn't been the strong one to bear the lashes of the Harpies. As if the arms that put the Seed to crib had not been the strong ones. Strong, Don Armando. Strong, Señor. Don't let them touch a hair on the Child, or they will see the strength that still lives in this angry flesh. She shakes off the snow white hand of the Father. She walks to the bottom of the hill and stands at the front of the sanctuary. Over my dead body, I tell you. You will be the sharpness of my sword. You will be the fire of my semblance. My name is María de la Candelaria Fresnet, and no one will enter the sanctuary where I twice rock the Son in my lap, accompanied by the sword of this rage that is me.

The Packard again drives off, blue sky on the road. The afternoon comes. Night falls. The old woman crouches by the entrance of the grotto. She hears steps from inside and moves to the door.

"Child, are you in there? I am alone."

"I am thirsty, Godmother. It has been two days since I have drunk anything."

"I'll bring you some food. I'll be right back. Stay hidden there."

"Oh, Godmother, what have I done?" She hears cries, snorts, labored breaths. She climbs the hill looking back. In there she will shelter him in her lap. Don't worry, Child, everything is going to be all right. She climbs the hill quickly and looks for a plate of cold vegetables with dry chicken. This is good enough; this will nourish the entrails of the Son. She readies to go down again. "I'm here, Child, open the door." The door starts to move on its hinges. Baggy green eyes, the tight curled hair a mess. His shirt is torn, stained with blood. They can't see him like this. Eat in peace; let me look for something for you to change into. She leaves the grotto open, dumb old woman, the door wide open while she skips toward the clothesline. She doesn't know how, but she didn't hear it, the crickets, the voices, she didn't even notice the Packard return and stop in front of the sanctuary. Snowy the shirt that she brought for the Son in her hands. She didn't hear it. She went back in and the attorney was there, inside.

Attack, María Candela, burn him with rage. The attorney reaches out his hand to the Son. "Roberto, what have you done?" Attack. "Father, is it true what they say? That I am the son of a whore? Tell me, is it true?" A smoky candle flame flickers. Attack. The Father takes a step closer. He takes the Son by the shoulders, presses him to his chest. They join in a long hug. He steals the old woman's hugs; don't fall apart now. He steals the hugs from she who gave him to eat and drink, she who kept watch over him all night in the sanctuary. Mantle of night his star. And you, old woman, a wallflower. The Virgin looks at her and laughs. The Son's shirt drops from the old woman's hands. A breeze drags her toward where the Father and Son step over her, examining each other on the way to the Packard.

I am alone, alone in my tribulations. The whole morning passes by. I am alone, alone without the Lord's mercy. The old woman makes as if to cook, no, as if to wash clothes, no, as if to do the dishes. Swim in your feeble mind, drown there, old woman. Did you think you were worth more than the almighty hand of the Father? Did you think that you would so erase the mark of the Señor? Oh, Mother, if you have brought me here, end this thing. She can't bear it any longer. The old woman will walk to the town. She will look under the stones of the plaza if necessary. She needs to know where they took her Child.

Full name: Roberto Fernando Fornarís. She changes from her thin robe into a Sunday dress. She slips on shoes that are too tight. Callused foot, old woman, all of you wrinkled and callused. She puts a pair of barrettes in her hair and looks for a parasol. She goes down the hill toward Camino Nuevo, crosses the Santuario neighborhood. She walks through the countryside until she comes to the front of the Church of Nuestra Señora de Montserrat. It is almost noon by the time she gets there. You're sweating, old tar woman, you're sweating and you stink. Whoever smells you won't talk to you. Who, I'd like to know, is going to tell you where the Child is, the way you stink? She walks to the plaza and on the far side finds the police station. Some vendors chat under the shadows of two rubber trees. "Don Eusebio's son survived by a hair. They have the other one at City Hall. He arrived with a lawyer and everything." Nobody knows that it is the Father who comes to save him. You should have stayed in your house. You are worthless to the Child. I am here because I am his Mother. The old woman climbs the steps of City Hall one by one. "Doña Montse." The attorney comes out of one of the offices. "Where is the Child? Tell me, for God's sake." The old woman collapses in the arms of the Holiest One. Juan, please, bring her some water. Yes, sir. The chauffeur runs off and the *patrón* sits her on a bench.

"Don't worry, Doña Montse, everything has been taken care of."

"I want to see the Child; I want to see my son."

"Not today."

"Where is he?"

"I had to send him to the Ramey base. He has to enlist as a soldier."

"The Child . . . yesyesyes."

"If I get him out of town, he won't have to spend a day in prison."

But the old woman has stopped listening; the Child is saved saved saved. I am alone alone alone. The old woman is no longer listening to the Father, who puts a glass of fresh water to her lips. Two fat drops of water fall through the crevices in her cheeks.

Three

THE LEADEN WATERS of the Delaware chilled his bones. No warmth, no invitation to peel off his shirt and walk thoughtfully on the shore. The current forced you to rush as well, a current worthy of the swift and volatile city. Luis Arsenio watched the river on the afternoon that he went to the dock. He smoked a Pall Mall in a frenzy, hurriedly, pulling up the collar of his coat. He had stopped smoking when he arrived in Philadelphia, but on this particular afternoon he bought a whole pack. A cold river. At four thirty in the afternoon, the *Coamo* would arrive from the island to spew out its cargo of passengers on the shore of the Delaware River. His grandparents would be traveling on it. It was cold that day, and the waters, a leaden blue, had dirty pieces of ice floating on the surface. Luis Arsenio finished smoking his cigarette and tossed it into the river. He walked toward the landing pier. He heard the accent of the island coming from dozens of mouths, trying to heat their hands with their breath. What was going on, what were so many *boricuas* doing there? The Viña-Viners were at the port also, and they greeted him enthusiastically. "Young man, you already look like a full-blooded American. And what are you smoking? Cigarettes, like the movie stars?" They had come to welcome Don Luis Fornarís and his wife as well.

On the stairs of the *Coamo*, the grandparents descended, all smiles. Don Luis was loaded down. Luis Arsenio approached him to help him with the luggage. "But first come here and give me a hug." He squeezed him tightly. In the arms of his grandfather, Luis Arsenio heard strange whimpers that escaped from the old man's chest, like the groans of a tired beast. But his green eyes shone against the cold afternoon of the port. It must be the fatigue from the long journey. The Viñas also approached to help.

"Time stands still for you, country boy."

"You don't look as good as I do, you Corsican, but it doesn't look like the tomb is calling. But it is Alicia who looks like a goddess."

"Always such a gentleman, Custodio."

"*Niña*, that's not his name anymore. Now he insists on being called Custer."

"I finally changed that screwed up, sissy church name. Damn the day they gave it to me. Call me Custer Viner. A name for a gentleman, a man of action."

Luis Arsenio had many plans for this visit. He would take his grandparents to eat with him alone, show them the city. But the Viñas insisted, "Don't even think about it, little man, you are all coming to our house right now. There will be plenty of time to see Philadelphia. But today, with this cold . . ." At the house, they treated them to an exquisite dinner. No turkey with cranberry dressing, or those desserts made with yam that made Luis Arsenio want to retch. The Viñas kept their roots in mind and prepared a roasted leg of pork with *criollo* season-ing, rice and black beans, sweet plantains in their own syrup. "*Óyeme*, it makes you want to lick your fingers; because I may have changed my name, but I never forget that I am Cuban." He had to wait for a moment when the hosts were out of the dining room.

"How are things going over there?"

"Well, you know, your mother . . ."

"Alicia, don't distract the boy with nonsense. Why don't you tell us how it is going at the university?"

Jake Barowski, the government classes, the elegant vesti-bules at Fischer Hassenfield. Luis Arsenio told them about ev-erything, everything but Maggie Carlisle.

They ate until they were stuffed. The men went to have a drink in Don Custer's studio and the ladies stayed in the kitchen, making coffee. "Fresh from our farm in Tibes. This is real coffee." Emilia Viner insisted that Luis Arsenio stay. "I have a room set up for you; don't be rude. Plus, this way we can make use of the day tomorrow and see the city. Don't you want to be a guide for your grandparents?" They convinced him.

It was a crisp morning to go out and see Philadelphia. It was sunny and cold at the same time. You could almost bite into the air as if it were an apple. "A perfect day to go out for a stroll. You won the lottery, Corsican, because around here December is a gray soup that takes away all desire to go out." They went to Old City, to Benjamin Franklin's house, to see people skate on the Schuylkill. They made the tourist rounds. Luis Arsenio showed his grandparents Constitution Hall, the geometric Mason door-frames of Carpenter Hall, the monuments of the first capital of the nation, defender of democracy and of the wealth of the world. "That's right, Corsican, of democracy and wealth, for here, he who struggles gets ahead. There are no tyrants to come and nationalize your lands or persecute you for your opinions. Damn the mother of that Machado . . ." Don Custer Viña sang the praises of his adopted country while the young man led his grandparents through the ample boulevard in front of the Free Library and the Museum of Natural History.

Luis Arsenio stayed at the house of the Viña-Viners for a week and a half. "We are going on to New York to visit some old friends from our country. Will you join us?" He really wanted to see the great city, the biggest of all, but Maggie Carlisle awaited him. During their break he had not been able to get in touch with her by phone. He called her from the post office and in secret twice. She replied in secret as well. "We went cross-country skiing with my cousin Kyle. He is such a bore." She told him about insignificant events. "My aunt gave me a horrendous scarf, not like yours, Louie; I'll show it to you when we see each other." But through the details seeped sighs that made Luis Arsenio's skin feverish. He wanted to kiss her until he was gasping for air, until his cold breath lodged itself in Maggie Carlisle's chest and stayed there, forever exiled.

"I have so much to go over before the semester starts. It's best if I get back to the university."

"No question, Luis. School comes first. But write your mother."

"Behave yourself, young man. And watch out for evil skirts."

"Alicia, stop treating him like a child. You know what to do. Stay in touch."

"Give a big hug to Papa."

SAM'S SODA WAS ALMOST EMPTY. Some townies drank their coffee; a mother bought a muffin with jimmies for her son.

The majority of the student population still had not returned to their dormitories. But they had agreed that Maggie would be there, waiting for him. Luis Arsenio got out of his car, made a stop in his room, and rushed off to Sam's Soda. She was at a corner table by the door. Red hair, alabaster skin. As soon as he saw her, he began to approach her slowly, but with his chest surging. Maggie smiled, jumping up like a spring from the chair. She hugged him. Her copper curls got caught in Luis Arsenio's lips. They left hand in hand, strolling slowly through the deserted streets. They crossed toward Mayer Hall, passed by the front of the Goldberg residence, and almost without noticing, toward Fischer Hassenfield. There was no one in the vestibule. Luis Arsenio looked at Maggie. Maggie, complicit, lowered her head. They scurried up the service stairs and went to Luis Arsenio's room. He drew the curtains, "Louie," and locked the doors. There was Maggie Carlisle, now, in his locked room. She allowed him to put his hands on her breasts, to kiss her ardently on the bed, he without his shirt on, she with her skirt above her waist, each piece of clothing cast off, a conquest and a promise. Maggie's thighs were a cold, longed-for sky. He didn't penetrate her, but it didn't matter. He was starving and his very life hurt in between his legs, but that was the price to pay for hours kissing her until they suffocated, tossing in the sheets, with his legs and his hard sex rubbing her thighs. She was the girl to wait for, the one to convince, the one to singe off his eyelashes studying for. She was the prize and that afternoon Luis Arsenio wanted to keep on being Louie Forneress until the end of time.

At the end of the month, a little packet arrived in the mail. When he opened it, he found an old wristwatch and a note from his father. "They came searching for me urgently at the office," he said in a letter. "I thought it was about your mother.

But it was your grandfather." He had kept the pains and aches in his heart well hidden from the rest of the family. The father had found out about this in the hospital, from the lips of a bald little old man. "I am Don Luis's doctor," he said, and he filled them in.

The patriarch had been complaining about pains in his chest for years. "I wanted him to get on a treatment, to take arsenic tablets, which in the right doses work well. But your father responded that why should he poison himself if death was at his heels. Let it surprise him. There was no way to convince him. That father of yours is stubborn as a mule." Was, Luis Arsenio thought. His grandfather was stubborn and distrustful. He hadn't even told his own son Fernando that he was full of debts. They would have to auction off the warehouse building to pay for tuition his second year, his father wrote.

The letter had taken three weeks to reach him with the unfortunate news. The grandfather would already have been buried, already the beginning of a feast for worms. Luis Arsenio would have liked to contemplate how his coffin sank into the bosom of the earth. For once, he would have liked to have taken the time to say his farewells to the people left behind on the island. But the letter was categorical. The grandfather had died. There was nothing to do but go on living.

The father's letter did more than cause an uneasiness to settle in his chest. The grandfather died and with him other things died. Auctioning off the warehouses. His education a continued expense. How much land did the family have left? How much property had to slip through their hands to ensure his lineage? Without land and without a surname he would end up being Don Nobody. A ton of syllables in the air similar to his name in these cities, Louie Forneress. He would be insignificant.

Jake found him in the room looking out the window.

"What a miracle that you are not with the redhead."

Luis Arsenio turned to look. He didn't know how, but Jake saw the abyss in his body.

"We're losing all our lands, Jake. We are in debt up to our souls. Perhaps the only thing left to do is to return to the island, at least stop being a burden on the family."

"Your grade average is good, Louie; apply for a scholarship, or at least an assistantship with some professor."

Scholarships? How do you apply for those? What words do you use to declare yourself one of the "needy"?

He bumped into Professor Allen in the halls of Ware. He was his favorite professor, the only who took time to talk to him and help him with specific questions. "You should consider specializing in the Judge Advocate General's Corps. It is a field growing very rapidly, because of the violent conflicts and the need for a personal mediator who has a vision in tune with the interests of the nation, but a wider, more sensible perspective of the changing military situations." He had asked him to write a special assignment for the class that Luis Arsenio did with great care. "Very impressive," he had commented. Professor Allen would be one of the ones he confided in that perhaps these were his last months as a student. "Hi, Professor." He greeted him and made up a question about the statutes that differentiated war crimes from crimes against humanity. The professor got caught up in a discussion about the law. "That is always open to interpretation, but there are offenses that are decidedly crimes against humanity. For example, the torture of a prisoner of war: that could be a crime or not. Depending on the issues of the chain of command, there is room for interpretation." Luis Arsenio pretended to listen, to follow the train of the argument. He would miss talking to such a mentor when he was studying in some far-off place. Crime against himself, crime of his stock against him. The criminal death of his grandfather had left his father so weakened. Suddenly, they were in front of the professor's office. It seemed that the conversation was coming to an end.

"If you'll excuse me, Professor, I have another issue to talk to you about."

"Another question?"

They walked in. A tenuous light entered through the window. Not like the light of his island in the south, a crushing light that burned at the possibility of finishing what he had started at the University of Pennsylvania.

"My family is in bad shape, Professor. My grandfather just died. My father has had to sell lands. I am afraid that I don't have the means to stay here."

"There are always means, Louie. Let me do some investigating and I'll get back to you in a few days. What is your status in your country?"

"What do you mean, Professor?"

"If you are an American citizen."

Luis Arsenio couldn't help but smile. "Yes," he answered, and kept the rest of the reply that he would have liked to offer to himself. "Since 1917, whether we like it or not," but he didn't want to risk exposing himself. He didn't have the inclination or the spirit to face the fact that even his only ally knew very little about his status in the world. And besides, it wasn't important. Who cared about the minutiae of some lost island of the Caribbean or any of its inhabitants? In relation to what empire, what history, what discussion was it pertinent? Luis Arsenio walked out of that office in Ware with his head down; an insignificant speck, a being without context. Even for his benefactor.

But Professor Allen surprised him. Two days after the conversation he asked to see him in the hall.

"Some of my colleagues are very involved in the central office of the Judge Advocate General's Corps. They have opened a branch here at the university. Many of their students are doing internships in that program. They offer tuition exemption plus a stipend. It's not much, but it's enough to finish your education."

Luis Arsenio's eyes beamed. Finally a solution to his dilemma. Not to have to go back.

"A thousand thanks, Professor."

"They only require one thing for the interns. You have to enlist in the armed forces. But I imagine that won't be a problem for you."

Four

It was time for Isaac to visit, as always, twice a month. Isabel began to make rice and soak the beans. She wanted to go to the plaza, to look for a good cut of meat for the stew. But it would have to be on the way back, because first she had to stop in the cathedral. She looked for two cents in her savings can. Two more to light a candle for the Virgin. "Holy Mother, made immaculate by the light, grant me this favor for the greater glory of God, your honor and my benefit."

She had been living with the soldier for almost a year. At the beginning of the courtship, Isabel followed Don Antón's advice, playing the part "of a proper young woman, so the gentleman will learn to value what you are and will be willing to pay the price for your intimacy. Don't forget your place, child." But those yellow eyes were asking for more. The truth was that she could not understand how the society girls could hold back for years. "Chaperones, my love, the strictest watch." It was so easy to let oneself go. Let there be pleasure, she wanted to say, but not yet. Isabel retained her composure. She left Isaac with the hunger in his eyes. "I don't want to do it in the bushes like the dogs, don't want to soil my dress." Isaac sighed deeply and pretended to understand. He took her by the hands again, bringing his fingers to her face, "You are right," giving her a tender kiss, like in the plaza. She didn't know where she got the strength to hold back.

"I have something for you. When I visit you again, you will be as surprised as anyone." Isaac had said this, and afterward, no matter how she begged and pleaded, said nothing else. With Leonor's help, she had put together a special outfit for that day. She took out some of the small sum of money she had hidden under the mattress. She bought a piece of cloth of the same hue of yellow as the soldier's eyes. The light cotton organza fell over her hips and highlighted them well, the hardy rump of a full-fledged woman, so that Isaac would notice them and desire them. It was a shame that the organza couldn't have been raw silk. She still didn't have anything to wear in that material. But soon. Who knew what the surprise that Isaac had in store was, maybe even a definitive engagement. Then she could enjoy a thousand luxuries.

Isaac arrived to pick her up at the steps of the room in the atelier. He gave her a small branch of forget-me-nots and planted a chaste kiss on her lips. Isabel took a few steps ahead so that Isaac would get a good look at her dress, how perfect the baggy folds at the chest and the back turned out, the imperceptible stitching of the appliqués. "Do you like it? I made it for you." Isaac was looking somewhere else, but he remained calm. They walked on Calle Salud, then up Castillo. They turned toward the Romaguerra after a few blocks, and at the beginning of the artisans' neighborhood, Isaac stopped. There was a little white house in front of them, with a porch made of tiles and balustrades. A vine of bougainvillea adorned the tiny entrance gate.

"What a pretty little house. Who are we visiting?"

"Nobody, Isabel. I rented it for you. The house is yours if you want it."

Isabel let herself be taken past the gate, over the steps of the porch, through the door, and into the living room of the wooden house. She looked at its high ceilings made of zinc, its floor tiles with painted arabesques. She measured the halfway point that separated the living room in two, one side for the vestibule and the other for the dining room, and she counted the bedrooms—one, two. "You can set up a seamstress's shop here." Isaac opened one of the doors. "I'll buy the furniture for you little by little." Then he took her to the fireplace with room for a stove and a tile top. There was a small patio with enough space to hang a clothesline, put in a sink, and grow something. Isabel imagined it as finished. She would plant rosebushes up against the fence, as there were in the patios of many señoras in town. She would cut them every week, and she would place a vase of fresh roses on a small table in the vestibule. She would sit on a straw sofa. She would sew embroidered linen tablecloths for the dining room. She would wax the floors every week and every week wash them with lye and flowery water so that the house always smelled fresh and no ill wind settled in its corners. This was her house. The house given to her by her soldier so that she did not have to live in the back of the shop.

Isaac Lowell, soldier of the Forty-second Regiment, stationed at the Loosey Point base, native of the island of St. Thomas, son of a Basque shopkeeper that he never knew and a seamstress from the islands, led Isabel Luberza to a closed room that he had not yet shown her. He pushed open the four painted boards that made the door. Inside, there was just a small table with uneven legs, a lit oil lamp, and a four-poster bed dressed in blue sheets. Isabel walked to the center of the room, which seemed to her the most luxurious place in the world. She carefully examined the walls, the little bed, the glass of water set next to the oil lamp on the table by the bed. She put her branch of forget-me-nots in the glass and then, with her back to Isaac, began to undo the buttons of her dress, one by one, slowly, until the yellow organza fell to the floor like the foam of a river. She took off her girdle, the garters that held up her stockings. And just so, she reached down to the floor, naked and with her back to him, to undo her shoes, to let Isaac watch her flexibility, a dark and round she-cat in the amplitude of her flesh. As if by accident, she exposed the pink and moist wound in between her legs. She felt Isaac's heart racing behind her, his flesh hardening, his clothes falling to the floor as well. Then she sat on the bed with the blue sheets. She felt Isaac's step approaching the place where her heart reverberated against her chest. Two hearts racing.

SHE WALKED ON THE STRETCH of Calle Salud. At the end of the avenue she saw the sign for Atelier Vilarís but kept on going. She was in a hurry that morning. Isaac would arrive at the stroke of noon. She wanted to have everything ready. If she stopped at the shop, Don Antón would distract her. She crossed the avenue toward Las Delicias. In the middle of Alamedas, the cathedral rose majestically. Its two steeples wounded the clear sky. Its serene altar received the prayers of the parishioners. This time she was going to go to the very pedestal of the Virgin. "Virgin of the Mercies, Virgin protector, watch over and take good care of this your slave . . ." No one would be able to stop her. It was nine in the morning and the Mass had ended; that

is, the señoras would have left the stage and gone back to harass
their servants. The church would be empty.

Isabel took out her embroidered shawl and covered her head.
She walked slowly through the nave, hearing her footsteps echo.
A deacon was pulling up the kneeling cushions and straighten-
ing the pews. In the back, the Immaculate Virgin raised her
eyes to the heavens, where she ascended surrounded by cherubs. Blond, serene in her blue gaze, her arms open, reaching in
her lightness toward the Highest. Isabel knelt. "Holy Virgin,
our Intercessor. Don't let my blood drop. I want to be fertile
for Isaac's visit."

France, Spain, New York. She would go everywhere. Hand
in hand with Isaac. In his arms. She would travel by train,
ship, even airplane. She would get in military cars. Beside him.
Private Isaac Lowell would be at the steering wheel. Later,
Sergeant Lowell would be driving, and then Lieutenant and
Captain Lowell. By then they would have children and live
far away from town, extremely far away, some place where the
heat would not be so crushing. Isabel would dress in creations
of Scottish wool, coats with leather collars and cuffs, which she
had seen in Don Antón's dressmaking magazines. They didn't
seem that difficult to make.

Moving out of the little room in the back of the store was
easy; the hard part was explaining it to Don Antón. When he
saw her picking up her belongings—"You, too, are abandoning me"—she didn't know how to explain the things that she
was thinking about. Don Antón put on a serious face, took in
a deep breath to consolidate the tragic air that was required
for his next intervention. Isabel sat on a bench to listen to the
speech that the dressmaker wanted to give her. She owed it to
him. For taking her off the streets, for offering a roof and a job,
and for helping her get herself together. She listened peacefully,

"Me, who expected you to marry in a white dress with a good man." But Don Antón's script was foreign to her. "Things are not like that for girls like me," she would have liked to tell him. "Things are not like that; nor do they need to be." Isaac was a good man; he had kept his word, making a home for her. She didn't need paraphernalia, or permission, or a party to celebrate whom she gave her body to. "It's that simple," she would have liked to explain to Don Antón, but instead she decided to assure him of her loyalty with something other than explanations.

"If you want, I can keep on working for you."

"Has your husband given you permission?"

It hadn't occurred to her to ask Isaac, but she knew the answer to the question. Of course, she could keep on working. Isabel nodded and Don Antón, in his tight-fitting pants, his lips curled as if he were a character in a tragic zarzuela, let out a deep sigh. "What are we to do? But don't think that I am under any illusions; I know, the first round belly and I'll never see you again." He buzzed inside the shop, the measuring tape around his neck. Isabel continued packing her things. She had thought there would be less stuff. Those two years with Don Antón had been prosperous.

Two embroidered shawls, five dresses for going out, plus the dresses that she used daily for work. Three pairs of shoes—the white ones that she sent out to dye, a pair of short black boots, and another pair for special occasions. She packed two sets of sheets, kitchen utensils, a tablecloth, a prayer book, and clippings from fashion magazines. She put away two bone barrettes and three little bottles of perfume. "Girl, we're going to have to call for a cart . . ." Leonor was helping her pack. Isabel smiled. She was leaving Don Antón's shop with enough possessions to build a new home. She was missing pots and pans, maybe some good curtains, but that would come soon. Isaac would provide for her, as he had provided the roof. For her, chosen among others. She had reason to smile. If only Godmother could see her.

Don Antón returned to the back of the store as if by chance. He was carrying a package in his hands. "Take this cloth; the owners have not come to claim it." It was three yards of very fine linen. Leonor's jaw came unhinged.

"Don Antón is certainly taken with you."

"I am going to make a tablecloth that will be the envy of all with this."

"I'll clean your whole house if you give me a little piece of that cloth."

"Of course, Leonor. And with the extra scraps, I'll make handkerchiefs for Isaac."

On the way back, she passed by the plaza in the Market and bought a nice piece of goat meat. She lit the wood on the fire and began to make a stew. She embroidered some orders for Don Antón, and before she knew it, it was past noon. Isabel waited for her soldier in the little porch with the forget-me-nots. The cart drivers passed in the middle of the street; the vendors returned home with empty baskets. She saw him turn the corner and smiled. Isaac. But there was a turbid look in his eyes. He went up the stairs and peeled off his jacket by the doorway, "I'll be right back." He went out again toward the town. He did not notice the smell of fresh stew in the house or Isabel's essence on her skin. He left her standing there, as if he had not even seen her.

Night had already fallen when he returned. "Abide, Isabel, abide." That's what the Virgin would have wanted. That she would abide, that she would be submissive, that she would throw herself in the bed ready for Isaac to climb on top of her. "The bleeding didn't come. Isn't that what you wanted?" But her rage did not allow her to proceed with her plan. "You want me to serve you dinner?" she asked her man, distant. Isaac had come back with reddened eyes and the stink of alcohol that soured the smell of his body. "I'm not hungry." She heard the rustle of clothes falling on the floor, and then, "Are you coming?" Her man was calling for her. "That animal is not going to put a finger on me." Isabel moved away from the bedroom. She stayed in the living room, keeping herself busy embroidering.

The following day she heard him washing in the back of the patio, changing his pants. She went to the kitchen to peel vegetables, but she could hear him. When she heard the sound of his boots enter the hallway of the house, Isabel stepped in front of him, blocking his path.

"Do you want to tell me what is going on? Because if I no longer interest you, I'll go in peace back to Don Antón and God's mercy." Isaac looked at Isabel as if that woman that he had made his were something less than the air in front of him, nothing, a body without a name and without precedent who had suddenly appeared there to annoy him. She saw his hands curled into fists by his waist. He looked her in the face, with a gesture ready for battle. But then his attitude changed. He took Isabel by the hand and sat her in one of the armchairs in the living room. "Girl, it's not what you think. It's because of Wilson." Little by little, words that Isabel did not understand poured out. President Wilson. The Peace of Versailles. The support for an antiwar campaign reducing military personnel.

"The colonel explained to us that there would be cuts, especially in the bases with minor presences. Guess, Isabel, where they start cutting."

Armaments, treaties, presidents. She lost Isaac in a world

that she could not imagine. He was lost to her and she could not be in his arms. He would be on the other side of a powerful and invisible frontier. She looked at her man's caramel arms, his hair in disheveled curls, his wide and fierce nose. You didn't have to know much about politics to know where the president would start cutting.

"And if we go abroad, to your grandfather's?"

"To live on what? If I could only get promoted . . . or be in a more important detachment. Here at Loosey Point we're lost in a void."

"But didn't you say that over there they kill black people; they lynch them like animals and set fire to them?"

"Fifty-eight lynchings last year."

"Here they don't lynch anybody."

"Because they don't let anyone become a real danger. Washerwomen, seamstresses, street vendors. We're not good enough to compete."

Then he told her: "They're transferring me to Panama." Isabel clutched her belly as if the words disemboweled her. "I'll go first, and as soon as I am set up, I'll send for you." A knot loosened. The air became a season of murmurs that reverberated against the walls of the house, against the recently mopped floor, against her empty stomach. "I have to go, because if not they throw me out of the division." Isaac kept on talking, but Isabel did not listen. She did not hear a single word that would comfort the heaviness in her belly, which she clutched firmly, trying to hold it together under the burden that spilled on her and forced her to falter. She walked slowly down the hall toward the stove, where she was simmering the meal that she had prepared for her man. "They say that Panama is a more strategic location . . ." With her back to him, she asked, "Do you want me to serve you some food?" Everything became strange, setting the table, watching Isaac eat peacefully, picking up the empty plates. Isaac rested from the meal by taking a siesta, convinced that he would do all that he had promised. Isabel began to wash the dishes, her hands strangers to everything, her chest out of place in that house.

Leonor found her brushing the stairs of the porch with complete devotion, as if in each corner of each step she was risking her life. For two weeks, she did nothing but clean. She stayed in the house moving things from place to place, the chairs, the sofas, the little table by the bed. Don Antón sent Leonor for some news of her.

"The soldier left, right?"

A droplet of sweat streaked down Isabel's face and fell, getting mixed up with the soapy water she was using to scrub the floor tiles. She counted the days of her blood. It had been a month since she had heard from Isaac.

"Now you are really going to have to work hard to keep the house. If you want, I'll move in with you."

She had to take laundry orders, going again by the back door as before. House to house, Isabel waited with the bundle of clean clothes for the señoras to attend to her, look over the shirts, the skirts, the girdles, and pay for the washing and ironing. The negotiation was done hurriedly, without due respect. "I need these clothes by Thursday, and don't forget to use a lot of starch, Isabel." "Yes, señora, don't worry, señora." She would take the bundle of clothes and hurry out of the house as quickly as possible. She left from all of them in a hurry, except from the Fornarís house. There were days when the young Fernando tried to start a conversation. "Don't call me *Don*; you make me feel like my father." He watched her from a peaceful, silent distance. Those green eyes, that chin where a dark beard was noticeable as soon as it was shaved. But Isabel wasn't interested. She wasn't interested in anyone, no señorito or lathe operator, no little white one or construction worker. "It's almost the end of the month. I have to pay rent." She had to keep on running from street to street, Gran Vía, Virtud, Salud, Reina Mora. She did not at all like those looks from Señorito Fornarís or the consequences that they could unleash. But Señorito Fornarís tried to establish conversation; she was needed for something that she could not quite specify.

The space was on the top floors of a building that the old man Fornarís used as warehouse for his shops. "Some day, I will open my private office there," he mentioned calmly. "But for now, I'm moving. This house is too small for me." Isabel was still not sure why Fernando Fornarís was telling her all this under the cornice of the patio. He looked at her straight on, without the manners of a *patrón,* and she found herself returning his gaze, equal to equal. "It has two bedrooms, a living room, a kitchen." Those eyes ensnared her.

"What I need is for someone to clean it a couple of times a week."

"I don't clean houses."

She told him without lowering her gaze, without softening her voice or making excuses. Before even thinking about it, she had responded to the señorito in her usual tone. The voice of Isabel Luberza Oppenheimer, with which she spoke to Don Antón, to his clients, so long ago, it seemed, in the shop. What was it about that man that made her speak this way? Isabel thought she saw a passing spark in the face of the señorito, as if he thought that her response had been a challenge. Which it had not been, not what she had meant it as.

"It's a shame; I am willing to pay well."

"Then there should be a lot of people interested."

"I pay three dollars a month. It's a lot."

It was a lot. That money would cover exactly the cost of the little house. It was what she made with the washing and ironing in five days. Her liberation from the back doors.

"Let me think about it, Don Fernando."

"Stop with the Don . . . just call me Fernando, that's it. If not, I'll take back my offer."

"I won't get used to it."

"Get used to what?"

"Calling you just by your first name."

"Who knows, Isabel? Don't get ahead of yourself."

She crossed Calle Virtud toward the Romaguerra. Inside her bra she was carrying the money for the last orders of washing and ironing. Three dollars a month. Isabel was making calculations. She arrived at the tree-lined avenues of Las Delicias and stopped at a shop to buy a notebook. Cutting out the laundry orders wouldn't have a great effect on her economic situation. Moreover, there was an idea slowly brewing in her head.

Illegal alcohol, that's where the money was. She saw it clearly in her head. She didn't know where the idea had come from, but she was sure. To hell with the soldier who would take her by the arm and lend support for the stroll. She would support herself. "With those three dollars a month . . . Fernando." The name of the attorney slipped out of her mouth like a surprise. She had to be careful with that man and the doors he opened for her. But she would accept the offer. Isabel felt as if a second skin began to grow on her, perhaps thicker than all of her skins before this. She let her mind wander to the horizon, in the numbers and figures that danced in her head. She would speak with Leonor as soon as she got home. They both would have to economize to begin the operations.

Sorrowful Mysteries

I AM IN the orchard of my afflictions. I am in Gethsemane. I am coiled in the branches of my sorrow. The Loved One always absent. The Son has gone and there is no witness to my shame. What have you left me with, Holy Mother? What have you left me with? What am I going to use to stop the sea of tears flooding me from within? A bitter liquor of fruits rotting and leading me to my rest, suffering in the twisted branches of my withered body. "Lord, grant me the true pain of my sins." First sorrowful mystery. But what was my error, my stigma? I was conceived to be snow-like, dawn-colored. I don't even know why, but you punished me. I don't even know, Mother, what I am accused of to be condemned to the most absolute solitude?

The worst. This is the worst. Because when the Son was in me, at least . . . Because when I cuddled him in my arms, when I gave him to eat and drink, my whole being had a function. The house was the sheltered nest. And although the Beloved did not arrive, the house protected me. The rumors remained outside, the absences remained outside. But inside, the Son and I breathed the airs that I made blow from the corners. A light and limpid air that eased the heaviness of the world. My word was law. "Carmela, the cupboards need to be cleaned," and the cupboards would be shining. "Delmira, someone needs to go the market," and the house was stocked. The orchards and the gardens and the Portuguese River, which drowns me, which I cannot cross, all remained outside. But now the house is empty. The Son is an unbearable absence. What good would it be to issue orders? Why would I want the cupboards stocked with fresh fruit from the earth that would not fit in a jar? I poured libations until I was left discarded, with no one to tell me you are the queen of all my lands, queen of my heart. "Lord, help me moderate my desires." No one will love me as much as my sacrifice merits. And I deserve that love. I deserve that love.

The branches of the orchard lash at my face, cover my brow with thorns. I pray and beg the Lord. But the Beloved does not listen. The Beloved has gone to the river looking for what he has not lost, to the countryside looking for what he has not lost. They say that there is a son in danger. But he is not the Real One, he is not the Real One, not the Son that was born from my entrails, the one whom I offered my breast, pink as an iris. He chewed on it until I bled and I, patiently, offered him the other one. I didn't want him to feed from any wet nurse. I didn't want any sooty milk to pass down his throat. Why can't the Beloved do what is customary, forget, offer the charity without letting his name touch the lips of the outlaw? Why can't he be like his Father, and his Father's Father? Force the Son to let his will be obeyed in him. And whose fault is it, Mother, if not that One who abandoned the Child? Who did not submit, as I submitted. Who did not open her breasts in milk and blood, who did not hide in the grotto, where she drags herself to pay for the pain of her sin. Because she was the real Sinner. She is certainly enveloped in blemishes, all of her, her body covered by the soot of her guilt.

It was probably her, Mother, curb my arrogance. Help me bear my Cross. They deserve each other, her and the Beloved. Two who know of no world except themselves, no hunger but that which they sate, leaving a thousand bodies in their drift, rivers of blood packed with fractures. Third and fourth sorrowful mysteries. How many will fall before she pays for her guilt? Why, Mother, must the design of her evil be fulfilled in me?

But to You and only You, Husband of mine, I commend my spirit. On you the entire burden of my misfortune will fall. For not listening to my calls, for not listening to my prayers, for abandoning me. For not separating from my lips the cup that is my blood transformed to rotted fruit. For allowing the Son to live outside my reach, torn from the island that is my home, that is this room where I die. The olive grove marks my face in mockery. This is me, Beloved, the Sorrowful One. And these are the slow workings of my pains. My sorrow will fall on your shoulders until it breaks them, as you have broken me, in two.

Five

WHEN HE RETURNED to the town, it was like going back in time, as if everything he had experienced, the snow, Sam's Soda Shop, Maggie's supremely white thighs, had not happened to him. A tulle was draped over his memory, smudging what just a few days before Luis Arsenio Fornarís had found so concrete. Amorous farewells, a tranquil contemplation through the window of the train as the firs and the shores of the Schuylkill passed by. All those things blurred in his mind as if they had happened years before and he was somebody else; Louie Forneress detached from Luis Arsenio Fornarís, who was now returning by car on the military highway toward the south. He arrived enveloped in a haze of fatigue and forgetfulness that he could not fathom. Maybe it was the heat.

It was May already when he got the message. He had been working for Professor Allen for exactly a year. The second semester was about to end. Luis Arsenio was studying in the library, looking over reference books. The letters were dancing in front of his eyes. "The Treaty of Versailles," "The Treaty of Britain." His head could not take any more. Past the windows of Simpson Hall night was beginning to fall. His stomach distracted him even more from his homework. He had to go back to Fischer Hassenfield, dress up a little bit, and run to the refectory in Ware before they closed it. Take some time at once to see Maggie. He picked some heavy volumes from his desk. He would take them to the room, where he would have time to go over them later.

The custodian stopped him on his way up the stairs to the room. "Forneress, Louie. You have some mail waiting for you. A telegram." He handed him a yellow envelope, where he could see some small letters through the opening of the address. These letters also began to dance. A telegram from his father.

URGENT STOP YOUR MOTHER IS VERY ILL STOP
COME BACK AS SOON AS YOU CAN STOP
FERNANDO FORNARÍS

The driver rounded the Plaza Las Delicias. Luis Arsenio looked at the line of trees, the cants and foundation of the church. He sighed without a hint of joy, but with a sense of relief. There was the ice cone vendor, the drivers of public cars, the shop. He recognized its context. Here, he was what he had always been. The son of the attorney, the good boy, the señorito from town returning. The people looked at him and recognized him. He would not have to try to please, to evade topics of conversation, to watch what he said. He had returned, if only for a moment, to his kingdom.

The car stopped at the front doors of the Fornarís house.

Luis Arsenio stood firm in front of the steps and gulped in some air. The chauffeur went ahead of him up the stairs, suitcase in hand. Luis Arsenio decided to follow him. Before he could cross the threshold, his father, Fernando Fornarís, came out to receive him.

Time became a formless thing in front of his eyes. How many years had he been gone? Two. Then, what was all that gray on his father's temples, all those ridges on his brow? Even the Fornarís beard, which always implacably covered the chins of the men of his stock, seemed sparse, made worse by a strange eruption that reddened around his father's jaw. A hug sealed the welcome. Luis Arsenio felt the fragile bones poking his skin. His father's eyes also seemed more downcast than usual, as if they were ill. But something was still present in that man who embraced him, who threw his arm over his shoulder and led him up the stairs. There perhaps, in the firmness of the embrace, lived a chance of resolution.

"How is Mama?"

"Rather ill."

"Don't you mean drunk?"

He didn't mean to, but the words slipped out. His intention for that journey was something other than to make evident the shame that his father surely felt, which he had to live with every day, and which he himself had escaped. Damn his tongue. However, to Luis Arsenio's surprise and before he could offer an apology, his father looked him directly in the eyes with a downcast smile.

"Her liver is inflamed, but that's not the worst part."

"What then?"

"Her mind, Luis Arsenio. Your mother can't stop shaking, uttering nonsense. I had to check her in to the Ladies Hospital using some family connections because they don't treat mental problems there. But at least they keep a watch over her twenty-four hours a day."

"What about Carmela and Delmira; can't they watch her?"

"The day that I sent you the telegram, I thought we had lost her. But come, sit down, you must be tired from your trip."

"No, Father, tell me . . ."

"She swallowed a whole bottle of sedatives. They had to pump her stomach."

"I want to see her."

"I'll take you to the hospital. But relax for now. Are you hungry?"

Delmira was in the kitchen. "How are you, señorito? Welcome." Her dark face closed in on itself, eyes turned away to what she was doing. The years did not catch up to her. She put out a bowl of lentil soup and Luis Arsenio remembered the fateful New Year's celebration that probably marked the beginning of this outcome he had returned to witness. He took a spoonful. Don Fernando sat next to him and again put his hand on his son's shoulder. Luis Arsenio opened his mouth to say something, but he realized that nothing he could say would live up to that moment. He had another spoonful of soup and his face grew hot, his eyes began to tear; the weight of that hand unknotted something in his chest. He had been carrying that pressure inside him for years, and now he felt it. He let go of the spoon. He covered his face with his hands and let the thing in his chest dissolve slowly. His father tightened the hold on his shoulder, still silent. He let his son weep.

HER HAIR DISHEVELED, WITH A yellowish paleness, Cristina Rangel lay on the bed of the Ladies Hospital. A *mulata* nurse combed her hair, which was also graying. Luis Arsenio walked in with a bunch of daisies that he had bought in the plaza. What had happened to his mother during those years? They had been barely two, a sigh that transformed Luis Arsenio into a fickle thing, with different names. He took a few steps, tenuously. He did not want to startle the woman whose hair they were combing. He approached the bed by her blind side, while his mother allowed her eyes to lose themselves in the view through the window, the dry country scene outside of the hospital.

"They didn't have white roses" was the only thing he could think to say when he reached his mother's bedside. Their eyes met. Cristina Rangel's were returning from a haze, as if they were crossing through a dark tunnel and came upon some other eyes that were connected to a voice that spoke to her from afar, "white roses," and mentioned a flower that she had once liked to smell in the crystal vase of the living room of her house. Where was her house now? Lost in that dark tunnel, likely. At the end of the voice were green eyes, vibrant, and a chin with a thick beard. At the end of the beard, some pieces of a white presence, very soft, which smelled like the water the ladies who watched her put on her. Her bed a fine glass where they would put those things, as if for eating because they smelled good. Could they be the roses, they didn't look like it, they were narrower, longer, with a different color in the center. But they were brought to her by eyes that smiled. She smiled, too, because they smelled good.

"Fernando?"

"No, Mama, it's me, Luis Arsenio."

Then it was only the sounds that remained and something broke in her chest. She no longer wanted the things that smelled. All she wanted to do was hug the one approaching her bed. She would not let go. She could not let him go, "Luis Arsenio," or let him escape, "son." She would take his hands, sit him beside her, hug him the whole time. Her eyes would not wander out the window anymore. She had to fix them on those other eyes, in the trimmed but fresh chin, in the hands that now caressed her hair, "I came to see you. Mother, I am here," like the ladies dressed in white who smell good, "I brought you some daisies," who comb her hair and fix the bed from which she no longer has the will to get up. But she will get up. She will go look for a vase to put her flowers in. "No, Mother, don't get up. I'll look for it. Do you want them near the bed?" And then she will tell Delmira to make her son Luis Arsenio some coffee, her son, who has returned. He has come to take her away from that bed forever, because he needs his lunch served, and his pants pressed, and his books set up. Now, she remembers. The boy has returned from school and she needs to get up from that bed, so he doesn't notice anything unusual, that she has no strength left, that she is withering, that something is irreparably broken inside. "Where's Delmira? Let her bring you coffee." Cristina sits up in bed. Tears fill his eyes. "No, Mother, don't worry. I've already had some." Her son has had his coffee and weeps upon seeing her. It is because he loves her. It is because he can't live without her. It is because he will never leave her alone.

"Are you sure you had some? Because if not, I'll get up right now and make you some. What beautiful flowers you brought me. They are my favorite."

"Your favorites are the white roses."

"Yes, white roses, how beautiful. Why don't you have some coffee? You must be hungry."

He had to ask the nurses to bring him a cup to prevent Doña Cristina from getting out of bed. He was afraid that she would fall apart in his arms. He had been gone for only two years. When he saw his father, he thought it could have been ten. But now, looking at his mother, he was sure that a whole lifetime had passed. Luis Arsenio could encircle both his mother's wrists with his fingers. He caressed her grayish hair, the golden streaks the remnants of the color it had been so long ago. The robe hung on her bony shoulders, which sunk into her chest and threatened to break the rhythm of her breath. There were wrinkles, but her face, nevertheless, was the same. Snowy, smooth, like a figure in a niche at church. That was the horrible thing, that the face of a passionate woman remained, framed by the withered body that was betraying her. What had happened to time? Had his mother allowed it to devour her so? The nurse arrived with the coffee. Luis Arsenio drank it in big gulps. He wanted it to burn him on the inside, so that it would put out the deafening cries that were stuck in his throat.

He spent the whole afternoon with his mother. He drank another cup of coffee and a glass of water. He read to her passages from a Bible that some nuns had left in the room. He went out to the hall twice to get some air and one of the times went down to the lobby while his mother napped, having dozed off while Luis Arsenio read the Sermon on the Mount. Down there, seated on the benches of the hospital's lobby, he was overcome with a desire to smoke. A Tiparillo, a Pall Mall, a hundred packs of Lucky Strikes. He had to settle for a home-made cigarette that a visitor offered him. The smoke let him breathe easier. He went up the stairs again to his mother's room. He wanted to be there when she woke up. He was afraid of the attack that might come over her if she noticed that her son was missing again.

Visiting hours came to an end. To his surprise, "God bless you, son," Cristina said her goodbyes calmly, as if Luis Arsenio was going off to sleep in the room next door. It was getting

dark when he left the Ladies Hospital. He felt like never returning, but he knew that he would be back the following day. He
wanted to make use of the time to be with his mother while his
courage held up. Because he knew that it would falter. A hunch
pulsated within him. One day, he would get dressed; he would
calmly descend the stairs of the house with his suitcase, which
he would give to the driver. He would go up to have some
juice, eat some bread. Then—"To the port"—he would leave
without even saying goodbye to his father. Everyone would
think he was at the hospital. But he would be en route to the
capital, with his ticket well tucked into the pocket of his vest.

On the way back to the house, they took the path that went
by the Gran Vía. The Fox Delicias movie theater was there, and
the fruit shops and the Rangel pharmacy. It was a corner that
he knew well, which he had passed through so many times,
with Esteban and Pedrito, or alone, looking for a way to kill
the slow-moving time that settled on every corner of the town.
Luis Arsenio asked the chauffeur to leave him there, at that
corner, that slowness. He wanted to get a little fresh air. Maybe
it would release some of the pressure in his chest, the turbu-
lences of time that he had had to endure. He was a man already.
A man with a woman and about to graduate from the university. Maggie Carlisle. A light breeze caressed his back as he
walked under the shade of the rubber trees. Hair in flames, alabaster face. His heels no longer felt so heavy against the pavement. Luis Arsenio decided to have a soda at the cafeteria of
the Hotel Melía. Perhaps from there he would call the Ferráns
house. Yes, to find out what was happening with Esteban. He
would pass by the house afterward.

Then he saw her. Sesame seed skin, sweet honey in the air.
Time took another dirty swipe at him. Minerva crossed on Calle
Isabel Segunda in the direction of Perla. Her hips had grown, as

well as her breasts. But it was the same frizzy hair taken up at the nape, the same color as her bee skin, and it was the same waist, swaying under the cotton dress, very tight-fitting on top, loose below, with a great skirt that the breeze toyed with. She was dressed in green, "Like your eyes." That vision froze his steps. Follow her, no. Say hello, no. Go see her later at Elizabeth's, never. Luis Arsenio had a concrete plan, unshakable. Maggie Carlisle was his prize. He could not let anything, or anybody, distract him. He would be in town a few weeks, visit with his family, his friends, the mother. He would dine with his father. Luis Arsenio turned abruptly and took long strides toward the house. Once there, fully stocked, he would wait out the storm that was Minerva. Let time take her away once again; let it transform her once more into the distant past, on a rural and barren road of the San Antón neighborhood.

That evening he had dinner with his father, alone in the empty house. They had always been three: the mother, the attorney, and the son; but now without Cristina it seemed as if a whole crowd was missing. But there was peace. There was, for example, a light bridge that spread between Don Fernando and Luis Arsenio, between the hands that ate the soup and the rhythm of the son's hands, which ate the soup as well, measuredly. A tenuous conversation developed between them. "It was difficult to see her." They seemed like two strange colleagues who had run into each other after a long journey. "At first it's upsetting, but then one gets used to it. It's not too horrible." There wasn't much to say to each other. The solitary air that had flooded the house was well received by the Fornarís men. It comforted them. They were, after all, two men talking about fate, solving problems, the two standing on their own two feet without the need to suffocate the other, to unleash the consequences of their lives on the other, to evade each other. There was no need for much talk, nor need to shut up in the silence of animosity. Delmira served them chicken casserole, rice, and green beans with *recao* and pumpkin. They drank wine.

"Let's hope she gets better."

"It's going to take time."

"I have to leave . . ."

"Of course you have to leave; don't think I'm going to allow you not to finish your courses."

"What about Mother?"

"That's my problem. I'll take care of her until God wills it. But tell me, how is it going at the university?"

They passed to the study, where they drank a cordial. "The ones that Cristina used to make." Luis Arsenio felt like laughing. And crying. He drank in honor of the slow destruction mounted on the fruit flavors and felt that his father drank for the same reasons. "I think I am going to specialize in military history." He started to explain how he had become the favorite of Professor Allen and how they dealt with criminal cases in the Judge Advocate General's Corps, but also with coastal trade and international law cases. That discipline would open the doors of the world for him. He could travel, get some experience, and then return to practice. "Don't think that I am going to abandon you." He would lay claim to what was his. He would take Maggie to see the world and then return with his pale, redheaded princess to fill a position of prominence within his clan. But this last bit he didn't tell the father. He didn't tell him about Maggie. There would be time for that later.

Don Fernando listened to his son's spare words, attentive. Intermittently, he nodded, a pleased smile sometimes spread on his face. "I had to sell one of the farms in San Antón," he said in passing. "Your mother's illness is costly." But otherwise everything was fine at the firm. There were new clients. The construction projects were multiplying and now they had opened a cement factory near the Canteras. All those contracts belonged to him. Luis Arsenio remembered the distant conversation in the Ferráns living room when Uncle Jaume had arrived on the island. He wanted to ask if the business belonged to that family but decided not to. His eyes felt heavy.

"You must be half asleep, son."

"Yes, it seems that way."

"Go on and rest; we'll talk some more tomorrow."

Luis Arsenio climbed the stairs toward his room when he thought he heard a muffled sound coming from the kitchen. He turned his head and found his father's silhouette in the dark, looking out the window, as always. What was he looking at? Maybe he would get the chance to ask him during this visit, to finally find out what it was that lived outside the house that had always laid claim to him, making him absent when he was inside, as if that were not the place where he really belonged. But not today. Today was finally over. Luis Arsenio pushed the door to his room, and almost before he took off his shirt, he threw himself on his boyhood bed, sure that he would fall into a heavy sleep that would let him rest.

But "yellow butterflies fluttering in the air, a dark hand that rises out of the thicket," the dream betrayed him. Once again he was lost in the lands of the farm of San Antón; once again his mother (this time he was sure, or was it Maggie?) called him from afar, and he lost himself in the underbrush to find himself with that black woman who pushed him against the grasses, who clutched him firmly in between the legs and licked him, while he was overcome with moans and stretched out on the ground, his arms spread, his body burning from saliva, a delightful nausea enveloped in a faint whiff of pumpkins that stuck to his body, another humor. Minerva. He saw her. The other woman was Minerva.

He awoke startled. He walked straight into the bathroom to rid himself of that memory from his skin. He washed himself vigorously, furiously. He also soaked the sheets under the shower. It was embarrassing. He was no longer a boy to have to slip into the bathroom in the shadows to wash sheets stained by a dream. But there was no other choice. He wasn't going to call Delmira or Carmela, go through the humiliation. He would figure out a way to bring down the wet sheets to the back of the pantry where they kept the dirty clothes baskets.

Just after breakfast, Esteban Ferráns appeared at the house. Seeing him—"My brother, what a joy to lay eyes on you. What are you doing here?"—was forgetting the frightening moment from the night before. "I was sick of Maryland. I took the exams early and fled. I heard a rumor that you were in town." Luis Arsenio hugged Esteban; he asked Carmela for something to eat and sat with him in the living room.

He was different. His face—"Have you lost weight?"— seemed sharper. His eyebrows were bushy, his brow furrowed, even as he kidded and laughed, in full concentration. He was more ponderous on the surface of things, on the chairs of the vestibule. "I don't like the pharmacy; I think I am going to change my concentration." There was something calculating about him now, an immediate measuring of things, as if he was always keeping count.

"Business, Arsenio, that's me. If it was up to me, I wouldn't go back to school. I would stay here, in charge of my father's industries. But he insists . . . He says the future belongs to the professionals. And what about you, how are things?"

"Good, good. I am leaning toward military law. And I have an American girlfriend."

"Really, man?"

He told him about Maggie, "Redhead, my brother," and his face flushed in a mixture of shyness and arrogance. He was talking about his intimate matters, and that made him uncomfortable, but, on the other hand, he could finally brag about his conquest to one of his own. "And how did you catch that phantom?" A door opened behind him and in walked Maggie and her friends at Sam's Soda Shop. He invited her to the movies. The rest is history. Water under the bridge. It was good to share stories about Maggie with Esteban. It would finally erase the memories of Minerva, the dream, the stain from his treasonous body. While he talked, Luis Arsenio observed Esteban looking at him smiling, and he thought that perhaps he wasn't so different at all. He had been imagining things. Esteban was his friend for life, a kid anxious to enter the manhood that was the custom of the Ferráns, but a good soul. There they both were, again recounting adventures, the small ritual that constitutes the complicated mission of wholeheartedly becoming a man. To prevail.

"Well, I haven't been so lucky. I spend my time with a Venezuelan and another Puerto Rican on the faculty."

"Don't worry, Esteban, now with that English you are mastering . . . the gringas will fall at your feet. I'm sure you will bring one back after you graduate."

"Not so, my brother, I have other plans. The year you left I kind of became the boyfriend of Ángela Castañer, of the Castañers from Guayanilla."

"The owners of the importing business?"

"Those."

"Good, then, here's to you. Are things serious? Are there plans for a wedding?"

"There's a lot of time to go before that. I have a lot of years of 'experimentation' left. Oh, and speaking of experiments, why don't we take a night to go to Elizabeth's? When are you leaving?"

The father returned that afternoon with plans to visit a client. They left for the Playa sector, where the ample offices of the ports had his commissions. They went into Ferráns Brothers, Inc. Brilliant, sweat-soaked bodies emptied the bellies of ships. Mechanical levers carried bundles in the air. "Now it is easier to get merchandise," he said. "But it all comes from the North. What we don't get are passengers. Businessmen. They all stay in San Juan." They continued toward the shore; Luis Arsenio tried to pay attention to the familiar conversation: "This Sunday we'll invite your cousins to the house so you can see them. They have grown like weeds." But the only thing that occupied his mind was how to get out of the invitation to go to Elizabeth's.

The next week flew by with visits to his mother, who was recovering from a urinary infection, with one, two lunches with Esteban and the boys. "Pedrito has grown immensely fat." Luis Arsenio invented excuses each time that Alejandro Villanúa and Esteban invited him out to party at night. "Shit, man, that redhead has you perched on your suitcase." He would say that he had headaches that persisted all afternoon after he returned from the hospital. He spent a lot if time in his father's office, as well, sharing with Don Fernando the silence among the law papers and books, imagining his life as a lawyer when he returned. He would build an office just like his father's, adjacent to it. He would take care of customers while his father attended to the simpler contracts, leaving for him, the enterprising young lawyer, the more complex ones. Proudly, he would watch him from afar, seeing how his son, the worthy specimen of his stock, took his place in the world.

His father was right. He had grown used to his mother's delirium, her bony hands, her lost gazes that struggled to maintain his. He had even grown used to the melancholy of missing her as she had been before—anxious, out of control, but alive. The time for him to leave grew near. Four more days and he would be in Pennsylvania. He would soon leave again, now that he had a father with whom he felt close and complicit. But he knew that he no longer had to stay at home to keep him close. A web bound them tightly. Perhaps it was the sorrow of losing someone together. He could go in peace. Four more days and he would be in Maggie's arms again, taking the last classes of his career, sure of what he needed to do, the steps to take.

That afternoon he went for a walk in the town with Esteban. And he made a decision. It was unplanned, just because. Luis Arsenio—"You know what, brother?"—took a deep breath and told his friend, "I'll go have a drink at Elizabeth's, just for memory's sake." They walked under the *capás* and poincianas that flanked the edges of Parque de Bombas. Red, black, red, black, red, the building rose with each wooden plank painted in the colors of the fair. Inside, two fire engines were being polished by diligent hands. His heart beat serenely in his chest. He was going to miss his town, those afternoon strolls, time standing still in the corners of the sea salt that bathed the plaza, the church dozing in the breezes past the alamedas.

Night fell over La Alhambra. Luis Arsenio began to get ready to go with Esteban to Elizabeth's. He knew he would see Minerva there, but he was not seventeen anymore. His beard was not the first sign of his manhood but its proof. He had nothing to fear. After all, he was almost set to apply for specialization in the School of Law; he would ask Professor Allen about it when he got there. And because of this, he, Luis Arsenio, shaved in the shower, dressed to the hilt, and waited for Esteban to come pick him up in the vestibule of his house. He had grown accustomed to the cold; he could go farther north to continue his studies. That would please Maggie's parents and convince her to introduce him to her society, and then, when they found out who he was and what he came from, they would not raise any obstacles to the wedding. Minerva was an ancient rite of passage, something that is always forgiven of the señoritos of his elegant stock, even in Philadelphia. Elizabeth's also. A forgivable place, an escape valve to be able to continue to bear the weight of who one is. He was a Fornarís, different and distant, when it came down to it, from that other thing that kept the island pulsating on the side of the unspeakable, the quiet rage that paralyzes it in time, as if waiting for vengeance.

They had expanded the back rooms at Elizabeth's. The entrance road was paved with tar well into the woods. The lighting was also better. It no longer depended on a hand-cranked generator. Two rococo lamps that did not match at all with the façade of the whorehouse bathed the entrance steps—no longer pounded earth or irregular stones from the shores of the Portuguese—in light. The whole floor was cement. It was evident that Isabel had prospered.

She had also redecorated the inside, but the ambience was the same. Elizabeth's continued to be a huge bandstand with an immense bar. Laughter, hip-swaying, relaxation. Esteban and Luis Arsenio, along with a certain Benigno Castañer, cousin of Esteban's girlfriend, looked for a table. Isabel was not seated on her straw throne, but the empty chair was there, at a corner of the bar, illuminated by a light from the ceiling. The hostess worked the cash register. Isabel was not there. She had gone to deal with some fat cat.

"What do you mean, fat cat?"

"They come around more all the time. They say that

they saw the new Liberal representative for the House the other day."

"Politicians, in here?"

"Well, we are here. What's the big deal if they come as well?"

That they were there was nothing out of the ordinary; that musicians came was to be expected. In the end they were workers who made money bringing life to parties of this sort. But for politicians to come . . . In the swift city of Philadelphia such things did not happen. Oh, yeah? How different were the politicians from the workers in their country? What's more, how different were all of them, the musicians, the landowners, the representatives, the madam, the river and the underbrush, the sea salt, and the brothel? In this small island where everything is crammed together, how far apart can any of its components be? Luis Arsenio did not know and did not want to think about it, especially at the instant that he saw—he could swear he saw her with a soldier in the middle of the dance floor—Minerva.

He ordered a whiskey on the rocks while he watched her. He swore he heard the distant laugh and a fluttering of clothes. It did not faze him. He took a sip of his drink and continued watching her. Minerva was dancing with her back to him. The soldier grabbed her below the waist, right at the top of the curves of her ass. Luis Arsenio's blood grew hot; he felt a tickling all over his body, the grazes he remembered in between his thighs, in his fingertips. A satin dress covered Minerva and revealed in each step of the dance flesh even firmer than before. Luis Arsenio sighed deeply. It seemed that he recognized the remnants of a faint pumpkin aroma amidst the fragrances of cheap perfume, sweat, and smoke. He smiled. There was nothing to fear. He could, if he wanted to, quell the fever in his blood, go to bed with one or another. Nothing would happen.

In four days he would return to Maggie, after allowing himself that matter-of-course indulgence.

He gulped down his whiskey. At the same moment, Minerva grabbed the soldier by the arm and led him to the new wing of back rooms. Luis Arsenio got up from his chair. He could see all the girls who were being offered. There was one with red hair, but with the skin of a *mulata*, or maybe just a bit lighter. Yes, lighter, he confirmed as he approached her, leaving Esteban and the cousin talking about how to maximize the profits of the import business. She was lighter than Minerva, had Maggie's red hair, and green eyes like him, freckles like his; her smile was somewhat crooked, a loose woman, because she was that, a woman, much older than Minerva and Maggie put together, as if they had combined them. Two bodies in one. A woman around forty. He took her out to the dance floor. "I haven't seen you around here, handsome." He passed his hands over her back and hid his face in the folds of her neck. It smelled like smoke, like sour cologne. The woman was looking to start a conversation, but Arsenio went directly to the language of the bodies. A quick look, a giggle, a handful of ass. "It looks like you know what you're doing, what you want. Are you going to tell me your name?" In response, Luis Arsenio stuck his tongue in the mouth of that other redheaded, freckled gift of a woman. He pressed against her so that she would feel him hard against her legs. The seduction was complete. The woman understood right away and prepared the path to lead him to the room that was hers that night. She was ahead of him, laughing. Luis Arsenio behind. At that exact moment, her ass against his belly, thighs touching, Arsenio felt the force of a look burning his profile. He closed his eyes for an instant; a gust emptied his head. He did not have to confirm his suspicions. That look belonged to Isabel. He almost felt the echo of laughter gathering behind him. He decided to fight and not slacken. "I think I am going to tell you my name." "You don't have to—" He interrupted the redhead with a categorical response and enunciated "Arsenio, my name is Luis Arsenio Fornarís." And then felt as if his feet were on solid ground once again.

He spent a long time in the redhead's room, over two hours. He paid generously so that she would remember him and went down to meet his friends, his shirt unbuttoned and his hair disheveled. He almost brushed Minerva when he passed by her, leaning on the bar and talking to the hostess. He didn't even say hello to her. What for? Esteban was dancing with a girl and the Castañer cousin was nowhere to be seen. Perhaps at that very moment he was snorting on top of some girl, relieving himself as he had relieved himself with the redhead. He sat triumphantly in his chair and asked the waitress for a double whiskey. Isabel herself brought it to the table.

"Back around these parts, señorito?"

He wouldn't let her catch him by surprise. Not this time. He responded to all of the questions that the madam asked, looking her straight in the face: that he was studying in Philadelphia, that he had come to visit his mother, who was feeling better after an illness. "And this is, as they say, my farewell party."

"You are leaving so soon?"

"I have been home almost a month." He told her so that she understood that he was a man who was not in danger, free of her sphere of influence. He told her from the heights of his surname and to show her its sway.

Isabel also looked at him directly in the eyes. Her eyes did not shift for a second during their conversation. With an empty smile she wished him a good trip and a quick recovery for his mother and went to take care of clients. The young man stretched out in his chair and finished his drink. Benigno

Castañer was coming down the stairs from the second floor and Esteban was approaching the table. It was time to go.

It was easier to leave than to arrive. From Elizabeth's, from the island, from the coast. A question of getting in the right vehicles, in the car with the chauffeur, in the ship with the captain, in the train with the conductor. Taking his mother by the wrist and kissing her, hugging his father and smiling silently, arranging to go visit Esteban in Maryland, or for him to come to Philadelphia. Leaving was the easiest thing he had done in his whole life. But returning to Philadelphia was another story.

He made good time toward the city. At the train station, he paid a *negrito* to carry his luggage to a taxi. He was coming back with more things than he had brought. He carried the suitcases and the packages up the stairs of Fischer Hassenfield calmly. He unpacked. He did not feel an urgency to run out looking for Maggie. He was coming back with another burden. So he went out whistling a song on Pine up to Fortieth, where he arrived at the soda shop. He wanted a chocolate malt. Nowhere did they make malts like at Sam's. As many times as he asked the young man at Meliá for it, giving him specifications, he could never reproduce it. He would sit at one of the tables with a view of the street. He would say hello to anyone who was there; hopefully Stevie would be there, the one from commercial law. But then something happened that never should have happened, that he never imagined would happen. Maggie walked by hand in hand with some other guy right in front of his eyes, on the sidewalk by Sam's. She walked by and looked at him as if he were a stranger. She kept on going down the street, holding hands with that other young man—tall, blond, distinguished. They were joined by a resolute air as they moved away from him with firm steps. It seemed that they were going somewhere specific, fixed. Luis Arsenio remained behind clutching his malt, as he watched them disappear on the corner of Spruce, his eyes adrift.

He waited for her at the corner of Schuyler Hall, and she walked in with her head lowered. For a fraction of a second he seemed to recognize her, undulating steps, a look of intense concentration on her brow, her arms folded over her chest to hold her books. That girl looked like his Maggie, the redheaded one who on some night had looked at him exaltedly from the sheets of his unmade bed. Maggie slowed down when she heard him calling from behind her. She lowered her head even more, that beautiful head of red hair. Luis Arsenio thought, "It was all a misunderstanding. She will speak and everything will be resolved, like before." But when she raised her head, Maggie showed him a face made of cardboard, with a malleable and vacuous expression. Outside, it was sprinkling against the glass of the hallway windows. What power worked so precisely that it could destroy so much in so little time?

"When were you going tell me?"

"Tell you what, Louie?"

"About your new love . . ."

"It all happened very unexpectedly. We met on a leisurely day that my uncle James organized by the lake. I didn't know where to write you, since you were over on your island . . ."

"You could have waited."

"Feelings don't wait, Louie. Besides, you never thought that we were really a couple, did you?"

Time turned in on itself. Luis Arsenio's head began to buzz. It would have been better to stay quiet, not have said anything. Maggie Carlisle's words reverberated in the hallway, hollow, like her face.

"Then what happened was my imagination?"

"Louie, I don't know how it is done in your country, but here things are not so serious at the beginning. A woman does not belong to a man just because she lets him kiss her."

"You reciprocated every kiss."

"And it doesn't mean anything. Besides, how was I going to introduce you to my family? 'Hi, this is Louie Forneress from some island. I don't know his parents. I don't know if he has the means to support me. We want to get married and live in the jungle, in a tree with the monkeys. He is not as tall as Johnny Weismuller, but . . . "Me, Jane, you Tarzan."'"

"You know who I am. My father is a lawyer. My grandfather owns half the town. You didn't want to meet him."

"And now even less. Look, Louie, what matters is that I am in love with someone else. The quicker you accept it, the better."

He saw her disappear toward the classroom and he didn't want to have anything else to do with her. Time tore open in Schuyler Hall. That afternoon he did not go to class, nor the next, nor the following. Shame prevented him from going. Not sadness, shame.

Six

THAT PAIN AND nothing to show for it in her hands. That burning inside if she coughed, if she breathed too deeply. She who had thought her path was open and protected. A woman with a plan. Now she was stretched out in a hospital bed with stitches in her belly. And with nothing worth showing in her hands.

But she had the land. And having what she needed to have in her hands was going to cost her too much to do what she needed to do. Leonor told her about it. "He's getting married, Isabel. Don Antón is making the dress for the bride." She had somehow been able to think in the middle of the disaster. "No one will touch me again." She wasn't referring to the body but to that other dense thing that was the Isabel within. No one would ever put a finger on that Isabel again. That's what she meant.

Arabesques in Richelieu stitches, silk floral appliqués adorned with mother-of-pearl beads, all around the edges of the train that extended a meter and a half beyond the wedding dress to impose its gallantry during the bride's walk up the nave of the church. "How these people throw away money in times like these," she thought. But all the better for her. That wedding could not be more opportune. It allowed her to earn some good money without having to expend too much of herself. She was almost finished with the dress when Leonor arrived at the house biting her lips.

"What happened, Don Antón didn't like the borders?"

"No, Isabel, it's not that."

"Good, because my fingers are worn out from embroidering. When is he paying us?"

"Hold on, woman, I have something to tell you."

The deciding chip fell in its place. Leonor chewed her words, "At first, I didn't really know what was going on." But she told Isabel, "Because at the shop, the only thing that was ever mentioned was the name of the bride . . ." Fernando Fornarís was getting married. The fiancée's name was Cristina Rangel. Fornarís, the attorney, the son, came with her that afternoon and while he was there he took the opportunity to order some alterations to the dress coat that he was wearing for the occasion. "That's the groom," one of the girls in the shop mentioned. And so Leonor told her. A wind whirled in Isabel's head. She had been sewing the wedding dress for the future Señora Fornarís. Luxury and shroud. That was the end of the tender moments between bodies, the sweaty afternoons on the floor of the man who explored from inside with his green eyes. And there she was, embroidering such luxury for another, at the same time carrying the child of the fiancé. Isabel saw her reflection in the brow of her friend. She wanted to fall apart. But a powerful woman possessed her from inside; she came to her rescue.

Municipal Hospital is a catalog of decay. In the beds next to her there is an endless number of sick whores, one who is so incontinent that she pisses on herself just breathing. The smell of urine and alcohol mixes in with the smell of blood, of the poisons that they put on the sores of the prostitutes to disinfect them, iodine, coagulation, sweat. Isabel taps her belly. At that exact moment, Fernando Fornarís is getting married. And she has just cheated death and given birth to a son. Is he alive? She doesn't want to know. All she wants to do is focus on the price of surviving all that this has cost her. And on the land that is waiting for the next step in her plan.

But then she wants to vomit . . .

AT FIRST SHE DIDN'T FEEL anything. She was cleaning the ceramic tiles in the kitchen, which came down from halfway up the wall to the floor. The corners were black with soot. "That cook is so . . . ," she thought. "Letting grease spill wherever and then one has to scrub until the fingers want to break." All she did was look behind her before she crouched, to make sure that there was no one there, when she noticed his silhouette against the doorframe of the kitchen. He was standing there, looking at her. Isabel pretended she hadn't seen him. She hiked up her skirt and exposed her skin wet with the soapy water, letting that bluish tint hidden just under the skin shine, like the savage brilliance that shines over the sea but that comes from below. The attorney was struck down by the vision. And she, serene as a bird suspended in mid-flight, kept to the pace of her own plans. It was a game, the same one she played in the Tous house, and that she had sometimes played with the soldier Lowell. But now she was more in charge, her strategies more developed. She felt that look on her body for a long time. But she wasn't fazed. She kept doing her thing until the attorney pulled away from the door, defeated. "Easy, Isabel," she told herself, and then she knew that she was on the hunt for the young attorney. She didn't know why she wanted to seduce him. What could she get out of such a thing? For the moment, it was enough to take the measure of her game, that is, her capability.

She splashed a bucketful of clean water and then another over the freshly scrubbed tiles and went to look for a rag to dry the floor. In the hall she ran into the señorito again who, when he saw her standing, could not return her gaze. She didn't even try to lower her eyes; she fixed them on his face. The attorney's face grew red immediately. *These little masters, always the same.* Isabel continued barefoot down the hallway, wet, with a sure step. After a few seconds, she felt the door closing. The attorney had fled.

She washed some dirty glasses, put away the ironed clothes in the bedroom armoires and the chest by the bed, tidied up in the living room. Then she sat down peacefully to arrange her hair and put on her shoes, readying to leave. On the bureau in the living room, a piece of paper danced to the rhythm of the breeze. Rolled up in the paper was the cleaning payment for the month, plus two extra dollars. "Thank you," the note said. He signed it, "Fernando," no surnames, no titles. Just Fernando. Isabel put away the bills in her bra and left, making sure to close the door tightly behind her. The game was fun and, better yet, came with a prize.

The retching had passed and the nausea vanished. Isabel dried the sweat on her brow, her neck, her breasts. She almost perished in her own fluids. "They are the effects of the anesthesia. Didn't you know that your uterus is inverted?" "That explains everything," Isabel thinks. Now she knows why everything turns out upside down for her with men. What other thing can a woman with her uterus head over heels expect?

She still has the taste of bile in her mouth. Leonor will arrive soon, she senses. The mewls of a cat. "What I want is that they take him away from here. Take him to the father." She should pull him away from her breasts, or if not, wait until life has done her the favor of turning her right side in again. Dying would be a relief, a luxury that she doesn't feel would be hers anytime soon. And to live with the proof of his deceit is too much for her right now, now that she knows what she has to do. To become finally what her womb dictates, Isabel "La Negra" Luberza.

Leonor went by the hospital to visit her, as Isabel had intuited. "Here, the girls sent you some pigeon soup." Isabel felt like retching again. She turned away. "Well then, drink this orange tea for the nerves. I mixed it with *anamú* to give strength to the mother in you."

"You know what they just told me? That my uterus is inverted."

"Honey, just your uterus?"

They laughed some, Isabel holding the stitches in her belly. Leonor told her about things. "The house is fine. But, woman, that Carmiña is always late with the payments. We are going to have to throw her out." In the middle of the conversation, Isabel thought that she heard that mewl again, like a cat's. Her heart reared up in her chest. She looked at Leonor with her soul in two, her eyes filled with a terror that she could not explain. Leonor took her hand. "Calm down, Chabela, they already took him away." She didn't want to know where. "The father came to pick him up."

"I don't want him to see me, Leonor, don't let him see me." Every step in the hallway of the hospital reverberated with an eternity of echoes, announcing the arrival of the attorney within the walls where she was trapped. Sweat on her brow, her neck, her chest. Leonor began to pass her hand over her fore-head. "Breathe. You are drowning in your own air. Come on, breathe . . ." Dying would have been a relief. But she's alive. She has to keep on living.

Always to keep on living, even in those days. Everywhere folks getting fired, businesses closing, people with nothing to do. That Friday she was crossing Las Delicias, heading for Sergeant Peña's post in the market of the Gran Vía, when she bumped into Don Antón. "The world is coming to an end, young lady. I have almost no one ordering clothes. It's a major disaster, my girl, a very bad disaster indeed . . ." Strikes everywhere. "And what rich folks have the time to think about luxuries in the middle of so many strikes? And look how these indigents waste their time. Even in the plaza, in the light of day, they dare to conspire." Isabel looked to where Don Antón raised his tiny left arm. Perched on a bench in Las Delicias—surrounded by coastal workers and those who had been fired from jobs—rose up the irate profile of Demetrio Sterling.

". . . because they rob us of our sweat and keep us living on their crumbs; because they keep us in ignorance to hide the fact that there are countries where the people, the workers, are free and sovereign . . ." The furor of that voice was heard throughout the alameda. But while Demetrio Sterling roared against the "oppressors who fatten their bellies while we starve to death," Isabel guessed at something else in his face. His buddies couldn't do enough, in the crowd selling *Unión Obrera, El Jacho, El Águila,* and other papers that supported the Federation. And Don Antón, "I don't know why he's screaming so much; there isn't a bit of the worker about him. Nobody wants to give him a job." So the rumors were true. All the *negro* Sterling did now was unionize. That was why he was so thin and wrapped up in such a terrible rage, as if possessed. Demetrio stood up on that makeshift stage. He addressed hundreds of people and Isabel knew that behind his complaints another need was being nourished. Up there, on the pulpit of the Federation meetings, Demetrio Sterling had a fixed place in which to call himself what he was, from which he could look at anyone face to face with that sanguine gaze of an avenging angel.

Isabel crossed the Gran Vía toward Cruz. In the corner of the intersection with Calle de la Torre, Sergeant Peña walked slowly, looking over toward Demetrio and the meeting of the Federation. He watched each movement of the worker, but biding in the shadows, so as not to soak his drill uniform in sweat. "Here, so you get yourself another one," Isabel told him, putting the payment of two pesos in his hand.

"Full payment, with a little bit extra. Business must be going well."

Things were going well, contrary to her expectations. So far that year they had closed down seven cigar factories, and the sugar mill at Merceditas had cut down on the amount of land harvested after the last strike by the Federation. Their administrators did not want to risk what had happened a couple of years before, when they lost four thousand tons of sugar after hectares of sugarcane fields were set on fire in vengeance. Pueblo Chiquito, Canteras, the workers' towns were all powder kegs on the verge of exploding. When the cart drivers, the stevedores, or the tobacco workers weren't picketing at a strike, they were looking to escape, even if it was at the bottom of a bottle. She provided the way. Yes, the moonshine business was going well, but she wasn't going to tell the guard.

"If I put in a little extra, it is to keep you happy."

"*Pues*, let me return the favor. I foresee a storm tonight. Take shelter, so it doesn't take you with it. Another round up of the whores, the hoi polloi. The plaza is packed with them."

Isabel watched the goings-on at Las Delicias. At the far end, the crowd that had been listening to Don Demetrio's speech started to disband. But life went on, business went on. You didn't stop working. Carts and covered wagons unloaded merchandise at the shops. Some employees helped to carry the boxes inside, who knows for how many cents. Meanwhile, in the corners, baggy-eyed looks waited anxiously for someone to call them for any kind of work, sweeping the sidewalk, washing the floor tiles of the entrances, loading the shelves. The street was full of coastal runners. The majority of them were women, girls recently arrived from the country who were looking for any kind of employment. When there was no other recourse, they sold themselves for pennies. They reminded Isabel of herself, or what she might have become without the moonshine and without the extra money that she earned from the attorney. Isabel knew that they would even work just for food; they would sell themselves to the shop owners for a dry corner where they could doze. And that even if their bellies were empty, they would seek Isabel out to buy a little shot of rum. She sometimes felt like giving it to them for free. "Are you crazy, woman? What about us?" Leonor reminded her. "Toughen up, Isabel." But she wasn't able to, not completely.

"Let them be, all they're doing is looking for something to eat," she told Peña.

"Tell that to the Civic Ladies or the Servants of Mary. They're not fooled."

"Of course, since they go to bed with a full belly."

"Loyal clientele, Isabel, that's what they have, a loyal and captive clientele. They are called husbands."

"Maybe I'll see if I can get me one of those, so I don't have to work so hard. See you later, Peña, stay in the shadow."

Isabel changed direction. She had made her daily payment. Now she was going to the home of the attorney.

The cleaning of floors for the attorney had become an empty pretext. Isabel went to see him just to have him all over her. And then he gave her the money. "To help you with your expenses," he joked. On top of the living room bureau he left some bills along with a note that he signed simply "Fernando." Isabel was bothered by the arrangement, but how could she put a stop to it? It was the flesh that burned and to which she responded to allow her to do all her other things, attend to her moonshine business, pay the municipal officials and guards, travel to San Antón to look for cheaper suppliers. Fernando Fornarís helped her to sleep better, to not feel so alone in all the delirium.

She turned on Calle de la Torre and covered the rest of the distance to the attorney's apartment. A weak sun shone, as on the day when everything began. Light blue linen dress with sleeves down to the elbow, a belt with a wide buckle over her waist, careful, keep to the shadows, not to ruin it with sweat. He opened the door in a long-sleeved shirt. She had wanted to see him dressed up, and that's why she hadn't changed. She walked around the apartment a few times, pretending to do things, in her street clothes. She didn't even know why she wanted to make her case. She was not some beggar starving to death. She was a woman of means, who worked and had a plan. She was not sure why she wanted to show the attorney that side, her secret self. But she showed him for a moment and then changed into her work clothes. She came out of the bathroom barefoot, with a simple cotton skirt and handkerchief on her head. She looked for the buckets, filled them with water, looked for the brush and the soap. She tossed sudsy water on the floors and began to scrub, on her hands and knees, her skirt balled up in between her legs. The attorney stood by the door.

This time he was silent, absorbed in thought. Isabel wanted to return his gaze, "that lonely gaze," and she turned. She looked at him straight on with her deep almond eyes. From the depths of her body she looked at him. The attorney crossed the length of the kitchen as if crossing a sea at full sail. Isabel turned around completely, on her back. And then she did not know what else to do but give herself to the weight of a warm body on top of hers. She opened her mouth; she opened herself completely. The soap suds made her back glide on the floor.

She told him as soon as he came to the door. "Look, Mr. Attorney, this can't go on like this." And he— "Go on how?"— was already reaching for her waist. "Either you let me clean your floors or I won't come back."

"Do what you want, Isabel." His lips settled like petals on her neck; his lips made her wet, his fingers butterflies in her stomach. And she, "Let me change, find the bucket."

"Of course," he whispered near her ear, not stopping her. She fell into the tangle of his hands.

"Wait, you're not letting me think."

"You don't need to." But she did need to. She needed to disentangle herself from those arms, to surface from those lips that drowned her with wetness and need. What was the name of her need?

And now, she did not want him to see her. May their paths never again cross. Leonor made herself comfortable by her bed. "Look, Isabel, it doesn't have to be now, but he told me that if you allowed him to visit you, he could explain everything. It doesn't have to be now; when you get a little better . . ." Leonor could not quite understand. That man could not ever come near her again. There was something in him, Isabel was not sure what it was called, that completely sucked up her will. And now she was going to need all of it. "Is it true that new soldiers are arriving?" She changed the topic. Her friend frowned. What were those questions from the bed of a woman who had been on the very brink of death, who had just renounced her son? Was she breaking down once and for all? But Isabel insisted she felt more like herself again. "Are there many soldiers arriving?"

"Less, now that the war is over in Europe."

"Those soldiers must be bored, then. Don't you think they would want to wander out of the fort? Take a little stroll, have a drink or two . . ."

Now she understood the gist of the conversation. Leonor looked at Isabel out of the corners of her eyes. How could her friend go so easily from being so broken to talking about things with such granite strength?

"Isabel, spit it out. What are you thinking?"

The words rose calmly out of her throat, as if it were not she who was speaking them. One by one they circled around Isabel's mouth, which effortlessly found the meaning of all of them. Now that she was returning from the utmost, now that she had not died, she could say that she, Isabel Luberza Oppenheimer, was the owner of a little less than three *cuerdas* of land on the shores of the Portuguese River. "A gift from the attorney." She began to explain things to Leonor in the lobby of the Municipal Hospital. "He arrived one day, without warning, with some papers under his arm. I don't know if it was because he had noticed my belly. But he gave them to me, Leonor. Tell him not to come around here anymore. Tell him that his account with me is settled." And she went silent. Her fingers passed over the stitching in her belly. She was again overcome with nausea. Once again she felt herself fainting on the mattress of her bed, like that day when Fernando drank a big gulp of coffee looking at her, and then another one, smiling, wanting to gulp her down. The attorney got in between her legs and then rose until he had her pressed under his weight, which he let fall completely on the solid flesh of the woman.

After the run-in with the flesh, the attorney ran out. Isabel got dressed to go. On the bureau of the living room was the property title of those lands and a little note signed, "Fernando." La Negra reached out her hand and took the title, picking it up with her fingers. "Isabel Luberza Oppenheimer," it read. ". . . landowner up to the boundary that adjoins the farms of the Fornarís family on one side," it stipulated. Now she was the owner of a property. She took the paper with her name and put it away with her things. Isabel changed and fixed her hair. She descended the stairs of the attorney's apartment, making sure that the doors were well locked. She would not say anything to Leonor about the title. She would not even ponder too much herself on the weight of that thing in her hands. She was going to keep on living like always, cleaning that floor, selling her moonshine, giving the municipal authorities their cut. She would save all the money that she could. It wouldn't be much, but drop by drop it would fill the carafe and who knows what else. Property owner. It might be in a hundred years, but she was sure that she would have her own roof over her head one day, a roof that she could claim as her own. Now nobody could take away that option. They would have to kill her first.

Visiting hours were coming to an end. An intern passed by on his rounds, took her temperature, prescribed antibiotics. "Since we had to sacrifice tubes, ovaries, we don't want you getting an infection." "I am an empty sack, never again a mother; I am a lightweight and empty sack," thought Isabel. A defeated will and something that hardened inside her. Those two forces were going to split her in two. But the other woman who possessed her took over.

"Don't let anyone know of the details. Go to San Antón and find a construction foreman through Demetrio," she told Leonor. "Make sure it's cheap. What I want is a simple construction, something like a ranch house. Something that doesn't seem ostentatious from the outside, that doesn't call attention to itself. Tell him to find you carpenters from the Federation. That as soon as I get out of here, we will sit down to seal the deal. We are going to open a dance hall, and we are going to be swimming in money, Leonor. A lot of money. The way we have lived up to now is over."

Alone

POOR LITTLE ONE, the three poor little ones that wanted to go down to town. They talk about a certain Isabel, very rich, they say, like I could have been if it wasn't for this sanctuary. It's probably the same one. It could have been me but for the Child. You, dumb old woman? You'll always be as mangy as a goat's knee. You'll never have anything to call yours, except for the floor of my sanctuary. That's what you think, Virgin of Shit. She has more glory and more power. I could have been her, with a mantle fancier than yours. She dresses in silk, she is as dark as charcoal, like you Doña Montse, yesyesyes, to hell with perdition, like the very Virgin, but she dresses like a film star. She has a house down there on the coast, a sanctuary.

Poor three little ones. From Tres Marías, which already looks like a stable for old horses. The roof is falling down; water leaks in from between the planks of the house. The poor girls have to do it in moth's nests. You see me, you see them. Like the bitches they are. What do you know, Montserrat, if the only thing with balls that has ever approached you is the bull that you frightened away from the cattle rancher? Does God have balls? Blasphemous old woman! Well, leave the girls alone. Poor three little ones. We're going down into the valley, they say. We're going to La Negra. And not to you, Montserrat, for not even the pilgrims come to see you anymore. We're going to Elizabeth's. I smile. They don't know that I know what they're talking about. She showed up one day, when I was with the Child in town because he had an infection. Poor little ones, they want to go down; I feel like going with them.

"She made herself a mansion and has a chauffeur and everything."

"I know her."

"What do you mean you know her, Doña Montse, if you spend your whole life in that grotto?"

"Don't think that I'm such a saint."

I told them. I saw her once. But they don't believe me.

THE CHILD IS FOUR YEARS old. "Don't worry, Señor, there is nothing wrong with the child," and the attorney doesn't know any better than to believe the Harpies. He didn't even go down to see him. He told me, "Doña Montse, I have some clothes for the child. Another white shirt, a knitted cap." The Child burning with a fever and he brings him a sailor's suit. "Montse, don't go worrying the attorney. Don't go telling him the Child is ill. He'll get better with *hierbabruja* anyway." And I, wicked, miserable, and filthy one, say nothing, and the attorney leaves, says nothing—and what doctor are we going to call at midnight? Do you remember, Montse? That was a long time ago. How long now, months ago, during the rainy season, and I, Purest Virgin, safeguard us, Patron of Heaven, protect us, with ice compresses and let the Child be eaten by ants. Yesyesyes, Montse, now what will the attorney say? She let Robertito get wet; she let him out in the cool evening air. And the Child, Godmother, his little hand red in mine, his feverish head on my lap, Black Virgin of those Harpies, they want you to die, but I will not allow it.

For days in the Kingdom of the Low Grounds hiding under my other name.

Me with the feverish boy in my lap. What's your name, *negra*? Montserrat. But the boy reminded me, that's not your name, and I told the truck driver, I told him. María de la Candelaria Fresnet, and I wanted to let go of the boy right there, throw him down a ravine, and climb on the truck driver's thighs, slip me on, you Christian, I am the apparition. I am Candela, the fire. Punish me, mighty Mother; protect me, merciful Mother; strengthen me, Mother of Humanity. It was Calvary, but the Child is fine now.

Freed from the Father, freed from the Son, freed from the Holy Spirit. It was pure hell when I had to go down to the Salesian brothers. They took me to the Charity Clinic. This boy is very ill; they took me to the clinic. Needles, cold metals on his chest, his pigeon's chest, pigeon's chest. Infection. Who is the father, and I was going to say I was, but I said the lawyer, and they sent a boy who brought him; and the mother, they asked, I was going to say it was me, but just then the attorney arrived and he murmured something underneath his breath, but I heard it clearly. He said the name of the Unnameable. And me yesyesyes, the Child, who puts his feverish little hand on me. Godmother, I am thirsty, and I run out looking for water, looking for lemon juice, looking for sweetened water with sesame, like my boy, like the mother who dresses in silk and I run through a town that I do not know.

Four days and nights and on the fifth day we left, freed by the Salesian fathers. Hail Mary, full of grace, the Lord, the Lord is with thee, blessed are thou amongst women and blessed is the fruit of thy womb, Jesus. Before leaving the town, we went to the cathedral of two peaks to give thanks. I have a name, Godmother. My name is Roberto Fernando. I wanted him to be named Rafael. My name is Roberto Fornarís, the nurse who took care of me told me. His little hand in my stinking hand, yesyesyes, in my common dismal hand, his penitent little hand in mine. I have a name, Godmother, and then the Señora appears. Right in the middle of the plaza, in the middle of the street, in the middle of the day. Blinding light that illuminates my face and the face of the Godson, which turns the color of quinces. His face solidified honey when the Señora appears and blocks our path. The Child becomes a mere boy again, but it's a matter of just looking at them, a matter of looking at the semblance in their faces, hers, his. Everything is revealed then. She is the Progenitress, she is the lover of the Holiest One, she is the one who proffers, proffers the candles for my sleeplessness. She doesn't recognize the Son who had been waiting years for her Revelation. Who is that woman, Godmother? Her name is Isabel and she is bad woman. A bad woman yesyesyes, when what I wanted to do was get on my knees and weep, here I am señora, do with me what you want, here I am with the boy in my lap. Take me with you, let me approach you.

I tell them I saw her once.

And from below, "Doña Montse, Doña Montse, Doña Montse." The pilgrims at the base of the hill. They should go play with their asses, but I go, to open the sanctuary so that they kneel before you. They say that she throws great parties, on the Feast of the Three Kings, and that then she wanders the countryside looking for *marucas* for her sanctuary. "She came around here and she took Saturnina. Here, at Tres Marías, not so long ago. It's better if we just go there." Poor little ones, the girls told me everything. I'm going with them. I'm closing this stinking cave. Don't you dare, you shriveled one. You, who is going to come near you? I'll help them with their toiletries, at least that I know about. "Good morning, Doña Montse, where do I put the offerings?" Better than adjusting the mantle of this dull Virgin. Better than adjusting your crown and your cape. At least those others attend to their parishioners. Opaque light, fire inside. The only thing you're good for is to listen to the complaints of these simpletons. You don't touch them, you don't soothe them, you're worthless. Black Virgin, white boy. The Child.

"Look, Godmother, it's not so bad." They'll show him a trade. "We're building a naval base. I learned how to place cable tubes and connect electricity outlets." That's what the Child told me when we spoke that one time. The attorney spent days on the Child's case. He took him out of the town. He saved him in his Packard. About a month later, he returned. It wasn't a month. What do you know, hollow Virgin, what do you know about how time passes? He returned about a month later and took me into town. He phoned the Child. I heard his voice. From Town Hall. "We get up at four in the morning to exercise. We run five miles and then we work like dogs building the base." About a month. You cried like a fool, quite a scene you made. "Don't you get tired, my love; how is your health?" That was a long time ago; you don't even realize it, dumb old woman. Don't you see how much the Child has grown? Don't mock me, Montserrat. I am no longer bound to the sanctuary. Don't mock me, because any day I'll grab my three rags and close up this house, and there won't be a hair left of me. You wouldn't dare. That's what you think. See who lights your candles when I split from here.

She counts the cents in the collection. A dollar and a half. The Child is coming yesyesyes. A measure of sugar. I am going to make a yam pie for him to take on the bus to the sugar mill. Holy Mother of God, it's not a sugar mill, it's a base. Same thing. I am going to make him a yam pie and sweetened sesame water so that he sees how much I think about him and miss him. The old woman leaves the grotto open. Another pilgrim kneels before the Virgin. Here in town nobody remembers about the cattle rancher. Here in town it was blood washed away by the river. Broken slabs, it washed it away. Perhaps it is time for the Child to return.

She walks toward the little house, climbs the steps. I am going to make him a yam pie. She passes by the Child's room. Full name, Roberto Fernando Fornarís. Private. "You have to start somewhere, Godmother." This Sunday he will come visit me. I better wash his bedsheets and his civilian clothes. He'll probably stop at Tres Marías. He won't even pay attention to you; he'll be so starving for women. I'll go with him then. And we'll drink and smoke. I'm going to make him a yam pie and sweetened sesame water, but later. I have to wash his clothes. The old woman takes a box from underneath the Child's bed. One poplin garment, three linen ones, a little pair of worn pants, with the button missing. The Child's little clothes. The Child whose ears never quite healed.

THIRD VISIT

But there are times when there is not time for all that close listening, all those exceptions, all that mercy. There is no time, so we fall back on the rule. And that is a great pity, the greatest pity. That is what you could have learned from Thucydides. It is a great pity when we find ourselves entering upon times like those. We should enter upon them with a sinking heart. They are by no means to be welcomed.

—J. M. Coetzee, *Age of Iron*

Magnificat Dominum anima
Madnam me facit Dominus

The Just Judge

(A WOMAN'S PRAYER)

MAY THE HOLY Company of God be with me and the Mantle of the Blessed Mary, his mother, shelter me and protect me from the dangers of evil. Hail, Mary, full of grace, Dominus is with thee, deliver me from all spirits, baptized and unbaptized. Christ triumphs. Christ reigns. Christ, defend me from the dangers of evil. By your leave I ask of the Lord and Just Judge, the only Son of the Holy Virgin Mary, He who was born on that solemn day, not to let me die, or let them wish me wrong. May those with eyes not see me, hands not touch me, iron not wound me, knots not bind me. Like God said to Libeón, they will not be able to harm me with three stones, me or anyone who loves me or defends me, even though they don't proclaim it. Amen, Jesus, Mary, and Joseph. *Dominus tecum herrum carrum.*

Merciful Holy Mary, mother of Our Lord Jesus Christ, who went into the Tartary Hills, who found the Great Serpent; and without great effort you bound it, with a swab of holy water dabbed it, and from the world removed it; soften my enemies' hearts. Let them have eyes but not see me, feet but not catch me, iron but not wound me, knots but not bind me. Let them fall by the swords of St. Julian, be dabbed by the milk of the Virgin, be buried in the Holy Sepulcher. Amen, Jesus, Mary, and Joseph, three Our Fathers for the passion and death of Our Lord Jesus Christ. This is the prayer of the Holy Shirt, of God's living Son, that I put on against my Enemies; let them have eyes but not see me, feet but not reach me, hands but not touch me, iron but not wound me, knots but not bind me. For the three crowns of the Patriarch Abraham, I offer this prayer in the union of my person. May my enemies come to me as tame as the Lord Jesus Christ went to the wood of the cross. St. Ildefonsus, holy confessor of our Lord Jesus Christ, you who blessed the host and the chalice in the Main Altar, bless my bed, my body, everything around me. Deliver me from bewitchers, from enchanters and people with ill intentions. By three I measure you, by three I break you, by the grace of God and the Holy Spirit. Amen, Jesus, Mary, and Joseph. This is the prayer of the Just Judge.

Pilgrimage

"I'M SHIPPING OUT, Godmother, I'm shipping out. They're sending me to Norfolk." And where is that, Child? Where, Holy Virgin? Likely very far from here. Beyond Hormigueros, beyond Hatillo del Mar, the old woman thinks. Is it beyond the sea? My forgiveness and the mercy of the Father. Kneel and ask for forgiveness, arrogant old woman. See what you did when you said that you were closing the sanctuary? See how you provoke the ire of the Lord? The old woman looks at the Child, who is there in front of her. They have cut off his tight curls. His little head reveals only points where there used to be hair. The color has risen in him. He is darker now, the color of a man that lives by his hands and sleeps in his sweat. But his eyes sparkle more than ever, and his beard grows thicker on his chin. Freckles have appeared. He has never looked so much like the Father.

"What about the attorney, Rafael?"

"He barely comes by the base. I took a public car."

"He didn't bring you in the Packard?"

"It's been months since I last saw him."

"Months?"

"But wasn't it yesterday that you stabbed the cattle rancher?" the old woman wants to ask, but something tells her, "You're wrong." Something that is not the Virgin, that overwhelms her even more than the voice of Montserrat in her head. Just yesterday, she sees herself going up the stretch of Camino Nuevo toward the town, passing by the Salsipuedes barrio before arriving at the Church of Nuestra Señora. "Where have they taken my Child?" And the attorney bringing her back in the Packard. Yesterday she also made a yam pie, yesterday also the Child was at Tres Marías spilling his rage. Yesterday also he arrived stinking of blood and liquor.

"You must be as hungry as a thousand devils. Should I make you lunch, Child?"

The old woman stops by the straw rocking chair on the balcony of the little house and trembles. She trembles toward the stairs and descends them one by one. "Let me help you, Godmother." The Child holds her. Private Roberto F. Fornarís. He should have been called . . . she forgets. You will fall under your own weight, Montserrat. You'll fall on the black earth, black as you. You will shatter into a thousand pieces and no one will be able to tell which pieces are your body and what is the mud or the cow dung. You will fall and no one will remember who you were. The old woman trembles on the way to the fire. "I made you some corn-flour empanadas. Let me open a *yuntita*; they're hot." The Child comes to her. "You shouldn't have, Madrina." If I shouldn't have, then what the hell am I doing still alive?

"So then when do you leave?"

"Next month, Godmother."

"During Holy Week."

"No, Godmother. It's the middle of September now."

Yesterday she was bringing down a bunch of braided palms for the Virgin. The pilgrims had asked the old woman, "Doña Montse, Doña Montse, why don't you give us the statuette of the Virgin? It will be a welcome rest for you." But the Virgin: don't you dare take me out of here, fetid old woman. This is my sanctuary. These lands are my possession. The Father gave them to me for watching over the Chosen One. How dare you, you piece of weather-beaten plaster. These lands are mine. You can't take them from me. Yesterday she threw some braided palm leaves in her face, the kind that they give parishioners at the beginning of Holy Week. And is it already September? Crazy old woman, you don't even know how time passes any-more. If they take me from the sanctuary, you'll no longer know what day it is or the hour when death arrives.

"You know, Child, they came to ask me for the Virgin. The little priests at the church are going to take her."

"I think it's a good idea, Godmother. You're too old for all that fuss."

THE CHILD EATS; SHE WATCHES him and smiles. His fingers get all greasy from the empanadas. "And besides, Godmother, they pay well. I'm going to send you the checks so you put the money away for me, and when I return, we'll build us another house in town, so you won't be so alone here." Yesyesyes. With this Virgin stuck inside my head. Take her out of my head, Child. Take her out because she doesn't even let me sleep in peace. "Don't worry, Godmother, I'm going to get you another house so that we can leave this place forever."

The Child finishes eating; he takes off his shirt and lies

down to take a little siesta. A breeze blows on the green of the hill and she sees him as if twice, entering the door of the sanctuary as well. She brushes off her eyes. The Child sleeps his siesta in the hammock of the porch. Then who is that other down in the grotto? Don't play dirty tricks on me, wicked one. Don't go putting visions in my head; not even for them will I come down to see you, just so you know. I am going to tell the priests yes, so that they come and take you from here forever. And then you're going to be as alone as a finger. As alone as shame. Because I'm leaving with the Child. Where, brilliant one, isn't the Child going off to war? Impossible. The Child came to visit me.

The old woman examines her godson's shirt. There is a little tear in the sleeve. She takes out her needle and spool and begins to mend it. The Child awakes from his siesta.

"Are you going to go by Tres Marías?"

"No, Godmother, the conditions were that I would not stop in town."

"What conditions, Child?"

"Don't you remember, because of the cattle rancher . . ."

The Child lowers his head. He becomes serious, turbid. "Virgin of Montserrat who protected the cattle rancher from a runaway bull, saving his life during the adversity. Black Virgin of Montserrat, white Child on her lap."

"It's better, then, that you don't go. Better that you stay here quietly until the attorney arrives."

"The attorney is not coming by here anymore. It worries me to leave you so alone."

"Aren't you coming next week?"

"No, Godmother, they're shipping me out. They're sending me to war."

The old woman thinks cattle rancher, thinks Virgin, thinks ears, thinks Harpies.

She looks at the Child, his skin so burnt by the sun, his scalp so cropped. She watches his callused hands. Holy Virgin, protect him, let him at last rest. The old woman opens her mouth and asks:

"But what other war are they sending you to?"

One

Don Demetrio looked at her crossly when he found out that she was going around town looking for builders to help her build a house with a few rooms by the shores of the river. Isabel had sent Leonor to tell him. But he did not want to act right away. The girl had lost a child; at least that is what he imagined when he saw Leonor arrive as she did, all contrite, with that strange message from Isabel.

"She wants you to get a master builder and some carpenters."

"But for what, *muchacha*?"

"Demetrio, who knows. I don't dare to contradict her, because she is very ill, recovering from the operation they had to perform on her."

"Do you think that it affected her mind?"

"I don't think so. There's some land in San Antón that is hers and she wants to build there. She said the sooner the better."

"Land that is hers? It can't be Maruca's and Casiana's because that parcel is already occupied."

"No, Don Demetrio, other land. You just find her a master builder. You know how Isabel is when she gets an idea in her head. Who knows if her zeal will last, but I'm not going to contradict her."

He wasn't contradicting, but it was difficult to take the message seriously. Land near the river? Everyone in San Antón knew that that was a private farm, owned by the businessman Fornarís. You didn't have to be too quick to understand what was going on. They had bought the girl's silence by giving her a little parcel of land to calm her down. That kid that Isabel had lost was either the father's or the son's. And Don Luis was too old for such things.

But then he ran into her in the barrio. "Leonor came looking for me," he commented when he saw her arrive at San Antón, with a measured step, holding her belly. He didn't want to ask about the pregnancy or the fruit of it. "She told me that you want to build a house by the shores of the river." Isabel nodded. "A place to meet, Don Demetrio. A place where the girls can work."

SHE HAD HEARD THEM ARGUE through the planks of the sewing room that they now occupied. Pedro and Leonor, Leonor and Pedro. Her friend had taken up a husband, at the exact time that Isabel had been hiding in secret as the lover of the attorney Fornarís. She didn't like this Pedro. Too much sweet talk, too much pampering and tumbles in the bed. Then he would disappear for whole weeks, leaving Leonor up in the air, waiting for him. Afterward, he returned to look for Leonor at the little house on Calle Romaguerra. "I had to go, my love, because there was work in Salinas and I stopped there. You know how bad things are, and there is so much competition among bricklayers in town." And Leonor, so that her steady one would not disappear, opened her purse of profits from the liquor sales. "I'm embarrassed to accept any more money from you, Leonor. But I need it for my expenses." Her friend fell for it every time. "Construction is bad, but you know that as soon as it picks up, I'll pay you everything I owe you, and I'll get you a better place than this one, a thousand times better." Isabel kept an eye on him, enraged. She measured each step of this Pedro, who began to wander like master and señor through the house that was not his but hers. He also played the fool at night, poking around the shelves in the kitchen. He pretended to be lost when Isabel lit the oil lamp. But he wasn't fooling her. He was looking for the jars of moonshine. She had to hide them in her room. She would have to talk to Leonor, before things got as dangerous as a nest of fire ants.

What changed color were the cheeks of her friend. From one day to the next. Her deep mahogany color turned to purple, a blow from a man to the cheekbone. Isabel was returning from making the rounds with the rum suppliers in San Antón. She arrived with two carafes and a basketful of liter jars to start distributing the liquor. She found Leonor in the living room holding a wet rag to her face. Reddened eyes, head downcast in shame. Isabel sat down beside her, crouched down to look at her. Leonor pulled her face away, but Isabel did not let her slip away. She lifted the rag from the side of her face. The skin was tight around the swollen and bloody cheekbone.

"You're going to let him treat you like this? Because if you let this go on without putting a stop to it, you're never going to be able to put a stop to it."

Leonor let out a long sigh, and then walked to her room and began packing the few things that the bricklayer kept in the house.

"Will you come with me?"

They both made their way to the Joya del Castillo barrio. They crossed the plaza and walked on Calle Estrella until they arrived. "They tell me that the bar where Pedro spends all his free hours is over there. Liar. Me thinking he was looking for work." On the way, they bumped into some young women. "Migrants," they murmured pityingly.

Joya del Castillo extended like a scar down the middle of the feudal town. A neighborhood of whores and *pleneros*. The porches of each of the houses opened their doors to the midafternoon. The women came out in their girdles to take in the fresh air, get the pieces of clothing used and washed the night before, which would be dry by that time. Leonor was wrapped up in a quiet fury, mumbling under her breath, "Look what he did to my face, that delinquent. Where was my head? I should have left him long ago. What was he good for? What is any man good for, Isabel . . ." Isabel listened to her friend and said nothing. Fernando, she thought. That man with whom she had an understanding, would he be good for something after all?

When they had almost arrived at the bar, they heard a ruckus.

"You bitch, take your ass to someone else to finish raising you."

It was Betania, an old hooker. Everyone in town knew about her temper. She had another hooker by the hair and was dragging her around from one end of the street to the other.

"I told you not to frighten my clientele. What do you come to sell here anyway, all bones, you?"

Other women surrounded them. Behind them, men holding liquor bottles stopped to watch. That was the entertainment for the afternoon. The girl that Betania jostled around was crying, begging to be released. "For the love of God, let me go!" Her eyes jumped out of her head, as if looking around in case someone she knew might show up. Isabel felt like jumping in to save her. But where to break the circle? How to fight against that ring of women who were experts in the attack, the blade, stronger than she? She had another duty, to help out Leonor. So the hookers were left behind.

They went into the bar.

"Has anyone seen Pedro the bricklayer?"

"He hasn't been around today."

"When you see him, tell him to look for somewhere else to live and somebody else's life to ruin. Not to bother looking for Leonor. Here is all his shit."

They went back together, walking slowly. The street was calm by now. Leonor took measured steps, wrapped up in her own thoughts. Isabel let her be. But on the return trip they bumped into the girl again. She was cast aside in a vestibule, examining the scratches from Betania. Helpless. That girl would not be able to compete. She would not be able to confront the tough women of Joya del Castillo, who covered the streets in the territory all the way up to the Plaza Las Delicias. She would starve to death first. But if she switched territories, if she stopped prowling the streets and offered the clients something those other women did not have, a quiet, discreet place, where any person (even the señoritos and—why not?—the attorneys) could go to set free their desires . . . then she might have a chance of surviving. They would need a person who would offer them what she had, who would give them a roof and take care of the clients. Someone who knew numbers and could buy and sell. Rum, services, girl migrant workers. It was all the same merchandise, after all. Better to sell oneself than to be sold, to be the owner of the merchandise. There's something to this, Isabel thought. Perhaps here was the missing piece for the good life.

WITH THE STITCHES IN HER belly, she went to conceive in full her task by the shores of the Portuguese River. At first she only imagined one house, with two floors, perhaps, and three or four bedrooms. Then she had the courage to imagine a place where she could do what she could not on Calle Romaguerra. Sell alcohol, take care of the girls . . . She worked up the courage to do more. She imagined a big hall where people would dance, just like the quarters of Bumbúm Oppeheimer, which were now a cobbler's workshop. Just like that, tall ceilings like that house, but in hers there would be chairs so that the clients could sit and give free rein to their leisure. She would need some good chairs and some tables, ice boxes, electric lights, and a generator. Her clients would enter a place of rest where they could drink, talk, and ask girls to dance.

Isabel contemplated the nature of the breezes and how they blew over her lands. A great boulder marked the first wetlands on the riverbank. She would make the windows face in that direction, so that the breezes from the riverbank soothed the sweaty bodies. By those windows she would put a stage, not too big, wide enough to hold a simple brass band, *pleneros*, local musicians. There were many in the barrio, the ones who played in the municipal band, in the small square at the plaza, or those who worked in the pit at La Perla Theater when they presented

zarzuelas or played for the society balls. She would hire them
for the weekends; the rest of the time the music would come
from the Victrola. The girls would work alongside it. Right
there at the bar to better hook the clients. But where would
they take them? It was necessary to build some bedrooms, with
windows also facing the river. "See if you can figure out how."
The woman within gave good advice. She would have to build
makeshift rooms so that the girls could take the clients to a safe
place. If not, she would get into quite a fix with the neighbors,
naked couples tiring the flesh in the pasture, or in the houses and
the patios, hitched to the gates like dogs. It was best to avoid such
difficulty and friction, to accept plainly that her place could be
nothing else but a house of assignations, a house with windows
facing the shores of the river. Only those who could pay would
enter that house. Yes, pay, no flesh would be free, and no desire
would turn treacherous against the body of another woman to
destroy her, or leave her starving and chewing on dust, cast her
down on the ground where she would have to beg for crumbs.
No misery, no misery, the misery of not being able to raise one's
chin. No one would have to lower their head in Isabel's place.

THE IDEA HAD taken her over once they had returned from Joya
del Castillo. All that was needed was to find some sacks, sew
them up, and give them out to everyone. Leonor would move
back into her room. In the sewing room there would be enough
space for four of the girl migrant workers. Not too many to start
off. They could pay a daily fee, twenty cents per space. Night
was falling. She was mending clothes on the porch of the house.
She seemed calm. Maybe it would be good to talk about it.

"Listen, Leonor, we're never going to use all the space in
this house and there are so many people out on the street . . ."

"We haven't finished throwing Pedro out and you already want to play the Good Samaritan."

"I'm serious. Just look how the streets are packed with people without any roof to live under. We might not have money left over, but we have enough space. What do you say we rent one of the rooms?"

"To whom, Isabel, to ladies of the night?"

Isabel's only response was a shrug because, calling things as they were, what had her exchanges with the attorney made her? A tepid thing that fused together inside, allegiances that startled her. Nevertheless, Isabel was still a woman who had to play the part of the cleaning girl. "I don't see any problem with it," she told her friend. It was going to be easy to manage those girls. "We tell them that they have to take their clients somewhere else. If they don't have anyplace, we arrange it with the other tenants and we rent, by the hour, our room in the back. At the same time we sell any leftover moonshine to their johns. They'll be very grateful, you'll see."

In a week they had divided up the labor. Leonor would go looking for sacks to make several jute beds. She would go out to recruit girls. She would put the word out to the unemployed. "I am only looking for four girls. Hard workers, levelheaded. I don't want drunks or gossips." Then she went by San Antón. Don Demetrio was fixing the thatch roof of his *bohío*.

"A sight for sore eyes, Isabel. What brings you around here?"

"I am looking for women to rent my room."

"Emancipated women?"

"And what is that, Demetrio?"

"Those who don't depend on husband or family."

"Those are exactly the ones."

"The only ones I know practice the profession."

"Refer them to me, Don Demetrio."

"You are going to become a madam now?"

"Not a madam, an emancipated woman."

"I always thought you the type."

"I'm surprised, Don Demetrio. Working for *patrones* is not any sort of emancipation."

When she got back, she found Leonor picking up their clothes to wash them. "I brought water from the pump and have the basin ready. Do you have any clothes to wash?" Isabel went to get her sack of dirty clothes. And then she remembered. It had been a long time since she had had her period: "It will come." She couldn't help worrying about it. She looked for a small mirror to see her face, her body, which shone with a strange splendor. Her breasts were full of a strange watery density and the nipples were ample and dark. She would not say anything to Leonor.

The weeks passed. There were two tenants living in the little house on Calle Romaguerra. Nobody in the neighborhood suspected what business was conducted there. Once in a while, one of the girls would come into the house with a "friend" who was visiting her. Leonor was in charge of combing them, "fixing them up a bit, so they don't wander the streets like souls in purgatory and can find some good johns. Besides, you know how much I love doing that." She went off with her lotions, her hot combs, her cosmetics, to see the girls who rented the tiny room. When she was finished with them, they looked like zarzuela performers. "*Mijitas*, like an old *patrón* of mine used to say, elegance has never done anyone any harm." The girls left for the plaza, on the prowl. They returned in the afternoon with their catch. Then Leonor sat on the porch with some task, whatever she could offer. And if not her, Isabel would do it.

One afternoon, they ran into each other in the little porch. Isabel was mending some clothes in the straw rocking chair. Leonor looked at her. Her friend's eyes were heavy on her face. Isabel stopped rocking. She arched her eyebrows. Leonor began to laugh. "What ever happened with the soldier, what luck! I bet I can guess who the father is?" she told her in a joking manner, but it was as if she had pushed Isabel to the floor. A dizzy spell threw her against the railing of the porch, which forced Leonor to hold her up against the rocking chair. "You are going to give birth to a *mulatito* for the attorney; you hide it very well . . ." Isabel had to run off to the back of the pantry, to vomit.

ISABEL CONTINUED TO VISIT THE parcel. She spent hours alone, looking off into the distance. The neighbors began to talk.

"La Negra has gone crazy. What does she want to build on all that underbrush?"

"Maybe she is opening up a business."

"It can't be a diner, because nobody is going to hike all the way out there to eat."

"But why open a business in such an isolated area?"

"And what if it's a house of ill repute?"

"What house of ill repute, even with eight rooms? Since when do the whores go out in the brush to look for clients? That's done in town, where people can move around."

"No, man, what La Negra is going to do is open a tavern to sell the moonshine that she buys from me and Lucho."

"All the way out there by the river? What that one has is a lover who bought those lands from the Fornaríses."

"Bought those lands? Or gave them to her because they were already his."

"*Ay*, Virgin of the Dove, a Fornarís set up La Negra in that house."

"But then why does she go around looking for so many bricklayers? It doesn't take that many hands to build a house."

"Maybe she wants to build a mansion for herself."

"No, man, I'm telling you, La Negra is fried."

DON DEMETRIO HEARD THE NEIGHBORS and went to Isabel. "Nobody even knows that it's a house of assignations and they are already skinning you alive in the barrio. I would think over this step you are about to take." But Isabel listened only to the voice from within. A hard voice that did not at all take into account outside comments or moral judgments. Not now. That voice was that other woman, and it had completely taken hold of Isabel. It took forty days for it to happen. Forty days while she was weak, silent, as if lost in a deep hole, almost bottomless, floating inside herself. Outside, everything was a faded, washed-out color. Leonor took care of her like a sister, "Eat some of this stew, Isabel; drink some of this warm milk; let's see, I'll bring the rocking chair to the porch so you can get some fresh air." In the mornings, she awoke from the burden of the previous day in between her ribs, rocking herself in her own arms, certain that she would vanish in that dark hole. Until one day the hole disappeared. She was alive. Perhaps being alive was that guilt and that pain, having a scar that split her in half and the mewling of a kitten resounding in her ears. Or perhaps life was the consequences of the small acts that were taken one after the other that brought her to the banks of this river. Returning to San Antón, but as someone else.

The work began. Don Demetrio finally decided to help her.

"I do it for you, because you are like family; but I don't agree with the plan."

"Work is work. Besides, I would be able to take from the salon a few donations to your Federation."

Her first purchase of favors as a local owner. She surprised herself, acting so coldly. She could walk fast again, and her steps became an obsession with speed on the dusty paths. Looking for girls, recruiting pupils. Having them line up when she opened the premises. What would she call it?

One, two, three, four. Isabel began to wander all through Las Delicias. "You came out of the hole in which you fell by yourself. Now look for your son." No. She was looking for something else. Forty days had passed. Every morning she had to struggle with that voice. Her steps led her to the shelter of the Salesian priests, to the orphanage, to climb the stairs of the clinic, asking, "Where did they take my son?" But the scar in her belly warned her, that son would be the death of her. They had to split her open to get him out, stitch her up afterward, a scar of shiny skin in the middle of her belly, a serpent of raised weaves like thick stitching, the openwork of her innards regrown. Her belly had turned against her, her hands, the hunger of her crotch had turned against her, and now her feet wanted to look for the son she had given away. But she trained her steps for other things. One, two, three, four . . . she walked around the Plaza Las Delicias. Toward the cart drivers, the knife sharpeners, the job distributors, the shoeshine men. "If you know of any girl who wants to rent a room, tell them to look for me on Calle Romaguerra." A hard woman took residence inside her and advised her. "Where are you going to take care of him?" she whispered in her ear. "How? Without taking his help again? Now what do you think you'll do? With what face are you going to present yourself so that he hates you as well, so that he, too, repudiates you?"

At the corner of the plaza, by the Town Hall, a crowd gathered. They had put up a stage. The municipal band played military music loudly. Some military men in very white uniforms accompanied the head of the civil guard and the mayor, who marched past the band and stopped in front of the podium. Isabel approached to see what was going on.

"What are they celebrating?"

"The arrival of some Yankee officer. Always soldiers coming and going. But don't drool over it, Negra. Soldiers and wars are not for women."

"No, in fact, I just realized that our war is something else."

The speeches by the politicians began. "Lieutenant Commander Nichols," the mayor lectured, "has just disembarked from the battleship *Elizabeth* to preside over the feast." Isabel left the military speeches behind. She crossed Calle Atocha on the way to the Market plaza. She would have to be careful not to run into the hookers from Joya del Castillo, but she had to take a chance. She would put the word out with the shopkeepers and street vendors. "If you know any of them who want to rent a decent room, tell them to come see me." And as she talked with Lucrecia the pastry woman, "Come look for me on Calle Romaguerra," and with Adela the vegetable woman, her feet became calm. The lieutenant commander had gotten off a ship with such a pretty name. *Elizabeth*. It sounded perfect to Isabel.

She went back to San Antón. She wanted to see how work was progressing. Don Demetrio and other workers from the Federation were in the house in front of the plaza. They were putting together a bundle of bulletins. In front of the house, a washerwoman passed by with a girl in her arms. A tiny girl who whimpered like a sad kitten. Perhaps from hunger. "Go get her, Isabel." La Negra shook her head. The smile came out like a rigid grimace. "Hello there, family." She stopped for a while to listen to the men's conversation as she went over a bulletin. In large type, like the print in a newspaper, she read: NO TO THE MILITARY ENLISTMENT.

"This one we'll lose, Demetrio."

"Half the workers from the port are already enlisted."

"As long as there is no declaration of war, it's a way to make a few cents."

"And to serve as meat for cannons. We have to make it clear to the people. The only ones who profit from war are the rich."

"But we look so nice with clean uniforms and dollars in our pockets, looking for where to spend them. Joya del Castillo is a hotbed of soldiers. Dances, women, rum. Anyone would want to enlist."

"Don Demetrio, I want to know if you need some more money to buy more materials."

Don Demetrio responded in a gloomy tone, with his head somewhere else. Isabel said goodbye and walked toward The riverbank. The sunlight ricocheted off the current, off the submerged stones that made the water murmur. Around the bend of the river rose the scaffolds of what would be her house. Great timing. If the soldiers wanted parties, they would find them there around the clock. Music, dancing, the gift of a few caresses. The voice inside dissolved in an echo. To the right would be the porches. And many windows so that the river cooled off the place. Once she had her girls ready, she would make her rounds in town again to tell the workers to recommend her place. Maybe she would have bulletins made, like the ones at the Federation but with a different message. In Spanish by word of mouth, in English through print. "Come. Come to Isabel's bar. Elizabeth's Dancing Place."

Now was not the time to raise a child. Now was her moment.

Two

LUIS ARSENIO, PERHAPS a little more emotional than he should have been, waited on Platform 8 and embraced Esteban. It was a relief to see a familiar face.

"I finished basic training, my brother. Stand at attention and salute, because you are in the presence of an officer of the navy."

"Go to hell, Luis Arsenio."

Esteban threw an arm over his shoulder. Amid guffaws they walked most of the length of the platform, as if those machines and the dispersing crowd were part of their retinue. That's how Luis Arsenio met his friend in Washington, D.C. Esteban was finally able to come for a visit. Luis Arsenio had spent the whole summer locked down in Fort Lee, two states away, doing his eight-week regulation military training. Eight weeks of rising at dawn to do warm-up exercises, then target practice at the range, and training with explosives and mortars. He exchanged the soft carpeting of Fischer Hassenfield for long hikes in military boots. His life as a child of privilege was left behind. Now Luis Arsenio proved himself in the territory of manliness. By himself. No one waited for him or cleared his path.

"Well, now that you belong with the Americans, let me introduce you to your capital."

"You're mistaken, Ferráns. I am just a humble officer in the navy hoping to graduate as a lawyer."

"Did you finish the courses on government?"

"Yes, sir, now I am transferring to the offices of the Judge Advocate General's Corps and to the law school at George Washington University."

"That's if war doesn't break out."

"It's not going to happen, brother!"

THEY HAD AGREED TO MEET in Washington, D.C., after Luis Arsenio moved there, leaving behind the halls of Fischer Hassenfield, the face of Maggie Carlisle, and his friend Jake, to whom he did not even say goodbye. He simply picked up his things and left Philadelphia, switching cities. He no longer cared where. But by chance, Esteban was near Washington, still studying in Maryland. "I can't take another semester. Either I graduate with my business degree or I leave. I'm sick of this land of Puritans. Not a single bar or a place to dance, even now that alcohol is legal again."

Everything had been arranged. Professor Allen had recommended a guesthouse on Ledroit Circle. He would return from Fort Lee to take up his position in the military law offices. In a year and a half he would finish his law degree, paying for it with six years of service as a naval officer. Six years in which he would see the world, gain experience. Even if it were a hundred, he was in no hurry to return to his town.

"Why don't we go eat something? Then pass by Capitol Hill, by the national parks . . ."

"Mother of God, Luis, it's clear you don't know Washington."

"And you do?"

"How do you think I survived in Maryland these three long years? To have any fun around here, you have to cross Boundary Street."

They took the electric streetcar to Ledroit Circle. It wasn't far from there to Number 64 on Allenway Road, where Luis Arsenio lived in a small room.

"Let me change, take a bath." And Esteban, "Well, hurry up, Boundary Street waits for no one."

Wide boulevards lined with poplars bordered the avenues. The residential streets flaunted Victorian houses on each side. But after the stop on Logan Street, the landscape began to change. Luis Arsenio and Esteban took a streetcar to the frontier of Boundary Street. The monumental avenues became narrow streets lined with garbage. Esteban asked to get off. The neighborhood near the trolley station was packed with immigrants. "Polish, Arsenio, and a lot of Italians." But Esteban took long strides past the street they left behind. Luis Arsenio felt as if they were entering a dangerous zone. Faces getting darker every moment, closed off and staring at the pavement. It was as if they had gone out the back door of one country and entered the back door of another. "Get ready to party, my brother." Esteban seemed to know where they were going. "We're entering Anacostia."

They turned a corner and there they were again, at Elizabeth's Dancing Place. Except that this one had a different name.

"Welcome to Joe's Outback."

"How did you find out about this place?"

"Necessity, my boy. I came here to study finance, not to become a missionary monk. Besides, I never had your luck with the gringas. Oh, that reminds me, how is your redhead?"

An uneasy feeling wrinkled Luis Arsenio's brow. He remembered swallowing broken glass. Maggie's silhouette dissolved anew around the corners of Anacostia.

"Water under the bridge. Now I'm single and with no commitments."

Under the shadow of that comment they entered Joe's. The bar, in a corner, reverberated, crowded with over-perfumed women, mostly black, in cheap satin dresses. Some of them swayed their hips to the rhythm of a melancholy tune that spilled out of the mouth of a guitarist, accompanied by a bassist and another one in the back who played a timid percussion. The smell of rotting sweat impregnated the air. Some faces looked with suspicion on the new presence of those two, Esteban and Luis Arsenio, the pigmentation of their skin in the minority. But they weren't the only white ones there. Here and there, in the shadows, you could glimpse one or another man with a similar skin tone caressing a girl while they sipped on their liquor. A familiar place.

Luis Arsenio began to feel more at ease. In a week, he would begin his law studies, to work until his eyes bled. With his work he would protect his father's lands, his future estate. Besides, he had survived ridicule by another woman. He had landed on his feet; it was time to celebrate with his childhood friend. This was the right place to return to his old skin. They found a table by the side of the makeshift stage, where someone sang the blues. They ordered moonshine.

"Today we have a double celebration. Did I tell you I was chosen as an intern for the legal office in Washington?"

"Naval officer and future lawyer. Damn, congratulations, Luis. But aren't you scared?"

"I already told you there's not going to be a war, Esteban. How long have they been killing our people in Europe and Roosevelt refuses to enter the combat?"

"That's just where the Allies come in."

"What?"

"Luis Arsenio, think about it. It's not just England and France; it's all the territories that the English control in the Pacific and the French in Asia and Arabia. If the Allies are weakened, these sly dogs take advantage of the situation and that's it. Oil, textiles, merchandise. Meanwhile, they sell to one, they sell to another, they strengthen their economies, and they sit back and wait."

"Business is not the only thing that makes the world go around."

"Oh, no?"

With a look, Esteban gestured for Luis Arsenio to review the very world of Joe's. There they were, in the middle of a place where flesh was trafficked. Some had a price; some had a hunger. But there also existed the world of the law, of order, of power. He could learn to control both worlds, reestablish the name of his family, if he paid attention to the hidden means that set the path over the rough terrain of power.

"Well, if there is a war, I'll have to go and fight."

"For democracy?"

"Why not? I'll get to travel, gain some experience."

"Then let's toast the future war hero, Captain Luis Arsenio Fornarís, and for the *negra* in that corner who wants a flag planted on her now."

He hadn't noticed, but yes. A woman watched them from the shadows of the bar. She wore a purple dress that clung to her

body. She seemed young, but above all she seemed to possess
the power of things that have just appeared, youth on the face
of the earth. Esteban raised his glass, and that gesture was all it
took for the woman to make her way to their table. A tide of
bodies opened to let her pass. Her eyes were directly—"Which
one of us is she looking at?"—affixed on her prey. When she
finally made it to the table, she whispered her name, "Lucille,"
and it scratched their chests. Luis Arsenio wanted to forget it.
He wasn't going to learn the name of any other woman while
he was in Washington, not before he graduated as a lawyer.
All of them would become a memory as soon as he met them.
Minerva, Maggie, whoever. He chugged back the rest of his
liquor and watched the moon through the window. It was early
in the night. The woman sat with them, not taking her eyes
off them. Esteban bit his lower lip, chewing on a curse. "I can't
take you anywhere, Arsenio; she's staring at you."

Laughter, alcohol, the taste of new flesh. Esteban disappears and reappears from the underbrush of bodies in that bar.
Another woman sits with them. Lucille, lunar, new woman,
a place to deposit the body, letting go of the vine, not having
to think. All you had to do was cross a boundary. Beyond the
boundary was Lucille, and her flesh was darker than before.
Beyond that was the other one, the one who was yellow and
moist like a garden vegetable and afterward was the color of
a red pumpkin, the one who now left the chocolate flavor of
wood in his mouth. There is Esteban. He has a drink in each
hand, as if they were the spoils from a battle. Drunk, he doesn't
want to remember.

They returned from Anacostia the following day. They stunk
of smoke and alcohol, but Luis Arsenio felt clean. Esteban insisted on talking about "the business, my brother, that shouldn't
cloud your mind, you have to be cold as stones, separate feelings

from commerce." Cold, yes. Luis Arsenio enjoyed the coolness of the early morning. They couldn't find any streetcar running at that hour in Anacostia. They had to cross Boundary Street, walking on the cobblestones, get to the Logan District, and from there take a cab to Ledroit. Luis Arsenio took off his shirt and threw himself on the wooden floor. It was cooler. And that's what he wanted, to soothe himself with something cool on his back, which was covered with scratches. What was the name of the clawer? Best if he didn't remember.

But there was no time to go back to Anacostia or to see Esteban again. Time hardened, suddenly becoming heavy. Hardened like a transatlantic steamship sinking in the middle of the sea. One day, in the middle of classes, all the radio stations in Washington relayed the same news. The *City of Benares* had been torpedoed by a Nazi submarine, taking with it, to the bottom of the ocean, the bodies of seventy-three French children. The Judge Advocate General's Corps office filled with a thick air. One of the supervisors of the division warned the interns about the imminence of war. "We still don't know anything, but be prepared to be transferred at any moment."

There were still a few more months before the massacre. In his office, Luis Arsenio watched and kept to himself. Every day internal mail arrived from various offices in the government. Nobody knew anything, but it felt as if something was going to happen soon. The entire university was sunk into an atmosphere of nerves that did not allow for calm exchanges or the revision of cases and treaties. There was nothing else to do but wait. On the morning of December 7, 1941, the wait ended. The Japanese had attacked Pearl Harbor.

Luis Arsenio embarked from Norfolk, Virginia. An aircraft carrier took him to Southeast Asia. He almost did not have time to telephone his father. But he did it, in the naval officers' club, hastily. "They're shipping me to Malaysia, Father. I'm calling to get your blessing." The mother was still sick, but he would not even find out. And he did not know when he would return from this venture, or if he would.

OTHER SOLDIERS, IN FILE, WERE also leaving for different points in the Pacific. Luis Arsenio went to his barracks to get his belongings to board the aircraft carrier *S.S. Seaborne*. But he felt the weight of a gaze on his body. It was for a fraction of a second, hurriedly, at full speed. His skin burned; he wasn't exactly sure why. Fear, uncertainty, cowardice. So he tried to focus on the steps that led to the stairs of the *S.S. Seaborne*. But that gaze weighed heavily on his flesh and he had to find its source. Then it seemed as if he saw himself doubled in the file of soldiers. There was another him over there, the same green eyes looking at him, a firmer body, but like his, same height, wide shoulders. He wore the green fatigues of a private. Tight curly hair recently cut, strong chin with the shadow of a thick beard that made him look older than he probably was, although they were probably the same age. His eyes were lost in his. Just for a moment. He was mulatto. Their eyes locked for a moment and then went on with the race to war. Luis Arsenio couldn't stop. He was sure that the feeling of expansion was an illusion of the atmosphere of battle.

WEEKS THAT SEEMED LIKE YEARS passed in roaming the vacuous time of the sea. The promise of an attack marked the many hours, the minutes; the rest were dead days lost in the immensity of the sea. On the deck of the *S.S. Seaborne*, soldiers swarmed, picking up pulleys, attending to planes. But a devouring also lay in wait. The imminent fangs could be sensed in the air. He wanted to escape the aircraft carrier, dive in the water, and swim to his island. But the island had become so lost among everything else, forcing him to bear witness as if from its shores, as always, from his cursed position, being unfulfilled on it or off of it. Some days before reaching Malaysia they had to change course. The Japanese had captured Kuala Lumpur. The *S.S. Seaborne* went on to the military bases in the Philippines.

Manila, Subic Bay. The base was right at the halfway point of the Bataan Peninsula, west of the capital. It was a no-man's-land. Soldiers and girls who sold themselves for pennies. The Japanese were around the corner, they said. Every day they waited for aerial attacks, bombings. The Filipinos with Japanese roots, which were more than a few, were organizing in the jungle to offer their support to the subjects of Emperor Hirohito if they landed. But on the base, the military police weren't sufficient to prevent the military personnel from disbanding. It was as if they could foresee the end. That premonition crawled on everyone's skin, pierced them to the bone. As it did with him, completely drunk and making the rounds of the bars inside the hovels near the base. Dirt floors, termite-eaten planks, and thatched or zinc roofs. Those houses provided alcohol and women to the military personnel to drive off the taste of imminent death. Many streets had no names. "Mothers" who arranged the parties swarmed through them. For five dollars, any soldier could get a meal and alcohol served by gaunt, defeated-looking creatures wrapped up in cheap taffeta. The mothers promised *Great fun, cheap, cheap.* They took the money up-front and led the soldiers down the middle of the muddy streets, full of dogs and transients, to a decrepit, unpainted house. They made them walk into a living room lacking everything except an occasional chair or table. Then they disappeared to the back of the house and reappeared with a "goddaughter" in hand. A girl made into an appetizer. Some of them were not even thirteen.

Those pigeon women unsettled him. Their flesh was slippery, nothing of the rotund hips of the women that he was accustomed to, nothing of their arched but firm backs under spent longings. The very flesh of those Oriental women was made of forgetfulness. Bloodless girls offered themselves in the streets of Manila for a few coins. Or their "mothers" approached with drooping heads, showing off merchandise that was all bones, all eyes that were absent. These women had surely lacked many things in life. He tried to sleep with some of them, but they felt like the wind.

But those fragile women were the number one problem for the base. Soldiers ate them up by the dozens. It might have been the heat, it might have been the feeling of being out of time, because that was Manila. Those unpaved backstreets were stormier than anything Luis Arsenio had experienced. Not even in San Antón or in Anacostia. The oblique silence of those people disconcerted him and stirred strange passions in the soldiers. It made them bloodthirsty.

He didn't stay in Manila for long. He barely got to know the city. His world was circumscribed by the lands bordering the base. That's where he saw him. Because he could swear that he saw him. Again, time played a prank on him. A soldier had murdered a native. The details of the case were the usual: He was with a lady of the night; you could argue self-defense. Violent Filipinos on their rounds for the night blocked his way, looking for a fight. Shouts, insults, "You fucking monkey nigger." A shot, a stab wound. Nothing of consequence. The soldier's file fell in his hands. "I.D. number 67544, twenty-one years old. Roberto Fernando Fornarís." His blood turned to ice in his veins.

He insisted on going to take declarations himself and in helping for the transfer of the accused from the military detention center. Among the dozens of soldiers, he saw him, head-on. Private Fornarís smoothed his short tangle of hair and stood at attention to salute his superiors—the legal officer, a Major Humbell whom he was assisting, and him. His captain's insignia, conferred as a result of his university degree, granted him superiority. The salute made the soldier direct his look above the head of Luis Arsenio. So the encounter was with another set of those eyes, eyes that always lost themselves beyond something, far away from their house in town, far away from the family dinner table, crossing the darkness of the office's boundary. That look in Manila and another one on the Caribbean met up in Luis Arsenio's memory. There was the chin with the heavy shadow of a beard, the medium but solid build, the listless look in the green eyes of all the men of his stock. But this Fornarís was a *negro*. The very dark hair wound in tight curls on a head that framed a set of lips a bit too thick, a nose a bit too wide.

He limited himself to taking the dictation of the deposition, "Around 2100 hours in a nameless alleyway behind the Ming bar . . ." Arsenio remembered Joe's Outback, remembered Elizabeth's. He thought that Roberto's eyes were watching him. Again that burdensome gaze, as in Norfolk. He wrote hastily, "There were three rather scrawny individuals. It was easy to overcome them. One of them had a knife." He spoke with propriety, correctness, but his English was not too good. He had a thick accent that forced Major Humbell to ask him to repeat what he had declared, to speak more slowly. Luis Arsenio wanted to act as translator, but he decided that it was not his place. "*Dirty nigger, people like you should be slaughtered like pigs*; and then I lost control." Now he was sure that Roberto's eyes were on him. "I saw the knife, and in self-defense I fired." And then a confusing succession of green-eyed looks in that military room. "The police arrived . . ." Roberto continued with his tale. Luis Arsenio did not take his eyes away from the soldier. He took notes, but he looked on; he couldn't help it. The other one kept talking in a neutral tone—"They ran off"—but there was something sparkling in his eyes, hard like metal. Luis Arsenio wanted to say something, to ask, "That thing that sparkles, is it hatred?" But how could he say anything in front of the major?

There was no doubt, though he did not have any proof. Soldier 67544, arrested for an attack in self-defense in the slums of Manila, was most certainly his brother.

Desolation

"Doña Montse."

"The sanctuary is closed."

"It's not that. I have a letter for you."

The old woman went down, grumbling about the slope up to the gate of the grotto. A man in a bus reached out an envelope to her. You don't know how to read, dumb old woman. She looked at the man with a blank expression.

"It's from the military office. It looks like it's from Roberto. Sign here."

"Where, *mijo*, how?"

"It's all right, Doña Montse, here on this line, make a mark. Two little crossed sticks."

The old woman took the pencil with her trembling hand. A letter from the Child, to tell me that he is coming back, that everything has been forgiven. He is all right. The first dash came out jittery. The second one she could not finish.

"That's fine, Doña Montse. Thank you."

She remained affixed to the spot by the gate with the envelope in hand. Holy Virgin, Mother of Mercy, let the Child be all right. Don't even bother opening it, old woman, it makes no difference, you won't know what the paper says. Shut up, Montserrat, I wasn't speaking with you. I am the Virgin; I am the Immaculate Mother. If you say a prayer, it comes directly to me. The old woman moved away from the grotto. The priests are coming for you soon; start saying your goodbyes, ungrateful Virgin. Her legs became watery on the way back. She went up the stairs slowly. She didn't want to put her hand on the railing, so as not to drop the envelope, or so that a breeze would not blow it out of her hands. When she got to the porch, she had to sit down. The envelope danced between her fingers.

You won't know what it says. She opened the flap carefully. The dark strokes on the white lined paper were big letters, as if written by a young child. Could it be the Child who writes to her? She had never known the slope of his writing. Could it be?

He is wounded; don't let it be, Mother.

Have they amputated a leg? Protect him, Lady.

He must be far away and says he cannot return; safeguard me in this difficult hour.

Could he have left messages for a companion to tell me when he died?

Don't let it be, don't let it be don't let it be.

All the sins of the Child are my doing. All the sins of anger, arrogance, vengeance, and desolation. Let my sinful flesh pay for them. Let these sooty wrinkles that I am pay for them, let the earth swallow me and the worms eat me alive, but not the Child, not the Child. By God the celestial Father, let the Child be sane and safe.

The old woman looked at the letter, those round lines. The

rough hand of the Child turned into a man pressing on a piece of charcoal to write to her. She wanted to understand this: "I am fine, Godmother, they are paying me a lot of money, I am coming back soon to take you away from the sanctuary." As much as she focused her eyes on the paper, as much as she tried to unravel the configuration of the letters, she could not understand a thing. I told you that you wouldn't understand anything, crazy old woman. You shouldn't even have bothered opening it. And you know how to read, you plaster pellet, you hollow Virgin in the closed-up sanctuary? I'll shut you up in that darkness like you have done with me in mine. Let the earth split open in two and swallow us if something has happened to the Child.

Letters, charcoal, anguish. Lines and circular things, strokes as dark as soot, silence is black, silence is that thing that sketches a word that she cannot know. You don't know anything, dumb old woman; you don't know that the murmur of thought leaves that stain, that blemish as black as any skin, those dirty, empty words. And she immaculate within—damn her, God—weepy, empty. White is deafness, the wandering gaze, the immensity of nothingness.

And now what are you going to do? She put on some shoes and the first dress she could find. Where do you think you are going? She didn't even know from where she summoned the strength. She made it all the way to the gate, through the entire stretch of Camino Nuevo. Don't leave me alone, Montserrat, don't abandon me to this desolation. I can't hear you, I can't hear you, I can't hear you. The old woman made it to the town hall. She has to get in touch with the Father; she has to find his friends. Yesyesyes someone is going to help me. "Excuse me, good Christian." Trembling, she stops the first person that comes out of the offices. She opens her mouth. The words pile up in her chest. The envelope shakes in her hands. "Look, excuse me." The man walks on. Another one comes. It's that these letters, the world tumbles past her eyes. Her blood bursts, Harpies, the Enemy wants to possess her, this paper is the Enemy's, these letters that entrap me in their soot. Hey, someone is asking you something. She opens her mouth but she cannot speak. I don't know what he's telling me, something else that closes up in my hands, something else I lose. Mother, how much are you going to take from me? I have never had anything, leftovers, a life torn to shreds, the leftovers of my son. Even that you strip from me? There is nothing left. The old woman's lungs are empty. That paper robbed her of all air, all the words that she can name. Señora, tell me how I can help you. Read this for me, good Christian, for the love of God. Read this to me and tell me the name of my misery.

"It's from a Roberto Fornarís. He is fine. That they are transferring him to another base because of a problem that he had in the Philippines. An enemy agent set a trap for him outside of a bar. It was self-defense, he says. They dropped the charges. But he asks if you know about the existence of a brother. If you know the whereabouts of the other son of the attorney. Let him know at this address. It is urgent."

Glorious Mysteries

I RISE FROM the dead, I will rise from the dead. White iris, Rose of Jericho. White are the roses that mark the way. Mary, be my Mother, the Lord is with me; I lift my arms and rise. Heaven is a lukewarm flight of stairs that takes me in. I ascend, I ascend, I am coming, I will now be the Absent One. What a relief, what a delight, what terrible anxiety. I leave all of them and weep on the outside. Everything has been inverted. I weep only on the outside. Inside, I am a sea of laughter and a liquid where I bathe naked. There is no need for cherubs. There is no need for waters to purify; I am myself the balm and the well. And all very dark. Saved, saved, the Lord is with you. Finally the Lord sits by me in these dying hours to watch me go. To go far away from the sword that pierces my heart. I am a woman dressed up in the sun, the moon under my feet and a crown of a dozen stars. But very dark within. I am the Mystery. A woman who triumphs over the tides of her misfortune and steps on the waning sickle that has devastated her. A woman who shines in the middle of the sky with an inverse light, free of her house and the room that holds her, free of the diminishing room that is her body, a growing body that extends toward all the galaxies, that marks her path and her exit. The Sun is the Eternal Lord. The Lord is the chest and His heart a light that blinds. My light is inverse, it doesn't burn, it chars within. I myself am the Lord and the irises open, the fruit of my womb matures, falls far from the branch, they spill their seed elsewhere. I am the one liberated from the Father, liberated from the Son. Among all women, I am the one who ascends. There is no need for cherubs, the one who ascends and leaves behind a trail of immaculate roses, the color of blood does not matter. I am the milk that I sprinkle to baptize with my Grace. My milk is my grace, another baptism, my milk is grace, my milk is irises and rose petals. Milk with no thorns. Mary, be my Mother, bathe me in your Redemptive Milk.

I am not Her, Mary, and I am.

I am not you and I am. The twelve stars the twelve tribes and the twelve rays of Milk. I am the one who wanders from the path and the one who follows it. I am the one who spends forty days in the desert dressed in rags. I am and I also deny my pain. The Church burns and no one rescues me. Soot covers my Immaculate face. And then I am the Solitary Soul. The wandering gypsy. *Nigra sum sed formosa*. I too am the Immaculate.

The Mystery of the Glory and the Grace of the Milk. He who shares my body will rise to the crown of all the mysteries. Perhaps they are a better prize than eternal life.

I die now and leave the men alone with their swords. I am free from all the battles. The battle that is to be silent and live in yearning. Now I rise and free myself and see all of them from above. The Father, the Son, and the Other One that I also shelter. I die in piece and yawn the great dream that I was. My will is done in me. I become Magnificent. Finally I meet up with my light.

Three

"Cloudy times encircle over our heads. Times of temptation and of sin that offer plenty of ways to wander from the path of the Lord. Right here, in this town, the sheep are constantly drifting away from the flock. And the Father watches them, watches their steps when they stray toward that den of iniquity in San Antón."

Another Sunday Mass is dedicated to her and her Dancing Place. Isabel shifts in her spot, catching a thousand gazes out of the corners of eyes. She sweats under the mantilla bought at the Padín shops. The most prestigious ones. She can afford it. She sweats beneath her silk underskirt. That Irish bishop has just arrived in town. How can she silence him?

"A woman should be a cradle of virtue, a mirror of morality, the pillar of the family. Wives, help your husbands not to stray among the ways of the flesh. Husbands, be true to your wives and to the promises that you made to render them the respect they deserve."

With Bishop Hernández it had been easy. Two or three donations to the Carmelite convent. Thousands of dollars for the orphanage. Perhaps among those children was hers. "Don't look for him, Isabel." Perhaps. And so she took care of the orphans of the archdiocese. And the bishop, "Don't think that I absolve you, Isabel. What you do is against the laws of God." But her, "I am not looking for absolution, Father. Let's just say that I come to pay my debt." She handed him the check and left, almost without looking at the faces of the children for whom she gave.

Bishop Hernández was the one who baptized Manolito, that child that she did take into her house, deciding to become his Godmother. She doesn't even know why she did it. She gave him to Olga, a girl whom she hired as soon as her mansion in the Bélgica sector was ready. She never loved him as a mother. She never grew close enough to him. But she had him there. She gave him food and a roof. She had him baptized.

They had to rip him from the hands of La Morena hours after he was born. She would not be able to raise him. "You're going to bleed to death, *muchacha*, let go of the boy; we have to rush you to the hospital as it is." Minerva lifted him from her lap and the newborn began to squeal like a baby bunny, a small animal falling apart in the arms of the girl. "La Morena is going to drop dead on us." Isabel was embroidering in the silence of her porch. She had spent the afternoon listening to the radio, which was covering the rallies of the cadets of the Republic. She knew a few of the boys who were going to march in the rally.

"Why are you looking for trouble?"

"It is going to be a peaceful demonstration, Doña Isabel."

"Don't give me that. It's a provocation. The only marches that the gringos applaud are the ones they organize themselves."

For once, she agreed with Demetrio. "What is left for our poor folk is the act of negotiation." Everything else became too abstract. It crumbled in words—liberty, sovereignty—just like that, writ large, so that they would enwrap the town, the island, the whole world. How could you negotiate liberty so that the weak were not burdened with paying the price? Demetrio came to visit her early that afternoon. Isabel sat to listen to the radio with him. "You have to admire that Pedro Albizu, but he's going down the wrong road. A lot of blood is going to be spilled to accomplish what he wants. The Americans are many and powerful. And they are preparing for a war as well. Now is not the time to be asking for liberty."

"And when is the right time to ask a master to leave you alone?" she had wanted to ask him. But for what? To negotiate. Isabel never stopped negotiating. In paying the ice boy, "It's three dollars, Doña Isabel," and the man with the carafes: "Pay me on Thursday for the week's liquor, or do we settle it today?" Demetrio talked on a level above her business, with the same gibberish: the united cause, workers without borders. Abstractions. She had a concrete world of negotiations to attend to.

The military strategy of the new masters had been excellent for her business. She had been open for only four years at her present spot, and it was already thriving. There were profits. She counted on Leonor. She built a house for both of them, with bathrooms and gardens, designed by the famous architect Antonin Nechodoma. She also had the San Antón place expanded. On the land that was hers. Hers alone. Scar of her womb.

"Besides, Isabel, Don Pedro's boys dressed like Nazis, with black shirts instead of brown. Their standard is an Iron Cross. They say that poverty will end when we get rid of the Americans."

"Well, I need their pennies."

"You're playing with fire. That spot is very visible."

"Everyone has to fight their own battles."

"I am going to the march, to see what these madmen are up to." Isabel watched Don Demetrio go down the road toward town. She shut off the radio. She had the rest of her life for provocations and confrontations.

BUT THE GIRLS ARRIVED SCREAMING. Isabel took out the dilapidated car that she had then. A Packard. She had insisted on trying to learn how to drive among the burs of San Antón. She had bought a brand-new one. "Run, Isabel, she'll die on us." Minerva was a little girl back then. She held the newborn against her little breasts while the other girls from Elizabeth's carried La Morena's weakened body to the car. "Her water broke this afternoon and the child has been born, but she won't stop bleeding." Isabel could not quite see the little bundle of flesh that Minerva held, but she could hear it cry. The squeals mixed with her steps on the ground, with the murmur of the river, the crickets that pierced the night with their song. Isabel reacted. She could not let one of her girls die. It would curse the place, making it impossible to use it for merrymaking, relief. She could imagine the priests' sermons once they found out. "That is where a woman who leads a sinful life dies, the price of her straying ways." She had to act, immediately.

Her Packard was crowded with women. She drove. In the backseat were Leonor, her staff, her support, Petra, and poor Morena, each moment growing more weary-eyed. When they arrived, they found the hospital blocked off by guards.

"It's an emergency."

"Someone else shot?"

"No, a birth."

They let them pass after examining the faces of the women in the car, one by one with a flashlight. Inside the lobby they came upon many stretchers and bustling nurses and doctors. "Has there been an accident?" Isabel then remembered the rally. While Petra gave the information to the doctors, La Negra wandered past the stretchers, looking for Don Demetrio. "It never fails. He's always getting into problems." But she did not see him. "They shot at us from above; they finished everybody off." She heard murmurs between the stretchers. The police took some young men prisoners, their bandages still soaked with blood. Don Demetrio was not there. Protect him, Divine Mother. Isabel squeezed the medallion of the Virgin of Charity between her fingers while she continued to wander the halls of the hospital.

She returned to the girls. "They took her to the operating room; it looks like they have to operate." They took turns. Petra would stay and wait for news. Leonor would return to the neighborhood with Isabel, to look for a cousin who knew La Morena, to tell her she was ill, in the hospital, in case she wanted to go see her. At the steering wheel of her Packard, Isabel could not stop looking over at the side of the road. The whole town was dark, like during a curfew. Outside, there were policemen on each corner. The war had erupted on the streets.

On the day they went to visit her, La Morena was gone. "They let her go this morning. She left without leaving a trace," Minerva told her. "Don't even worry about looking for her. She won't be back." Isabel got all the girls from Elizabeth's together. Between all of them they had taken care of the boy, but now that La Morena wouldn't be returning, they had to make a decision.

"I have two that my mother cares for."

"I don't even have enough for my own expenses. How am I going to feed another mouth?"

"Don't worry, I'll take him to an orphanage. Besides, this is no place to raise a child."

There was nothing else to talk about. But when she took Manolín in her arms and saw that same look that he had since the moment of his birth, as if looking for where to anchor himself, Isabel could not make up her mind. Another desire began to take shape in her arms that held tiny Manolín, with his little hands clutching her ring fingers. She decided to stay with him, for the moment. She would see what she would do afterward.

"Cloudy times encircle our heads. Times that require peace and brotherhood," Antonio Hernández spoke from the pulpit. "This is a good priest, Isabel, he won't get wrapped up in things." Petra had taken her to Sunday Mass. "It's true that now and then he preaches against the business, but it's out of goodness. Besides, we have to baptize that child to give him some relations, because he won't have any other family." They waited until the end of the Mass, and they followed the priest to the parish house. Petra made signs for Isabel to follow her.

"Excuse me, Father."

"You don't have to tell me who you are. Do you come to confess?"

"No, to baptize this child."

"Who are the parents?"

"He doesn't have any."

"Then who will be the godparent?"

He looked at her with a stern but clear look. One didn't have to lower one's head with this priest, contritely kneel, *mea culpa*, things she would never do anyway. She could look him in the eyes. The words came out of her mouth before she could pause to think about them.

"Me."

"I don't know if you are the best person for that."

"I know I am not, Father. But the child has no one else."

But this other bishop lacked that look. Red, chubby, his eyebrows almost white. The gringos had posted him in the archdiocese after the end of the war. The town was full of the paralytic, the crippled, and the mad. The Protestants sent missionaries. The rural roads grew crowded with small Pentecostal churches screaming Hallelujah against the wind. But what to do with the Catholic elite? What to do to strengthen their grip on the reins of power?

So in the mid-1940s, Bishop James E. MacManus arrived. Irish man. Red, like God's ire. He began thundering as soon as he set foot in the archdiocese. "There is a house of assignations on the outskirts of that barrio of workers who are looking for the guidance of the Lord. Innocent and primitive people who let themselves be derailed by women of questionable character who make them stray from their true morality. And it is not just they who allow themselves to be derailed, but fathers of families as well, pillars of society. Just one rotten apple can spoil a whole harvest of souls." During the Mass, Isabel's face burned under her mantilla. Shut up, MacManus, shut up.

It had been many years since she had gone to Mass. But she decided to break up her Sunday and go to the cathedral only because little Ruth had asked her. The very same Ruth Fernández, singer and granddaughter of the well-known medium from the Bélgica barrio, Doña Adela Quiñónez, Adela the Divine. Leonor had introduced them. She looked like an experienced woman, though she was barely more than a girl. But she had buried a mother, had a divorce under her belt, and had just embarked on a career as a soloist. "She left Mingo and his Whoopie Kids, and even the Orquesta de los Salones Elegantes, and she wants me as her dresser." La Negra controlled herself. So this hoarse *negrita* wants to steal Leonor from me? But she reached out her hand. "You know that I take the style of my dresses from yours," Ruth told her at first, not holding back. She won Isabel over at that very moment.

"Mamita Adela told me that a spirit of light appeared to her in her dreams. It told her that for me to succeed this time around, I have to do a novena of Masses."

Ruth told them everything. They had finally invited her to sing at the Panama Hilton. A great opportunity to promote her career. She was going to appear in one of the hotels that was opening in that city full of commerce, with banks that sprouted daily like mushrooms in the miasmas. Bank of Hong Kong, Lufhausser Bank of Alsace, Bank of America, from places throbbing with the business that the ships brought in through the canal. And hotels to close the deals and celebrate the victory of profits.

"Daniel told me that the Panama is utter luxury. Full of Venezuelan oilmen who light their cigars with hundred-dollar bills."

"Bullshit. You believe that Daniel?"

"How am I not going to believe Daniel Santos?"

Behind her, Leonor and Little Ruth chatted. She had gone a few pews ahead. She did not want to harm them with her presence. She should not have agreed to go to that Mass. The only thing she wanted to was to get out of that church fast. But outside the looks persisted. The crowd of parishioners parted to let her pass. She was a pestilence, a plague. The women took their husbands by the arm, holding on to them tightly. The husbands let themselves be taken without looking at her face. Señor Tous, Villanúa, and Méndez Vigo the businessman. They all came to Elizabeth's. "Isabel, a pleasure to see you," they would greet her upon entering. But that Sunday at Mass they denied her, inside they denied her, and outside in the plaza they denied her.

"Isabel, slow down, woman."

"Damn, that little bishop is an ass."

"Perhaps you have to make one of your grand donations."

"He looks like a hard nut to crack."

"Don't worry, Isabel, it will pass soon. You'll see, by the time we return from Panama it will be water under the bridge."

Panama. She was going with Leonor. For the first time in her life she finally had money to spend. Money to travel, to buy things. She had always wanted to travel. This would be the first of her trips.

Leonor fixed Ruth Fernández's hair in a tight bun at the nape with a great organza flower adorning the right side of her head. The spotlight bathed her in a light that made her seem an apparition. She was wrapped in a dress with a long ruffled train. Isabel had given it to her along with a sequined dress that she would wear for her second show. The diamond choker that Ruth was wearing was also hers. A bolero slipped out of her honeyed throat. "My dear audience," a voice thundered from the microphone, "the Panama Hilton is pleased to present Ruth Fernández, the soul of America made into song."

"That was my idea."

Her friend listened to the first *son*, but then she ran off to the dressing room. "Too bad I can't stay with you, but after this session Ruth comes back to change." Isabel got herself comfortable at the center table Ruth had reserved for her to watch the show. Isabel was alone but she was enjoying herself. She ordered the most expensive bottle of champagne. A Spanish banker started a conversation with her.

"I have been in your land, child; I have family there. A cousin who has some quarries there. Jaime Pujols, at your service."

"Isabel Luberza."

"Are you related to the singer?"

"Not exactly. Let's just say that I am a friend and benefactress."

"Well, let's put our tables together. It's not good to see these shows by oneself."

She didn't sleep all night. Although they partied with the musicians after the show, Isabel was up early. Jaime Pujols had arranged a meeting with another banker friend of his from Panama. After the third bottle of champagne, he gave her the advice of her life. "What you have to do is open various bank accounts here in Panama, where they allow you to save money in dollars. Don't even think about leaving it in your country, because you'll lose it all if the national treasury takes you to court. I have a savings account in Santo Domingo from which you can make the transaction."

Things were going along faster than expected. "But opportunity only comes knocking once," Isabel encouraged herself. No time for timidity. She had to prepare herself to act. She called the banker, confirmed her appointment. They would meet for lunch. Isabel arrived in the banking sector and went with her potential partner to a light lunch. They agreed to contact each other before she left. She asked him to call a taxi for her and decided to return to the tourist zone to buy something to mark the occasion, maybe a diamond brooch. It was a luxury that she would allow herself. In fact, according to what she had just learned, jewels were more than a luxury, they were an investment.

Water crashed against the stone and wooden barricades that protected the road. The seawater was dirty, muddy after sifting onto the flat coast, with no waves. "It's river water, señora, the kind that takes the blue out of the sea," the taxi driver explained to her. They approached the narrow streets of the colonial city. To Isabel they seemed like ruins that she already knew. The lower floors of the buildings consisted of stones and masonry. On the upper floors were wooden barracks rotted by the humidity. The street was filled with devastation and misery. The taxi turned into a little street and Isabel found herself in front of the cathedral plaza. Then it turned into another street and a Chinese market spread before her for three blocks. She had never seen anything like it.

A Chinese neighborhood snaked right through the middle of that decrepit city. Restaurants, silk flower vendors, and others with merchandise of all kinds attracted a multitude that swam through the tables and under the tarps like startled fish. A strange smell of grease grimed the air. Oriental faces mixed with black faces, Indian faces, mestizo faces that let other traits be seen, other sources. Not everything that they sold there was Chinese. From one spot to another, sesame sweets and tropical fruits announced the presence of merchants of other origins.

She stopped the taxi. Among the vendors was a fat lady with a face like a dish who in accented Spanish was hawking silk stockings at a ridiculous price. They were probably contraband. She would buy two dozen for the girls; some she would give to Little Ruth and Leonor. At the next spot, a mulatto with almond-shaped eyes and frizzy hair sold religious images. Black Christ of Portobello, Virgin of Mercedes, Virgin of Providence. Chinese stockings and plaster images that portrayed terrible suffering. Everything at reduced prices.

Four Virgins, the Black Christ, and dozens of pairs of stockings. She was almost done with her shopping when she saw the girl. She walked down the street swaying her flesh, the flesh of a thin but blazing she-cat. She passed by close to the vendor stall and with one swipe grabbed a pair of stockings that she hid

under her skirt. But the vendor caught the move. She grabbed
the girl's arm and slapped her twice in the face. She was going
to land another blow when Isabel found herself grabbing the
girl's other arm.

"Stop, señora, I'll pay for them."

She couldn't explain it. And she didn't know, either, how
she convinced the girl to get in a taxi with her. Perhaps it was
because she recognized the neglect in her own face, the rage in
her own eyes. Isabel felt like taking the girl with her.

"What's your name, child?"

"Mae Lin."

When they arrived at the hotel room, Isabel informed Leonor
that they were going back with another passenger. "But are you
crazy?" her friend screamed. "With so many things going on
back home you decide to bring back a stranger. How are we
going to take her out of the country?" The madam smiled.
"In this world, money takes care of everything." She would
call her new friend, the banker, to see if he had some contact
who could help her with the problem of taking the *chinita* out
of the country. Better than a diamond choker. The girl looked
at Isabel with her eyes empty and guarded against some rage.
Isabel called room service and gave the girl something to eat,
leaving her gasping in the delirium of a sated hunger. She called
the travel agency and booked a ticket. She would figure out a
way to get her through immigration, she was sure of it.

The trip had been planned originally only for a week, but
they had extended Little Ruth's contract. An entire month and
a half. Isabel extended her stay for another week and finalized
the details with Pujols. When she got back, she would transfer
a substantial part of her profits to the savings account in Santo
Domingo. She had to get back. Only Leonor held her there.

"Stay a little while longer. You and I have never taken a vacation."

"Vacation for me, Leonor. You are here as a dresser. You like it, right?"

"Very much."

"This is your chance; stay here."

"And the girls? Who is going to fix them up for the clients? And what about you, Isabel?"

"You have taken care of me plenty. Ruth needs you, and you her. I'll take Mae Lin. When you come back, we'll be waiting for you at home."

In the plane with her *chinita*, she found no resistance. Some pesos under the table to an agent solved the problem. "You are going to like the island, you'll see." Mae Lin looked at her anxiously. She didn't let Isabel take her hand, or let go of the large leather suitcases that Isabel had purchased at a boutique in the hotel.

But when she got back, she found a disaster. Two of the girls had left Elizabeth's. Three more were on the verge of gathering their belongings and leaving San Antón. All because of Bishop MacManus, the whip of rage.

"Now he points us out when we go to church. He set the servants of Mary on us. From the pulpit he calls out our first and last names."

She had to fix this. In her house in Bélgica, among the toys of Manolín and Olga and now her Panamanian *chinita*, she began to plot her strategy. She had to break in two the empire that MacManus was building against her. Double her donations to the orphanage. Take advantage of the business-men who came to the Dancing Place. She was going to put all that money that was left over to work. Invest, as Pujols had advised her. But the girls, how could she convince them to stay?

The following day she drove her Packard to San Antón. Don Demetrio. She would bring him a box of cigars that she bought in Panama. And she would make him a proposition.

"Don Demetrio, I need the bricklayers of the Federation again. I'm going to build a grotto. So that the girls can seek comfort in peace."

"But Isabel, why are you adding fuel to the fire? A grotto next to the Dancing Place. For many it will be a provocation."

"Well, let it be that, Don Demetrio. The girls have to pray in peace. Besides, I need protection against that bishop. Let him cast his angels at me. I'll raise my virgins on this end. We'll see which of the two sides wins."

Four

LUIS WAITS FOR a passenger. A new partner, an excellent opportunity to get the Fornaríses out of the hole, make some business with the lands they have left. The gringo was from Louisiana; he wanted to open an importing firm for truck parts and needed warehouses with close access to the roads north that connected easily with the ports. Although all the land on the shores of the river had changed hands, he still had a parcel left, bordering San Antón, which long ago had ceased to be a town of sugarcane workers and had become a slum. He would build the warehouses there. That would be the base from which the trucks would transport merchandise. He would put up the lands, the permits, and an initial investment. The gringo from Louisiana would give him exclusive rights to the parts and, with luck, the supply that was needed to buy his own fleet. Once the business fell into place, Luis Arsenio would put his plan into effect.

San Antón. There were still some wooden houses left and

sparse spots where wild sugarcane grew; but all its properties
had been converted into workshops and residences. That field
of his infancy had disappeared. Among the patios there were
still some small strips of land, some somnolent outbuildings
with thatched or zinc roofs, but most of the buildings were now
an uneven stretch of wood and cement. Here and there in the
neighborhood were workshops of all kinds, for tinplating and
paint, sign making, upholstering, general mechanics. The main
road was paved. There were wire poles on the side of the three
roads that divided the town in a fan shape toward the middle,
toward the remnants of the vacant sugarcane field where they
had recently erected high tension lines that extended an oscil-
lating and dark tangle of cables toward the sky. On the far side
of the towers, the river hid behind wild vegetation. The town
looked so vacant without its sugarcane, fenced in cement. The
military road snaked by on the other side. There was talk of
plans to widen it and turn it into a great highway, a task that
would take years. Let the Ferránses take that on. He didn't want
to dirty his hands like that. But that's how fortunes were made
in these lands. With cement. Luis Arsenio could not believe
how the cement grew, eating up the greenery that constituted
the fences of his youth. That green and migrating growth that
had not let him breathe.

The loudspeaker announced arrivals from San José, Panama
City, and Florida. The attorney Fornarís put out his Tiparillo.
Ever since he returned to the island he had begun to smoke
them again. He approached the airline counter to confirm that
his information was correct. "We're sorry, but there was a flight
delay." They did not have a definite time of arrival. It didn't
matter. Now that everything had been set, he knew what he
had to do step by step. He had nothing but time left over.

It seemed impossible, but it had been years since he had returned. His father had gone to pick him up at the airport on a day like this one, not too sunny or too cloudy, a midmorning in December. Luis Arsenio had recognized him in an instant, as soon as he stepped into the passageway with a canvas roof that led the passengers to the hot room where they picked up their luggage. He would have liked to have not recognized his father right away, to have made him out piece by piece until forming a complete picture and saying to himself, "It's him," and embracing him. But Don Fernando Fornarís showed up at the terminal stirring up the stormy weather of his old age with an arm that was extremely thin and tired. This was what was left of his father. Arsenio forgot about picking up his luggage and stood in front of him. His mother had died, and his grandmother. He shouldn't have let him bury so many people on his own. With one arm he brought him to his chest. From Fernando Fornarís arose that odor of an ancient baby, of talcum powder with sweat, of rancid milk, that the bodies of the old emit. The son almost did not have the courage to kiss him on the cheek.

"Adrián is looking for parking. Is this all you brought?"

"There's more inside."

"Go get it. Here, I'll watch this bag for you."

He knew then that it was his duty to come back. He had finally finished his law degree and was returning to take charge, to look for solutions for the well-being and growth of the dishonored clan. Of the old there was almost no one left alive and almost nothing left in their hands. On the death of the grandmother, they had to sell the last of the warehouses to divide the inheritance among distant relatives. There were some cousins left, like Adrián, who took interest in the family's welfare. Every once in a while he helped the old man with little problems, like coming to pick up his returning son. Nobody even mentioned the word *chauffeur* anymore. Of the sons of old Fernando there were Luis Arsenio himself and the one that he knew was a secret. He was coming back to look for him, as well.

After having returned with all his luggage—some boxes of books and a suitcase containing the few civilian clothes he owned—he was able to speak with his father without getting choked up.

"You look good," he lied.

"And you have become a man."

"I've come to stay, Father . . ."

"You've come alone?"

"I didn't want to bring back anything that would be a burden."

His father looked at him from head to toe and smiled within. His son was coming back without a wife, without children, with nothing else but the years that had placed wrinkles around his eyes. Luis Arsenio looked at himself in his father's smile. Underneath the gray hair, the stature shortened by a slight stoop, beneath even the eyes, now more the color of dry pastures, he saw a splendor. Perhaps he was returning in time, perhaps he would have a father for some time yet.

"Let's see if you are ready now to hand over the law firm."

"You'll have to pry it from my hands. But don't worry, I have several fat accounts waiting for you."

"At least partners, no?"

"When haven't we been?"

They walked toward the car, Luis Arsenio carrying the military bag and suitcase with his things. His father tried to carry his coat and his hand luggage. The way back had been long, but now he was here, finally home.

To kill time, the airport offered two options: going into the military club to have some drinks or the cafeteria to get some coffee. The attorney Luis Arsenio Fornarís would wait for the fat fish to arrive and then would invite him for some good liquor. A little rum to get things going. At the same time he'd make a show of his former rank as officer in the navy. Perhaps that would help to arrange things in his favor. For the moment, however, his taste buds yearned for the second option. Airports always made him want to drink coffee. Only coffee. Cup in hand, he sat down once more to wait and could not help but remember that last time he had been a passenger. He had traveled a lot after the Philippines, to Normandy, Tunisia, Brittany. But the journey that he now remembered was the definitive one.

He had made the voyage with only a cup of coffee in his intestines. That is how he had become accustomed to fly in the military, when he had to travel at a moment's notice from base to base, to resolve some legal problem over new regulations or to draw up contracts for reconstruction that had to be mediated by the office of the Judge Advocate General's Corps. He was never a pilot, always a passenger, but from the pilots he had learned the habit of flying on an empty stomach. "There'll be time to eat something when you're on solid ground." He did not want to suffer the embarrassment of having his stomach turn on him in the cabin of the plane.

That Pan Am flight had all the passengers reciting the rosary. Seven hours in the air. Each jolt elicited screams from his traveling companions. Pockets of air shook the plane like a firecracker. The propellers deafened the passengers, making their eardrums vibrate and sending them to the brink of tears. They were all sick with nausea, the urge to vomit ever-present in their throats, pale as can be, except for the two or three who were too drunk to recognize the danger. But as the belly of the plane swelled, Luis Arsenio looked around and could not stop asking himself where so many passengers had come from, crossing the air in this direction.

"I'm going back to see the old lady, who's dying on me. I went to New Jersey in forty-eight to pick tomatoes. I've been at it for six years. I'm used to living there."

"Although sometimes one needs a little heat, right? And you, young man, what are you returning for? You have the look of a veteran."

Two men, darkened by a sun that was not the tropical one, he was sure, were talking to him. Their skin had the dry cast of those who work in inclement freezing weather. But they talked to him as if he were family. And he responded calmly, without getting worked up or angry. He told them about his conquests in Tunisia, in France, of the battles he saw in the Philippines. "She had the eyes of a cat in heat, I swear." The words drained out of his mouth effortlessly. The little shots of legal rum—"Palo Viejo, you see?"—that the men poured out of a canister into the snack cups, while the stewardesses had their backs to them, helped. They kept asking him for stories in between the airplane's jolts and invited him to yet another drink, "To soothe the nerves, because this monstrosity is putting us in a bind." They weren't going to die, Luis Arsenio assured them. He put his snout to the little cup, like them, and spoke with a freedom whose origin he did not know.

He finished his coffee and went out again to watch the planes land. In an hour he would go back to the airline counter; meanwhile, he would bide his time, consulting the gold wristwatch that his grandfather had left him in the will. With it he measured time, each minute, each second, and the steps he had to take. Although it had been on his wrist for years, time still escaped without his realizing it. A sign of how that other time passes, the one that can't be measured. He spent more than ten years at sea. That's how he burned through the war and then the aftermath. He remained on the other side of the ocean, in

Caen, Normandy, helping with the reconstruction. He learned
to draw up contracts between American and French partners,
always to the advantage of the first. Sale of cement, steel, car-
goes of tools and manufacturing goods; with the closing of
each successive contract it became clear that Europe was ruined
and the American industrialists strengthened from war.

He had burned through more than ten years and did not
even realize it. The women became all the same. In Caen, it
was Lorene, the one with very dark eyes who was called La
Chouette. In Tunisia she was called Maura, who filled the
dingy room where they pressed together with musk as soon
as he lifted up her skirt to penetrate her. He spent a year and a
half in the region of Ventimiglia. Única, Lusiana, and Marilé
shared his bed during this time. None of them permanent;
that's the way that Luis Arsenio wanted it. His journey was an
apprenticeship; he was a bird passing through. His father's lands
awaited him on the other side of the ocean. But he had to finish
what was pending first.

He could pay for one last year at school through the G.I.
Bill. And that was the plan. One fine day he decided to return.
He asked to be transferred to Fort Brooks. At the fort he sought
out options. He was sent to New Haven. That city that wasn't
at all a city, rising in Gothic spires in the middle of a cement
plain with newly built houses. It was made to easily delight
men of his ilk; men without women, wanderers who put the
plan of progress and postwar stability in danger. Because that is
what spread beyond the center of town, beyond the towers of
Yale University, the gasoline stations, tire stores, butchers, cafés.
Stability, progress. The suburbs. Families and more families re-
produced in slope-roofed houses, with the whitest of fences
marking off the territory. The bars were on the other side of the
train tracks, ill-smelling hovels full of cripples and sad whores

who fell asleep against the jukebox. Luis was returning from the other side of the world, and once again he found himself in a country where he did not fit in.

The habit of going from port to port rid him of his disposition to study. He found the classes antiquated; he couldn't help but compare what his books said with experience, with the way that the law becomes water in the hands of he who practices it and turns it into a living thing, a jumble of words that changes density the moment it drains from one mouth to another, from one paper to another, from the hand that, clutching a pen, wants to make it more definitive. The law is made of wind and the price for trying to nail it down is determined by the highest bidder. But Luis Arsenio had made a promise and he meant to keep it.

Now he had returned on that flight to his country with a cup of coffee warming his innards. Drunk from drinking rum with two strangers, a brother to people who years before he would have avoided. It didn't matter. Nothing mattered at that moment. Luis Arsenio continued to laugh beside those two leathery hicks, as if finally settling in to his true stature as a man. He felt good in the average stature of his body. He no longer needed a first name or a last name, nor even the certainty that there were still lands that belonged to the family. All he needed was his wide-shouldered and anonymous body to contain him, his thick beard, the skin over his ribs. The war had changed him. It had shown him what people were capable of, black, white, yellow, powerful or lacking, protected by the law or by the fire bred from rancor and a machine gun. As long as they didn't have to eat dirt, as long as they could make anyone pay for their own vulnerability, they were capable of selling and plundering, entrapping and immolating others, whether it be newborns, or those who were alone, or those left to the elements. He had seen people do anything for food, or for a business exchange, or for a pretty dress. Or simply and straightforwardly, to feel as if they had defeated that adversary who had become so intimate that they no longer knew who it was or what he was called. They found him everywhere and everywhere they wanted to humiliate him. "Enough." Luis Arsenio doesn't even remember when he said it first, in Tunisia or in the Philippines or in Caen. "Enough of this," he definitely remembers thinking that midmorning in December, seated on the B-49 en route to San Juan, Puerto Rico, drinking rum and not eating breakfast with two emigrants who had broken their backs on some tomato farm in New Jersey. Something inside him said, "Enough," for real that time. The somber weight of silence dissolved in the pit of his stomach. And nothing else had been needed for him to return home.

He went back to the counter and found out that the plane was about to land. Now he had to get ready to set his plan in motion. He lit a Tiparillo. Dozens of people descended from the metal guts. Carton boxes bound with rope, sacks reinforced with jute, and a few leather bags were set down in the pushcarts that took the luggage to the terminal. From the bridge, Luis Arsenio made out his prey. He came out with a briefcase in hand, drying the sweat that reddened his chubby cheeks and neck with a white handkerchief. Bald. Too tall for the tropics, too much mass on him. This was his partner from Louisiana. It was time for the attorney Fornarís to get to work.

"Mr. Douglas, this way. Let me help you. How was your flight?"

"A nightmare. But here we are."

"Don't you worry, I'll make it up to you."

"I hope so . . ."

"Wait until you see the location of the land and the plans

for the warehouses. But you seem hot. Would you like a little whiskey?"

"Man, you sure read my mind."

They walked toward the officers' club in the military hangar. The attorney showed his I.D. and got a quick, "Go ahead, captian." He explained his rank to his partner. They looked for a cool and quiet corner and ordered their drinks with lots of ice. The attorney smiled, relaxing. Something told him that the winds were favorable for this undertaking.

"You know that the government is offering incentives for the establishment of new businesses on the island."

"That's only for factories."

"But also for industries with high employment. Tuna fish plants, distilleries, packagers. If we add a transporting component to our parts warehouse, and administration personnel and material warehousing on an industrial scale . . ."

"We already have a branch in the capital."

"But that branch doesn't meet the demand for heavy construction machinery parts. What I'm proposing is to duplicate that space with another industrial center in the south of the island, specializing in pieces and service for big machinery. There are a lot of construction projects coming at this time. I know it from a good source."

"And who would be our clients?"

"At first, the contractors that the government employs. Many of them are clients of my law firm. This is a small island in the middle of a growth spurt, Mr. Douglas. It's impossible not to have connections."

Everything he said was a lie. His connections were not so vast, nor were the clients so bound to him. And although he did keep an account of building proposals, if this deal went through, he would do just the opposite of what he said. This time he was not going to negotiate for the benefit of others. He was not going to sell favors or pretend he did not notice things. He identified a pocket that no one had thought about, and now he was going to use it for the advantage of himself and his own. It was only now that the idea of who exactly were his own had taken shape.

That midmorning when his father had received him, Luis Arsenio was desperate for his arrival. The four hours were almost entirely spent crossing through the mountains. They stopped only, at the father's insistence, at the side of the road where they sold *sacos de china* and avocados. They stocked up. "When you were a boy, I spent all my time crossing this road from north to south. The curves left everyone dizzy; cars flew off the roads every once in a while. A calamity. La Puquiña. But for me this countryside was a stretch of rough seas that I crossed again and again, to solve cases, represent clients in the tribunals of the city. My father cast off to sea, and I to the countryside. Toward the inside. I like it around here. I also made a lot of good business deals in these parts, believe it or not." Luis Arsenio said, "What deals, Father?" And Don Fernando replied, "Land deals. In Hormigueros. San Germán. Now that you're back, we'll get on the road one day and I'll show you." Hills in all shades of green spread out like living skin, as the clouds sketched patterns of light and shadow on the ravines. Luis Arsenio suddenly thought of Minerva. Why her? "When I die, bury me up here. There's nothing for me in the municipal cemetery."

The son rested for a day, and that was plenty. He immediately set up his things in his father's office. Everything went so naturally. Don Fernando did not make him jump through any hoops and did not cling to his power. On the contrary, he gave up the keys to the office and opened the accounting books of the law firm one by one. One by one, he spoke to his son clearly about the financial state of the family. "Your mother's illness was long and costly. The Rangels never forgave me for putting her in the hospital. They bad-mouthed me. So in the last years I brought her home from the hospital and hired private nurses around the clock. I had to transform the house, put up railings, locks, set up a hospital bed. Adapt it to live with the illness." The complete picture passed through Luis Arsenio's mind. His father lowered his head and took a deep breath, as if he were finally letting out trapped air. "In town, we lost almost everything, but we still have some property in the highlands."

What did interest Luis Arsenio was who the new owners of the family's goods were. "The Ferránses offered to buy the farm by the river at a price well below market value; but we needed the money, son." Conversations crossed the son's mind; "You have to be cold, Luis Arsenio." He could not help thinking ill of Esteban. Why didn't he tell him, send him some signal, even if it were just made of smoke?

There were the books, spread out on his father's desk in the office. Numbers of the contracts, the costs of approvals, services. One percent on closing for both purchases and sales. The Marcels needed excavation contracts for aqueducts and sewers; the Vega Urrutias for auctions to replace the stone and sand that they supplied the town the year before, and the year before that, and before that. The Cardosos for permits to build bridges in two sectors by Pueblo Chiquito and for the reparation of roads in La Piquiña. With the Ferránses, the list became long. Construction auctions, permits to develop stretches of rural roads, a bridge over the Morrell Ravine, dredging in the Morrell Ravine, auctions for stone and sand, once, twice, seven times to the town. And the sale of the Fornarís lands. All of it by the banks of the river, and by the military road, they acquired for less than its assessed value, hectares and hectares passed from hand to hand. From the hand of the Fornaríses to the hand of the Ferránses.

"But, Father, didn't you keep their books?"

"Almost all of them."

"Then you must have known they were getting ready to do serious business. Why didn't you try to get in on it with them?"

"Your mother, the law firm. My head was somewhere else."

"You could see the signs from a mile away."

"Dredging the river, widening the military road. They've been plotting it for a long time, but the project is so big that it gets hung up with each administration. Perhaps with this one they'll come to an agreement."

"And none of them invited you in on it, instead of ripping your lands from your hands?"

"I thought that the war had taught you that lesson, Mr. Attorney? That's not the way you play this game and my blood was never cold enough to play it."

"Nor mine," said the son under his breath. But they had to fix the finances. And that's how he had done it, step by step, to this very day, when he would put the finishing touches on his plan. Mr. Douglas finished drinking his whiskey on ice and looking at him with his crafty eyes over the lip of the glass. The attorney Fornarís did not move from his spot. He was waiting for the signal so that the partner would feel like he was the engine driving the events that would unfold.

"And when can I see the plans for the warehouses?"

"Whenever you want, Mr. Douglas."

"The sooner the better."

"What do you say I drop you off at the hotel so you can freshen up? Relax a little bit?"

"Look, Mr. Attorney, I came for one reason. When do we head down south?"

"Why don't we go there now?"

From the airport, they took a small plane to Isla Grande. Once again, an unusual carpet of green spread out below. Señor Douglas almost did not fit in the craft and did not stop sweating, although the windows let in a crisp breeze through a round hatch-like slot. But the gringo was also not unresponsive to the colors below, that sinuous green that looked like the spectrum of all the greens imaginable. "Pretty," he murmured. Luis Arsenio liked this gringo. The attorney Fornarís was content with looking out his window.

The pilot announced spots nearby. In some twenty minutes they would be flying over San Antón. There was a good breeze, and toward the sea the sunlight made visible the small islands of the southern inlet. In one of those nooks was his brother, Roberto Fornarís.

Captain Fornarís lived in a four-room cement house that he had bought with his soldier's pension. His family grew wild from the womb of a country girl with whom he had fallen in love on one of his visits to the island. Lisandra. "She was the one who settled me down." He married her while he was still in the armed forces but left her in Hormigueros, in his Godmother's house; afterward he took her to Germany. From there to Fort Allen, where he was last stationed. Then he retired. Little by little he became a contractor. He was never able to get his degree as an engineer, which he had promised the army, but his sons would do it. There was already one about to graduate from high school, with much potential to be accepted in the new engineering school of the university, around Mayaguez.

"There's nothing like having your children finish the path that you began."

His brother had told him this when Luis Aresnio finally worked up the courage to go see him.

During the war, weeks after Luis Arsenio had taken that terrible deposition concerning his brother, the Japanese had attacked the Philippines. The defense held out for a few weeks, but the offensive did not let up. Eisenhower ordered a retreat and Luis Arsenio missed his chance to look for Roberto. He wanted to tell him that he knew something, it wasn't definitive, he didn't have proof, but he knew. He wasn't the only one of his species, and to top it off his species had mutated. But instead of aggravating him, this made him happy. It filled him with a strange peace that he could not explain and he wanted to tell Roberto about it, to talk to him and finally dismember the silence. "The grandfather is dead," he wanted to tell him. "And Mama is mad as a goat. I imagine that you drove her to it or what you represented in her head, that she stopped being if you existed. Or worse, if your mother existed. How old are you? Was my father married when you were born? And tell me, who was your mother?" He wanted to hear from his mouth. Finally hear the name of the woman who for so long had made him an orphan as well, almost not there in the distant gaze of his father, in the hysteric fits of his mother. That woman who was never his, but who gave birth to the man he became, child of silence, in between the legs of Minerva, of Lucile, in between the legs of so many other women that he avoided, always fleeing from them.

But Manila fell and he lost track of his brother. Soldier 67544.

Roberto Fernando Fornarís. Burma fell and he no longer knew where to look for him. Luis Arsenio was a hero in the battle of Guadalcanal. Stationed in Tripoli and promoted to lieutenant for his work in helping France take back Algeria. He kept looking among the military uniforms. Stationed under the command of Admiral Vernon, assistant to General Clark during the landing in Sicily and the conquest of Naples. Even when he tried to forget, he looked for him in each tavern, each port where he stopped. Normandy fell; the Allies liberated Calais. Now and then he received a letter from his father, conversations with an absent one who now was doubly so. Luis Arsenio asked himself if Roberto was not at that moment some place on the globe, his other half, leaning on a table, reading a similar letter, or a letter diametrically different, as if written on another surface. His chest filled with a strange nostalgia. Luis Arsenio and Roberto Fernando, one brother and another, Fornarís skin to skin. Who knew if they could find a way to dispel the fog of fear and suspicion, of the silence of those who did not know how to let them be brothers?

And then, finally, he was face to face with his brother. The contractor Roberto Fernando Fornarís looked at him, green to green, right in the centers of his eyes. The full words of his story rose easily from his throat. "I became a captain in the army. They were going to award me yet another medal, but the war robbed me of whatever courage I had left. Lisandra must have the medals put away somewhere. Ever since I was a child I have always been a pest, but seeing so many broken people changes one.

"I asked to be transferred. And then I went up to the mountain to look for Godmother. She was old, crazy. She spoke to me of vengeance and of payback with blood and all this other foolishness; I returned sick of seeing so much blood spilled. She threw Lisandra out of the house; she said it was her fault that I had changed. That I was as much a traitor as my mother. And then she told me her name. Isabel Luberza Oppenheimer." He spoke with the same tone of voice as years before, when Luis Arsenio had taken his deposition in the Philippines. But this time his brother's eyes did not avoid Luis Arsenio's, did not shine with rage. He looked at him straight on as he spoke, paying attention to each breath.

"The things one sees in war, right? What one is capable of doing? Do you remember my case in the Philippines?"

"You knew about me in the Philippines?"

"Since forty-one. I saw you before you even knew that I existed."

"Why didn't you come to me?"

"I didn't know what I would say. How about you?"

"The same."

They both smiled, but a lump formed in Luis Arsenio's throat. They had not been able to find the words, or they had been too narrow, and because of that, it took them years to find out how much they could have kept each other company. But then his older brother gave him a tender look. "Things happen when they have to happen. Like the day I saw you getting off the aircraft carrier. I was on the regulation line to get on board. The naval forces would help with the transfer. The *S.S. Seaborne* had docked because Malaysia had fallen. Hundreds of soldiers passed by our line. It wasn't even me who noticed you. It was Moncho, a friend from the same barrio whom I found over there. 'My God, Roberto, look at that guy, your double, but white.' That's how it was, as if I were looking at myself in a mirror, with that same face, that same distant gaze, looking for what one has not lost and then come on back to touch base and so advance, little by little. The same square body, you thinner, but the same. The same shadow of a thick beard that makes one look older. But it was the eyes that told me. You passed by and didn't even notice that I was looking at you. That's why I didn't dare when you were in front of me in the detention hall. Perhaps you knew more than me, although I always suspected that the attorney had another family. Perhaps the attorney had told you, and you were forced to be there and did not want to approach me."

"Then it wasn't hatred that I saw in your eyes."

"Hatred? No, sir, it was nervousness, wanting to approach you."

"I thought you hated me."

"No, brother. I hated myself."

Luis Arsenio watched his brother's hands, exactly like his father's. They rested peacefully on the arms of the rocking chair of the porch where they sat to talk. Hands at rest, like Fernando Fornarís's, seated in his Packard. Hands of years crossing La Piquiña to go see that other son who grew up in Hormigueros. "I wanted nothing to do with it, but I couldn't stay away. Your grandfather reproached me about it enough. 'A man has a right to stray from the fold now and then, your wife better get used to it. Unclaimed sons, I have three or four, and aside from passing on a few cents, they never see my face or feel the weight of my last name.' But the mother abandoned him as a newborn. Didn't even want to breastfeed him. Then she opened the dance hall in those same lands that I gave her and didn't pay attention to any of my messages. I don't know why I loved her, but I loved her, is the thing. I loved both of them and it shattered my life. But what was I going to do with her? Where would I have her live? How would I make her accept that place that was the only thing I could give her? I couldn't convince her. Your mother noticed right away. She smelled it on me, all the times that I tried to convince Isabel to accept the child, another house in another town, I would take care of it. And well, you know the rest."

They spoke for a long time that afternoon, comparing stories. Luis Arsenio brought one from the mouth of his father and he measured it with the one that Roberto told.

"So that's how all of the family's lands were lost. I'm sorry."

"Don't worry about me. Work is going well. Besides, we have the little farm left in Hormigueros. When Godmother died, they passed on to me without my having to lift a finger. I imagine it was the attorney's doing. And also my mother . . ."

"Isabel?"

"Wants to see me."

"And what do you want?"

"I don't know. I'm afraid the rage will return."

A silence opened up between them, the first one of the afternoon. But there was a series of questions yet to ask and Luis Arsenio was not going to go without putting them on the table.

"Did you ever see her?"

"Once, when I was little, but Godmother did not want me to approach her. She was very elegant. 'That woman is evil,' she told me, and we kept on walking."

"Did you miss her?"

"One doesn't miss what one never had. That's how she wanted it."

"Do you believe that, Roberto? I am not asking to annoy you, but do you believe that that's how she wanted it?"

"No, now I don't. Half my life proves it. I have spent it doing things I did not want to do."

"Then why don't you go see her?"

"I have always lived under the shadow of that abandonment. It's time for other things to mark what I am."

When Luis Arsenio and Señor Douglas landed, the midday

sun was out in full. There was no time to lose. They had a light lunch and he took his client to see the lands in San Antón. Señor Douglas would put up a percentage of the investment and would give the attorney exclusive rights to the parts. The construction of the warehouses should begin immediately if they wanted to have everything ready for operation by the end of the fiscal year. Now the last piece fell into place, the piece that Luis Arsenio had chased all his life.

"Who will be in charge of the construction phase of the project?"

"I have a contractor partner who will build the warehouses before the next cock crows."

"And to whom do I make out the check?"

"Make it out to Luis Arsenio and Roberto Fornarís, Brothers S.A."

Last Prayer

AND THEN I took him so they could free him of all delusions. I
took him so that he, too, would hold on to rancor. Your mother
is like the whores of the Wind, your mother sells herself for
nothing. I didn't tell him, but I showed him. The attorney did
not want to pay attention to me. "I am busy, Doña Montse."
He didn't want to tell me about the other brother. Now I am
dying and can't answer the message that you sent me. The old
woman tosses in the bed. She is alone in the little house. She
sees a shadow approach. Is it you, Mother? Let's not fight anymore. Doña Montse, Doña Montse, Doña Montse, Virgin in
her throne, Black Virgin with white Son on her lap. Don't
worry, Montse, you are not alone. That is not my name. My
name is María de la Candelaria Fresnet and this is the hour of
my hour. And only ask one favor from you, Mother. Tell Him
that he is my whole life.

"Godmother, it is me. Roberto."

"Rafael."

"I am here, I am here, take my hand."

Son of the Father and the Holy Spirit, the Child returns from war made into a Man, made into an Angel incarnate in his fatigues. I am tired of so much struggling. *Ay*, Godmother, said the one who returned from the war, and he wept. The Child made man wept. "I don't want to fight anymore." Godmother Montse, I have returned home, saved; I don't want to hate. I caressed his curls, poured out my eyes, kissed his hands.

Yesyesyes, I, María Candelaria Fresnet, kiss the hands of the Son who wants to forgive the Father, who wants to embrace the Mother, who wants to reach out to the brother who never came by the grotto to ease the wasteland of my solitude. Let them go to the Harpies, let him betray the destiny that I wove for him with such care. Let him abandon me as well. But inside I cursed him, I cursed him. I curse you.

Before departing I curse this land. I, the one who provides, who safeguards, who incites the bull of Shame. I curse the Son and die from old age and with the rage intact in my breast. I curse the Father and die with the rage turned into a fetid cyst. I curse the Mother and take her with me beyond Death. Because she is beside me in my guilt. She will die with me in this finale. In this finale I am the victor and I take her with me, take her take her. She is the Virgin whore that I have in my bones. My bones are the grave, it is their only place. The long candles burn in reverse in the heavens, where she is Angel and Demon, where she is Montserrat and Isabel, where she is María Candelaria and the rage of the heavens that burn themselves out, leaving her cleansed of the fingers of the Absent One. Let God descend and bless the fury of the one who never dared say more than yesyesyes, who let herself be eaten by the crocodiles, by the vermin of the mountains of her spite. I take her and win this battle. The hour of the final hour is here. Light candles forever and ever, Amen.

From your lap, Lady, inverse water, black black black. Give me the black water to drink. Give me the night that you are, Lady. Now that I am old and dying. Come, you build a shrine for me. Make me what I made you. Charge your pretty pennies for exhibiting me, let the drooling pilgrims see me seated on a throne of *marabú* feathers, open your legs, Virgin, see her. See her for twenty-five cents, let them kneel and see me in the most luxurious silks, enveloped in odorous smoke, in your sanctuary in Hormigueros, in San Antón, let them toss in the ant hill of my saliva, you Virgin whore, me Black Virgin with white boy on her lap. Where did you get that boy? Defeat the enemy that beats in my head, the Enemy was the Señor and it was me, yesyesyes Montserrat, Montserrat, Doña Montse. What's my name? Godmother. María de la Candelaria Fresnet. Magnanimous María Candelaria Fresnet of the Night like all the virgins of the world when I could have remained without last names or nicknames, without mantles or crowns, without sons of the Holy One, the very one. Mary Woman of the Mountains and without Mary, let them leave me alone now that I am dying and take the rage with me to my grave because of what the Harpies did not let me be.

ROBERTO HOLDS THE OLD WOMAN's hand. He measures her breathing. He weeps. His Godmother is going to die. Roberto sees her move her mouth. He thinks that she is praying. The old woman's eyes are lost.

You are all I have left, yesyesyes, Mother, yes. Take in this old woman who kneels before you in the hour of her death. Shelter me in this empty farm and don't let my end be delayed. I await thee, Mother, I await you, Fountain of Patience, Messenger from Heaven, Benevolent Mother. Let the ants devour me, let them rip off my skin at this Last Hour. What good has it been to me? This old woman who no longer wants to be confused, Candela, the mocking of her wound, her absolution. They mocked me, Mother, until I was without a name, without a face, looking more like you, Black Virgin with white boy on her lap, Holiest Mother of the Reckless, Dark Madonna, Holy Virgin of Montserrat. Protect me, Lady, for I no longer want to be Debased. All I want to do is to rest.

THE END OF VANITY

Final Litany

HOLY VIRGIN, IN your days of glory, do not forget the sorrows of the earth. Cast a benevolent eye on those who suffer, who struggle against adversity and spend their days wetting their lips with the difficulties of life.

Have mercy on those who loved and were separated.

Have mercy on the isolation of the heart.

Have mercy on the weakness of faith.

Save us from our love, save us from our narrow love.

Have mercy on those who weep, those who tremble, give them peace and hope.

Virgin of Solitude, pray for us.

Virgin of the Novena, pray for us.

Virgin of the Rosary, pray for us.

Virgin of the Light, pray for us.

Virgin of Good Counsel, pray for us.

Virgin of Mercy, pray for us.

Virgin of Abandonment, pray for us.

Virgin of Consolation, pray for us.

Virgin of Transfers, pray for us.

Egyptian Mary, Gypsy Mary.

Mary Magdalene, black like Rage, like the most fertile night where the Son grows, where he plunges his flowering crook of the revived Father,

Tota Pulchra es María et Mácula Originalis non est in te
Nigra sum sed formosa.

One

THE FIRST TIME that Isabel Luberza Oppenheimer saw the son of the attorney Fornarís, she almost devoured him with her eyes. The kid walked right down the middle of the bar, swaying his medium height and heavy beard. Ever since she had opened the doors of Elizabeth's she had seen hundreds of candidates for manhood stroll though her place in that manner. Her place. Some were feckless soldiers, more disoriented than cross-eyed land crabs, who didn't know how they had ended up on the coast of this country where they didn't even know their names. Others were boys playing champions of this or that strike, or sprout-like men celebrating the fact that now they had a little money to pay for their debut in the professional sheets of the most famous whorehouse on the island. Elizabeth's Dancing Place. Oh, yes, in English, so from the time they saw it people would know that her house was a place well worth it.

The son of the attorney came to make his debut. You could tell from his deliberate walk. Like all of them who came for the first time, he walked with a heavy step so as not to betray himself and take off running. He had the same green eyes of all the Fornaríses, of the father, and he was named after Don Luis, the grandfather. Another three striplings were with him. She saw them talking, inspiring each other to approach her throne of woven straw, where she smoked a cigarette in a holder. "They know the rules. They have to come and say hello to me." She saw them coming, the chests out, and stop in front of her. "Good evening, Doña Isabel." She didn't know it then, but one of them is now the Enemy. She should have let loose that night, thrown him like meat to one of her more experienced lionesses to keep under watch and supervision. But who could have imagined that one of those kids would have grown up to be her incessant adversary? They looked so meek, startled but with their chests stuck out, each with his vest buttoned, hair full of Yardley's Hair Tonic, Tiparillos in their hands. But she could smell the mother's milk behind the ears. Still nourishing them. And they had come here, escaped, that very night they had come to lean precisely on her bar. Precisely them, precisely the son of the attorney. She almost devoured them with her eyes. "Fornarís," she said. "I know your family well, although they don't frequent my house." She couldn't peel her pupils from his face, his square chin, his freckled cheeks, and his very black hair, the color of jet. The boy melted under her gaze; he almost had a fainting spell from not breathing. But she clung to his features. The same perhaps of her son now, if she had had him there, beside her, introducing himself.

Around that time he appeared to her in her dreams, in the middle of a field of yellow butterflies, the same ones that she had painted on one of the walls of Elizabeth's. "Come, my son, come back to me, don't lose yourself." But the son paid no attention. He hid in the thick underbrush of the riverbank.

And then she desperately followed him. With each step, she thought she caught a glimpse of his shoulder, a stride, a shirt-sleeve. The wings of the butterflies obstructed her view. And then she extended her view to a clearing in the woods. In the underbrush there were two supine bodies that smelled of legumes, something lukewarm and oily that emitted sweat. It was her and him, the father attorney, enjoying themselves like dogs in the bushes. She did not want to see it, but there she was, another her, but there, far from her son who once again escaped through the bushes of the Portuguese River.

Perhaps darker, more of mulatto, but with the same features. That's how he looked in her dreams. That is why, when she saw the young man, she could not take her eyes off him. The boy had nothing in him to withstand the deep almond burden of her eyes or the density of her dream. Isabel anxiously penetrated each pore on his face, each trembling of his chin. The other three boys began to play with their ties, nervously. The one who is now the Enemy said something, but she can't remember what. No, that boy did not know anything. Isabel fell into the depth of herself and someone else appeared, the woman seated on her straw throne, who rose out of a cloud of smoke like an apparition. Glossy blue skin streaked with yellow.

"Order whatever you want, *muchachos*. The first round is on the house."

One more year at the most and she would have her son, that son of her dream, the one that she was forced to lose. Now she would reclaim that loss.

The bar was full to capacity. Isabel lit another cigarette. She didn't like the flavor of tobacco in her mouth, but she made use of the effect, a woman covered in a fog of smoke that suddenly disappears. Her cloud became the stage of her apparition. From there she could watch. See, for example, how the boys took a table in the back. None of them dared move, to pick out a girl to dance with. They restricted themselves to looking at the gathering, perhaps afraid that someone would recognize them. But her bar was full of important people. There in the back, a senator from the new Unionist coalition drank with a federal judge. In the opposite corner, Representative Merced from the Fourth District discussed party strategies with the leader of the chamber of commerce. The hostess had just opened the door to two other influential personages. And those kids, hidden in the shadows as if their presence would unleash a cataclysm. That's how it always is with the boys from good families. They think that everyone is looking at them.

She made a gesture to Altagracia so that she would go take the order. "Brought here from Cibao, and it wasn't easy. If it had not been for Don Jaume's connections . . ." She picked her up off the streets, starving and full of parasites. But since then, she had been completely devoted. "For you, Doña Isabel, I would do anything." She was one of the other set of eyes and ears for the place, Isabel's multiple antennae. Elizabeth's Dancing Place was full of them. Strategic antennae picking up what was taking shape in her salon—business transactions, political pacts, party alliances. She found out everything, and then: "Senator, you see, the news has reached my ears of your party's plan to renovate the plaza. I would like to make a donation. Anonymously, of course." She had learned it in her past life. You had to win the hearts of those influential men who came to Elizabeth's by chance. She did not seek them out; they came on their own, in caravans, attracted by the out-of-the-way bar, and by the cool breezes of the flesh and the river. She wanted to know what the boys were talking about, the son of the attorney. Let Altagracia take their order. She would supply them with the best alcohol; maybe that would loosen their tongues.

One of them stood from the table, buttoned his vest. He was getting ready for battle. "Now, one by one, all of them will go toward the girls." She was wrong. The attorney's son could not make up his mind. "Don't worry, boy, I'll do it for you." She made a signal to Minerva. She was the most beautiful of the girls from San Antón that she had in her pack. She had saved her from an uncle who was making her miserable. Minerva responded to the signal and approached the table where the loner let his eyes wander on the walls, the ceiling. He smoothed his pants, sucked on the cigarette mightily. Minerva advanced like a cat. Isabel nodded from her throne. "There you go, my cheeky one, don't even give him time to think." She saw her girl crouch to the exact height of the ear. She watched her whisper a phrase, assault the young man when he was not expecting it, that hardy *mulata* bursting out at the tip of his ear—"Why waste time with preambles?"—turning to face him—"From the moment you walked in, I could not look at anybody else." He let himself be led docilely to the slaughterhouse of Minerva's thighs. Isabel La Negra, the Señora of San Antón, the Patrona, smiled, satisfied. The son of the attorney took the bait, because Minerva had something that hooked men. Once they tasted her, they could not detach themselves from her touch. The poor girl was not even aware of it. But that's why Isabel was there, to make sure that the girls would make the best use of their talents. And Minerva's talent was to retain them. And that's what Isabel wanted, to retain the son of the attorney under her dominion for a while. She had no idea why, but that's what she needed.

The dream of the butterflies. It became more and more frequent, but during those months she awoke from it with a voice resounding in her chest. It was more like a murmur, the remains of something more resounding. A cat's mewl, a newborn animal. She woke up knowing it was there, deep within. She, suffering, watching herself like a mongrel bitch, fitted under the attorney's legs, while her son escaped thorough the underbrush and the butterflies. She awoke to those phantom sounds agitating her breath. The days after the dreams were always bad days. She could not orient herself.

BUT THERE WAS THE OTHER one, the counterpart of her guilt and her stigma. There in Elizabeth's Dancing Place was Luis Arsenio Fornarís, son of the attorney and the one that was the cause of her inverted womb. From her straw throne she watched Minerva take him to the back rooms. To "initiate" him, to make him a man. The same old ritual would begin again there, to devour his first *mulata, negra*, and then attempt to leave her behind. There he goes, and his flesh will split in two, his desire in two, she feels it. On one side the true affections; on the other, the fear of what his body is asking of him. But you walk away from the beds immune. She knows that now, she who is now the Divided One, Isabel of a Thousand Names, La Negra, the Patrona, Protector and Tempter of the Wanderer. She who saves and she who leads astray, that's her. Seated on her straw throne, she watched the son of the attorney lose himself in the shadows of her house. She let out a thick mouthful of smoke from her cigarette holder. If only she could disappear like that, behind the smoke. But no, her house lay claim on her. Two other clients were approaching her. They looked like businessmen. I have to attend to them as well. "They, too, know the rules," she thought as they neared.

"*Señores*, welcome to Elizabeth's Dancing Place, make yourselves comfortable. A pleasure to have you in my house."

Two

ON THE THIRD of January 1974, at ten thirty at night, Isabel Luberza La Negra died in the front of her establishment. The impact of two bullets ended her life, the first plunging into the shoulder blade, the second entering her right side and lodging too near the heart. The sound of the shots alarmed everyone at the bar. It was a slow night. Manolito Hernández, an adopted son of the deceased, was coming in through the back door to return a transistor radio he had been listening to, the baseball game between the Ponce Lions and the Arrecibo Pirates, eleven to eight in nine; no extra innings had been necessary for the victory. There were two explosions and Manolito thought that it was the hooligans from the Chico River trying out the illegal firecrackers that had been left over from the New Year's celebration. He walked toward the bar, worried about his adoptive mother, who for the umpteenth time was going to have to bribe the district judge to avoid having to present herself to the tribunals to face a new accusation of trafficking illegals and prostitution. Isabel had gone that same afternoon to bring him the transistor radio and to tell him that everything had been arranged, not to worry. She knew how the game was played; it was not by chance that she had endured for more than fifty years in the business that she would soon leave as an inheritance, "to you and one other person."

She had been behaving strangely during the previous weeks, more isolated than usual, holing up for hours in her office, with her ear to the telephone receiver. Manolito admits that he had been intrigued by the previous warning and that he decided to go to the bar with the pretext of returning the transistor radio to get more information out of Isabel about the other mysterious heir. "It seemed that he felt something might happen," the press declared.

The deceased's attorney, Chiro Canggiano, advised Manolito Hernández not to say anything else. In the television report Manolito went on to recount how he had heard new explosions and decided to go out the front door of Elizabeth's Dancing Place to scare away the boys who were lighting the firecrackers. Then he found his adoptive mother on the ground, spread out in a pool of blood. He ran to her aid. When he made it to her side, he had the opportunity to hear her last words. "Son, call him . . ." and the air went out of Isabel's lungs. But with her mute lips not emitting sound, she kept on talking. Manolito understood. In his hand she left a wrinkled scrap of paper with a telephone number written on it. The lawyer interrupted again.

In the living room of his house, Luis Arsenio Fornarís turned off the television. He noticed the trembling in his wrist when he pulled his hand from the controls and he could not tell exactly if it was a symptom of aging or the feelings that overcame him when he heard the news. Isabel Luberza Oppenheimer had died. He had to go back to San Antón.

"Who murdered her? Who had her murdered?" Arsenio murmured under his breath on the road, speaking to himself in the car while he heard over the radio the thousand declarations that people were making about Isabel La Negra. Juanito Rosario sang part of a *plena* that he had written for the deceased in the same voice in which he had sung the novenas to the Three Kings that Isabel had paid him to perform during her famous parties in the barrio of San Antón. Police commissioners accused her of perverting minors and trafficking girls, many of whom arrived with falsified papers and ages, from Panama, Curaçao, and the Dominican Republic. The great Ruth Fernández declared that Isabel Luberza had been her friend, one of the first who helped her in her career. "A very cultured woman, very generous to others." The report went on to name dozens of acts of charity sponsored out of the pockets of La Negra—the renovation of the old age home run by the town's archdiocese, a quarter of a million dollars donated to the Red Cross, the elementary school in San Antón. "Who had her murdered?" Luis Arsenio repeated, and a chill ran up his chest. His hands once again trembled as he steered the car.

It had been decided. The bishop refused to let the vigil for the body of the benefactress take place within the confines of the church. "Her dubious morality" put her on a different plane from the ladies from the good families, those other ladies who preferred a modest life rather than selling themselves and others to obtain luxuries and acceptance. When a reporter asked for a declaration from the bishop as to why he had accepted the countless donations of the *patrona*, the prelate refused to answer. Luis Arsenio could not avoid a guffaw. Someone should have warned poor Isabel.

The body would be kept in vigil in her old house in the Bélgica barrio, the baronial mansion that Isabel had the Czech

Antonin Nechodoma design for the admiration and envy of the rich in town. Nechodoma almost ended up losing his august clientele. How dare he lend his talents in the services of a madam? "The end justifies the means," the architect had responded, "and my end is to revolutionize the architecture of this place." That was all he answered to anyone who dared to restrain him. Nechodoma did his job well and gave Isabel a house where she could feel proud. There in her mansion, they would keep the vigil. The entourage would leave for the municipal cemetery in a procession at three in the afternoon. The burial would be at five. Luis Arsenio made a note of it in his head.

It rained the entire afternoon of the burial. The skies opened at exactly eleven o'clock in the morning. After twelve noon, the shower abated, becoming a formless drizzle that lasted until Isabel had slept her last sleep in the very bosom of the earth. But still, a large crowd showed up at the house in the Bélgica barrio. There were people from every walk of life there. Girl prostitutes and matrons, old clients who still owed Isabel some favor, representatives from all the political parties, old men and washerwomen, small-time singers, and artists with international reputations. All of them came to say their last goodbyes to La Negra. The line to get into the prayer session was enormous, as was the entourage outside awaiting the journey across the town. The porch of the mansion filled with people under umbrellas, and the large crowd waited silently.

He went to the house in the Bélgica barrio, but he did not want to go in. From outside he spotted those who were closest to Isabel. An old Chinese woman dressed in mourning who let out puffs of smoke over the very coffin of the deceased. He recognized her; it had to be her, Mae Lin. A young man rested his hand on the shoulder of a robust mulatto with the face of an abandoned child. Manolito Hernández, adopted son. The whole town knew he had been born of a girl worker whom Isabel always refused to identify. Behind Manolito, standing, the one in charge of the bar whimpered, a certain Altagracia Riberia, who, according to the news reports, while she was still an adolescent, had been helped by Isabel into Puerto Rico illegally. She had screamed that she had wanted to help with the burial, that if they wanted, they could deport her afterward.

Luis Arsenio continued with his inventory through the funeral room. Startled, his eyes came to rest on a mourner. There he was, hiding behind the Dominican employee and taking his place behind the attorney Canggiano. He had not put on his retired captain's uniform.

There was his brother. All he had inherited from Isabel was her skin color. He remembered how with cigarette in hand he had finally heard him tell the whole story of his life, telling him his own, tying up loose ends, finally being able to forgive the father and the mother, the whole town. His chest filled with the warmth of relief.

"Who had her murdered?" he asked himself again aloud, leaning on the front doorframe of the mansion. From all around he could hear rumors that they had arrested two thugs who supposedly were the gunmen. Under questioning their stories matched: they pulled the triggers thinking that the person coming out was the bodyguard of the place, with whom they had had an altercation the night before. There were also rumors that no, that's not how it was, that the bodyguard had thrown them out for a reason, that they were dealers whom Isabel did not allow to sell on her premises, because "you know how she was about drugs." But Luis Arsenio feared something else.

La Negra trafficked in secrets. Had she sought to do business with someone too big? You know how it is, they took her out . . .

BUT ISABEL HAD CONNECTIONS, INFLUENCE.

But even influence can be spent.

Luis Arsenio's hands trembled again. He approached a woman who was lighting a cigarette and asked her for one.

"You're a Fornarís, from here in town, right?"

Luis Arsenio smiled as he inhaled. He asked the doña how she knew. "The same face as the grandfather, the same eyes . . ." A mouthful of nicotine escaped from his chest.

The entourage came out carrying the coffin. The original intent was to parade the body in a funeral carriage from Bélgica to San Antón, and from there to the church in town. Pass in front of the archbishopric, to dramatize the affront that Isabel's body was not allowed in the parish that she herself had helped build. But the crowd wanted to carry the coffin, so the carriage went on ahead, empty. Manolito Hernández led without letting go of the handle. Women and men adjusted themselves next to the casket, to relieve the penitents or take the place of anyone who grew tired on the way. Luis Arsenio approached it slowly, looking for a spot nearest the dead body.

It drizzled, but no one seemed to notice. They were nearing San Antón when a pealing of whores joined the entourage. They belted out celebratory *plenas* in the name of Isabel. Dozens of *pleneros* joined to sing the whole way to the town, stopping as they neared the plaza approaching the church. Then Manolito, who had not taken a rest since they left Bélgica, let himself fall, exhausted by the weight of his dead mother.

Before the knees of the adopted son touched the ground,

two strong, dark hands took his place. Luis Arsenio got closer
to the coffin. He offered to carry it exactly at the opposite side
of that man who took on the head of the entourage and whom
nobody knew. Someone protested, shouting, "Some respect, the
head is only for those who were close to her." Manolito made
a gesture so they would let him take his place. "He is family,"
he screamed, "he is family." His voice cracked. Luis Arsenio
took the opportunity to grab the coffin himself. Meanwhile,
the people looked at the substitute, his green eyes, his heavy
beard, his square chin, and asked themselves who it might be,
because his face was so recognizable. There were even those
who looked at him and then rested their eyes on Luis Arsenio
to find an astonishing resemblance. Two strong arms, one white
and one black, carrying the coffin at the same time.

Luis Arsenio looked at his brother. For a moment, he thought
that he had again inadvertently spoken the question about Isabel's death out loud. But there were so many who were guilty
of that death. He focused again on his eyes, which he guided
like darts until that man on the other side of the coffin turned
to look at him, to open his eyes wide, to recognize him. As
they rounded the curve approaching the cemetery, Luis Arsenio offered him a smile. He thought his brother complicitly
returned it. He was there as a representative, as his father would
have liked to have been, if he had loved with more courage.
Other hands came to relieve them.

The two Fornarís brothers walked slowly past the graves.
Isabel La Negra's was opened in a corner of the cemetery. Manolito sat with the relatives. Roberto, his brother, did also. Luis
Arsenio decided to remain standing. No priest spoke, no representative of the church. The attorney Canggiano offered to say
a few words, talking about false moralities, taking the chance to
accuse those who had used La Negra to later forget her in that

hole in the ground. "She never had the respect she deserved."
Luis Arsenio saw how some faces contracted with grimaces of
disgust, whispers that "now that she is dead, she is a heroine,"
and "what about the ones La Negra used?"

The service was short and the drizzle stopped, as people
began to leave. The *pleneros* took out their tambourines again
and played some *plena*s for Isabel. The crowd was dispersing,
the people saying their goodbyes. There were even some who
offered their condolences to Manolito, to his brother, and to
him. In the distance you could hear the murmur of the wind
and a jukebox playing boleros.